if we

lived

here

Also by Lindsey J. Palmer

PRETTY IN INK

Published by Kensington Publishing Corporation

if we

lived

here

Lindsey J. Palmer

KENSINGTON BOOKS
www.kensingtonbooks.com

KENSINGTON BOOKS are published by

Kensington Publishing Corp.
119 West 40th Street
New York, NY 10018

All Kensington titles, imprints, and distributed lines are available at special quantity discounts for bulk purchases for sales promotion, premiums, fund-raising, and educational or institutional use.

Special book excerpts or customized printings can also be created to fit specific needs. For details, write or phone the office of the Kensington Special Sales Manager: Kensington Publishing Corp., 119 West 40th Street, New York, NY 10018. Attn. Special Sales Department. Phone: 1-800-221-2647.

Kensington and the K logo Reg. U.S. Pat. & TM Off.

eISBN-13: 978-0-7582-9436-4
eISBN-10: 0-7582-9436-0
First Kensington Electronic Edition: April 2015

ISBN-13: 978-0-7582-9435-7
ISBN-10: 0-7582-9435-2
First Kensington Trade Paperback Printing: April 2015

10 9 8 7 6 5 4 3 2 1

Printed in the United States of America

To Damian, my home

Chapter 1

The apartment's location was ideal, and the rent was within their range, but it was discovering the pair of walk-in closets that prompted Emma to start fantasizing about the article that would appear in the *New York Times* Habitats section, that trove of adorably obnoxious stories about New Yorkers landing their perfect homes:

> Emma Feit, 30, and Nicholas O'Hare, 34, had set out with cautious optimism to find their first joint domicile. Lucky for them, their dream spot proved to be just one Craigslist ad away.

Emma stepped her entire body inside one of the closets, whispered, "Space!" and heard an actual echo. She performed a jumping jack, confirming that her arms at full wingspan wouldn't brush up against the walls; the walk-in was only slightly smaller than the size of Emma's whole bedroom in Manhattan. She ran her palm along the built-in shelves, which must have been teak, or cedar, or some other solid, expensive wood that real carpenters used to build real furniture. Emma breathed in—the scent made her think of camping trips and farm-to-table restaurants, nothing like her current closet's flimsy plywood that smelled vaguely of chemicals.

Anxious that their moderate rental budget wouldn't get them much more than a glorified studio, the pair had anticipated a stressful search. "But it couldn't have been simpler," noted Mr. O'Hare, his blue eyes sparkling.

Emma exited the closet and moseyed over to its twin. The spaces were mirror images, this one's wall of shelves back to back with the others. Emma pictured herself getting ready for work, reaching for a scarf or a purse or one of many books she'd be reading all at once, while Nick would be opposite her, grabbing a belt or a sweater or one of his many Yankees hats. They'd be in their own little inlets, yet just a foot apart, both separate and together.

Not only did the duo hit real-estate Nirvana with their discovery of a stately floor-through brownstone in Prospect Heights, Brooklyn, but the 800-square-foot charmer boasts walk-in his-and-her closets. "There's none of his sports gear getting mixed up with my workout things," noted Ms. Feit. "And we're never tripping over each other getting dressed in the morning."

"Em, is that you?"

Emma peeked her head out to see her boyfriend, Nick, abutted by the landlady, a stout, middle-aged woman who had introduced herself as Mrs. Caroline. "Who are you talking to in there?"

"Oh, no one." Had she been narrating aloud? "This place is incredible, right?" Emma pulled Nick into the closet, realizing there was definitely enough room for physical fun. "Look, shelves!" She could easily prop a leg up onto one.

"Fancy. Did you see the dishwasher?"

"Ooh, we can have dinner parties!"

"Or, you know, just clean forks," Nick said. Neither of them was too diligent about dish washing.

"Plus there's the extra room. It's perfect for an office, or storage—"

"Or a man cave." Emma knew he'd said it just to get a rise out of her; at the top of her list of most despised concepts was that of the "man cave."

"Or maybe a nursery." She raised her eyebrows. If the landlady weren't standing right there, Nick probably would've been yanking at her ponytail.

"Or a ball pit," he said.

"Like at Chuck E. Cheese's?"

"Exactly."

"What about a yoga nook?"

"Or we could rent it out to a small family of immigrants."

"Or to a heavy metal band, for their practice space."

"Ahem."

They might have kept going, but Mrs. Caroline was now beside them—three people in one closet! "You know I don't permit sublets, correct?"

"Oh, of course," Emma said in her best responsible-adult tone, instinctively straightening her shirt, which weirdly she was thinking of as a blouse. "We're just enjoying some lighthearted banter." Nick smirked; Emma's eagerness to please sounded ridiculous even to herself.

"Very sweet," said Mrs. Caroline flatly. "Should I draw up an application?"

"I just want to check out the shower," said Emma.

Inside the bathroom—spacious, tasteful, with lots of medicine cabinet storage and no sign of tile mold—Emma cranked at the shower knob. The water pounded against her palm. "Nick, feel this. It's massage quality." When her boyfriend put his hand under the stream, Emma took the opportunity to splash his face. He tried to retaliate, but she ducked away, all smiles at the landlady.

"You could bathe an elephant in there," Nick said.

"But you kids wouldn't try a stunt like that?" Mrs. Caroline asked, her tone inscrutable.

"You mean, would we locate an elephant in need of a bath, transport him or her up the stairs to this apartment, and—"

"Of course not," Emma said, cutting Nick off. "We're very responsible."

"So, the application?"

Emma and Nick nodded like idiots, and followed Mrs. Caroline, who was shuffling in platform flip-flops, into the kitchen—state-of-the-art appliances, plenty of counter space, an eat-in bar, and a separate nook for table and chairs. A wide window looked out onto Prospect Park and Grand Army Plaza, where Emma could make out the stately arch; bronze statues of soldiers and their handsome horses were frozen in poses of triumph. It seemed like a sign, the arch an entrance and a beckoning to Emma and Nick: *This will be your home.* Nick's tug on her shirtsleeve pulled her out of her daydream. Mrs. Caroline was waiting, clipboard in hand.

"So, what's the relationship between you two?"

Emma had a strange urge to lie, but Nick spoke first: "Boyfriend-girlfriend." The description made Emma wince; although accurate, it sounded like it was out of a nursery rhyme, singsongy and juvenile.

"We're very committed," she added, reaching for Nick's hand, as clammy as her own. "We've been dating for three years."

"But you've never lived together?"

"That's correct," said Emma. Since she was more adept at this put-your-best-selves-forward routine, she and Nick had agreed she would do most of the talking with prospective landlords. But the act was making her squirm. Who was this interrogator across the table? Might she next ask Emma to divulge her most shameful memory, or Nick to state his preference for boxers or briefs?

"I see." It sounded judgmental. Emma couldn't tell if it was because they were planning to cohabitate before marrying or because they'd waited so long to shack up in the first place. "Do you have all the necessary documents?"

Nick pulled the packet from his bag, their lives summed up in a neat little stack—bank statements and pay stubs, credit reports, personal and professional references, Nick's letter of employment from P.S. 899's principal, Emma's letter of employment from the CEO of *1, 2, 3 . . . Ivies!* When Nick relinquished the paper trail into Mrs. Caroline's stubby fingers, Emma had to suppress an instinct to grab it back. *This woman could steal our identities,* she thought, plastering a grin to her face.

Mrs. Caroline perched a pair of spectacles on the tip of her nose, then began thumbing through the pages. "My last tenants made more money." The remark hung in the air, stagnant. She peered up at Nick, the glasses in danger of slipping off her face. "So what kind of earning potential do teachers have?"

"I get an annual raise." Emma placed a hand on Nick's thigh and hoped the landlord couldn't detect his defensiveness. He was sensitive about his salary.

"Nick is tenured," Emma said, "so unlike the rest of us, he has real job security."

Mrs. Caroline glanced back at the papers, then fixed her gaze on Emma. "I see you've been at your position for less than a year."

Emma felt her cheeks grow hot. She willed herself to keep her eyes on the prize: two walk-in closets, a dishwasher, ample counter space, a killer view.

"Emma is always changing things up and seeking out a new challenge," Nick offered. Immediately, Emma knew it was the wrong thing to say.

"Is she?" The implication seemed to be that she was perhaps not very dependable.

Emma jumped in: "My job is great. I help high school students through the college application process, which is quite a booming business. Every parent these days wants their child to get into a top school, no matter who the kid is or what his grades look like. So I help my clients see that vision through, making sure my students stand out to admissions officers. It's very rewarding, and my boss would certainly vouch for my reliability. Feel free to reach out to any of our references. We're good, responsible, upstanding citizens, I can assure you." Emma realized she was rambling, and she also had a sense these were the kind of assurances a serial killer might make.

"Well, it's been good to meet you. You're a very nice couple. I'll be in touch." Mrs. Caroline ushered them outside, where they each offered her a hearty handshake.

Emma and Nick stood on the sidewalk in front of the brownstone for a long time, blinking up at the windows they hoped would

6 Lindsey J. Palmer

soon be theirs. An autumn crisp had snuck its way into the August air, and it felt like relief—another sign, Emma told herself, although her stomach was clenched into knots.

"I feel like I just went on an awkward first date," Nick said.

"I know. What was I thinking, telling her we're good, upstanding citizens?"

"Did we blow it?"

"No. Or, I don't know. Maybe. But damn it, we *are* good, upstanding citizens."

"We'll just have to wait and see whether we'll get our man-cave-storage-space-nursery-ball-pit-heavy-metal-band-practice-room."

"You forgot yoga nook," Emma said. "You know what? I think we'll get it. I can feel it. Mrs. Caroline will think it over and she'll realize we're the perfect tenants."

"And what exactly does that kind of certainty feel like?"

"Like blisters, actually. Wearing these sensible heels is torture." Emma slipped a swollen foot out of a pump. "Did you see her in those awful flip-flops? I mean, they had rhinestones. We clearly deserve this place."

"We do."

With that settled, Emma and Nick strolled down the street. Canopied by trees and buzzing with birds, it was so different from Emma's current block, which was strewn with garbage and noisy with taxi horns and drunken NYU students. The couple's silence was easy. After months of discussion and negotiation about this potential move-in, it was a comfort to know that, at least for this particular moment, they both wished for the same thing with the same degree of fervor; no ambivalence or hesitation clouded their joint wanting. What a relief, after all their tense talk of feelings and future, to finally focus on concrete details like street address and amenities.

Emma continued drafting the Habitats article in her head:

> Certain they would have to settle for a less desirable
> location, a not-quite-gentrified Bedford-Stuyvesant
> or a deep-in-Brooklyn Sunset Park, the couple had

been shocked to discover an affordable haven within their top-choice neighborhood of Prospect Heights. An area replete with trendy restaurants and upscale boutiques, and sidewalks bustling with hipsters and stroller-toting parents alike, the couple could imagine staying put through several life stages—Ms. Feit may well one day become one of those stroller-toting moms.

Well, not quite. Emma had gotten carried away with her pretend article—whose style, after all, was much too flowery for the *Times*—and the certainty she expressed within its imagined lines was just that: imagined. Already she felt the familiar anxieties seeping into her head. Were she and Nick really ready to move in together? Would the pros of cohabitation outweigh the cons of forfeiting their freedom? What would spending so much time together do to their sex life? What if they broke up and one of them had to sleep on the couch until they rode out the lease? And who would clean the toilet?

Nick had stopped. His head was cocked, gaze turned to the sky. "Look," he said. "Parakeets." Emma peered where he was pointing, and there they were—elegant creatures dancing around the branches, their lime-green bodies nearly blending in with the leaves. Nick had a sensitive eye for the lovely and rare, and it delighted Emma when he shared his sightings with her; they added a golden sheen to her everyday life. Here was the person she loved, the one whom she wanted, now in this moment, to share a home with.

"Parakeets in Prospect Heights," she said, kissing Nick on the cheek. "Perfect."

Aboard the subway, Emma perused the map. She'd hop off at Grand Street, then Nick would continue one more stop, switch to the 6 train, then shoot up the East Side to Twenty-eighth Street. They'd be thirty-five blocks apart, each in their own home. The distance spanned about a foot on the map, the same space between those walk-in closets.

"So?" Nick pinched at Emma's waist.

"Huh?"

"I said, do you want to crash at my place tonight?"

"Oh, nah, I don't have another dress there to go with these shoes."

"Okay, then we've arrived at your destination. Stand clear of the closing doors and all that. Love you."

Emma slipped through the train doors, then navigated the two crowded blocks to her building. She climbed the four flights that were responsible for her powerful glutes but that always reeked of cat pee and occasionally housed an actual hissing alley cat (thankfully not tonight). Opening her front door, Emma was hit by a wall of heat. The apartment had a talent for holding on to the day's swelter long through a cool evening. She flicked on a fan and yelled out, "Hello?" knowing she'd get no response. Her roommate was an architect who lived and sometimes also slept at her office. If not for the occasional appearance or disappearance of a rolled-up blueprint or a fat textbook on electrical wiring, Emma would've sworn she didn't exist. Emma didn't mind, though; in fact, she'd chosen the girl because she seemed like the busiest of all the Craigslist applicants. Emma now wondered what it would be like to have a more present roommate, to share with Nick a set of keys, an address, a view out the window, a permanent bed. It thrilled and frightened her both.

The kitchen sink swelled with the remains of last night's stir-fry, and Emma, for the first time feeling sullen over her lack of a dishwasher, set about tackling the dishes. As she soaped and scrubbed, her forehead gleaming with sweat, she dreamed of her new home in Brooklyn, where she and Nick would likely live come October first, just five short weeks away.

"And we've never been happier," Ms. Feit noted of the couple's new digs.

"It's true," Mr. O'Hare concurred. "We made the right choice. Everything worked out for the best."

Chapter 2

Genevieve poked her head into Emma's office. "Hey, Feit, your ten a.m.'s here." Genevieve straightened out the *1, 2, 3 . . . Ivies!* button that she was required to wear on her lapel, and winked, like this whole receptionist gig was a joke. Emma had helped Gen land the job a few months ago after Gen had once again declared she'd given up on acting. Genevieve claimed she was filling out applications for nursing school, but Emma guessed her friend would return to auditioning within the year, as she always had shortly after previous "I'm through!" declarations.

"Thanks, Gen."

"If you need anything—faxes, Post-its, sexual favors—you know where to find me." She batted her eyelashes, and Emma chucked a pencil at her. "Hey, no need to get feisty. I'm leaving."

Emma flipped through the dossier on her new client—male, Tribeca born and bred, enrolled at Stuyvesant. As always, she hoped that only the student would show, but 90 percent of the time the parents flanked their child like twin parasites, primed to run the show and suck most of the life out of their kid. This appointment proved to be no exception, as Emma rose to greet the boy and saw that both Hellis were accounted for. ("Helli" was Emma's shorthand for Mom or Dad, a cross between "Helicopter Parent" and "hell-raiser.") Dad looked business casual in a button-down but no tie, and Mom wore an eighties-style power suit, dragging Son along like a timid puppy. The boy, a head taller than his parents but still prepubescent, was all limbs in an oversized T-shirt he probably wished he could disappear into.

"You must be the Spencers. Please take a seat. I'm Emma Feit, and I'll be your college advisory counselor, prepared to hold Paul's hand through every step of the admissions process. Soon you'll be off to the university of your dreams." Usually Emma blew off this introductory stump speech, but when her door was open and she sensed her boss nearby, she went for it. "One note before we begin: I seem to be missing Paul's high school transcripts and PSAT scores."

"Oh, Paul is just entering his freshman year." This from Mom, tap-tap-tapping her sling-back heel against a well-muscled calf. "We figured we'd get a bit of a jump on the process." The boy smiled meekly.

"I see." Emma had learned that when it came to their kids' success, nothing was too crazy for Manhattan parents. That very morning she'd received a voicemail asking if she'd be willing to tutor a girl during her track practice, providing she could keep up with an eight-minute mile. So if these Hellis wanted their son to run SAT practice drills for the next three and a half years, who was Emma to deny herself all the billable hours?

"The Yorks gave you glowing reviews. They told us your nickname was Eight, since you got into all the Ivies. Very clever." Mrs. Spencer said this like it was her own witticism, and Emma resisted an eye-roll. Her boss, Quinn, had pried this info out of Emma during her interview at *1, 2, 3 . . . Ivies!* Even after Emma insisted she'd benefited from some lucky admissions fluke, Quinn had burdened her on the spot with the so-called nickname. "Although I wondered, after reading your bio, why on earth would you choose Brown over Harvard or Yale?" This woman was worse than Emma's own mother.

"Honey, come on." Mr. Spencer offered Emma an apologetic look.

"That's all right," Emma said. "Brown has an excellent Linguistics department. At the time I hoped to pursue a Ph.D. in World

Languages. But here I've landed, and now I can help Paul get into any school he wants, then he can disappoint you guys by picking the wrong one, just like I have." There—the first inkling of a smirk from the boy. Emma was in. She'd explain to them all of their options, from the Basic Package of SAT and Essay Skills, to the Deluxe Deal that included Interview Prep, Extracurricular Bolstering, Personality Development, Social Media Training, and more. The Hellis would spring for the works, of course. And because Emma had shown with her quip that she was on Paul's and not his parents' side, he'd leave slightly less terrified than he'd been when he walked in, and he'd reluctantly agree to go Deluxe. Done and done—and all before eleven a.m.

On cue at five before the hour, Genevieve appeared in the doorframe. "Ms. Feit, your next clients have arrived." Emma was booked back-to-back today. The cusp of the school year was the busy season.

"In hot demand, I see," Mrs. Spencer said, clutching her purse. "I guess we'll have to carve out some of your precious time before it's all snatched up."

"Wonderful to meet you." Emma shook all three hands—Mom's a death grip, Dad's and Son's both like putty—and guided them out of her office.

Emma's next client, Sophia Cole, sat cross-legged on the waiting room floor, drawing. Emma's view of the sketchpad was blocked, but from the way Sophia kept not-so-slyly glancing up at the set of Hellis and Son seated opposite her, all in crisp Ralph Lauren polos, Emma guessed the trio was involuntarily sitting for a family portrait.

"Sophia, so nice to see you." Emma greeted every client with some version of this statement, but she actually meant it with Sophia Cole. Sophia had been seeing her for the past six months, ever since she got a 600, the lowest possible score, on the SATs. Her first session, Sophia had slunk into Emma's office on her own, sans Hellis. Besides telling Emma that her mother had threatened to take away her art supplies if she didn't show up, she'd refused to speak. But Emma had suspected from the start that she was not dealing with a moron; quite the opposite. After a few futile attempts to engage the girl, Emma had let her be with her pad and pencil. With five minutes left of the session, Emma had tried again: "So, what happened during the test?" Sophia, eyeing her warily, had slid over her notepad: In beautifully rendered detail was an illustration of a middle-aged man in a leather jacket and fedora, a cigarette dangling from his sneer; below that, the same man was pictured, now naked, penetrating a buxom woman from behind; at the bottom of the page, the man was shown curled up on the ground, lying in a pool of blood.

Emma had guessed Sophia expected a disapproving reaction, but she'd said simply, "You're quite the artist."

"Dad be a bad cad. Bed a babe. Dad dead."

"Excuse me?"

The girl repeated herself: "Dad be a bad cad. Bed a babe. Dad dead."

Emma had glanced back at the drawing, then up at Sophia, whose eyebrows were arched with satisfaction. Then Emma burst into laughter. "So that's how you answered the multiple choice, D-A-D B-E A B-A-D C-A-D, et cetera, right? Clever. I mean quite dumb, but clever, too. Your mom mentioned something about the proctor confiscating a picture." In fact, Emma had realized, it took nearly as much skill to get zero answers correct as it took to get them all right.

Sophia's eyes had glinted, and Emma had known they'd get along thereafter. She'd passed the girl's test, plus Sophia seemed like the type of teen Emma wished she'd had the guts to be back in high school. Since that first session, Sophia had agreed to complete just one practice exam, and she'd scored perfectly, proving she probably needed a shrink, not Emma. But at Mrs. Cole's insistence, Emma was charged with convincing Sophia that college was key to life success. Because she liked the girl, Emma had agreed to the mission, playing halfhearted ambassador to the illustrious life of a university coed.

Now Sophia looked up from the waiting room floor and angled her drawing to face Emma. Pictured on the page were three cartoon wasps, all in matching polo shirts and accessorized—a strand of pearls for the female wasp, a Rolex for the male, and a golf club for the child. Despite being insects, the drawings bore strong resemblances to the human trio sitting across the room.

"Get it?" asked Sophia. "White Anglo-Saxon—"

"Yeah." Emma cut her off, eyeing the family anxiously. "Okay, troublemaker, let's go. I want to tell you about this really interesting program at RISD."

"Feit, *psst!*" It was Genevieve, beckoning from the front desk. Emma wondered if her friend had glimpsed Sophia's caricatures or overheard their exchange.

"Meet you in a minute," Emma said to Sophia, then approached Gen. "What's up?"

"So what, do you have a stalker now?"

"Excuse me?"

"I got a call from a, let's see"—she flipped through her messages dramatically, wrinkling her forehead as if she was about to report on a client's poor SAT scores—"a Mrs. Caroline. She claimed to be a landlady, but sounded more like a psychopath. So when she asked for your boss I just pretended to be Quinn." Gen began impersonating the CEO's raspy voice and overly articulated vowels, which made Emma laugh. "Why does she need to know how tidy you keep your office, your day-to-day mood patterns, and—what was it?—whether I predict you'll still be working here ten years down the line?"

"*Ten years?*" Emma couldn't help the outburst. The thought of still doing this job a decade from now made her imagine a leap from their twelfth-floor office; come 2022, Manhattan parents would probably start signing up their kindergarteners for *1, 2, 3 . . . Ivies!* Plus, Emma had trouble committing to plans more than a week in advance, never mind a decade; she liked to keep her options open.

"Tell me about it. So who is this Caroline lady?"

"She actually is who she says. And her apartment is beyond incredible."

"So incredible that you'd put up with her as your landlady?"

"Yep."

"And what does that dreamy boyfriend of yours think of this Mrs. Caroline?"

"Nick agrees. Trust me, this is the place for us."

"All right, then. By the way, I told her I'm considering signing you up for *Hoarders* and that you're *this* close to getting fired."

"Gee thanks, Gen. You're a gem."

"By the way, that family out there is your twelve o'clock. That kid's some kind of football legend at Horace Mann, but his grades are appalling. The parents want him in tutoring six days a week."

"Oy, did you tell them we're closed weekends? And that they don't need to arrive more than an hour early?"

"Hey, I just answer the phones." Gen smiled mischievously. Emma appreciated that her friend had the ears of a bat; she was a pro at eavesdropping on the waiting room chatter while pretending to look busy. If she ever returned to the stage, she'd kill it playing some snooty Manhattan mom or spoiled city kid; she'd done extensive field research. "Now up you go, off to work."

"Sophia's probably pulling a Michelangelo as we speak, painting a mural on my ceiling."

"Better go nip that in the bud. I'm not sure the WASPs would appreciate nude art in your office." So then she had seen Sophia's drawing—what a sneak.

"On it." Emma scurried down the hall, pumped for her weekly spar session with the sullen girl genius.

Nick examined his scrawling on the chalkboard, lamenting the fact that his handwriting looked about as grown-up as his fifth graders':

Class 232 Rules:

1. Treat others how you want to be treated, with kindness and respect!
2. Take responsibility for yourself and your actions.
3. Arrive ready to learn and to have fun!

If only everyone everywhere followed these rules, Nick thought, *the world would be a much happier place.* Not that his classroom was any kind of utopia—he shuddered to imagine what kind of curveballs would come at him this year. Ten-year-olds who still peed their pants? Boys and girls trying to figure out how sex worked, first-hand in the supply closet? Parents complaining that certain units—dinosaurs, the Civil War, fractions, you name it—were incompatible with their religion or politics? In his twelve years of teaching, Nick had weathered it all. Still, it was gratifying for him to establish a set of rules at the outset and at least aim to build a genuine community.

Nick had asked all the parents of his incoming class to send photos of their kids during a happy moment—photos that he was now tacking up over each name. Last year Nick had participated, too, posting a picture of Emma and him paddle-boarding in Costa Rica. They'd spent most of that vacation laid out on the beach reading aloud to each other, she from *Pride and Prejudice* (decent, if a little dry) and he from *Lord of the Rings* (mind-blowing, even the third time); that was Nick's happy place. But his students had ribbed him mercilessly about the girl in the blue bikini, chanting during chaotic moments, "Mr. O'Hare and his girlfriend sitting in a tree, K-I-S-S-I-N-G . . ." Then Nick would have to become a taskmaster, a role he hated, and point the kids back to Rule #1. Eventually he'd taken down the photo and was thankful that none of the kids seemed to notice.

"What next, Mensa?" Nick poked a finger into the cage and tapped the gerbil's furry head. He wondered how the little guy would adjust to the new batch of kids who would come storming in the following week. Mensa began spinning wildly in his wheel.

"I know, it's a thrill," said Nick. "Another year, another fresh start." The wheel's squeaking didn't bother Nick, but it drove Emma bonkers. He kept Mensa at home over the summer, and even from the other end of the apartment with a cloth over the cage, Emma complained that the wheel's turning kept her up at night. Nick was relieved that their cohabitation would coincide with the start of the school year, when students would take turns pet-sitting the gerbil on nights and weekends.

Nick scanned his classroom, and decided to set out the seeds and soil and paper cups that the kids would need for the bean plant experiment. It was amazing, really, how varying the rate of water-ing or the amount of sunlight made such a difference: a lush, healthy plant beaming in the sun, versus its gangly, shriveled counterpoint languishing in the shade. Science was awesome.

Badoop! Nick checked his phone—a text from Emma: *Scored client this a.m. 14 yrs old, mom = nutcase. Also, Mrs. C called Gen for rec. TOTAL nutcase. But she's calling references, so a good sign, right?*

He thought about calling back, but Emma kept her cell on silent at work, and reaching her office line required a ten-minute chat with Genevieve first; Nick wasn't in the mood. He texted back: *Brava on the client. You're a star! Good sign, yes.*

A twinge of nausea gripped at Nick's gut and he dropped into one of the child-sized chairs. Mrs. Caroline was a concern—he worried how she'd respond if he and Emma needed an exterminator or a plumbing repair. But the queasiness felt like more than just nerves over a landlady.

It was a new variable—living with Emma. Nick breathed deeply, wondering whether the new arrangement would be like adding sunlight or taking it away. Would their relationship flourish or wither? He wished he could keep a control going, too. Because Nick liked the control. He was wary of taking their strong relationship and testing it under new conditions, as if their lives were some kind of science experiment.

To calm himself, Nick glanced at the schedule he'd mapped out for his class—each day divided into forty-five-minute blocks of reading, math, et cetera—a routine that was soothing in its structure. Nick marveled when Emma rattled off all she had going on in a particular day, always different from the previous one. She loved the unpredictable and—as much as she complained about it—relished the crises of her high-strung clients.

Sweet, brilliant, wonderful Emma, who'd been pushing for months to share a home with him. It was true they were both sick of lugging clothes and toiletries and everything else back and forth from one apartment to the other, uptown and downtown and back. And it did seem ludicrous to be shelling out two separate rents when on most nights one of their beds lay fallow. These were the sorts of details they discussed, and the kinds of reasons Nick's buddies cited for shacking up with their girlfriends. And yet, Nick wasn't convinced these minor annoyances added up to a case for such a major life change. Again, why shake up what was working well?

Nick peered into Mensa's cage. "It's me and you, buddy." Glassy eyes blinked back at him. When Nick had bought the pet two years ago, he was told gerbils were social creatures and preferred to live in pairs. So he'd gotten Mensa a companion. But the duo had been vicious together, hissing and fighting until Nick had been forced to give one away to a teacher down the hall.

Nick believed there was something to his pea-brained pet's preference for his own space. Nick, too, had been living alone for nearly a decade, and he was wary of abandoning what Emma derisively called his bachelor pad. He knew the stereotype—that men were commitment-phobes, from Mars, et cetera—but Nick felt the opposite. He believed himself so committed that he felt terrified of moving in with Emma and having her discover some so-called deal-breaker. It was one thing for her to crash at his place and have to navigate piles of comic books, or to spot a month-old block of tofu festering in his fridge, or an X-rated clip loaded up on his laptop (she minded the rotting food more than the porn). But it was quite another thing for Nick's unwholesome habits to contaminate Emma's own home. A home that would also be his, in a new location with a new layout and new quirks and surprises and frustrations. Nick's stomach flipped. Still, all of these worries had become moot when Emma eventually made it clear that, if he didn't give in to the experiment in cohabitation, Nick was going to lose her.

The loudspeaker emitted a beep, then hissed with static. "Attention, empty school. Paging Mr. O'Hare. Mr. Nicholas O'Hare, please report to the principal's office, on the double!" Nick grunted. The voice belonged to Carl, who'd just been promoted to assistant principal. But Nick didn't mind the excuse for a break, and when he arrived at Carl's office, his friend had his feet propped on the desk and was cracking open a beer. "Want one? It's just past noon, so we're good."

"Where's Lara?"

"Our beloved principal is at some workshop all day. Something about the state's new standards of excellence—in other words, blow me. They tried to make me go, but I talked my way out of it. More important matters to attend to here." Carl raised his can.

"Clearly. Pass me one of those."

"So, I hear Emma's finally roped you into the next big step of relationship-hood."

"Did that landlady call you?"

"Oh, you mean the C.I.A. agent with the epic list of questions about your personal character and criminal record? Yes, she certainly did. Congrats, dude."

"Thanks."

"With me and Suze, it only took six months for her to wear me down into living together. Two years in, we were bound for life and Suze had grown obese with the fetus that would become our whiny, diarrhea-prone, bank account–draining progeny."

"Nice talk, Carl."

"I love the rugrat, of course."

"Of course."

"But you're a tougher case, Mr. Totebag-carrying, Tree-hugging Marlboro Man, always going on about how much you care about those snot-covered students of ours. You're not an easy one to wrangle in, are you?"

"Is there a point to this meeting, or were you just testing out how your voice sounded over the loudspeaker?"

"Mostly the latter."

"Narcissist."

"I'll admit it, Nicky boy, the power's gone to my head. *Mwa-ha-ha!*" He threw his head back. "But I also wanted to toast your blind leap into the deep pit that some call relationship maturity. Cheers, to you and Emma!"

They glugged the remainder of their beers, and Carl unleashed a powerful belch.

"So," Nick asked, "what did you say to that landlady, anyway?"

"I told her the truth, that you're a gentleman and a scholar." Nick felt a small blip of joy. If he was resigned to move in with Emma, at least they'd end up in that apartment that was almost too good to be true.

Chapter 3

Emma drew seven tiles from the Scrabble pouch, then arranged and rearranged the letters on her rack until a seven-letter word emerged: BURGERS. A bingo on her first turn! She laid the tiles down on the board, and tallied her points: 76.

"On second thought, I think I'm too tired to play," said Nick.

"No way, dude! You're the one who convinced me."

Nick sighed, examined his tiles, then dropped FAX above and slightly to the left of BURGERS, also creating AB and XU vertically.

"Thirty points, not bad."

When three of the next five of Emma's words were diner-related— FRIES, SHAKE, and CHEESE—Nick said, "Any chance you're hungry?"

"Affirmative." Emma liked to send messages via Scrabble moves. Nick preferred a more straightforward mode of play, laying down a boring but strategic two- or three-letter word and cleaning up in points. "Let's do takeout from the Meatball Shop."

"Em, you're averaging once a day there. Soon you might turn into a meatball."

"I'm just trying to enjoy as much meat as possible before I'm sentenced to a life of seitan and portobellos." It was one of Emma's concessions for the move-in, that she'd respect Nick's preference for a meat-free apartment. "Although I am looking forward to the slimming results of tofu and kale. Five or six veggie balls for you?"

"Five's good."

Emma swiped open her phone, but heard no dial tone. "Hello?"

"Ems, thank God you're there."

"Annie?" It was her best friend, sounding more frantic than usual. "What, do you live in my phone now?"

"Huh? Listen, I just found out there's a weight limit for my suitcase, and I need you to help me figure out which shoes to ditch: hiking boots, wedges, or kitten heels?"

"I thought you guys were going on an African safari."

"We are, but there's supposed to be this big banquet at the end. I want to look cute! I've spent months putting together my honeymoon wardrobe, and only now do I find out I can't bring it all. This is a disaster."

"Annie, this is not a disaster. Tomorrow we'll go over it together, okay? I'm with Nick tonight."

"Hey, remind him to bring a flask this weekend. I don't know what the guys have planned, but Eli said a flask was imperative."

"The flask?" Nick whispered. "She's already e-mailed me twice about it."

"Flask packed, check! Anything else?" Emma's stomach was growling.

"Yeah, about a million things. I'm only getting married in seventy-two hours!"

"Put a pin in those concerns and we'll deal with every little thing in the morning."

"You're the best maid of honor ever."

"I know I am. I'll talk to you tomorrow." Emma hung up, called in the dinner order, then flopped onto the couch.

"How's she holding it together?" Nick asked.

"Just barely. But who expected anything other than Annie Bridezilla Blum?"

"She's why you're so good at your job, you know. You can deal with all those crazy parents because you've had a lifetime of practice with Annie."

"You're right. Prepping for a dozen college interviews is nothing compared to what Annie used to put me through before a middle school Snowball Dance."

"Yeesh, Annie as a preteen." Nick shook his head. "It's your turn."

Emma switched her theme: She laid down the words VEIL and SPEECH, then cleaned up with BOUQUETS, right through the triple-word score for 116 points.

"Think it's safe to say I won?" Emma asked.

"I do."

"I do, too."

"You set me up for that," Nick said.

"I did. Just like you set me up for the triple-word score, and the win. Boo-ya!"

"And now, you may kiss your poor opponent." And they did, until it was time to pick up their food.

On Emma's way to the Meatball Shop, Annie called again. "I didn't know you found an apartment!" Her shrieking made Emma jerk the phone away from her ear.

"You have a lot going on, Annie. I didn't want to add—"

"Thanks for listing me as a reference, by the way. It's an honor and a privilege. And the place sounds unreal! I know you were worried about having enough space to breathe with Nick, and what did she say, eight hundred square feet? Wow! With hardwood floors and a skylight? Killer! I'm a little concerned that the bathroom hasn't been redone since the eighties, but we can re-grout and spruce it right up. Have you thought about paint colors? I've seen this gorgeous Robin's Egg swatch that I think would be great for the bedroom, seems very you and Nick. I'll bring it this weekend."

"Annie, slow down. First of all, you are not bringing paint swatches for my apartment to your own wedding. Secondly, how do you know all this stuff?"

"Oh, Mrs. C and I got to chatting. We have a lot in common. We both prefer the Whitney over MoMA and we both want to be best friends with the Dowager Countess on *Downton Abbey*—no offense to my real bestie. Mrs. Caroline seems like she really cares about you guys. She was so interested. I think you're a shoo-in."

"I knew you could charm her." This is why Emma loved Annie, because as impossible as she could be, she would also do anything for a friend. Emma spotted the hostess and, covering her speaker, whispered, "Yes, Emma Feit. Five veggie, six lamb."

"Ems, you are *not* eating meatballs three days before my wedding, are you? That dress of yours is skintight."

"I plead the Fifth."

"*Blerg*. Okay, enjoy your greasy dinner. Kindly go for a run afterward. Ta-ta!"

Back home Emma found Nick crouched over a notepad. "So I concede that you won either way," he said, "but with our superior version of point scoring, you only beat me by thirty-two, instead of the sixty-eight-point slaughtering you delivered with traditional scoring."

"*Only* thirty-two, huh?" Emma kissed Nick on the forehead and dug into the take-out bag.

Together Emma and Nick had developed what they thought was a fairer way to score Scrabble. Based on facility of use and frequency of appearance, they believed that Qs and Zs should be worth eight, not ten, points; that Cs should be four, not three; that Ys should be five, not four; and that Us should be two, not one. They disagreed only on the V; Emma thought it should be five, but Nick felt it was aptly weighted at four points. For her twenty-ninth birthday last year, Nick had designed Emma a poster of their scoring (he valued the V at 4.5), framed it, and hung it above her bed. Emma was so touched that she'd insisted on showing off the poster to everyone who came over. Most people deemed it super-sweet or super-dorky. Except Emma's brother and his wife, that is.

"Oh, we used to have board game nights, didn't we, Max?" Alysse, Emma's sister-in-law, had remarked during a visit. "Gin rummy and Monopoly." *Those games aren't at all like Scrabble*, Emma had thought but not said. "That was before we had real responsibilities, of course."

"Well, I think it's cute that you guys spend so much time playing games," Max had added, patting Emma's head like she was a puppy instead of his younger sister. "It's whimsical." The implication seemed to be that the way she spent her time was insubstantial, and Emma had fumed. Her brother often managed to diminish whatever she felt proud of or excited about. That memory still gave Emma a twinge.

"You know," Nick said now, reaching for his dinner, "I think our point system has subconsciously affected my play. Whenever I recalculate the score using our version I always come out ahead."

"So that's your excuse, huh?" Emma dug into a lamb meatball, and with mouth full, added, "How many more times do you think I'll hear from Annie tonight?"

As if on cue, her phone rang. She swiped it open and, still chewing, said, "Annie, I told you we'd figure it all out tomorrow."

"Excuse me, Emma?"

Emma nearly choked on her food. "Oh, Mrs. Goldstein, I'm so sorry. I thought you were someone else. How are you this evening?" Ever the professional, Emma had all her clients' voices memorized. It was important to let the Hellis know how much she valued them. She chastised herself for being so careless.

"Good. Well, listen, we have somewhat of a doozy on our hands. We just received Isaac's fall course schedule, and he got Mr. Trundle for A.P. World."

"I see." Emma had dealt with this issue before with her students from Riverdale; she knew that Mr. Trundle didn't believe in grade inflation, and—arguably a graver crime for her clients—didn't tolerate overinvolved parents.

"I'm sure he's a fine teacher," Mrs. Goldstein continued, "but I've heard rumors about suspect comments he's made regarding the Israel-Palestine situation. And this class covers World War II, you know, *the Holocaust*"—this last part she whispered—"so I wouldn't want to put Isaac in any uncomfortable situations. . . ." She trailed off, and Emma rolled her eyes. There was no way Riverdale would hire an anti-Semite to its faculty, as Mrs. Goldstein seemed to be insinuating, but these parents always had to feel justified in their special requests.

"I hear you," Emma said. "Let me put a call into the school. Mr. Trundle tends to teach A.P. in the afternoons, and I've had luck in the past suggesting that a student's right-brain processing is keener in the morning."

"Emma Feit, you're a star. I don't know what we'd do without you."

Without me, you'd have a kid who'd know what it was like to get a B, a kid who'd have an easier time dealing with real life someday when he won't just be able to hire someone to make all his problems go away. Emma didn't say this, of course, especially since she knew she was part of the problem. But she also knew that some of these kids *would* in fact grow up to live in a world where they *could* keep hiring someone to disappear their problems; so, she figured, why not take advantage for a cut of the profits? Anyway, that's what Emma told herself when she was up in a cold sweat in the middle of the night debating the ethics of her job and questioning her long-ago flight from academia. (At other times, Emma found these twinges of guilt reassuring—they would make it easier one day when she'd decide to flee this job, as she inevitably would when some shiny new opportunity presented itself.)

As soon as Emma got rid of Mrs. Goldstein, her phone rang again. This time she checked the caller ID: *Annie.*

"So Eli's staying at his parents' place. They said they want to bond with him as a single man for the last time. Lame-slash-sweet, right? Ems, will you please come sleep over at my place? I'm freaking out and don't want to be alone tonight."

"Well, Nick is down here at my apartment."

"Tell Nick he can get a six-pack and an on-demand movie, my treat. Or leave him your Facebook password so he can cybersnoop. Come on, please?"

Nick was furiously shaking his head. Emma turned away. "All right, fine. I'll be over there soon."

She hung up, and Nick groaned. "If that girl asked you to hide the body of someone she just murdered, you'd start clearing out your closet."

"If it was three days before her wedding, yeah, I probably would. But guess what? She'd do the same for me."

"I should've brought Mensa over to keep me company. He could watch me play video games and then we'd cuddle together under your covers."

"Gross." Emma shuddered at the thought.

"The little guy would be so cozy, curled up on your pillow."
Nick contorted his facial features into a surprisingly realistic de-
piction of a gerbil, and Emma pelted a plastic fork at him. "Nice,
Em. I actually think I'll head home. Come on, I'll walk you out."

When Annie swung open the door, the fact that her face was
covered in blue goop didn't stop her from leaning in to kiss Emma
hello. She was wearing oversized shorts (probably Eli's) and a
sports bra, and her hair was twisted up into a shower cap.
   "Why does it reek of mayonnaise in here?" Emma asked. "I
thought you'd sworn off fat all month."
   "To eat, yes. That's my hair mask. It's for shine and luster, and
condiments are cheaper than the spa stuff."
   "Yuck."
   "I have ten minutes left of my Insanity workout. Come and
squat with me."
   "No way, my butt isn't doing anything but planting itself onto
your couch. But first I'm raiding the fridge." In the freezer Emma
found a rice-milk coconut bar, probably the closest thing to junk
food Eli and Annie had. She tore it open and plunked onto the
couch, which afforded her a first-rate view of Annie's calorie-blasting
contortions.
   "Eli would kill you if he saw you eating that there," Annie said
between gasps.
   "Good thing he's not here then. Who buys a white leather sofa,
anyway?"
   "Eli's boss has the same one, and he was inspired. It's imported
from Italy."
   "Of course it is. Whatever happened to that futon from your old
place, the one we scored on Avenue A after that mile-long bar
crawl about a million years ago? Remember we paid those guys ten
bucks to haul it up five flights to your apartment?"
   "God, they should've insisted on at least twenty. When I moved
I put that ratty old thing right back where it came from, down on
the curb. Good riddance."
   "It's exhausting me just looking at you." Annie had moved on to
burpees, manically launching herself into the air, squatting down,

flinging her legs back into a plank, performing a push-up, then catapulting her body back up for more. "Does Eli freak out that you're sweating on the rug, which he probably had airlifted in from Persia?"

"Ha ha. You forget, my friend, I don't sweat."

Emma reached out a foot and nudged Annie mid-jump, causing her to stumble. "Hey, clumsy, you don't sweat, and apparently you don't have any coordination, either."

"Ems, how dare you!" Annie stopped and caught her breath. Her flush overlaid with the blue goop gave her face a green sheen. "If I broke my ankle right then, you'd be responsible for carrying me down the aisle on Sunday."

"And I'd do it with pleasure and panache. So, wanna go through your suitcase?"

"Nah. I know you'll make me ditch all the fun stuff, like my mood candles and hot rollers."

"You're flying to South Africa with hot rollers?"

"See? Let's do something fun instead. Ooh, I know. Wait here."

Annie scurried off. Moments later she returned, her face scrubbed clean and a flash drive between her fingers.

"Eli converted all my old VHS tapes. You are not going to believe what I found."

Cozying up next to Emma, Annie opened her laptop, and moments later Emma was staring at moving images of the two of them from half a lifetime ago. There they were in Annie's childhood basement—Emma recognized the teal wallpaper—both in off-the-shoulder dresses, practicing their pouts. Emma could almost smell the rich rosiness of Heather Moon, the Clinique lipstick they both wore back then. Watching her teenage self make kissy faces to the camera, Emma felt half-convinced that this scene was from just last week; it was as if the last fifteen years had never happened, or had simply whooshed by in a dream, her brain's invention during a particularly intense bout of REM sleep.

"This is what I'm going to do all over Doug's face tonight," on-camera Annie said, her voice the same as now. She smooched Emma's cheek, and Emma grimaced at the camera. Emma remembered the lead-up to this night. Though they'd only been freshmen, Annie had strategically scored them invites to Prom. For months she'd been "running into" senior Doug Parker in the halls, at the mall, wherever, and reeling him in with her charm and her well-developed chest. This effort was made partly because Doug was a hot football player and Annie could imagine nothing more incredible than slow dancing with him at Prom, but also because she'd known that his best friend, Joey Puck, would be too shy to get himself a date, and then Emma could come, too.

"How far are you gonna go with Joey tonight, Ems? First base? Second?" Video Annie tugged fast at the zipper on her friend's dress, exposing Emma's suddenly bare top half to the camera.

She shrieked. "Annie, what the hell! You better destroy this tape tonight." Her teenage squawk made Emma wince; she hoped she'd grown out of it.

"I will, I will." Emma flashed a look at her present-day friend, who was wheezing laughter identically to how her fifteen-year-old self was currently doing on-screen.

"You're lucky I didn't post it online," present-day Annie said, as her younger counterpart remarked, "I'm telling Doug he has to take me out at least ten times before I'll go all the way. That's how to get respect from a guy. And then he'll want to marry me and have a dozen little babies with me."

"You want to marry Doug Parker? Yuck!" Emma was no longer in the shot, presumably off fixing her dress.

"Why not? Our wedding would be unreal. I'd wear one of those mermaid gowns, and the bridesmaids would be in pink and green, and you'd be my maid of honor, natch."

Emma watched the screen, rapt. She'd played plus-one at all of Annie's bridal appointments this past spring, and when her friend had stepped out of the Bloomie's dressing room in the Carolina Herrera mermaid number, they'd both known it was totally Annie, tiara to train. For Emma's maid-of-honor getup, her friend had picked a green sheath dress with a pink sash.

"You're a psycho, Annie." Emma was back in the shot, her dress now crooked.

"Oh come on, don't tell me you don't dream about your wedding day."

"I don't!"

"Well, who's the freak now? When you're off studying Advanced Calculus and A.P. Astro-whatever, the rest of us are choreographing our first dances with our future grooms." Teenage Annie grabbed Emma's hands, and off they went, sashaying through Annie's basement, in and out of the camera view. "You must fantasize about the future."

"Of course I do. About doing something amazing with my life. Also, having a maid so I'll never have to do laundry again, and owning a soft-serve machine."

"And making out with Joey Puck tonight, right?" Annie dipped Emma and made kissy noises at her. "Ems, my wedding is going to be a hundred times better than Prom. Picture us fifteen years from now, ancient at thirty, two old married ladies reminiscing about Prom. We probably won't even remember whether or not we kissed our dates."

Emma felt herself heating up, her thighs sticky with sweat against Eli's expensive leather sofa. But next to her, Annie was squealing. "Can you believe this shit? And here I am, tying the knot just under the wire, one week before my thirtieth birthday. God, I must've been psychic back then."

Emma smiled, but she felt slightly sick. She'd turned thirty back in March, five months earlier. Plus, she *did* remember what had happened that night: Joey Puck had managed to maneuver his slobbery tongue around her mouth for the entirety of Toni Braxton's "Un-Break My Heart," and Annie had snuck out of the dance early to go lose her virginity in the back of Doug Parker's mother's minivan. "Let's turn this off."

"Oh, come on, the best part is coming up. The boys arrive and we all pose for pictures super-awkwardly. Doug has that awful bowl haircut. Can you believe I wanted to marry that guy? I think he still lives with his parents."

"Annie, I don't think I can bear any more of my teenage self."

"Yeah, that green taffeta is a nightmare. Okay, fine. Ooh, I know."

Annie pecked at her keyboard a few times, until another scene appeared onscreen, the two girls, aged six or seven, in Emma's childhood living room, wearing oversized blazers that they'd probably nabbed from her father's closet.

"Hello, we are Emma Feit and Annie Blum, world-famous chemists," Emma announced to the camera. "We recently invented a brand-new element that will transform the face of modern science. Behold element number 119, which we have named Em-An." Emma gestured at a bowl of ice cubes that looked to be dyed with orange food coloring.

"Em-An is the best element the world has ever seen," Annie added.

"Yes. It will be key to curing both cancer and the common cold. In fact, our sources have just informed us that we've won this year's Nobel Prize for Chemistry."

"Wahoo, go us! And the celebration ball is tonight," said Annie. "The menu will be pigs in blankets and prime rib and chocolate cake, and the New Kids on the Block will be performing. Watch out, world, these scientists will be partying down tonight."

On screen, Annie began Electric Sliding and Emma frowned at her friend, adding, "To learn more about the many benefits of Em-An, tune in tomorrow to Science Talk. This has been Nobel Prize–winning chemists Emma and Annie, signing off."

"Toodle-loo!"

Annie paused the clip. "Hilarious, right? I mean, the New Kids on the Block!"

"I think back then I really believed I might win a Nobel Prize one day."

"I wouldn't put it past you, Ems."

Emma smiled, grateful for her ever-supportive friend; she pushed out of her mind the fact that she prepared kids for standardized tests for a living.

"Now come help me wash this mayo out of my hair, and then we'll veg out in a bubble bath."

Changing into a bathing suit in Annie's room, Emma tested herself to see if she could still recite the periodic table of elements. She started struggling in the forties. At ruthenium, Annie called out, "Come on, I've got the jets going!" so Emma gave up and gave in to the idea of a soothing bath.

Annie and Eli's bathroom was slightly smaller than Emma's entire apartment, all white marble and soft lighting, with fresh flowers in vases beside the double sinks and an actual sitting area in the corner. The claw-foot tub looked vintage, but was tricked out with enough amenities to rival a high-end spa. "It's still hard for me to believe you actually live here," Emma said to her friend.

"I know. And lucky you, you get to come over and play anytime you want!" Emma had once Googled Eli's address and discovered the apartment's market value: $2.6 million. She knew Eli had paid to break Annie's lease when she'd moved in with him back in May. Emma began wondering if Annie contributed at all to the mortgage, then forced herself to stop; this line of thought was a slippery slope. Plus, she wanted to keep feeling excited about the prospect of a dishwasher and his-and-her closets in her own place. She plunged into the water—piping hot.

"Nice, right?" Annie dunked under, popping up a moment later covered in soap bubbles. "I feel just like Julia Roberts in *Pretty Woman*."

"Like a prostitute in a client's hotel room?"

Annie splashed her. "No, dumbass, like I'm living in a fairy tale and all of my dreams are coming true."

"Ah." There was some truth to that. Annie had been dreaming about her wedding since age five, and in Eli Silber she'd managed to find a sweet, well-off guy, and Jewish, to boot. Emma wasn't jealous of Eli—he was too much the M.B.A. guy's guy to interest her—but she envied the fact that Annie knew exactly what she wanted in the world and had gone for it, heart and soul all in. Emma could feel less sure about a pants purchase than Annie seemed to feel about the sum of her life's choices. It was exhausting to consider—and so for the moment she decided not to. She took a deep breath and dipped under the surface, letting her unsettling thoughts drift away, drowned out by the gurgle of the turbo jets.

Chapter 4

Emma had cleared her Friday appointments for maid-of-honor duty, but she'd still managed to field two client phone calls, plus convince the dean of Riverdale to switch Isaac Goldstein's history class, all before Annie blinked awake at nine-thirty.

Annie blended them kale-quinoa-ginger juices (Emma discreetly poured the majority of hers down the drain), then they suited up in bikinis and hit the roofdeck. "We are not lying out for leisure," Annie declared, slathering herself in a pungent tanning oil that Emma suspected was not FDA-approved. "This is our very last opportunity to soak up some sun before the wedding, and I want to be positively golden. Plus, my vows are a mess. Please tell me you're in the mood to ghostwrite."

Emma slathered on SPF 30—Annie called it "sad pale person potion"—and asked, "What do you have so far?" Emma wasn't thrilled with the idea of authoring her best friend's wedding vows, but it couldn't be much different from helping her students write their college essays. It was just a matter of pulling out the right anecdotes and sentiment to convey a certain message, in this case, eternal love.

Annie handed over a mess of papers, which Emma saw was a series of templates printed out from bridal Web sites. "Are you planning to do this Mad Libs–style? Okay, give me three adjectives and a verb, and I'll fill it in."

"That's not a bad idea," Annie said. "Sexy, shocking, aquamarine. Serenade."

"Let's see, 'You are the most sexy, shocking, and aquamarine person I have ever met, and I promise to always serenade you.' Well, I've heard worse."

"Ems, please help."

"Look, you want your vows to sound like you and Eli, not just any old couple. So talk about your relationship in specific ways. Like, what have you done for each other's birthdays?"

Annie shrugged. "Nothing."

"Seriously?"

"We haven't had them yet. We started dating last November. My birthday's next week and Eli's is in October."

"Wow." Emma thought about the first birthday she'd spent with Nick, her twenty-eighth. He'd given her a silver bracelet with a star dangling from it, and ever since on birthdays and Valentine's Days and other holidays he'd added a charm. The bracelet was heavy now; it clanked when Emma wore it. Depending on her mood, this either delighted or depressed her. She couldn't even remember all the gifts she'd given Nick for his various birthdays. "Then how about your favorite date? Or a memory that stands out?"

Annie shrugged. "We always just go to dinner, or to the movies, or out to bars. I know you and Nick take cooking classes and have game nights, and that's totally adorable, but we're not like that. Give me Eli, a meal, and a rom-com, and I'm happy."

"You're making this difficult, Annie. Um, when you let your mind wander, what comes to mind about Eli?"

"It's pretty simple. I love Eli and I always will. I have no idea where it comes from, but it's something I feel deep in my heart and know in my head, too. We haven't been dating that long, but when you feel it, you feel it. You could say that's just a stupid hunch, but it's the strongest one I've ever had, and anyway, I trust my feelings one hundred percent. I love Eli, I just do."

Annie shrugged, and Emma felt a funny urge to cry. Annie's

words weren't witty or clever or even original, and they had zilch in common with the kind of vows Emma imagined herself writing one day for her own wedding. But they were honest, and exactly right for Annie. "Say that," Emma said, just as her phone started ringing. "Write it down now, quick, before you forget. I'm going to get this—it's probably one of the Hellis."

"Hello?" She wandered to the other side of the deck.

"Hey, Feit, I cannot believe you flaked on work." It was Genevieve. "I'm trapped all alone in this pressure cooker of adolescent angst and parental stress. Help! SOS! Get your butt over here right now and rescue me!"

"Gen, come on, you'll be fine. I told you I'm with Annie today."

"Oh, right, the blushing bride and her *aah-maaazing* wedding." She was doing her sarcastic voice. Despite Emma's many efforts to get her two closest friends to be mutual friends, Genevieve and Annie had only ever politely tolerated each other; Emma couldn't figure out why they didn't gel. "I guess that means you can't come out with me this weekend. I'll have to hit the bars without my favorite wing-woman."

"Sorry, Gen. Next weekend, I promise." In truth Emma had grown tired of New York City nightlife. Years ago she and Genevieve had gone out to the bars each weekend practically glowing with the thrill of a night's potential, whereas these days Emma preferred to stay in on the couch with Nick, a bottle of wine, and a well-stocked DVR. But she felt guilty that Gen didn't have a Nick of her own, so she occasionally braved the too-loud music, the overpriced drinks, and the string of guys Genevieve sized up through a veneer of flirtation. Emma suspected Gen was sick of the scene, too, although without much of a viable alternative for meeting a man—Gen inexplicably refused to try online dating—she wouldn't have admitted it.

"Fine, fine," said Gen. "Tell the bride I say break a femur."

"Absolutely not. Talk to you later."

After hanging up, Emma immediately felt her phone buzz again. She picked up and spat out an impatient hello.

"Emma, hi, it's Mrs. Caroline."

"Oh hi." Emma plopped down into a lounge chair.

"I've heard some nice things about you and Nick over the past few days."

"That's great. I hope you weren't expecting anything different." Emma laughed nervously.

"No, no. Listen, I have a question for you."

"All right."

"Do you and Nick talk about the future, like plans and dreams, maybe marriage and kids, things like that?"

"Excuse me?" It was windy on the roof, and Emma was hoping she'd misheard. The truth was that she had trouble planning beyond the next weekend, but that had nothing to do with her and Nick.

Mrs. Caroline continued: "What I'm trying to say is, because I feel I must be honest . . . I'm having trouble—how shall I put it?—placing you and Nick."

"Placing us?"

"I've rented to married couples, and to single folks, and even to two friends—they had this very clever setup with these folding Chinese curtains as room dividers. Do you know what I'm talking about, those accordion thingies? They can look very elegant."

"Uh-huh." Emma was impatient. She couldn't care less how Mrs. Caroline's former tenants had set up the apartment. And whatever this woman was getting at, Emma felt it was only fair for her to come right out and say it.

"Anyway, and I only mean to be looking out for you—" Mrs. Caroline paused, and a chill shivered down Emma's spine. She hugged her arms around her torso.

"Yes?"

"Well, what will you do if, say, you and Nick split up?" Mrs. Caroline whispered the words, as if decreasing her volume would reduce her rudeness. "You'll be on a lease together. Are you certain it's smart to move in with a man who hasn't proposed yet?"

Now Emma was furious. This was almost worse than rejection. She knew if she relayed this conversation to Nick (which she already knew she wouldn't), he'd say, Forget about the apartment and let's find a place whose landlady doesn't think she's their couples counselor. And yet, Emma wanted this home.

So she strategized how to respond in the most appealing and convincing way, humiliating as it was. She cleared her throat, trying to shore up some semblance of dignity; the noise made Annie look up from her vows and wave. "Technically," Emma said into the phone, "it's not your problem if Nick and I break up, since we'll both be on the lease, therefore legally obligated to pay the rent. But you asked if I feel certain, and I do." (She worried she didn't sound at all certain.) "I hope speaking to our references confirmed for you how committed Nick and I are. If there's something else I can do—"

"That's the concern. You've really done all you can, but . . ."

"But what?"

"I've got this feeling I can't quite put my finger on."

Emma was tempted to chuck her phone over the deck down onto Houston Street. She wanted to howl, to jump up and down, go ballistic with rage. Later, she'd wonder why she hadn't done any of those things, why instead she'd put up with Mrs. Caroline's insults, why she'd waited patiently for the woman to articulate herself and then responded with a simple, civilized, "I see." What she would briefly conclude, and then push out of her mind before she had time to dwell on it, was that Mrs. Caroline had been onto something in her ungracious speech. As Annie sat on the other side of the roof scribbling down her complete and total devotion to her husband-to-be, Emma had stood there unsure of her own relationship. She'd marveled at the fact that she and Nick's ambivalence— their many late-night talks expressing worry about commitment and fear about making the kinds of serious, adult decisions that had serious, adult consequences in their lives—had been so blatant to this near-stranger. And that for some reason that tough stuff had cast a shadow over her and Nick's love and devotion to each other, when to Emma the latter felt so much more meaningful and substantial.

But before Emma had time to do anything daring or even to think these thoughts, Mrs. Caroline chimed in again: "You know what? Let's do it. Let's throw caution to the wind and do it!"

"So we're getting the apartment?" Emma's skin sprouted with goose bumps and she leaped into the air. She felt the tie to her bikini top go slack, but didn't even care that she was now flashing half of lower Manhattan. Later she would think about Mrs. Caroline's wording, and wonder, *How was this throwing caution to the wind? The woman had pored over their financial documents and called every major person in their lives and received only ringing endorsements.* But for now, Emma was simply thrilled.

"I'll prepare the lease and you two can stop by to sign it tomorrow."

"Oh, tomorrow we're going to a wedding."

"Then the next day?"

"We won't be back in town until Monday night, and Tuesday is Nick's first day of school. How about Tuesday evening?"

"That's a long time to wait." Emma started panicking. Should they return early from the wedding? Could Mrs. Caroline scan the lease and fax it to them to sign? *Whoa, calm down,* she told herself; *they'd gotten the apartment.* "But if we must wait until Tuesday, we simply must wait."

"Great!" Emma ran to Annie to tell her the news, and they squealed like kids.

"I wrote my vows, you got your apartment, and we're on top of the world," Annie said, gesturing to the Manhattan skyline laid out before them like a grand buffet. She grabbed Emma's hands and spun her around just as she had in the Prom video. "That juice didn't quite fill me up. Should we mix up some Bloody Marys?"

Emma flashed guiltily on Genevieve, stuck at *1, 2, 3 . . . Ivies!* reception while she and Annie were spending the day like spoiled socialites. Oh well, Emma thought; if Gen wasn't so cool to Annie then she could be here with them, too. "Yes, Bloody Marys, stat."

Nick was busy battling a bioterrorism-induced zombie outbreak when Emma called to tell him about the apartment.

"Take that, flesh-eating douche." He'd said it under his breath, but she'd heard.

"Video games?"

"Check. I just got my hands on *Resident Evil 6*." Nick had spent a fairly successful morning destroying a fleet of C-virus-infected cruise missiles and picking off human-hungry zombies. Big accomplishments, considering he hadn't even put on pants.

"All those kids so scared to go back to school on Tuesday, if only they knew their teacher was home playing his Nintendo whatchamacallit, just like they probably are."

"GameCube. And, Em, you've gotta respect the ritual. It's my last day of freedom, and I'm one hundred percent committed to being a complete and total waste of space. Besides, didn't you say you were tanning with Annie?"

"She'd tell you that's for work, not pleasure."

"And she'd be crazy."

"I'm getting the signal that it's time to flip to our stomachs. Don't tell Mrs. Caroline I'm soaking up cancerous rays all day, and I won't tell her you're rotting your brain killing vampires."

"Zombies. Virus-ridden zombies intent on destroying our planet. It's very important work, Em. I think even Mrs. Caroline might concede the point."

"I see a career change on your horizon. Zombie killer."

"I wonder what the benefits are like. I'd probably have to go freelance."

"Whatever makes you happy, babe, as long as you can pay the rent."

"Thanks, love."

A growling stomach finally jolted Nick out of the gaming universe. In the fridge, he found the veggies he and Emma had hauled back from the farmers' market last weekend. But no, this last day of freedom was not for leafy greens. Nick paged through his take-out menus, decided on Thai, and, fifteen minutes later and still in boxers, he answered the door to accept the brown bag. He knew if Emma had been there, she would've been mortified. She would've spent the whole meal obsessing over what the delivery guy had thought of Nick's state of undress, wondering how traumatized he'd been by their crass American culture (she always assumed delivery guys were immigrants, even though Nick himself had delivered pizza in college).

But Emma wasn't there, so Nick turned on ESPN and wolfed down his Pad Thai, burping at his leisure and zoning out to a recap of last night's Yankees game. See all the things he could do alone in his own place?

But Nick wasn't being fair, he knew, in writing Emma off as the disapproving girlfriend. In fact, she'd once told him she wished she could produce the same thunderous belches that he managed. Still, Nick needed a target for his general anxiety, and his girlfriend was an easy pick. Which was also why, at three p.m., he got dressed and set out to find a bar, happily resenting the reaction he imagined from Emma.

Nick believed daytime drinking was acceptable in the following situations: at brunch, while watching sports, on vacation, and after a particularly rough school day. He reasoned he could add one more occasion to the list: the day you officially found out you were shacking up with the old ball and chain. . . . There, he caught himself doing it again, casting Emma as some kind of sitcom girlfriend. If anyone was a ball and chain, it was Nick, always trying to convince Emma to ditch a night out with Genevieve and reel her back home to hang out with him. Still, he needed a drink.

The Irish pub he eventually chose was less depressing than the first two he'd passed, whose few dazed patrons looked as if they spent most of their weekdays planted on a barstool. But it wasn't exactly cheerful, either, with sticky floors and air heavy with stale beer and lemony disinfectant. Inside the dark space, sunlight seemed like a mirage.

Nick sipped at a Guinness and half watched an ancient *Seinfeld* episode on mute. It was the one where Kramer starts multitasking in the shower—washing dishes as he also washes himself. *No wonder none of the* Seinfeld *characters ended up in real relationships,* Nick thought; he couldn't imagine bickering with Emma over who left the lettuce by the loofah. It was funny to think how Nick had grown up watching this show, worshipping the jokes about Jewish New York that couldn't have been more foreign to small-town Ohio. In retrospect, it seemed like soaking up all that culture had been preparation for eventually meeting Emma. The first time he'd joined the Feits for dinner, during one of Emma's parents' rare trips back to New York from their home in Spain, her mom had served an actual chocolate babka for dessert.

Halfway through Nick's second beer—he'd switched to the IPA—a trio of women poured in to the bar, all chatter and flowery perfume. They claimed the three stools to Nick's right and ordered a round of tequila shots. Nick smiled noncommittally. They were of an age that would make the normally confident Emma suspicious—twenty-six or twenty-seven. That was how old Emma had been when they'd met, so she assumed it was the age Nick preferred most in women. "It's only natural, evolution-wise," she'd once explained in that know-it-all way of hers that usually masked nerves. This had been right around her thirtieth birthday. "Men want their women young and fertile. If they started lusting after more mature ladies, the human race would be in trouble, right?" Nick had felt like Emma was blaming him for some imagined wrong, yet he'd still denied it, citing Halle Berry, Naomi Watts, and Sofia Vergara as examples of older women he would happily go to bed with.

Still, though Nick never would've admitted it, there was some truth to what Emma had said. But it wasn't for the reasons she'd cited. In Nick's experience, women in their mid-twenties generally weren't too concerned with what he'd dubbed the stage-of-life calculus—meaning where they stood career- and relationship-wise, who was ahead of whom, and where they felt they should be or deserved to be by that particular age. Whereas, the closer a woman crept toward thirty, the more obsessed she became with checking off the boxes that someone somewhere at some point in time had decided made for a fulfilling, successful life: the job promotions, the relationship advancement, the procreation. And Nick couldn't stand that kind of thinking. To him, all that stuff flew in the face of the happiness that came from living in the now and appreciating where you were and who you were, not to mention who you were with.

"Cheers?"

Nick looked up to see one of the women handling two shots, one extended to him.

"Thanks," he said, accepting the glass. "Though it's kind of early for the hard stuff, am I right?"

"It's a three-day weekend, last one of the summer. That means celebration!"

"Sure, why not?" Nick threw back the shot along with the women. "So where are you ladies headed for Labor Day, the Hamptons?"

"Yeah, right. More like Coney Island."

"That's more my style, too. Funnel cake and carnival rides. Though they got rid of Shoot the Freak, didn't they?"

"Yeah, but there are still plenty of dirty old Russian men hanging around." This from the prettiest one, whose green eyes were now glinting at Nick as she sidled over to the stool on his left. Now he was surrounded. He glanced at the others. Well, it was hard to say who was prettiest. They were all sweet and sweet-smelling, talking over one another about weekend plans.

"We're doing a day trip to Beacon for the art museum, and another one out to Long Beach to go surfing."

"That's ambitious," said Nick.

"Eh, we'll probably just end up sleeping off our hangovers and wasting the day watching *Real Housewives* marathons."

Nick laughed. Emma was the only person he knew who, without fail, followed through on any plan she set; it was admirable, but it could also be exhausting. He ordered the four of them another round, intent on getting a little tipsy.

Nick knew one of the girls would eventually ask him what he did for a living; it happened after the third tequila. "I teach fifth grade," he said, and then waited for the inevitable: the three of them oohing and aahing like he was some kind of saint.

Back when he'd started out in education, long before he met Emma, Nick's friend Carl had welcomed him to the brotherhood by explaining the girl-related perks. "Mention you're a teacher, and as long as she's not a gold digger or a lesbian, she'll fall all over you," Carl had said. "One-night stands only, though. As soon as they realize you have to be in bed by ten every night and that you can't afford to take them to the latest Momofuku outpost, they'll leave you for a lawyer."

Carl's advice had been on target, and over time Nick had honed his seduction technique. Over drinks he'd talk about how much his students inspired him; he'd divulge just enough to draw admiration, then he'd transition to it's-getting-late banter. Nick had told himself he was too busy to get involved in a real relationship. But then he'd met Emma, who'd proved immune to his charms. When he'd mentioned a student who'd been struggling with cursive, hoping to elicit an affectionate "Aw!" Emma had instead snapped, "God, I can't believe you're still teaching that junk. It's so twentieth century. If kids want to have any chance of future success, they need to learn how to brand themselves and create a savvy Web presence." Emma had been working in P.R. at the time, and Nick couldn't tell whether or not she'd been joking. He'd had no choice but to be smitten.

"That has to be the sweetest job ever!" cooed the green-eyed girl now. Nick nodded, feeling a surge of delight; how simple and entertaining this was. From deep in the recesses of his brain he pulled out the old anecdotes, the ones so many girls (but not Emma) had eaten up. The stories still worked, apparently; as he performed the raps he'd written to help kids with spelling, the girls edged their stools nearer, closing in on him.

Eventually Nick noticed his empty stomach. He asked his companions if they were up for a bite.

"I could eat." It was the pretty one. "How about takeout, maybe at my place?" She touched Nick's thigh, which sent little buzzes of electricity up his leg. Nick gaped at her, wondering if her eyes' sparkling was a trick of the light. He wouldn't soon forget that gaze, a seduction much more potent than his heroic teacher routine.

Nick snapped to attention. "Shit. The wedding. Emma. I have to pack."

"Ahem, it's Mallory."

"Huh? No, not you." Nick didn't feel drunk, but when he tried to think of a breezy way to explain himself or smooth over this situation, his brain churned like sludge. He said simply, "Emma's my girlfriend." His stomach cartwheeled; the walls wavered.

"Seriously?" The girl's voice dropped an octave. "I've been wasting my time for the past six hours talking to a guy with a *girlfriend?*" *Six hours?* Nick glanced at his watch and was shocked to discover the hour and minute hands pointed jointly at the 12. It was like he'd tripped into some twisted version of "Cinderella": midnight an accusation.

"Shit, I've got to go. I'm sorry." On his way out he heard one of the girls say, "Forget about that asshole. He's just like every other dirtbag we meet here."

Back home, Nick stumbled out of his clothing, then collapsed naked into bed. A thought drifted through his head—was he really like every other dirtbag, as the girl had accused him? He was snoring before he could formulate an answer.

Chapter 5

Nick jolted awake to his ringtone's victorious pumping of the *Rocky* theme song. He was sprawled naked across his bed, and his head shivered a sensation he greeted with reluctant resignation. He eyed his phone: nine missed calls from Emma, another one coming in now. "Hello?" he squeaked, his throat parched.

"Where the hell are you? We were supposed to meet at nine. Our train leaves in twenty—no, nineteen minutes. I've been trying you all morning. Tell me you're, like, ten feet away from me and about to swoop in from behind for one of those romantic train station reunions. Please say I didn't just wake you up."

Nick cleared his throat, swiping a nugget of sleep from his eye. "No, I'm up, I'm up."

"And you're ready to go, right?"

"Of course." In fact, Nick wasn't even sure if his suit was clean; he'd been meaning to check all week.

"Okay, then you might just be able to make it. Don't bother telling me now what happened. Grab a cab and get your ass to Penn, ASAP."

A wave of nausea rippled through Nick's insides. He doubled over. "Em?"

"Yeah?"

"I'm not going to make the train. I'm so sorry."

* * *

Emma sat slumped on her suitcase, her maid-of-honor dress draped across her lap and probably growing reprehensibly wrinkled. She sucked at a too-sweet orange shake, which she'd bought from Smoothie King out of self-pity. Waiting for her delinquent boyfriend at Penn Station, she'd seen the arrivals and departures boards update themselves several times over and was lamenting the fact that two more D.C.-bound trains had come and gone since the one they'd been scheduled to board. The crowd around her had also turned over at least twice. Everyone was hurrying this way or that, intent on this or that gate, headed to this subway or that cab line, all knowing exactly where they needed to go. It seemed unnatural to stay still for so long in a train station. Emma was a loiterer, and despite the fact that Nick was supposedly now on his way, she felt officially neglected.

Not for the first time, Emma began imagining herself as the character Lily Bart in the opening scene of Edith Wharton's classic novel *The House of Mirth*, a single woman in a New York train station, anxious and alone and probably being judged by every passerby. Emma didn't kid herself that she possessed the protagonist's infamous beauty, but she did identify with Miss Bart's nerves—about making the right moves, and fearing mistakes, and figuring out how to parlay her assets into a life of success and happiness.

Emma had first encountered Lily Bart during her debut week of grad school, in a Twentieth-Century Women's Novel survey, and something about that train station moment had struck her as particularly poignant (she'd dreaded solo train travel ever since). In fact, that first scene in *The House of Mirth* was partially responsible both for Emma's decision to focus her doctoral studies on Edith Wharton's novels and for her later decision to abandon those same studies. Emma had initially homed in on Wharton's comedies of manners because she'd been fascinated with the strict, antiquated social conventions that governed that 1920s universe of Manhattan high society. How bizarre that those young women poured all of their talents and energies into the hunt for a suitable partner! How absurd to have one's life dictated and restricted by such a long list of esoteric rules, to have one's choices so limited, to have the slightest misstep spell ruin from a solid reputation and a life of respectability! And how clever and savvy Wharton had been to both satirize and celebrate this world, often within a single sentence.

These were the kinds of explanations Emma had rattled off when people asked her about her doctoral studies at the glum little cocktail parties thrown by Cornell's English department. And yet, if Emma had been brutally honest—with others or with herself—she would've admitted that partly she was intrigued by a world that handed so many answers to its denizens on a tastefully decorated silver platter. It was a world in which everyone knew exactly what was expected of them, exactly what they were to wear and say on any given occasion, and exactly what a good life looked like. Never mind that Wharton took pains to uncover how insipid this so-called good life could be—Emma was still intrigued, and more than a little envious of those debutantes whose lives were bound so tightly by corsets and curfews.

Emma, of course, had grown up being told that she could be whatever she wanted to be and, earning top grades and honors whenever they were doled out, she'd actually believed it. Never once had she seriously considered that at some point she'd have to decide what that "whatever" would actually be. Even in college she hadn't had to choose; Brown let you sample whatever classes you wanted and then labeled the collective dabbling a degree in General Studies and sent you on your way. And so, after four years of acing her courses but never settling on any one area of interest, on graduation day Emma had stood on the side of the commencement stage, clutching her *summa cum laude* diploma and paralyzed with terror. Packing up her college apartment, she'd bathed herself in tears of self-pity. It had all been a lie, she'd moaned to her roommates, those gifts of freedom and possibility, those tales about the sky being the limit.

This epiphany had sent Emma into a tailspin that resulted in two months spent nestled under a comforter in her childhood bedroom devouring hefty paperbacks. Although Emma's retreat into story had been motivated by a simple desire to escape the real world, her mother had mistaken it for a passion for fiction and, fed up after a summer of waiting hand and foot on her college-degree-holding daughter, had dropped on Emma's bed a stack of applications for Ph.D. programs in English Literature. (A year later, when her parents had suddenly sold the house to Emma's brother, Max, and transplanted their lives from Westchester to Madrid, Emma had wondered if this push for grad school had been premeditated as a way to get her out of the way.)

At the time, Emma had flipped through the pamphlets, comforted by the familiar photos of stately architecture and verdant quadrangles. She'd shrugged "Why not?," then committed herself to completing the applications with the same level of rigor she devoted to any task she set her mind to. Though the idea of a life in academia didn't exactly thrill her, Emma had felt anxious to be back in school again, learning and achieving and impressing her professors and classmates. When she'd been accepted to Cornell's prestigious program, she took it as a sign that it was the right path. So it was more than surprising when, cracking open the first book of her first semester, which happened to be Edith Wharton's *The House of Mirth*, Emma had found herself falling fast in love.

But that love hadn't lasted. Years spent monomaniacally immersed in Wharton's world—analyzing and reanalyzing the texts, and then analyzing others' analyses and counter-analyses of those same texts—all while living in isolating and often snow-submerged upstate New York, had changed Emma. By the time she was twenty-five, four years into her program and more inclined to mop the bathroom floor than attempt to make sense of her dissertation notes, Emma had started to feel overwhelmed by all those train station moments in Edith Wharton World. She'd had trouble remembering that she was studying fictional accounts of a century-old society, and not immersed in the society herself. For a while she believed she could walk through campus and happen upon Undine Spragg or Ellen Olenska or countless other characters from Wharton's oeuvre. That is, if she ever did walk through campus; going outside had become a rarer and rarer event. Hiding out in hibernation, surviving mostly on the care packages of pastries her parents sent from their bakery in Madrid, Emma had found herself unspooling into vertigo, twisted up with dread, disoriented by where she was living and what she was doing with her life.

And if that wasn't enough to contend with, Emma had also started reconsidering her girlfriends and their melodramatic concerns that she'd once dismissed as beneath her attention—the obsession over pretty dresses and makeup, and the scheming supposedly necessary to snatch up a good guy. What if these things weren't in fact trivial but instead of utmost importance? Marinating in a single pair of sweatpants for a week at a time, Emma would scare herself with a long list of what ifs. What if she became one of Wharton's heroines, pushing thirty, still on her own, and all but put out by society? What if she suddenly realized how blind she'd been to the workings of the world and only understood much too late the importance of acting in certain ways and working toward certain milestones? Only in the breeziest ways had Emma relayed these fears over the phone to Annie. Her friend had been working as an executive assistant at the time, planted behind a sleek desk in stilettos and a suit, wiling away her days checking Facebook and flirting with both her boss and her intern. Still, Annie had detected something was seriously wrong with her best friend.

"This is why people in academia are all nuts," Annie had said. "They spend all their time buried in books, studying stuff no one else could give a shit about, and they forget that there's actual life happening here in the real world. Earth to Ems, more than a hundred years have passed since Edith Wharton wrote that stuff! I can't even imagine where you'd go these days to find the kinds of outfits they wore—probably some hipster Williamsburg hat shop."

"Haberdashery," Emma said.

"What?"

Emma mumbled the word again, realizing she sounded crazy. Annie ignored her and went on. "Also: Hello, none of the stories are real! Nobody's going to jilt you at the opera, or accuse you of being a floozy for visiting some guy's apartment late at night. Times changed, oh, about a century ago, and now you can do whatever the hell you want! Get with the program, Ems!"

This outburst had actually cheered Emma up, because Annie was the last person she'd imagined would argue against society's codes of convention. Still, it hadn't been enough. With only fifty pages left to write of her dissertation, Emma had dropped out of the Ph.D. program and moved to Manhattan, where Annie had hooked her up with a job in P.R. The gig, all surface and spin, had seemed at the time like the perfect antidote to the brain-bending work of her doctoral studies. She'd met Genevieve around then, who'd been working as the office's part-time messenger in between auditions, and they'd developed mutual girl crushes—Gen taken with Emma's dramatic abandonment of academia in favor of publicity's glitz and glamour, and Emma taken with Gen's devotion to what seemed like an impossible dream career. Emma's sense of relief at her new job path had lasted about six months, until she again grew restless and panicked, intent on finding the next solution to her Lily Bart–esque dread.

Now here Emma was, going on her second hour of waiting for Nick at Penn Station, feeling worse off than the doomed Miss Bart. Lily was tragically at risk of spinsterhood and societal ostracism at age twenty-nine, and yet Emma had already hurtled past the treacherous threshold of thirty. She had a boyfriend, sure, but where was he when she needed him, i.e. now? Emma had sworn she'd arrive two hours early to Annie's rehearsal dinner to help set up. She knew it was ridiculous to stress about not being on hand for flower arrangements and centerpiece construction, but she'd made a promise to her best friend. She was the maid of honor, after all.

Not that Nick was usually unreliable. And yet Emma sometimes felt like one of those lab rats who got used to a routine, but then every once in a while—*zap!*—was tricked (*I thought pushing this lever led to a piece of cheese, not an electroshock!*) and then started to go insane. That was Emma's experience of dating Nick—90 percent of the time he was a committed and conscientious boyfriend; but there was that other 10 percent, the oversleeping, hungover, overgrown-teenager part of Nick. Then again, Emma knew she had a habit of holding the people in her life to unreasonably high standards. Just because she'd never been late to anything, and just because she believed it was inappropriate to cancel plans except in cases of high fever or stomach flu (and maybe this was why she struggled with making plans in the first place), she realized other people didn't operate by such strict principles. And that didn't make them all hopeless flakes. Just as Emma was starting to soften toward Nick, she felt him wrap his arms around her from behind and say in her ear, "Hey, bad news."

"Good morning to you, too. What's the matter now?" Emma's stomach started gurgling, like it was preparing to take in something sour. Admittedly she'd just ingested thirty-two ounces of sugar from a "size small" shake.

"Our tickets were nonrefundable, and it was going to cost another three hundred dollars to buy new ones, day of."

"So you found a teleporting machine to zip us down to D.C.?"

"Close. I booked us on Greyhound."

"You're kidding." Again, Emma felt herself slipping into the role of Lily Bart, indignant over being wronged. And she wasn't just acting like a diva. Buses made Emma ill—literally. Once, on a ride to Boston with a driver whose two modes of movement were gunning the gas and slamming the breaks, Emma had been subjected to a seatmate sloshing a pint of beef bouillon onto her lap. Not only had she spent twenty minutes vomiting in the bathroom, but because there was only hand sanitizer and not a sink with running water, she'd had to sit for three more hours stewing in a fusion of broth and alcoholic rub, willing her stomach not to erupt again. Emma detested the bus.

"I wish I were kidding," Nick said. "I screwed up. And believe me, I'm paying for it." He rubbed his temples, and for the first time that day Emma got a good look at her boyfriend. His skin was sallow, his eyes bloodshot and covered with a cloudy film. The part of Emma that wasn't furious wanted to pull him into a comforting embrace.

"What happened to you exactly?" she asked.

"You know, alarm-clock trouble. Hey, look, a Krispy Kreme!"

"All right, I'll fall for your very subtle sleight of hand." As much as Emma had been fuming, and even as she suspected that Nick had done something that likely deserved her scorn, it seemed easier to let it go. "I'll take a chocolate glazed, please."

"One chocolate-glazed donut to go, and one bus ticket for the lady."

"And one Dramamine."

"Coming right up!"

The traffic was bumper-to-bumper, and Emma was trying to gaze beyond the window's grimy streaks and concentrate on the horizon. It had taken nearly an hour to make it through the Holland Tunnel, and they'd spent the past forty-five minutes inching so gradually down the New Jersey Turnpike that it seemed like life was playing in slo-mo.

Emma glanced at her watch: two p.m., meaning their original train was just pulling in to Union Station in D.C. She pictured passengers gathering bags after a pleasant trip; she felt particularly resentful toward the two people who, due to the vacancies left by Emma's and Nick's absences, had probably sprawled out across double-seaters for naps.

The screen on Emma's phone flashed *Landlady!*, which she'd inputted yesterday for Mrs. Caroline. She picked up: "Hey, Mrs. Caroline, how's it going?" The man in front of Emma swiveled around to glare, which seemed unfair considering he'd spent the past half hour loudly recounting a synopsis of last week's *Girls* to his seatmate.

"Listen, we need to talk." Her tone was ominous. Emma was struck with the sinking feeling specific to knowing you're about to get dumped; she realized she'd been half expecting this all along. "I'm going to have to rescind my offer on the apartment."

Emma let her head fall against the dirty window beside her. She closed her eyes.

"Hello, are you there? Emma?"

"Yes." Her voice was a whisper. Nick placed a hand on her shoulder, scrunching his face into a look of concern. Emma shrugged him off.

"I know we agreed, but I've had a funny feeling about it ever since. It's been affecting my sleep, and I'm someone who needs to get my eight hours. Another couple came by to see the apartment. They're newlyweds. She's a law professor and he makes a great income as some kind of engineer for Google, and—"

"Enough, please stop." There were many things Emma wanted to say to Mrs. Caroline—how she was a bad person; and how the last thing Emma wanted to hear about was the wealthier, more successful, more committed couple who were her lucky new tenants; and how it was ridiculous to ask people to refer to you as "Mrs." along with your first name. But she also didn't want to waste another moment in conversation with her.

Click. Emma hung up. She yearned to thrust her hand through the glass beside her, then stick her head out and drink in the fresh air. Also, she wanted to talk to her mother. But because of the intercontinental time difference, they always made Skype dates, catching up once a week at predetermined times with that weird computer screen delay. Her mom's phone didn't even take international calls.

"What does Annie want now?" Nick said. "I hope you told her it's too late to get the tablecloths monogrammed according to each guest's seating placement."

Emma didn't even attempt a smile. "The apartment's out." She didn't bother filling him in on the reason. Meanwhile, the man in front of her jerked his seat back to recline fully.

"Oh, Emma." Nick pulled her into his arms as best as he could in the cramped two-seater. "I admit I'm sort of relieved. That woman was a nutcase."

"Yeah, but—"

"I know you're disappointed. But we still have plenty of time."

"I guess." Emma did the math—they had three weeks until their respective leases were up. But in three days' time Nick would be back in school and return home an exhausted lump each afternoon; evenings would be needed for planning and parent calls. Finding their future apartment, Emma sensed, would be a burden entirely hers to bear.

"Slam." Nick nudged her arm. She was unresponsive. "Come on, Em, slam."

"Fine. Slap," she said, not thrilled to be playing Scrabble Slam. The game involved taking turns changing one letter in a word in order to create a new one. Emma usually enjoyed it.

"Slip."

"Slim."

"Slit."

"Shit." Emma said it loudly, and the man in front of her shot her a look of disdain. This from someone who had recently eliminated all of her legroom.

"Shit is right," Nick said. "This trip is the worst. Shin." Nick made a motion to kick the offending passenger.

"It is. Thin." Emma sucked in her stomach.

"At *this* rate, we won't arrive until halfway through the rehearsal dinner. *Thus*, I wish you hadn't been so irresponsible and slept through our original train." Nick grinned.

"Oh, shush."

"*Shush* doesn't work, Em. You can't add two letters."

Emma elbowed her boyfriend, then reached for her vibrating phone. It was her brother, Max, no doubt calling to offer his weekly Shabbat Shalom tidings. Emma wasn't up for it, so she let the call ring through to voicemail, then dialed to hear the message. The sharp sopranos of her niece and nephew, Aimee and Caleb, accosted Emma's eardrums. They were singing some Hebrew school song. Aimee's lisp was cute, but otherwise the song made Emma roll her eyes: "On Shabbat we are happy, we are bursting full of joy! For Shabbat is a festive day for every girl and boy!"

Emma worried that her sister-in-law, Alysse, was the type of mother who wouldn't allow her children to act anything but happy. Here the kids were, ages three and four, singing about their joy on Shabbat, but Emma wondered whether they even knew what the holiday was. She also thought it was no coincidence that Max called her every week after synagogue. His voice interrupted the children's on the message: "Hey, Emmy, I hope you're having a great weekend at the wedding. We just heard a very moving sermon from Rabbi Shimon and it made me think of you. Shabbat Shalom!"

Emma noted her brother's put-on Hebrew lilt. "The Shabbat police, calling to check in," she said to Nick.

"I think it's nice," he replied. Nick had been raised in one of those laid-back Unitarian homes, and so had no idea about all the subtle, guilt-inducing tactics Jewish families employed. But while most of Emma's Jewish friends shouldered heaps of guilt from their mothers, she found it disturbing that for her it was her brother, just three years older than she, who had taken it upon himself to be the family's religion monitor. Emma suspected a lot of it was for show, some kind of "keeping up with the Jacobsons" thing. Even their mom, whose business was selling kosher-style pastries to the Jewish Madrileños, poked fun at Max's and Alysse's insistence on calling on a Christian neighbor to flip their light switches on and off during Shabbat. If all that weren't bad enough, it made Emma seethe that, back when their parents had broached the idea of selling their house and shipping out to Europe, Max had pounced; within six months, he'd bought them out and moved himself into the house Emma had grown up calling home. All of the doorframes now bore colorful mezuzahs that Alysse had picked up at JCC craft fairs, and Emma's niece now slept in her old bedroom, redecorated in Alysse's matchy-matchy aesthetic. A giant poster of Noah's ark replaced the photo collage Emma had updated through high school and college and then pleaded with her parents to preserve like a museum display after she'd moved away.

Emma and Nick did occasionally trek up to Westchester to spend Jewish holidays with her brother's family. And when she didn't let herself get worked up over Alysse's pointed comments— "Isn't it refreshing to get out of the city and breathe clean air for a change?" "By the time I was your age, the only thing on my mind was babies, babies, babies. It's funny how people are different."— Emma did find herself comforted by the old rituals. They gathered around the family room, which Max must've lobbied to keep as it was before, and lit the candles. They sang the same songs she and Max had sung as kids, the ancient tunes bursting up like buds from their childhood, lovelier for their deep roots. They tore off chunks of the same fluffy challah from Weintrob's, sipped at the same syrupy Manischewitz wine, and then took turns sharing a highlight from the past week and a hope for the coming week. This last tradition was a new one, created by Max for his family, and it was sweet, something Emma could imagine Aimee and Caleb might repeat decades down the line with their own future

families. Emma didn't go in for any of the God stuff, and she'd yet
to meet anyone who was anything but horribly scarred from their
childhood Hebrew school experience, but she could see the appeal of this weekly touchstone, the ritual coming together of family for an official day of rest.

Considering Max's Shabbat ritual made Emma wonder what
kinds of rituals she and Nick would create now that they'd be living together. When Annie had moved to an old apartment, she'd
brought in a feng shui expert to perform a move-in ceremony with
incense and yoga and, much to Emma's amusement, Annie had
followed the instructions and repeated the procedure each full
moon thereafter. Now Annie and Eli practiced mindful meditation
each morning. (Annie was flexible in her spirituality.) Emma knew
her parents had a bimonthly tradition of compiling care packages
of sweets and Spanish tchotchkes to send to their kids, their intercontinental expression of parental love. And Genevieve had once
confessed to a post-one-night-stand ritual of flooding her room
with musky incense and Drake tunes in order to seal in what she
called her "sexual mojo."

Emma began dreaming up new traditions for her and Nick—a
weekly Scrabble tournament at the breakfast nook overlooking
Grand Army Plaza, or a shelf in each of the his-and-hers closets
where they'd leave little trinkets for each other. But wait. She
bolted up in her seat, remembering that that particular home had
vanished. She and Nick were back to square one. Acid anxiety
swirled through Emma's stomach. She breathed deeply, willing
herself to feel a hint of excitement, the thrilling potential born of
the unknown.

The bus jolted forward and a fishy stench invaded the air.
Emma stared stubbornly ahead, gaze fixed on the horizon, and
thought, *We're almost there, we've got to be almost there.*

Chapter 6

"Em, it's time."

Emma blinked awake, disconcerted by the darkness. She had that half-relieved, half-unsettled feeling of jolting out of a nightmare: In her sleep, she and Nick had been setting up a new apartment, laying down masking tape to indicate which half of the space belonged to each of them, and then Emma had discovered her closet was jammed full of her teenage clients, all freaking out about the SATs.

"What time is it?" she asked.

"Eight. I called Eli and they know we're running behind. We'll rush to the hotel—"

"Let's just head right to the dinner. We're already so late. We can pop into a bathroom and change."

But when their cab pulled up to the restaurant and Nick and Emma raced in with their bags, a distracted concierge directed them left instead of right, not to the bathrooms but straight into the reception hall. They pushed through a set of double doors and, both still in their hoodies and jeans, found themselves gaping at hundreds of Eli and Annie's guests, everyone suited up and cocktail-attired, chic and tailored and so very appropriate.

"Ah, Nick and Emma finally make an appearance!" The words echoed through the ballroom in surround sound. "I was just discussing you two." It was Connor, Eli's best man, perched on a platform at the front of the room and speaking into a microphone. Hundreds of heads swiveled to face the entrance, where Emma and Nick stood frozen. Emma waved awkwardly, searching in vain for Annie's face to gauge her friend's level of fury.

Connor went on: "I was saying how if it weren't for you guys, there'd be no Eli and Annie, and none of us would've had to schlep all the way down to humid, hazy D.C. and have the last weekend of our summers ruined." Polite laughter all around. Emma wished Connor would stop pointing in their direction; half the crowd was still eyeing her, probably noticing her unwashed hair, maybe even detecting a faint stink of Greyhound.

"So what's with the late entrance?" Connor continued, a glint in his eye. Connor was known as a jokester among Nick's and Eli's college friends, but what others regarded as "edgy" humor Emma found to be plain not nice. "I hear you guys are moving in together after only—what?—three or four years? Nice work stalling, Nick. You should've offered Eli here some tips. Looks like you could've used even more stalling tonight to pull together some decent outfits. Eli, man, next time you get married, make sure to write 'No sweatshirts' on the invitations. Apparently that wasn't clear. Well, ladies and gentlemen, let's raise our glasses to our maid of honor and her boyfriend, fashionably late in not-so-fashionable attire, and to all of you gathered here tonight, and of course to the couple of the hour, who knew within months that they were meant to be together forever. Hear, hear, to Annie and Eli! *L'chaim!*"

No sympathizer surfaced to hand Nick and Emma drinks. So, as all of the room's flutes raised and everyone sipped at champagne, the two of them stood in the doorway empty-handed. Emma tried to cover her humiliation with a smile and, noticing her fingers clenched into fists, unfurled them. She whispered to Nick, "Is he drunk or just awful?"

"It's hard to say. Probably both."

"Can we escape now?"

"Yes, let's go."

They found the bathroom, and were quiet as they changed from bus-casual to party attire. The halter dress Emma had chosen because it accentuated her tanned shoulders now looked off in the mirror, like she was playing dress-up in a big sister's closet; though she supposed it didn't really matter, since everyone had already seen her in ratty jeans. Her hair was frizzy and her eyes kept tearing up, making it difficult to apply mascara.

"Em, don't listen to anything Connor says. He's never in his life had a girlfriend for more than three weeks. He's just jealous of people in happy relationships."

"He's an asshole is what he is."

"He probably spent the rest of the speech ribbing each and every other person in the room. It's just his style."

"Charming. I can't believe you're friends with that guy."

"*Was* friends with him. Back in college, ages ago. He's not *my* best man."

"Yeah, because you're not getting married, because you're apparently so skilled at stalling me." Emma muttered it under her breath with more conviction than she felt.

"What was that?"

"Nothing, never mind. Come on, let's go face the music."

Emma was angry, although unclear over who or what was its target. She wanted desperately to talk to Annie to sort things out, but spotting her best friend across the room, Emma saw she was blocked three bodies deep by well-wishers. She and Nick had missed the dinner, and the only available chairs were at a table of old ladies. They took their seats amid a cloud of perfume, and Emma attacked the dessert, shoveling down two slabs of carrot cake to feed both her hunger and her hurt. "Is someone eating for two, perhaps?" asked the most shrunken of the ladies, her arthritic talon tapping at Emma's shoulder. "Or is this just the hearty appetite of a growing girl?" Emma silently mouthed a response, cruelly wishing the woman might believe her hearing to blame for the noiselessness. She reached for another piece of cake.

Emma was creating waves with her fork in the frosting, practically daring her seatmates to scold her for playing with her food, when she heard the opening beats to Cee Lo Green's "Fuck You" sound through the speakers. She looked up, and there was Annie looking right at her, beckoning her and Nick. Emma nudged Nick up to the stage.

"Attention, everybody, this here is my amazing maid of honor, Emma, and her dashing beau, and look, don't they clean up nice?" Annie paused for the applause, urging Emma to curtsy. "Ems has been my friend since forever. It's thanks to her that I made it through school, since she let me cheat off her pretty much all the way through. That's what friends are for, right? And then she was *this* close to becoming Dr. Emma Feit, Ph.D., but I of course convinced her to jump ship and come keep me company in Manhattan instead. Anyway, something you may not know is that these two have so kindly agreed to share their big day with Eli and me. See, tomorrow marks the three-year anniversary of when Emma and Nick met, in a room much like this one, at a wedding kind of like this one, only less classy and perfect, of course."

Emma leaned in to the mike. "She can only say that because that bride's not here." Both had lost touch with the childhood friend since her wedding three years ago.

"Anyway, Emma and I were dancing to this very song when we spotted him, this dashing, blue-eyed guy at the bar. Emma ditched me on the dance floor to go find her prince, and the rest is history. So here's to you guys, *mazel tov!*" Annie pecked the cheeks of both Emma and Nick, and Emma smiled even though her friend's version of that night wasn't quite accurate. The music pumped louder, and Eli swooped in to spin his bride to be. Other couples began dotting the dance floor, and Nick took Emma's waist. As Eli dipped his fiancée, Annie winked at Emma and mouthed the lyrics about being sorry she couldn't afford a Ferrari.

Emma crooned back halfheartedly, declaring herself not an Xbox but an Atari. She dropped her head onto Nick's shoulder, blocking out her flitting friend. There was something very different about singing this song with Annie when it had come out years ago—back then, belting out their bitterness at being broke and living in wretched apartments and regularly freaking out about their bank balances—and singing it together now, the night before Annie's hundred-thousand-dollar wedding to her financier fiancé.

"Are you okay?" Nick asked.

"Just hold me, please." Emma sang along to the chorus, delighting in the fact that for the moment it seemed socially acceptable to be yelling out expletives at a fancy party.

In the cab back to the hotel, Emma slouched against Nick and watched the car's clock strike 11:59. "Happy almost-anniversary, babe. Remember that night we first met?"

"Barely. I do remember you got me wasted, and then I made an idiot of myself in front of my family." It was true. Nick, whose second cousin had been the groom at that wedding, had moonwalked across the dance floor and crashed right into his parents.

"I'd been watching you all night. Your Hora was hilarious."

"Are you joking? I'm a pro at that dance—it's just like the grapevine."

"Whatever you say, babe. And then I saw you in a corner, scribbling on all those napkins. I thought you must've been some kind of lunatic. Or a detective, or something."

"I was lesson planning, Em. I know you Jews all love to have your weddings over Labor Day weekend so you can do it on a Sunday night and avoid Shabbat, but it's rough going for a teacher, partying right before the start of the school year."

"Oh, poor you. I remember I went over to talk to you, and you started in on this made-for-TV crap about how inspirational your job was. I thought I'd never heard so much B.S., which is saying a lot considering I was working in P.R."

"You were not very nice about it, actually."

"Aw, baby." Emma squeezed his hand. "But then I had the genius idea to challenge you to a multiplication tables race, which I'd always dominated in grade school. Then you got to see what a smarty-pants I was."

"We tied, as I remember it."

"No way."

"Yes way, Em. And you were so turned on by my brilliant math skills that you hopped directly into bed with me."

"Correction, my friend: It was the other way around. I couldn't fend you off."

"Well, one thing's for sure. By the time I woke up, you'd disappeared. I assumed you'd sobered up, decided I wasn't as cute as you'd thought the night before, and fled."

"But in the end, you couldn't get rid of me." Emma nestled her head into the nook of Nick's shoulder, and remembered back to that morning after the hookup. She'd woken up queasy—she never did shots, but something about Nick had driven her to order several—and she'd glanced at the guy in the bed, snoring softly, his face slack with sleep. She'd dreaded his awakening, worrying he might look at her with scorn or triumph or sarcasm or some other equally distasteful emotion, fearing that what she'd imagined as sparkly and special the night before might dissolve in the light of day.

Although she'd hated to admit it, Emma had still been feeling the weight of her doctoral studies at the time. She'd flashed on Wharton's novel *The Age of Innocence*, and felt herself to be the Ellen Oleska character, scandalizing society with her loose ways. Emma had winced to imagine how she and Nick had behaved the night before, and what people must've been saying about her that morning. Because of course the girl was always blamed. Remembering the book's plot—how the free-spirited Ellen returns to Europe shamed and alone, while the object of her desire remains proudly protected in his proper marriage, unscathed in the eyes of society—Emma had quickly dressed and ducked out, skipping brunch. Resolving to act more appropriately the next time she met a guy she liked, she'd pledged to forget all about the previous night, and Nick along with it.

Of course, Emma hadn't been able to excise Nick and his ocean-y eyes from her mind. Then Annie called to say she'd snagged the phone number of "that hookup guy" for her at the brunch, and reassured Emma that she was crazy to think anyone cared about what she'd done or whom she'd done it with the previous night. Emma demanded the number and memorized it on the spot. The next day she and Nick were strolling through the Brooklyn Botanic Garden, seeking inspiration for a unit on *The Se-*

cret Garden for his class. It was in the bonsai enclave where Emma had first felt she was falling in love.

"Em? We're here, come on. You keep falling asleep on me today."

"Huh?" Nick was tugging at her arm, urging her out of the cab. The next thing Emma remembered, she was dreaming of bonsais, those miniature trees so delicate in their pots, their wire-thin branches splaying out into bright bursts of bloom.

Chapter 7

"Where is that fucking florist?" Annie snapped. She was perched upon what looked to be a throne, being attended to by a team of helpers—the hair guy was manipulating her straight strands into tight curls, the makeup girl was arming her lashes with turbo tear-resistant mascara, the wedding planner was attacking her slip with a lint roller, and Annie's mother was flitting about, fanning the flames of her daughter's panic.

"She was supposed to arrive one full hour ago," Mrs. Blum fumed, stabbing Re-dial on her phone with long lacquered nails. "This is very unprofessional."

Emma was also part of the team of helpers, though with a less clearly defined role; she thought of herself as moral support. Knowing Mrs. Blum was most comfortable in crisis mode, Emma didn't offer the obvious comment that the wedding was still three hours away, meaning the lack of flowers did not yet qualify as a crisis. But Emma *was* concerned about Annie's freak-out, mostly since there was a steaming-hot iron an inch from her friend's skull and a razor-sharp implement even closer to her eyeball. "If I were you," she whispered in Annie's ear, "I'd be more concerned with the state of your hair. Did you ask to look like a cross between Shirley Temple and the Bride of Frankenstein?"

Annie whipped her head around, and Emma let out an involuntary yelp: The bride looked like a horror movie villain, half of her hair teased perpendicular and the other half kinked into coils, one eye without makeup and the other bulging out of spidery lashes. Annie seemed to understand her effect, and erupted into the wheezing laughter Emma had loved for nearly three decades. "Emma the Bitch," Annie said, delighted.

"You also have food in your teeth. You're a total mess." Emma knew full well that Annie hadn't eaten anything all day, and that her friend's curls would eventually be pinned up and dotted with diamonds to create a masterful updo—Emma had attended both practice runs and rhapsodized on cue. "I think a month without carbs has gone to your head. Your body's in ketosis, literally eating itself for fuel, so naturally you're flipping out about a little hiccup with the flowers. Listen, if the florist doesn't show, I will personally haul ass over to the National Mall and pick a bunch of bouquets from the presidential gardens, even if Michelle Obama herself comes running after me and punches me out with her powerhouse arms. Deal?"

Annie erupted into more giggles. "Okay, deal."

"Also, I got you a bagel. Please don't fight me on this." Emma fed the bread to her friend, whose moans of pleasure at the food embarrassed everyone present. She was spitting crumbs, causing the makeup girl to tighten her smile.

"Attention, everyone!" A beaming Mrs. Blum bounded into the room. "The flowers are here!" She shoved into Emma's hand a bouquet nearly two feet in diameter and so heavy Emma felt like she should perform bicep curls. The blooms looked almost obscene in their ripeness, orchids gaping and hydrangeas fecund; Emma had to look away. Her gaze settled on Annie, whose eyes were both now heavily painted. *Over the top*, Emma thought. Everywhere she looked—at the sumptuous spread of croissants laid out on silver, at the treasure trove of pots and palettes in the makeup girl's trunk, at the salon's worth of high-end hair products crowding the vanity, at the garish patterns on her own nails that Annie had coerced her into getting that morning—it was all over the top.

"Excuse me for a moment," she said, and handed off the heft of flowers to the mother of the bride. She ducked into the suite's walk-in closet and dialed Nick. "Hey, how's lunch with the guys?"

"Very meaty. The restaurant's entryway has you walking through a locker of animal carcasses, and the menu is literally all steak. Our waiter had to ask the kitchen if they could scrounge together a salad for me. I'm eating carrot sticks and a wedge of iceberg—Connor's calling me Bugs Bunny—plus I'm sure we're splitting the check, so I'll be shelling out forty bucks for lettuce. Oh, and the guys are giving me shit for forgetting my flask. Eli smuggled in a handle of whiskey, so the meal's de facto BYOB."

"Jeez, sounds like fun. Well, I'm here playing referee between the hysterical bride and her ticking timebomb of a mother." Emma noticed she was crouching on the trail of Annie's wedding gown, and shifted over.

"We should've armed ourselves with benzos."

"Or horse tranquilizers. Okay, I've got to go. I hear Momzilla freaking out about the rainy forecast. Clearly the weather should respect that it's Annie Blum's big day."

"Clearly. Bye, love." Emma cozied up to the hanging gown and ran her cheek along its delicate material, relishing the silence of the space. She'd been looking forward to Annie's wedding, but now that it was here, Emma felt a little lonely, like it would be a farewell to her friend. She sighed, smoothed out the gown's lace, and returned to the fray.

Emma thought she might faint, standing beside the chuppah with spine erect, shoulders thrust back, and right foot planted slightly in front of left, as the wedding planner had demonstrated during the rehearsal. The air hung heavy, as if someone had sprinkled cornstarch into the heat, smothering out most of the oxygen and thickening the atmosphere to paste. Emma was supposed to keep her elbows bent ninety degrees, flowers held just below her boobs—"at high stomach," the wedding planner had said—but the bouquet seemed to be gaining a pound a minute. Emma's forearms trembled.

It was during the opening line of Annie's reading when Emma

started to feel like her sash was suffocating her. She thought she'd been in on all of the plans, but it turned out the bride had kept one detail from her, the fact that she'd be reciting Emma's favorite poem at the ceremony. When Annie had asked her months ago, offhandedly, to suggest a great love poem, Emma had quoted from memory Edith Wharton's "Happiness":

> THIS perfect love can find no words to say.
> What words are left, still sacred for our use,
> That have not suffered the sad world's abuse,
> And figure forth a gladness dimmed and gray?

Emma had continued on through that stanza and the next, and then blathered on about the poem's perfect sentiment: how only through silence could the language of love emerge, richer than any spoken tongue. She'd shut up only when she'd noticed Annie texting. Now Emma realized her friend must've been recording the name of the poem. Annie had only just met Eli, but she'd already been plotting for their wedding.

It irked Emma that Annie was now practically shouting the lines that called for quiet. The poem's mood was all wrong for Annie and Eli's love, which was loud and neon, not hushed and subtle. Emma hoped her annoyance didn't bleed through her fixed-on smile, and she was almost grateful for the light-headedness that made it difficult to concentrate on the words. She scanned the crowd to catch eyes with Nick, who winked. He, too, must've realized that Annie had co-opted the poem: Emma often recited it to him during their stints of mutual insomnia, hoping the words would calm their restlessness. As Annie now read out the last lines, Emma saw Nick's lips move along with the bride's: "The song the morning stars together sing, / The sound of deep that calleth unto deep."

The bouquet was becoming nearly unbearable. In her head Emma cursed the extravagance. She remembered back to Annie's third or fourth florist visit, when Emma had mentioned an idea for her own someday wedding: bonsais for table centerpieces.

"You mean those gnarled-up little trees?" Annie had responded.

"They're beautiful and delicate."

"I dunno, Ems. Bonsais have their growth stunted, right? They remind me of the Chinese binding girls' feet. It's creepy. They get to be, like, five hundred years old and still look like they never got it together to grow. Not such a nice metaphor for love, if you ask me."

As often happened, Annie had surprised Emma with her insight. Emma had never thought about bonsais that way. Now, she let her arms drop, which she knew ruined the symmetry of the bridesmaids' stances. She considered that maybe Annie had it right with the overblown bouquets, with the thirteen-piece band, and the filet mignon dinner that she knew were forthcoming, with the hundreds of acquaintances there to witness the vows that Emma had coaxed out of her friend and that Annie was now reciting through teary whimpers. Maybe it was best to have a love that was big and loud and uncontainable.

No wonder Emma and Nick, with their more reserved affection and meeker love, had been passed over for their dream apartment. Emma never would've gotten on stage and declared that she'd never experienced a moment's doubt about her relationship, as Annie was doing now; she never would've claimed to have known she and Nick would end up together from the first moment they met. Probably that couple who'd gotten the apartment had walked in, all bedroom eyes and public displays of affection, the woman's diamond ring and the man's flashy watch winking under the skylights. Probably they hadn't had to sit at Mrs. Caroline's table begging her to believe them that they were solidly in love.

Now Eli was reciting his vows to Annie. They were the stuff of Hallmark, laden with cliché, and yet tears brimmed his eyes. Why was it, Emma wondered, that guys like Eli, who had ruthless jobs where the sole goal was to amass money, were also the most sentimental? Perhaps there was a connection—more was more, for wealth *and* for schmaltz. Nick, on the other hand, who expressed his feelings in two- and three-word notes, who deconstructed every ad for how it played on viewers' emotions, had the kind of job some might call stagnant. He'd confided that one of the appeals of teaching was the opportunity to do the same thing again and again, but with each iteration to revise and hopefully improve. Because how often in life did you get another chance to go back and try a new tack? For over a decade Nick had been perfecting his approach to the fifth grade. Emma respected this kind of repetition, the purpose and thought that went into it. And yet, now she wondered what Annie's and Eli's take on this would be—another kind of stunted growth, a bonsai of a job. (Emma didn't even want to consider her own career in this light.) When Emma had mentioned her bonsai centerpiece idea, Annie had made another good point: "They'd be pathetic in the pictures. You want to be able to look back at your wedding album and remember the day as larger-than-life." Emma had to admit, the ostentatious bouquet she was struggling to hold would look gorgeous in the photos.

She sighed, re-bent her elbows, and beamed up at the freshly married pair, who were now locked together in an R-rated kiss, prompting whoops and whistles from the hundreds of onlookers. The couple eventually detached, then Eli stamped hard on a wineglass, sending up a spray of shards that scintillated in the sun.

Chapter 8

"Hey, Happy Anniversary, man!"

"Yeah, what is it, three years now? That's epic."

"Your girl must be expecting a proposal one of these days. Time to grow a pair and get down on one knee, right?"

"Whatever, don't listen to them. I dated my wife six years before I bought a ring."

"Yeah, marriage is a completely outdated institution. Weddings, too. I hear Eli and Annie blew six figures on this thing. That's like 30 K an hour. Fucking crazy."

"Three whole years! You two must be thinking about next steps."

Nick had been deflecting these remarks all night, in a few cases from people he could've sworn were strangers. Though as cocktail hour gave way to dancing and speeches, and he'd lubricated his gut with a couple of drinks, and then a few more, Nick started feeling more equipped to respond—mostly with non-responses, patting the person on the back and then excusing himself for the bar. He'd never understood why people felt it was acceptable to comment on the status and progress of other people's relationships, and why as a rule the less close they were to the people in question the nosier they became. To Nick, this felt about as appropriate as asking after an acquaintance's sex life—which positions did he and his partner go in for, how often did they do it, what were their feelings about vibrators? What would happen, Nick wondered, if he were to answer any of these people in a genuine way? What if he were to reveal to near-strangers that he and Emma were in some ways anxious about formally and legally hitching each other's wagons together; that they felt both totally, wonderfully dependent on each other, but also sort of freaked out by that dependence; that in his hardest, darkest moments Nick sometimes entertained the thought that maybe it was inertia rather than love that was keeping them together; and that they sometimes had a tendency to stoke and exacerbate rather than alleviate each other's frustrations and fears about life and growing up and figuring out the types of people they wanted to be.

Whoa, Nick thought, *get a grip*. He was retreating too much into his thoughts—hitting on that morbid, middle-of-the-night panic that lived in the deepest pits of his brain. He abandoned his half-finished drink, intent on giving the booze a rest. But then he wasn't sure what to do with his hands, and he felt jumpy, and soon he found himself back at the bar. Without his asking, the bartender served him up a bourbon, neat. Nick raised his glass in cheers, having run out of singles for tips.

Sipping at his drink, Nick watched Eli feed a bite of risotto to Annie. They sat at a private table perched on an elevated platform and highlighted by an actual spotlight—*ridiculous*. Emma had told him this was called a "sweetheart table," which seemed even dumber than calling a couch a loveseat. The funny thing, Nick thought, was that everyone was going on about how head over heels Annie and Eli must be to sprint so quickly to the altar, but Nick knew it hadn't been that romantic.

When Eli had been plotting his move from Los Angeles to New York the previous year, he'd confided in Nick that he'd felt ready to get hitched but hadn't found West Coast women to be marriage material. He'd decided he wanted one of those sharp, motivated New Yorkers, a girl with a job she liked but wouldn't mind quitting, and who'd happily manage their social life and eventually their family life with the same vigor she'd previously devoted to Manhattan nightlife. Eli described his life like a puzzle with one

piece missing—he had all the trappings of the upper-crust existence he'd envisioned for himself, all but the girl. Nick had tried
to talk some sense into his friend, explaining that no girl, whether
the kind of New Yorker Eli imagined he'd meet or not, was going
to be that exact puzzle piece he was seeking; love wasn't that neat.
And yet when Eli had moved to New York, and Nick and Emma
brought Annie to his welcome party, he'd practically pounced.
Annie had caught on quickly and done an expert job of reshaping
herself into what Eli wanted. Then, *voilà!*—the puzzle was complete. Call him naïve, but this didn't sound like Nick's idea of perfect love.

Nick was sucking with a straw at his almost-empty glass when
Connor clapped him on the back. "She's doing great up there."
Looking up, Nick spotted Emma at the front of the room, delivering the speech he'd watched her write and rewrite for the past
month.

"One of my favorite memories with Annie is our spring break
trip to Jamaica, back in '07." Emma looked beautiful up there—ra-
diant. "We're at some little reggae club, flushed with sunburn and
rum drinks, and we start hanging out with a group of Jamaican
guys. They're teaching us dance moves and the words to all the
songs, and they start asking us questions about our lives. Eventually they get to our kids—how many we have, boys or girls, what
ages. We're twenty-five, by the way, and these guys literally can't
believe it when we say we don't have any kids. *But aren't you in
your mid-twenties?* they're asking. Uh-huh. They make it very clear
how worried they are for our dwindling fertility, and then—most of
you can probably guess what happens next—Annie spends the
rest of the night drunkenly crying into her piña coladas, going on
about how she'll never meet the right guy to marry or have kids
with. She had her hair braided that day, and all those neon-colored
beads are clinking against one another as she sobs. Folks, she
looked ridiculous. I had to take photos. I had to! Even she laughed
about it the next morning.

"Because that's so Annie, right?—spending her vacation in the
most laid-back country in the world, freaking out about her life
plans and taking these guys' crazy comments seriously, but then

making fun of herself for it, too. As many of you know, Annie has been dreaming about this day and her future family long before we jetted off to Jamaica. In kindergarten recess, I'd be swinging from the monkey bars probably thinking about chocolate milk and *3-2-1 Contact*, and meanwhile Annie would be off in the sandbox, designing the perfect tiered wedding cake, decorating it with sticks and pebbles.

"Well, Annie, my best friend in the world, you've finally made it to the altar, and with the perfect guy, too. He plucked you up off the streets of Manhattan like the prince revived a slumbering Snow White in the forest. How lucky you are, and how lucky I am, too, to be your maid of honor on this fantasy day, and to live mere blocks away from you in real life. I plan to bask in your happy marital glow forevermore. I love you guys!"

The applause reached a crescendo and Annie stormed the stage to bear-hug Emma. "And p.s., I'll be hiding out in your suitcase so I can join you on your safari."

Annie snatched the mike away. "Sorry, Ems, I'm bringing half my wardrobe so there's no room for you in the luggage. Drop ten pounds and then we'll talk."

Nick wanted to get to Emma. He wanted to tell her that she'd nailed it—depicting Annie exactly how she liked to think of herself, serious but with a zany side, a princess who'd been rescued by her prince. (Nick had lobbied against the Snow White allusion—it freaked him out to picture a guy falling for a comatose girl in a coffin, but he had to admit it had gone over very well.) But Emma was all the way on the other side of the room, entwined in some kind of a friendship pretzel with Annie that looked vaguely sexual. Hordes of people were closing in on them for congratulations. They looked like a mob of predators, poised for attack. Nick felt himself break out into sweat. He wanted no part of this. He also suspected he maybe wasn't thinking straight. He beamed a mental "Good job" to Emma, downed the rest of his drink, then slipped out of the ballroom.

Outside provided little relief—the air had been a net for the day's worth of stink and sweat and dust—but at least it was quiet and dark. Nick lit a cigarette, which he'd bummed off one of the groomsmen. Emma would smell it on him later, and be angry; when they'd quit together two years ago, they'd made a pact that if either of them caved they'd invite the other along for the indulgence.

Nick wandered over to the patio where they'd held the ceremony. The tiki lamps were gone, or were at least no longer lit, and a stack of folded chairs took Nick's shin by surprise. He managed to catch his trip before toppling over, and as he reached for his throbbing leg, he spotted what looked like a flag whipping in the wind. He edged toward it. The gusts were picking up, whistling and whining in his ears. Getting closer, he saw that the material was part of the chuppah. It was still intact from the ceremony, although if the weather got any wilder Nick imagined the structure's four stakes might lift free from the ground and hurl themselves across the patio. The chuppah was supposed to represent the home that the newlyweds would build together—spend enough time around Jews and you learned things like this. Nick could picture Annie's look of angry horror as the symbol of her new marital home went careening, torn and tattered, through the storm. Better that than their actual home, those 1,500 square feet of luxury space in prime SoHo. How ridiculous, Nick thought, that a sheet and a few poles were supposed to be a stand-in for that multimillion-dollar property.

Nick found himself mesmerized by the chuppah's cloth, its muscled movements in the wind like performance art. He remembered Annie blathering on about which fabric store was the best. He and Emma had laughed—*who would notice or care whether the fabric was the finest or a salvaged scrap?*—but now he saw how beautifully the material blew and billowed. It was perfect. Annoyingly so. It had probably cost them four figures. "Perfect, perfect, *puuurrrfect*," Nick whined aloud. He recalled something he'd read about Persian rugs, how the weavers always stitched in a small irregularity because they believed only God was perfect; it would've been haughty to create a perfect earthly thing. Eli and Annie should've followed those rug makers' lead, Nick thought, and not aimed for the perfect wedding, the perfect marriage, all this goddamned perfection that made Nick want to bend over and retch. He had a brilliant idea: He would help them out. He'd give the chuppah an irregularity. He took his cigarette and stubbed it out on the cloth.

Nick had intended to create a perfectly imperfect hole that the Persian weavers would've approved of. Instead, he watched as the ash seared its way speedily across the material. He was mesmerized, staring at the smoke coiling up in the wind. The smell of singe hit his nostrils. Just as it was occurring to Nick to worry, a torrent of rain released from the sky. It was full blast, like someone had cranked on a faucet. The fire smoldered and then died under the damp, and within moments the burnt fabric collapsed under the water's weight, toppling a stake along with it. As Nick was trying to decide whether to flee or make some effort to hide the evidence of his arson, he felt a wet slap on his back.

"My man O'Hare, what are you doing out here? Plotting for your own sacrifice at the altar?" It was Connor. He wore a smug grin, and Nick felt tempted to punch it away; he'd only been in one fistfight before, during a much-too-late-night misunderstanding back in college. Perhaps sensing danger, Connor shoved a bottle of Jim Beam into Nick's grip. "Purloined, my friend."

"Thanks." Nick untwisted the cap and took a long swig. The liquid's burn down his throat reminded him of the cigarette burn across the cloth.

"Join us on a romp through the rain. Even the groom's on board." Connor pointed to a colony of suited men, whipping through the water across the grounds.

Nick wouldn't have thought he had it in him to run right then. But off he went, one foot flying in front of the other, relying on the rhythm of soles squashing into earth to propel him forward. He ran and ran, gulping from the bottle that Connor had not reclaimed, and whooping it up along with the pack. His voice echoed full and fierce in the wet air. He felt fantastic, leaping and spinning and skipping through the night. He imagined he was one of those African phenoms who could sprint entire marathons, their lanky limbs like liquid steel. On and on, the ground disappearing fast behind him.

Nick wasn't sure how long had passed when he realized that the rest of the guys were missing. Where were they, and where was he?

He found himself surrounded by trees of nightmares, massive with gnarled trunks and branches like tentacles. Spooky shadows seemed to be playing tricks on him. He was shaking and shivering. He halted his run and made a move to turn around. But his toe went sliding on something mossy, which sent the bottom half of his body flying out in front of the top half. The last thing he heard was the sharp shatter of glass against hard ground, and the soft splash of bourbon.

Chapter 9

In retrospect, Emma couldn't understand why it had taken her so long to notice Nick's absence. That she felt guilty was an understatement, but she was also troubled by her lack of scrutiny. She was usually a noticer, sharply attentive to details. Besides, she was at a wedding whose soundtrack was saturated with love songs, music that would've usually sent her clinging to her boyfriend's frame, head heavy against his shoulder.

Still, Emma had been preoccupied. Delivering her speech had elated her. After its favorable reception, she was already fantasizing about abandoning her snotty teen clients in favor of a more glamorous career in speech writing. Maybe she could specialize in wedding toasts; a package deal could bundle in the vows and the programs—plus bonus recommendations for poetry at the ceremony (though *not* Edith Wharton).

Plus, Emma had been busy. After Annie had pumped her full of champagne, she'd made a beeline for the bathroom, where she'd gotten caught up experimenting with all the toiletries and goodies in the baskets by the sinks. She'd floofed her hair back up with military-grade hairspray, and then was painting over her nail art with sparkly silver when Annie found her and dragged her back to the dance floor to sway with her to "At Last." Emma crooned along with the bride, the two of them doing their best Etta James impersonations (embarrassingly off-key). They made it through two verses before it occurred to Emma to ask, "Where's Eli?"

"All the guys went running like madmen into the storm," Annie said, flinging Emma off to the side, then spinning her back in. "They tried to get me to come, but ruin this incredible updo by choice? They've got to be kidding." Annie expertly dipped Emma, who shrieked with glee, feeling as if all the bubbles from her many glasses of champagne were now pop-pop-popping in her upside-down head. Her nose tickled, too.

Only when Eli and Connor and the rest of the groomsmen burst back into the ballroom did Emma realize that Nick had also been gone. But he was not among the guys now literally wringing out their shirtsleeves to create little puddles at their feet. One by one Emma questioned the group: Where was Nick? They shrugged, or said "Who?" or "We must've lost track of him," or "I bet he'll be back in a minute."

The late-night sliders were served, the band announced the last dance, and guests began lining up to retrieve their shawls and jackets from the coat check. Still no Nick. Emma didn't want to unload her worry on Annie, who seemed to be savoring the last moments of her wedding by drawing smiley faces on the foggy windows with the flower girls. She approached Eli instead: "I can't find Nick. Have you seen him?"

"Oh, he probably went back to the hotel." Eli pronounced this with his trademark confidence. But before Emma had a chance to counter that that wouldn't make any sense, Eli had wandered off to a group of departing couples to shake hands (heartily, no doubt). Emma wondered if this was how Eli was in every situation, so cocksure, so resolute even when he didn't have reason to be, never, ever doubting himself. He'd probably taken a business school course on perfecting his greetings and good-byes. Emma cringed to consider that Annie might find these qualities attractive in her new husband.

So Emma was left alone, standing unsteady in her dyed-to-match heels, incapacitated by uncertainty. She considered calling Genevieve, but she knew her friend couldn't help her from so far away. Plus she worried Gen would think her pathetically dependent on her boyfriend, freaking out over briefly losing him amidst the party crowd. Emma could sense her nerves gearing up for a panic. She knew she should distract herself, maybe with another glass of champagne, or something stronger, or—

Emma felt fingers latch onto her upper arm. She teetered around to see Annie's mother, Mrs. Blum. "Wait right here, dear, and eat this. It'll soak up some of the liquor." Emma took the dinner roll and began chewing like an obedient child. When Mrs. Blum reappeared five minutes later, she was sporting a yellow poncho over her gown and matching rubber boots. She handed an identical set of rain gear to Emma, and shined a flashlight in her face. "Goody, it works."

Emma couldn't help gaping; she'd only ever seen Mrs. Blum in the most elegant of older-woman outfits, all Eileen Fisher and Ann Taylor. (Annie claimed her mom even had her nightgowns tailored.) Here she was dressed like a cartoon duck. "What are you looking at?" she snapped. "I'm the mother of the bride, prepared for anything. Come on, suit up. Then you and I are going on a search party for your lost boyfriend."

The rain was still falling steadily and, much to Emma's surprise, Mrs. Blum didn't seem fazed by her updo's fast transformation into fallen frizz. Emma's boots, a size too large, suctioned into and slipped about the wet earth. This made it difficult to keep up with Mrs. Blum's clip—although the effort was a distraction from her fear.

"I told Annie it was ridiculous to have the wedding here, an estate with a hundred acres of woods. Of course we'd lose track of someone. But everything must always be so extravagant with my daughter." Emma appreciated the chatter, which was clearly voiced for her sake; she knew Mrs. Blum had been the biggest proponent of this venue.

The longer they trekked across the grounds, the harder Emma's heart knocked about in her chest. Worry wobbled her thoughts into worse and worse scenarios—a fallen tree trapping one of Nick's legs, a stumble off an unseen cliff, a pack of hungry bears. Emma had witnessed Nick's many visits to the bar that night. She hoped the wind was muffling her whimpering.

Emma had completely lost her bearings—part of her suspected they were walking in circles—when Mrs. Blum let out a sharp puff of air and stopped short. "I believe we've found our missing person."

Emma looked down. There was Nick, his body curled into itself like a fetus. He looked peaceful, despite the fact that he was lying in a puddle of mud. Emma wanted to believe he was simply taking a nap.

"Let's see what we've got here." Mrs. Blum knelt down and nudged Nick. No response. "Help me, dear." Emma crouched down, and together they gripped Nick's sides and rolled him onto his back. The newly revealed side of his head was painted crimson with blood. That guttural sound must've come from Emma's own throat. She collapsed onto her boyfriend's body, tracing her fingers along the branches of red that spread across his cheek. His skin was frigid.

"What a mess." Mrs. Blum's voice was matter-of-fact, like she'd opened a closet and found it untidy. "But it's not as bad as it looks. See, all of the blood originates from that one gash right there." She pointed to a cut across Nick's eyebrow.

"Nick." Emma shook her boyfriend. The hood of her raincoat slipped off, and her face was instantly soaked, from rain or tears or both.

"Gentle, dear."

"Nick, wake up!"

After a moment, he blinked, the eye below the gash a slit. A sleepy smile crept across his face, cracking the dried blood. "Hi, my love," he said, words slurred. "Ouch, I've got a killer headache."

"No shit, you cut your freaking head open. How'd you think that would feel?" Emma realized she was yelling only when Mrs. Blum rested a hand on her back.

"Shh. Let's hold the hysterics and focus on what needs to be done. First step, we'll get him up and back to the building. Next, we'll find the nearest decent hospital. Nick, my friend, do you think you can walk?"

His smile was charming, but he made no move to get up.

"I guess that's our answer," said Mrs. Blum. "Come on, Emma, now's the time to show off your fierce upper-body strength." Each of them grabbed under one of Nick's armpits and together they hoisted him to his feet. Emma was grateful Mrs. Blum didn't mention the stench of alcohol screaming from his pores.

For the long walk back, Nick stumbled along between the two women's grips. Emma tried to focus on the fact that she was literally being a supportive girlfriend. She also tried to tune out Nick's blathering—he was cursing Connor and then rambling about marathon times and then assuming a falsetto voice to wish Emma a happy anniversary. He was difficult to ignore, and Emma consoled herself that she could only feel so terrified when she was also feeling mortified. Mrs. Blum hummed quietly to herself.

Mrs. Blum hopped into the front of the cab, and Emma squeezed in next to Nick, who'd sprawled himself across the backseat. For a while they rode in silence, the driver stealing glances in the rearview mirror, no doubt wondering if his passenger would leave bloodstains on the upholstery. When Nick began moaning, Mrs. Blum craned around to face Emma. "It was a nice wedding, wasn't it?"

Emma nodded from her cramped corner. "It was." For a moment she let herself forget the present, and instead pictured Annie's antics on the dance floor. Nick's arm thrashed sideways, bonking her square in the nose, as if in punishment for her straying attention. "Except for all this . . ." She trailed off, attempting to restrain Nick's flailing.

"You know, dear, I feel I ought to tell you something."

"Okay." Emma braced herself for some kind of lecture.

"Well, Mr. Blum and I never tied the knot."

"Excuse me?" Emma sat up straight. Mrs. Blum was the most traditional woman she knew. She was the kind of mom who, during Emma's childhood, had thrown a fit anytime other parents insisted Annie call them by first name.

"We'd meant to. Especially after we had Annie. But something or other always came up. Plus I could never quite decide on how I wanted the wedding to be—the planning, the seating arrangements, all that nonsense always sent me into a tizzy. If only I'd known about Xanax back then, right? Anyway, somewhere along the way I found out I could change my name without all the ceremonial hoopla, and that was that."

"What about your ring?" The joke was, Annie could see her mom's diamond from the next town over; of course, the one now on Annie's finger outsparkled her mother's.

"A sham, I'm afraid. I bought it for myself on a trip to Monaco."

"Does Annie know about this?"

"Yes, my dear, and it's the greatest shame of her life to be burdened with unwed parents. No wonder she went sprinting to the altar—and with that phony, too. Oops! I suppose I'm a little tipsy, aren't I?" Mrs. Blum's smile was sly, and Emma couldn't help giggling along with her. Who was this woman she'd supposedly known all her life?

Still, Emma felt the need to defend her friend. "Oh, Eli's sweet."

Mrs. Blum shrugged. "He's just not whom I expected. . . . Well, it's exhausting to live up to everyone else's expectations, isn't it? That's the point I was trying to get at."

"Yeah."

"Although," Mrs. Blum said, glancing at Nick. He'd fallen asleep with his mouth open and was now emitting sounds that approximated a blender's range of settings. "Perhaps it *is* reasonable to expect one's date to not disappear halfway through a party, and also to not single-handedly drain most of the liquor supply. Perhaps both of those things are reasonable, even in cases when one's relationship has been unfairly roasted in public speeches. Mr. Blum and I are the ones bankrolling all that booze, you know."

"Yeah. I'm sorry about that."

Mrs. Blum shook her head. "Never mind, dear." The cab pulled up to the hospital, and the two women reenacted their awkward shuffling along of Nick inside to the ER.

It took fifteen minutes for Emma to insist that Mrs. Blum go back to the hotel and at least attempt a nap before the morning brunch; making her case required physically pushing the mother of the bride out the hospital's automatic doors and into a taxi.

"Please call me if you need anything. I'll keep my phone on."

"Bye, Mrs. Blum. I can't thank you enough."

As the cab pulled away, Emma lingered on the curb, waving at the woman who was like a fairy godmother. She knew she had to return inside to face her boyfriend, but for a moment she paused, relishing being alone in the night air, soft and damp like a sigh.

Chapter 10

The check-in nurse approached the waiting area with a clipboard. "Nicholas O'Hare," she announced, "and you can come, too, prom queen." Emma looked down at her pink-and-green dress now streaked with mud. In any other circumstance she would've been embarrassed, but she and Nick were surrounded by people much worse off than they were: body parts twisted in the wrong direction, skin bubbled up with burn, a drugstore's worth of gauze and bandage mercifully hiding who knew what kinds of wounds.

"Two things you gotta do while you wait for the doctor," the nurse told Emma, as Nick slept beside her. "Keep him awake in case of concussion"—she flicked Nick's arm and his eyes floated open—"and make sure he doesn't touch his face. You don't want that nasty business getting any nastier with infection."

"How long of a wait might it be?" Emma asked. The nurse gave her a look like, *Don't get your hopes up, girl.*

Both of the tasks Emma had been charged with proved nearly impossible. Nick dozed off about two times per minute, so Emma had to jostle him nonstop. And since each time he awoke his hands went straight to the gash on his head, Emma was trapped in an endless loop of keep-away. "What's happening? Why won't you let me rest?" Nick whined his questions again and again, forgetting Emma's responses moments after she'd finished explaining. Exhausted, Emma was reminded of what it was like to try and reason with her niece and nephew; but at least they were cute and smelled like talcum powder, whereas Nick was a full-grown man who reeked of booze and blood.

Nick's prospects of seeing a doctor seemed to grow grimmer the longer they waited. It became clear that the system wasn't first-come, first-served, but rather who-was-most-likely-to-die-if-they-weren't-attended-to? A mother and her clammy child had joined their ranks; the former held an orange Tupperware in front of the latter's mouth, which erupted like clockwork every five minutes with choking blasts of vomit. Another man looked like maybe he'd been shot in the shoulder, although Emma couldn't let herself look close enough to confirm the suspicion. When two guys shuffled in and from all the way across the room managed to stink worse than Nick, the nurse explained to Emma, "We get a lot of bums on rainy nights. Better to camp out in a hospital waiting room, even a sorry-ass one like this, than out in the elements. Some won't even bother to claim they're sick or hurt, but we can't turn them away." Emma flashed on the black-tie crowd she'd been mingling with mere hours ago and cringed at her current surroundings.

As the night's darkness thinned out and dawn began peeking through the windows, Emma dipped into despair. She felt she couldn't possibly continue to keep Nick awake. She began to wish hateful things upon the check-in nurse, whom she suspected had only assigned her these Sisyphean tasks in order to distract her from the reality of having a bloodied boyfriend in the ER. Emma could barely keep her own eyes open, and the flimsy plastic chairs started looking more and more viable as mattress substitutes. So when the nurse finally called out "Nicholas O'Hare," Emma's eyes welled up with tears, so overcome was she with the hours of singing songs and inventing secret handshakes and doing everything she could to keep Nick conscious and safe.

The doctor was a tall woman with porcelain skin who looked about twenty-five years old. Emma's thought—*God, I'm old*—was immediately overshadowed by another—*God, I'm shallow to think about that now.*

"Can you tell me who the President is?" the doctor asked Nick.

"Who is Mr. Barack H. Obama?" Nick answered, *Jeopardy*-style, flashing a grin at Emma. She felt her muscles relax a notch, only then realizing how tensed they'd been.

"Can you tell me how to spell 'world' backward?"

"W-O-R—"

"Now can you try it backward?"

The doctor was patient as Nick worried his brow. "Uh, D, O, L, W . . ." Nick trailed off, peering at his shoes. The doctor jotted something onto her paper.

"Let's try this; repeat after me." She listed a series of simple words, and Emma zoned out as Nick, like a special-needs kindergartener, struggled to echo the short list.

"Do you know where you are?" the doctor asked.

"New York City," Nick answered with assurance.

"Did you attend a special event last night?"

Nick's shrug hit Emma like a punch to the gut. This was clearly not just the booze. Even after half a dozen whiskeys Nick could kick her butt in Trivial Pursuit; drunker than that, he was still a formidable opponent in Scrabble.

"We'll do a CT scan," the doctor said. As he was wheeled away, Nick waved jauntily to Emma, as if he believed he was off for an ice-cream cone.

As soon as he was gone, all remaining energy drained from Emma's body, and she collapsed across two plastic chairs. She fell asleep and dreamed of a double wedding, she and Nick alongside Mr. and Mrs. Blum at the altar, Mrs. Blum in a yellow gown made of rain slicker material. When it was time for "I dos," all four of them dispersed in hysterics, flailing their arms and wailing about not being ready for the commitment. Emma reeled about in circles, until she slipped on a branch and—*bam!*—hit her head. She woke up.

The young doctor had a hand on her shoulder. "Your boyfriend has a pretty serious concussion, and we detected bleeding in his brain. Mild hemorrhaging is a common result of the kind of trauma he's experienced."

When the doctor stopped talking, Emma heard only a low hum.

Her body felt frozen. From the gurney Nick took her hand and patted it gently, as if he was the one who was supposed to be caring for her. "It's okay, Em." His speech was like sludge.

The doctor started in on the medical jargon, and Emma forced herself to imagine it was a foreign tongue from some beautiful faraway land. Her mind wandered back to her dream. She saw herself sprinting from the altar, breathless with anxiety. Would Nick be forever stuck in this space, blood seeping into his brain, unable to spell words or place himself in time and space? Emma pulsed with fear.

She realized the doctor was looking at her expectantly. "Come again?"

"I said, we'll need to monitor him for a couple of days, okay?"

"Oh, um, yeah." Was she supposed to protest or ask for more details? Emma didn't know.

They moved Nick into a private room, and a male nurse in *Star Wars* scrubs helped him out of his rumpled suit and into a thin hospital gown. The doctor reappeared, and Emma watched as she removed a needle and thread from her supply kit and then went to work embroidering Nick's eyebrow. Emma thought of Edith Wharton's world: fair maidens in fancy dress passing the time with needlepoint, honing the ladylike hobby and, along with it, their eligibility for marriage. And yet, here was this woman in her prime, wearing baggy scrubs and hunched over Nick's wound, threading a needle in and out of human flesh. Emma found herself wondering if the doctor was married, and whether having such a prestigious job would make it easier or harder to get a guy.

"There we go, Nick. You're all stitched up." She turned to Emma. "We've got him on morphine and a diuretic to reduce the swelling. A nurse will come by to adjust the meds. In the meantime, he should sleep, and we'll wake him occasionally to make sure he's improving. Two days of monitoring here, and then most likely you'll be off, good as new, only Nick'll have a gnarly new scar to show off to all his friends."

Emma nodded, torn between thinking that this news was cause for alarm (*two whole days in the hospital!*) and that it was cause for celebration (*just two days in the hospital after a brain injury!*). It was

Monday, Labor Day. Nick was supposed to start school tomorrow, and Emma had ten clients lined up. Nick was already snoring, and Emma panicked for a good thirty seconds before, exhausted, she, too, drifted off to sleep in her chair. She dreamed of blood—gobs and gobs of it, flowing in gushes and coating everything with its sour stickiness, leaving a metallic taste on Emma's tongue.

When she finally awakened, it was from a knock, and then the *Star Wars*–clad nurse reappeared, carrying a covered tray. Emma wondered what would happen if she showed up to a *1, 2, 3 . . . Ivies!* appointment wearing patterned pajamas. The nurse nudged Nick—"Wake up, buddy"—and then peeled plastic wrap off a series of casserole dishes: steak and white rice, a side of wilted french fries, and a big slab of chocolate layer cake. They served this junk at a hospital? And why hadn't Emma told them that Nick was a vegetarian? She felt a pang of guilt.

The nurse asked Nick the same series of questions—who is the President, how do you spell "world" backward, can you repeat these words, and where are you?

"In the doghouse," Nick responded to the last one.

"Excuse me?"

"In the doghouse with my girlfriend."

Emma smiled. Nick was back, sort of. He looked like a mess and his boozy stench had hardly dissipated, but he was making a joke about his situation, so that had to be something. Emma imagined Nick's brain like those preserved ones in science class, pink as bubblegum, bobbing gently in a jar of formaldehyde.

The nurse pointed to the bedside phone on his way out: "To call outside of the hospital, just dial nine before the number."

Nick's parents, Emma thought. *Why hadn't she gotten in touch with them?* But just as soon as the thought flashed through her head, Emma pictured Mr. and Mrs. O'Hare receiving her call. They'd be sitting in their twin armchairs, and silently take in the news about their son's fall and the bleeding in his brain. They'd be too polite to admit their terror, and from five hundred miles away, unable to help. Though they were just a few years older than Emma's own parents, Mr. and Mrs. O'Hare seemed of an earlier generation, frail and gray. Emma couldn't bear the thought of the call. Plus, she decided it would be best for Nick to be the one to reach out. She'd mention it when he was feeling a bit better.

"Hand me the phone," Nick said. "I'm gonna call Mrs. Caroline and tell her what happened." *Oh no, did he not remember?* He waited a moment before saying, "That bitch." Emma sighed with relief. "Come here, Em. You can have the cake."

Emma ate and ate, letting the rich frosting coat her twisted stomach. By the time she was finished, Nick was asleep again, and Emma felt utterly alone. Now she considered calling her own parents, unloading all that had happened in the past twenty-four hours and begging them to come solve everything. Emma pictured her mom bustling around the bakery, happily selling her challah and rugelach to the Spaniards, who, just awake from their siestas, craved something sweet. Emma's parents had built up a loyal clientele in their seven years abroad, neighborhood folks charmed by the quirky American Jews who'd appeared in their midst. Many were non-Jews, since the goods were kosher-style, not kosher. ("Don't tell your brother," her mom had once confided, "but the secret ingredient is lard!") The patrons must have found her parents adorable, as everyone always did. Throughout her childhood, Emma had watched in awe as her parents laughed and hugged and practically danced their way through life. Together they'd launched business after successful business, all of which were great fun *and* gave back. There were the personalized jewelry boxes whose profits supported dress-up parties for the daughters of battered women, the Keds knockoffs whose every purchase funded another pair for a needy child (and this was way before TOMS), and the Mommy's Night Out wine tastings, whose leftover cheese plates were donated to a food pantry—and on and on, until they tired of one venture and moved on to the next.

As a child, Emma remembered asking her mother how come she and her dad were so happy. Her mom would get a mysterious look on her face and then spout off blithe relationship wisdom, like, "You have to try on many men until you find one that fits," without offering any instructions for how to tell if one actually fit. Or, "The trick is to find a partner who complements your assets," at an age when Emma had no idea what her assets were or if she actually had any. So, even as everyone was always gushing to Emma how lucky she was to have parents still so in love, she'd grown up baffled as to how it all worked. When she'd started dating Nick and found herself reeling in the aftermath of a fight, she'd sometimes wonder how her parents would've handled the situation; then she'd realize that she couldn't recall them fighting. This was a revelation that also worried Emma. It made her question whether she really knew how to be in a relationship.

Ever since her parents had sold off all they owned and shipped out to Spain for, as they called it, their "empty-nester adventure abroad," Emma had found them even more baffling. So much distance—their only contact was weekly Skype conversations and a rare visit home—had morphed them into caricatures that Emma suspected weren't quite accurate. Her mother only ever seemed to want to know whether she was happy or not. If she were to call her mom now, Emma could've told her about how gorgeous the bride and the venue had been, and how she'd spent a wonderful anniversary with Nick, and her mom would've cooed with delight; or, Emma could've sobbed about Nick's fall and the hospital and how terrified she felt at the moment, and her mom would've commiserated expertly. But there was no way for Emma to tell her the good along with the bad. She felt that somehow her mother couldn't take in the shades of gray. As a result, Emma realized that during their next scheduled talk she would share only inconsequential details about her weekend. She would keep the conversation light and breezy, surface level. Her mom would ask if she was okay, and she would nod vaguely and say, "Sure." This made Emma feel terribly lonely, and even farther apart than the 3,500 miles from her mother.

The nurse re-administered morphine just in time for visiting hours, so that when Annie strolled in with her entourage of Eli and the rest of the wedding party, Nick was glassy-eyed and wearing a Willy Wonka grin.

"I'm sad to say you missed caviar and crème fraîche at the brunch," Annie trilled. She hoisted herself up on the arm of Emma's chair, while the guys surrounded Nick, slapping him on the back. "Ems, I was so worried about you! Mom told me everything. Oh, this is from her." She handed Emma a flashlight, the same one she'd used the night before. The note read, *Here's to an easy recovery and bright, shiny things to come.*

Annie continued: "My mom tried to convince us not to come. She thought Nick would want to rest. But we *had* to see you." Emma glanced at Nick, whose eyes were at half-mast. Connor was tugging at his hospital gown; his laugh had an edge. "Ooh, I almost forgot. I brought these from the bridal suite." Annie hopped up, opened her handbag, and started scattering rose petals across Nick's bed.

The petals made Emma think of drops of blood, but Nick's eyes grew wide, and he gathered them up and flung them into the air. They fluttered in a heap on the floor. "The ground's slippery with roses," Nick said. "Don't anyone slip. Or we'll sue you, Annie. Her husband can afford it, right, Em?" Eli laughed, but Emma felt mortified.

"One more thing," Annie said, ignoring Nick and reaching into her purse again. "We pulled together some provisions." She handed Emma a stack of plastic containers: mushroom risotto and zucchini tartlets and Brussels sprout salad, the same food Emma had watched Nick upchuck the night before. Her stomach stirred. "And here." Annie shoved a family-sized container of Purell at Emma. "The germs must be insane here."

"Gee, thanks."

Annie deposited a large dollop of the hand sanitizer into her palm, then vigorously rubbed her palms before reaching down to hug Nick.

"I think it's time for us to go, hon." Eli took hold of his new wife's shoulders. Emma was thankful, worried that next Annie would pull some Happy-Anniversary-slash-Get-Well-Soon gift from her Mary Poppins purse.

On their way out, Annie leaned into Emma. "Ems, you look like shit. How are you really?"

"Oh, I'm okay. We'll be fine." Before this weekend, Emma would've opened up to her best friend, confiding all the fear and loneliness and shame of the past twelve hours; but somehow, now that Annie was standing there in her just-right post-wedding sundress and cardigan, it felt different. It was like Annie had crossed over some divide, leaving a chasm between them.

"Listen, Eli got me this phone that I can use in Africa. It supposedly gets service even way the fuck out on safari, so please call me and keep me posted on everything going on. And look on the bright side: You've got this amazing apartment to look forward to back in New York. A dishwasher and skylights, right? Kiss, kiss!"

Emma forgot that she hadn't told Annie they'd lost the apartment. Her friend was already halfway down the hall, shooting a disapproving look at the nurse's *Star Wars* duds, so Emma just waved.

Back in the room, Emma perched herself beside Nick, who had nodded off again. She examined the spidery stitches that crawled their way across his brow. She ran her fingers along them, feeling out their wiry prickles like Braille, wondering what terrible word they might spell.

Nick blinked awake. "Mensa," he said.

"What?" Emma thought he might've been caught in a dream conversation.

"What about Mensa? Who will feed him?" Nick's gerbil, right. Emma wiped away the dots of sweat from her boyfriend's skin. It was sweet, if a little disconcerting, that he seemed more concerned about his pet's welfare than his own.

"I'll call Carl." Emma paused. "But, Nick—"

"Hey, Em?" She knew he'd recognized her tone, the one that indicated the need for a serious conversation.

"Yeah?"

"Let's not have a *talk* talk, okay? At least not right now."

Emma nodded. The truth was, as much as she knew they *should* have a *talk* talk, about Nick's drinking and their apartment hunt and all that had happened, she wasn't up for it either. So they sat in silence. They took in the mechanical beeps and hums like they were cicadas' calls, both of them picturing that they were out at someone's country house for a Labor Day picnic, soaking up the sun and sipping at cold lemonade, instead of cooped up here in the hospital, so far away from home.

Chapter 11

Emma was supposedly on a search for a cell-phone-permitted zone, although she'd been wandering the hospital halls for twenty minutes, peeking her head into patients' rooms and guessing at what they were in for, and still no luck. Clearly she was dreading calling the Hellis. Canceling their next-day appointments would mean offering an explanation (and an especially good one, considering some were first-timers). Emma preferred her *1, 2, 3 . . . Ivies!* clients to think she lived and breathed the business of getting their kids into the best colleges; she was not thrilled to have them picture her in her current predicament.

"Girl, what exactly are you looking for?" It was the check-in nurse from the previous night. "You've walked by here three times now. You're giving me the creeps."

"Oh, sorry. Where might I be able to make a call?"

"Cafeteria's straight down the hall, take a right."

Now Emma had no excuse. She would tell her clients her uncle had died. Everyone had uncles—right?—and sometimes they died. It didn't detract from her professionalism to have an uncle die.

Emma continued putting off the work calls by first dialing Genevieve. She filled her friend in on the whole weekend saga, then added, "By the way, I can't believe you're thinking of applying to nursing school. Hospitals are the worst."

"Obviously I'd prefer to play a nurse in a movie," Gen responded, "but apparently that is not to be. But don't you find it sort of romantic to see Nick so in need, to know he's relying on you so much?"

"Um." Try as she might, Emma could not adopt that benevolent perspective.

"Well, I happen to like helping people heal. It beats hanging around with the Hellis, that's for sure."

"You're better than I, Gen Nightingale. Remind me again why you're single?"

"Because I don't want any man tying me down."

"Right. Instead you want to change the bandages of *many* men, and spoon-feed soup to a range of male mouths."

"Exactly." This had been Genevieve's stance for as long as Emma had known her—happily, steadfastly single. But as they'd edged into their late twenties and most of their friends had settled into relationships, Emma had started to suspect Gen's happy-go-lucky independence had become a bit of an act; this made her sad. She knew it wasn't helpful to remark upon the absurdity of her friend's single status; the comment had simply slipped out. "Anyway," said Gen, "I wish Nick a speedy recovery, and I can't wait to smother you in hugs once you're back. Stay strong, and don't forget to fluff up his pillows occasionally."

"Thanks, Gen. Love you."

Emma sighed. There was no more delaying facing the Hellis. She reached Mrs. Goldstein first, and wasn't prepared for the woman's response: "Okay, where is the funeral—is it in the tristate area? I can put Isaac on a train in the morning to come meet you. Surely you'll have some downtime. My condolences, of course."

The Spencers insisted on a discount for the next session—after all, Mrs. Spencer had canceled appointments of her own to attend her son's first appointment (despite Emma discouraging parents from participating in their children's sessions, she couldn't outright ban the people who were writing the checks).

When Emma reached Sophia Cole, she hadn't even started in on her explanation when the girl broke in, "Fantastic! But don't tell my mom, okay?"

"Sophia, I have to, so she doesn't pay for the missed session."

"Come on, please? I promise I won't rat you out. If Mom knows you canceled, she'll force me to do a mock college interview with her. She'll make me wear a suit."

Oy, Sophia's mother was intense. "Fine, I'll use the money on a gift certificate for you to Lee's Art. But you should really draft a personal essay before our next appointment."

"Blah, blah, okay. I'll write about colluding with my college counselor to extort art supply money from my mother."

"Lovely. Make sure to use descriptive detail and specific anecdotes."

"Aye-aye, captain."

"And watch those comma splices. Bye, Sophia."

Emma shook her head, then looked up the next client to call: Mrs. York, who pulled out her *1, 2, 3 . . . Ivies!* contract and read aloud the twenty-four-hour cancellation policy. They settled on a phone session—which is how Emma found herself back in the cafeteria the next morning, sitting among the families of the sick and injured, drilling Dylan York on rhetorical devices. At least the boy was hardworking.

"The hospital says the drunk can't leave until he's sobered up," Emma said.

"Metonymy," Dylan answered, "since the hospital didn't actually say it. Next?"

"The more beer you drink, the more fun you'll have."

"Easy: sophistry."

"People who run drunk through the woods in the middle of the night are dumb. The boy runs drunk through the woods in the middle of the night, so the boy is dumb."

"Syllogism. What is this, some kind of public service announcement? Did my mom tell you she caught me with that six-pack?"

"Sorry, no, just a coincidence. But you've really studied, nice work!"

"Thanks, my girlfriend's been testing me. Our plan is to both go to Columbia."

"That's great. How long have you been dating?"

"Eleven weeks." Emma almost laughed—the long-term plans of teenage lovers were ridiculous—but then she remembered

Connor's cruel laughter mocking her own relationship, and kept quiet.

"Well, it sounds like she's a keeper. Next time we'll practice math."

"I'm sorry about your uncle, by the way."

"Oh, thanks." Emma wanted to own up to her lie, but refrained, fearing that the boy's mother would find out. "See you next week, Dylan. And go easy on the beer."

Emma hadn't even bothered trying to get out of her appointment with the Griffins. Mr. Griffin had written her three angry e-mails about his son's score on the SAT practice test—100 points lower than the last one. Emma had improvised something about how bolstering one's auditory skills could ultimately enhance one's reading comprehension, and much to her surprise, Mr. Griffin had bought it and agreed to the phone session.

"Hey, Lucas, are you there?" All Emma heard over the line was heavy breathing.

"You've gotta help me." The boy's whisper was scratchy. "My dad grounded me for my test scores. No matter what I do, I can't break 2,100."

Emma knew this family well—a couple of years ago she'd tutored Lucas's older brother, who'd scored a perfect 2,400 on his SATs, fives on all of his Advanced Placement exams, and an early admissions ticket to Harvard, all of which he would've achieved with or without Emma's help. Lucas was not the student that his brother was, although in Emma's opinion he was the kinder and more interesting of the two. Unfortunately his father didn't seem to see past the test scores. And Lucas's mother, whom Emma imagined to be a compassionate, gentle woman (an impression based solely on wishful thinking), was out of the picture, living somewhere in South America.

Emma had an idea. "Okay, Lucas, let's try something different." Channeling her best yoga teacher voice, she instructed the boy to focus on his breath, to tune out his surroundings, and to pay attention only to his inhales and exhales.

She could hear Lucas's breathing slow down. Emma did the exercise, too, focusing her attention on the air passing in and out of her lungs. It was relaxing. She found she was actually able to let go of her surroundings—the hospital, Nick's injury, being 200-plus miles from home.

"What the hell is going on here?" The gruff voice accosted Emma's eardrums, and her stomach seized. It was Mr. Griffin. He must have been tapping the line. The man's rage ramped up: "I'm paying your company $120 an hour for you to practice *breathing* with my son? Is this some kind of joke?"

"Dad, it's helpful." Lucas sounded far away.

"That's it. No wonder Lucas's scores are plummeting. I guess he's too busy concentrating on the challenging task of inhaling oxygen to study. If you ask me, Ms. Feit, your methodology has really slipped. I wouldn't have thought *1, 2, 3 . . . Ivies!* would fall for this hippie crap, but clearly I was wrong. We're done here. I expect a refund for half of this session." *Click.* Fired.

Emma sat very still, her vision bleary with tears. She was startled by a hand on her back, and then a stranger's reassurance: "Hang in there." She felt silly, then. Someone had thought she was misty-eyed over a sick friend or relative, and here she was letting a Helli get to her. These parents had preposterous expectations, and Emma became a punching bag for all their own disappointments and anxieties. Usually she remembered these things; usually she could laugh off their crazy behavior.

But now, Emma questioned herself. This Helli-shaming made her wonder, why had simply breathing along with Lucas just now felt like one of her most satisfying experiences on the job? She'd always suspected yoga was a bit of a fraud. She figured at some point the practice must've hired a fantastic P.R. firm to convince the masses that it was reasonable to choke up twenty bucks for an hour of guided breathing and stretching, plus another $100 for the right pants to do it in. But now Emma sort of got it. Life had gotten so stressful that people actually had to carve out time in their day to chill out. When she was generous with herself, Emma liked to think of her job as opening doors for kids. Now she wondered if all she was doing was piling on more pressure—raising the bar for everyone so that more students would have to seek out similar services to be successful, and then graduate to further stresses and successes . . . and the cycle would go on and on.

Emma flashed on herself at age seventeen, the spring of her senior year when all those fat college acceptance packets had arrived in the mail. When her brother, Max, heard she'd been admitted to Yale, where he was enrolled as a junior, he'd sent her a sweatshirt stamped with the university mascot, a bulldog that seemed to be scowling at Emma. She'd been so sure of herself when she chose Brown, the school renowned for its lack of requirements and a student body that actually cared about learning. She'd wanted to forge her own path to success, whatever that meant, outside of the pressure cooker that nearly everyone else had accepted as the norm.

So where and when had she gone wrong? Emma was suddenly back to Lily Bart, near the end of *The House of Mirth* when the protagonist had fallen so far. Despite her beauty and her wardrobe and all her potential, a series of small missteps left Miss Bart alone and penniless, abandoned by her friends and shamed by society. Emma reveled in her own self-pity. Today was the day after Labor Day, the unofficial start of getting back to business, and here Emma was forcing down a sad sandwich of dry turkey and wilted lettuce, wearing dirty clothes (at least Annie had brought her her suitcase, so she could change out of her muddy maid-of-honor dress), and waiting for the bleeding to abate in her boyfriend's brain. She felt alone. Annie and Eli were off to Africa, Genevieve was back in New York, Nick was sleeping off his head trauma, her parents were an ocean away, and Mr. Griffin had cursed her out for being bad at her job. To top it all off, in a few weeks, she and Nick would become homeless.

Emma tore open a carton of chocolate milk, which she'd bought in an attempt to comfort herself. Her sip tasted sour, and she sprayed it out across her tray. She checked the expiration date: August 15. Of course her milk would be bad, she thought, pouting. She heard laughter, and turned around to see a table of kids, most bald and all skeletally thin, playing cards. Emma chastised herself for her self-absorption. She imagined Gen telling her to buck up, so she stood up, tossed out the milk, and headed back to her boyfriend.

"Great news," Nick said, greeting her with a kiss. "I'm good to go."

Chapter 12

The discharge nurse had warned Emma it would take weeks for Nick's brain to recover, meaning his main job for now would be to rest. He seemed to split his days between sleeping and sitting on his couch munching Saltines. He wouldn't be cleared to go back to school for at least another week—the D.C. doctor had put him in touch with a colleague at NYU for a follow-up. Maybe they feared Nick would keel over and collapse in front of his students, Emma wasn't sure. But whatever the legitimate reasons for Nick's extended respite, she couldn't help feeling envious, wishing she too had a doctor's note excusing her from everyday life. Alas, she couldn't call in a sub to take over her responsibilities. And those responsibilities—nine clients, plus the manic refreshing of Craigslist apartment listings during rare breaks—along with Nick's fragile state, provided Emma with enough fodder to keep putting off the serious talk she knew they needed to have.

In truth, Emma wouldn't have known where to begin. She felt angry and resentful, but was unsure whether she had a right to be. After all, Nick was seriously injured. Plus, she knew he would've rather been back at school. He talked about it regularly in his sleep, tongue thick with lesson plans as she shook him awake to ask him those inane questions about spelling words and the President. When the nurse had told Emma how important it was to monitor Nick's brain recovery, and then prescribed a strict regimen of middle-of-the-night wake-ups, Emma had nodded like a hyperactive string puppet. But it was exhausting work. Genevieve had volunteered to help with some of the caretaking, but so far Emma had felt reluctant to rope her friend into Nick's stale-smelling den of recovery. And although when Nick finally called his parents they'd offered to fly out, Nick had insisted it wasn't necessary, and they'd quickly conceded. Instead they'd sent a modest fruit basket of apples and oranges, a preprinted Get Well Soon! placard toothpicked into one of the Granny Smiths.

So Emma was on her own tending to Nick night after night, with no break to escape to her own apartment for a stretch of solitude or uninterrupted sleep. If this was a preview of what it would be like to shack up for good with Nick, Emma was not thrilled.

Still, Emma soldiered on, lining up back-to-back apartment visits after work each day. After two hours spent drilling Isaac on SAT geometry (Mrs. Goldstein had booked her son a double session), Emma rushed out to visit what sounded like a promising pad—a Park Slope one-bedroom with exposed brick and a claw-foot tub, one block from Atlantic Center and all the major subways. When Emma arrived, she double-checked the address. The apartment jutted out of a building's second floor and hung directly over the three-way junction of Atlantic, Flatbush, and Fourth Avenues, cars careening all around. Emma imagined her wake-up there: a surround-sound alarm clock of honking horns and a thousand commuters, plus construction noise of the stadium going up across the street. When Emma pictured moving to Brooklyn, it was not to live on one of the borough's busiest intersections, neighbor to a 20,000-seat arena. She didn't even make it inside.

At her next appointment, Emma arrived at a South Slope building and, while distracted looking for the right bell, was startled by a *"Psst."* A couple skulked out from behind a bush. "Whatever you do, do not move in here," the woman hissed. "The place will seem great at first—high ceilings and hardwood floors, the whole deal. But the landlord's a psychopath. The building's infested with rats, and if you complain, he'll turn off your heat in retaliation. Half the units have sued him in housing court. Seriously, Google the address." The man handed Emma a card that read *Prospect Ave Tenants for Fair Housing*, then said, "We broke our lease, and it cost us thousands of dollars. We're just here as volunteers, trying to help others avoid the same hell we went through."

"Alrighty," Emma said, fidgeting the card, not sure what to make of the creeping duo. She decided whether it was the landlord or this bug-eyed pair who were crazy, she wasn't going to risk involvement. She thanked them and walked away.

Next up, Emma ventured to Gowanus to check out a loft with rooftop access. She met the realtor and together they ducked inside. Emma perused what must have been the foyer, narrow but neat with a futon and side table against one wall, and oddly featuring a sink and stove tucked into a corner.

"So what do you think?" asked the realtor.

"Good so far." Emma looked up expectantly.

"Oh, the bathroom's off this way. It's cozy, but it does the trick. Quaint, right?"

Emma peered around—so this was it? The space barely fit the two of them standing side by side. "The ad said 825 square feet."

"That's right, my mistake. I meant to write 285. I'm dyslexic, so, you know." The realtor clicked his pen open and shut, open and shut.

Emma wanted to throw a tantrum. She wanted to let loose on this slimeball with a middle-man's moocher of an occupation. He probably thought he was so clever to trick innocent people into wasting their time to come see the world's smallest—sorry, "quaintest," "coziest"—apartment, then claim a learning disability, so that calling him out on his asshole-ness would make her seem like the asshole. Instead, Emma took a deep breath, shook the guy's hand, and managed, "Good luck renting this gem." She slammed the door on her way out.

The next day, Emma arranged visits to apartments in Clinton Hill, since she was scheduled later to accompany Sophia to an info session at nearby Pratt Institute. (Mrs. Cole was paying Emma simply to sit there with her daughter in order to make sure the girl actually attended.) Since Sophia showed up wearing a paint-splattered tracksuit and looking like she hadn't washed her hair in a week,

Emma directed them to seats in the back. "Pay attention, okay?" she whispered. Sophia pretended to pass out in her chair.

The presentation began, and as the admissions officer rattled on about state-of-the-art studio spaces and majors in sculpture, ceramics, and more, Emma fantasized about returning to school to study art. She pictured late nights in the pottery studio, throwing vases and bowls, maybe meeting a talented mentor who shared her artistic vision, and—Emma stopped herself when she realized she was plagiarizing the fantasy from the movie *Ghost*. She flashed guiltily on an image of Nick at home in his haze of recovery.

She glanced over at Sophia, who was absorbed in covering her Pratt pamphlet with doodles of the presenter. Emma was about to snap her to attention, when she noticed that most every other kid in the room was similarly occupied. Emma felt a blip of excitement for Sophia, hoping the girl also realized that she was in the right place.

"So what did you think?" Emma asked her at the end.

"I think it seems pretty dumb to throw away 50K a year just to do the art I'd be doing anyway."

Emma nodded. She resisted pointing out what Sophia knew to be true, that fifty thousand dollars meant very little to her mother, who was heiress to her late father's multimillion-dollar estate; as Sophia had explained it to Emma, her grandfather had started a line of bacon-infused snack food that Kraft eventually bought up for a killing. Emma decided to bag the rest of the rah-rah college pitch. She honestly wasn't even sure college was the right path for Sophia. "Anyway, I have to run to see an apartment. Are you okay getting home?"

"Can I come?"

"Excuse me?"

"Can I come see the apartment with you? My mom texted me that she Netflixed that Banksy documentary. I'd do anything to avoid a movie date with my mother."

"Um, okay, I guess so." Emma felt put on the spot. "As long as you understand that this is not going to be some Newport mansion tour."

"Duh, we're in gritty Brooklyn."

Emma suppressed a laugh. They were standing on a pristine campus cloaked by a canopy of oak trees, surrounded by beautiful, stately buildings; only someone who lived in a doorman building on Park Avenue would call this gritty. "Seriously though, if you're going to tag along you'll have to suspend your usual judgment. No snark."

"Snark officially suspended. So where are we headed?"

"Let's see, up to Myrtle."

"Ooh, sounds like the name of some eccentric great-aunt. Let's go!"

A week earlier, Emma never would've suspected she'd be apartment-hunting with her seventeen-year-old client, instead of with her boyfriend, but little had gone as planned lately. When she and Sophia arrived at the address she'd texted to herself, there didn't seem to be a buzzer. Emma knocked on the door, hollering, "Hello?"

An old man in a suit and tie leaned his belly out of an upstairs window. "Greetings, my friends. Catch!" Emma reacted fast, snatching a key from the air just before it would've landed on the bridge of her nose. The key's chain bore a bloody Jesus on a cross.

"It's the top lock," the man yelled down. "Turn it counter-clockwise and meet me upstairs." His accent had a musical lilt that was maybe Caribbean; embarrassingly, it made Emma think of frozen daiquiris and sunbathing.

Inside, the house smelled musty and looked like a funeral home. A vase of fake flowers sat on a mahogany bureau and a gaudy mirror filled half the wall. Emma and Sophia tentatively approached the staircase, which was lined with red velvet carpeting. Emma squeezed her client's shoulder. "If this guy turns out to be an ax murderer, your mother is going to kill me."

"We'd already be dead, right? So no sweat."

The door at the top of the stairs bore a series of bumper stickers, each dictating a command: "America, don't forget to thank God!" "Pray today!" and "Love Him now!"

"Love who? Where's the antecedent to that pronoun, am I right?" said Sophia, and the door swung open before Emma had a chance to praise the point but also correct her: It was "love *whom*."

"Hello, my friends. What a fine day we've been blessed with today. Come in."

The first thing Emma noticed was the plastic—all three couches were covered in it. Next she saw the teddy bears. There must've been at least a dozen of them, gracing the surface of every cabinet and table. The man noticed Emma looking, and said, "They're collector's items, very hard to track down." He held up a bear and Emma saw that a small set of wings extended from its furry shoulders. "My angel bears watch over our home."

Emma decided to change the subject: "So what's the square footage here?"

"Oh, I don't know, we didn't measure. But it's the whole floor. Right now my wife and I live up here. As soon as we rent it out, we'll move downstairs with our daughters and their families. Take a look around."

"Have you had any problems with vermin?" Sophia asked, then added under her breath, "Or perhaps silver-tongued serpents?" Emma pinched her.

They wandered the rooms, which were large and filled with light, if a bit run-down. In her mind, Emma tried to remove the clutter of old-fashioned furniture and stuffed animals, and she found she could imagine a pretty nice apartment.

Sophia held up an angel bear, and put on a childish voice: "Thou shall not kill, thou shall not commit adultery, thou shall not—"

"Stop it," Emma snapped, spotting the landlord. She swatted away Sophia's hand.

"So, friends, what are your thoughts?" he asked. "I should tell you we lowered the price since we put up the ad—to $1,600 per month. Our priority is to rent it out quickly."

Wow, Emma thought. The apartment was hundreds of dollars cheaper than other places she'd seen, and twice as large. So what if the landlord seemed like a religious nut? So what if he'd be living—

"So, do you and your daughter go to church regularly?" he asked, interrupting her thoughts.

Sophia whispered, "He means me." Jesus, how old did this guy think Emma was?

"Mom and I have fallen a bit off the Christ bandwagon these days," Sophia said. "We've moved more into agnostic territory."

Emma glared at her, relieved that at least she hadn't mentioned Judaism.

"Well," said the landlord, resting his hands atop his belly, "my wife and I run a Bible group that meets every Tuesday. We certainly hope our tenants will attend. It's very important to us to maintain a positive Christian atmosphere in our home. It would be a pleasure for us to help save your souls." His smile made him look like a Cheshire cat.

"Thanks, we'll think about it," Emma said quickly, then shook the man's hand. Bargain rent or not, she was out of there, dragging Sophia behind her.

Outside, Emma felt a wave of self-pity, slipping back into Lily Bart despair.

"Cheer up, my sister," Sophia sang out, like a Pentecostal preacher. "I'll take you to a revival meeting, we'll praise the Lord Jesus, and all your troubles will melt away." She dropped the sermon routine: "Or, if your evil plot to ship me off to college succeeds, then you and your man can bunk up in my old bedroom. Although having my mom as a roommate would probably be worse than living above that psycho dude."

"All right, Ms. Smarty-Pants, I think it's time for you to mosey on back to Manhattan." But Sophia had managed to cheer her up; Emma was glad the girl had tagged along. Emma escorted her to the subway, then checked her agenda: She was supposed to see a 1.5-bedroom in what the ad claimed was Boerum Hill, but which, based on price and vagueness of listed location, Emma suspected actually abutted the nearby housing project. These realtors clearly had the same kind of training she'd gotten in P.R., filling their posts with spin and euphemism to mask every imperfection and emphasize any puny perk, spooning out the happy images of home that hopeful renters ate up. Well, right now Emma wasn't biting. She blew off the appointment and headed home to Nick.

It wasn't yet dark when Emma let herself in to Nick's apartment, but her boyfriend was already asleep. The sight of him sprawled out on the couch, jaw slack and thin film of drool stream-ing from his lip, made Emma wish she'd suggested dinner with Sophia, and delayed both of their trips home. She decided that to-morrow she'd take Gen up on her offer to help with Nick—even if just to hang out with him for a couple of hours. Nick had avoided reaching out to his friends since his injury, and it would be good for him to see someone other than Emma, someone who wasn't so burnt-out on benevolence.

"Come on, babe, up we go." Emma eased Nick, half-asleep, to his room and into bed. She planted a kiss on his forehead and checked the clock: 8:04 p.m. She had three hours before she'd have to rouse him awake with the questions, her very last round after a week of prescribed interrogations. Nick was already snoring when she tiptoed away.

Emma changed the channel from ESPN to FOX, which was air-ing *New Girl*. Jess was bantering with one of her attractive male roommates, a flirtation Emma suspected would last two seasons max before they finally got together and the show got dull; happy couples didn't make good TV. At the commercial break, Emma logged into Seamless and, in an act of carnivorous rebellion, or-dered herself a cheeseburger from Five Guys.

When Emma later went outside to dump the evidence of her meat eating, on a whim, she kept walking until she ended up in a pub. She perched herself on a barstool and ordered a Stella, then nursed it, fidgeting and watching the other patrons. Back before Emma had met Nick, she'd sometimes ventured out alone to bars. She'd hoped she might attract a different kind of guy from the fratty dudes who approached her when she was out with Annie or the hipsters she met while with Gen. And she'd been right, al-though the guys who'd sought her out solo tended to be married men in their forties—not Emma's thing. Now she tried to be incon-spicuous, as she watched a group of early-twenty-somethings chat-ting and flirting and flitting around one another like butterflies. She guessed this was the start of their night, and who knows where they'd end up in two hours. Emma knew exactly what she'd be doing: easing Nick awake to check on the progress of his healing.

She ordered another beer, then immediately regretted it. One of the girls from the group leaned over the bar, exposing serious cleavage as she waved down the bartender. The girl's tube top seemed silly in this dive bar, but she did look fantastic. Emma herself had on a worn button-down; she tried to remember the last time she'd donned a tube top—years ago. She was starting to feel like a cross between a Peeping Tom and a parasite, creepy and pathetic for trying to suck some vicarious fun out of a group of strangers. She finished off her beer and slinked out.

At eleven on the dot, Emma jostled her boyfriend awake. She began with the usual suspects—"Who's the President?" "What's the date?"—which Nick aced. Emma wondered if he could spell a more challenging word backward and, giving in to her curiosity, channeled her best impression of a spelling bee host: "Please spell 'paradigm' backward. That's 'paradigm,' noun, as in 'You are proving to be a paradigm of recovery.'" Nick struggled, but eventually, with brow furrowed in concentration, he managed the word. Emma kissed him on the nose, delighted that he'd successfully performed the trick, like a circus animal. She dismissed what she imagined as Gen's horrified reaction, not quite caring that she was being a little cruel. She improvised a couple more questions: "Do you love me?" ("Of course"), and "Are you happy being my boyfriend?" ("Yes, I want to spend the rest of my life with you.") Emma's heart fluttered, and she felt a pang of what had been lying dormant since Nick's fall in the woods—lust.

"Are you awake, baby?" she asked, rubbing Nick's shoulders.

"Mmm," he answered, unconvincingly. His breath was ripe, but the smell drew Emma in closer, until she was pressing her lips to his and then moving to his stubbly cheek.

She hesitated only briefly before pulling off Nick's shirt, and then her own. As she drew her body into his, Nick moaned quietly, eyes shut. He was soon ready, and then Emma eased her hips over his, rocking herself against him, letting her shoulders relax and her head slip back. The shuddering release overtook her quickly, arriving like a treat she hadn't known she'd been missing. She remained still, connected to Nick, delighting in the warm after-buzz coursing through her body. "I love you," she said eventually, leaning her face close to Nick's and easing his mouth open with her tongue.

"Mmm-hmm," Nick murmured.

Emma realized this was the first sex they'd had since Nick's fall. The last time they'd done it, they believed they'd be moving to that Prospect Heights pad—Emma had already been fantasizing about making love under those skylights and in the walk-in closets. She eased herself off Nick, who was already snoring, and lay supine next to him, focusing her gaze on a crack creeping across his ceiling. For a moment, she let herself wonder if it wasn't just Nick's injury that had caused them to lie chastely beside each other all week, neither one reaching out for the other. Sex had softened something inside of her, which was perhaps what let her recognize that another part of her was still seething at all that had happened, furious at Nick and the landlords of New York and the world at large. She tried to tamp down her rage, but quickly gave up. When a sleeping Nick draped an arm across her waist, Emma eased out from under it and got up. On her laptop she loaded up Craigslist.

Chapter 13

W aking up, Nick felt heavy with the same film of fogginess he'd been feeling each morning since his fall—a hangover from the painkillers, he knew. But today he felt something else, too, a looseness, like his muscles were all at ease. It was a relief, this strange peace. Despite how he knew it looked to Emma (who wasn't very subtle in letting her feelings be known), this past week hadn't been a breezy break for him. Never before had he experienced this level of exhaustion. Peeling open his eyelids felt like lifting weights, and his limbs ached with a weariness that he imagined was a preview of old age. That coupled with the headaches, the waves of nausea, and the moments of confusion when he tried to remember what he'd just watched on TV or whom he'd just spoken to on the phone but came up with only a void that was lonely and cold and terrifying—all of this so-called healing had kept Nick suspended in a state of murky misery.

But now, that faint scent of apple shampoo and the rumple of sheets next to him, like an afterimage of his girlfriend—it both calmed and energized him. He had a vague memory of Emma's presence in his bed, but she was long gone now, as she'd been every morning when he awoke this week. He sat up, and took notice of his nakedness. It didn't surprise him exactly—with his recent blips of blackout, he was starting to accept odd occurrences as the norm. He pulled on boxers and dragged himself to the kitchen, where he saw a note on the counter: *Cereal in the cabinet, milk in the fridge. Love you, babe!* A swell of solace rose up from Nick's general state of sludge.

Breakfast in hand, he slouched over to the couch and switched on his Nintendo GameCube. Nick always became briefly obsessive when he got a new game, and *Resident Evil 6* was no exception. The plot wasn't as strong as previous chapters, and the constant switching of camera angles was pretty annoying, especially considering his throbbing head, but still Nick found himself sucked into this world so separate from his own. Dealing with a global bioterrorism crisis on-screen minimized all of Nick's real problems—his slow recovery, the apartment predicament, and the tension between Emma and him. Plus, his character, Captain Chris Redfield, was hampered with serious cases of both alcoholism and amnesia, which made Nick feel better about his own recent drinking and memory lapses.

"Take that!" Nick shouted, pressing like mad at his controller. A strange beep sent his heart racing, and it took him a moment to realize it was coming not from the game but from his phone. He pressed Pause to read the text: *Found a DREAM apt, 2BR in Boerum Hill, not too $$$, going to C 2nite. xoxo.*

Nick felt a wave of sick and reached for the sleeve of Saltines beside him. He munched and munched, indifferent to the crumbs raining down on him. The nausea didn't pass, so he grabbed a ginger ale from the fridge, though he suspected that wouldn't help, either. He was considering something he'd done earlier in the week: called his landlady to ask whether he might extend his lease. Nick knew the management company was planning to renovate, so they probably hadn't yet rented it out to someone else. "Of course you can stay," she'd exclaimed, delighted; Nick had always been a model tenant. He said he'd let her know.

But Nick hadn't gotten back to her, nor had he mentioned this possibility to Emma. He'd meant to, but he couldn't figure out quite how to say it. He knew it sounded stupid to suggest that his fall had been a sign. (He could hear Emma's retort in his head: "You mean like a sign of your drunkenness? I agree.") But he did wonder, had this injury been an obstacle put along his path for a reason, a signal that the move-in was a bad idea? Ever since the accident, Emma had been on edge, seemingly annoyed by everything Nick said or did. This was precisely what he feared about living together—that spending so much time in close proximity would make Emma rethink their relationship and then retreat. Rationally Nick knew he wasn't always the heap of hurt that he'd been this past week; he also knew his self-esteem had taken a real hit by being stuck at home while the school year started up and bustled ahead without him. Nevertheless, he was worried.

Then again, Nick considered Emma's note about breakfast, and the glimpse of vitality he'd felt this morning. Maybe everything would be fine. Maybe Emma *had* found them a dream home, where they would be happy. And so before he could change his mind, Nick typed, *Great, good luck! Love you!* But as he was about to press Send, his phone beeped again, another text from Emma: *BTW, Gen popping by with groceries.*

Nick stared at the screen, transfixed, trying to consider this turn of events. It struck him not as wonderful or worrisome, but as merely unimaginable that Emma's pretty, peppy friend would make a middle-of-the-day pop-in to his apartment. He couldn't square the idea of that girl—all perfume and playfulness—in this space, which had started to feel like a black hole of headache and fatigue and unwashed dishes. Much of the time Genevieve annoyed Nick; reaching Emma at work required first going through Gen's receptionist line, which meant humoring her penchant for sustained small talk. But if Nick were being totally honest with himself, "annoyed" would not exactly describe his feelings toward his girlfriend's friend; "annoyed" was perhaps an easier way of characterizing something a little more complicated. In fact, on more than one occasion Nick had caught himself inventing a reason to call Emma during the day, looking forward to that initial chat with Genevieve. Gen listened, asked questions, and laughed at Nick's not-quite-jokes that magically turned funny in her ears. Even if the attention was merely a result of her acting training (and Nick had considered that), it was a welcome change from Emma, who was often impatient, and who became distracted if she felt Nick's conversational contributions weren't interesting or important enough.

It occurred to Nick that he was wearing a stained T-shirt covered in crumbs, and that he hadn't washed himself in days. He mustered up the energy to shower. It made him slightly resentful toward Emma, whose manner all week had implied that if he'd just put forth a little effort, he'd be less of a lump; he pictured her "I told you so" look, the raised eyebrow and twisted lip. Although, maybe she had a point; maybe that had been her ulterior motive for getting Gen to visit him. On a roll of productivity, Nick decided to clean the apartment, scrubbing and sweeping and even mopping. After an hour, and still no sign of Gen, a wave of weariness overtook him and he lay down for a nap.

Nick awoke to Genevieve's wavy hair tickling his cheek. "Hello, sleepyhead, I come bearing sustenance." She eased Nick up, and then gaped at his eyebrow. "Wow, that's a nasty cut. Poor thing, you must really be having a rough time."

Gen set him up in front of the TV with a blanket and slippers, and then bustled about the kitchen stocking the fridge with supplies. She droned on about who knows what, occasionally interrupting herself to ask if Nick needed some tea or another pillow. He didn't need a thing, but he appreciated the asking. "I don't know why Emma said it was a sty in here," she said breezily; it made Nick bristle, even if he knew that up until an hour ago the description had been apt. "I brought Windex and a Swiffer, but it seems like you already enlisted another admiring fan to come clean." She fixed Nick with her one-hundred-watt smile. "I clocked out for the afternoon, so I guess I'll have to find some other way to be useful. How about food?" Gen presented him with a plate, a hummus wrap secured with a toothpick. Notably to Nick, she didn't rib him about how it would taste better with some lamb, as Emma might've done, and for the first time in days Nick's stomach growled for a real meal.

"Eat up." Genevieve plopped down next to him on the couch. "But save me some. I had to work through lunch. This client's mom's phone died, and I was helping her make calls to her team of helpers—manicurist, waxer, therapist, and what was it?—"

"Um, acupuncturist?"

"Close—masseuse. God, I could use a massage, sitting in that terrible office chair all day." Gen twisted her waist and performed stretches, and Nick felt himself tense up.

"Want a bite?" He handed her the sandwich.

Gen spoke while chewing: "Emma's lucky to be with someone so health conscious. Every guy I date ends up being the beer-and-wings type, and I can't help picturing them with big old bowling-ball bellies by the time they're forty. Yuck. Not you—you'll be as trim and cute as ever." She patted Nick on the knee, and her smile was sympathetic but not pitying. Nick was grateful, since he knew his scar made him look gruesome. He felt cheered up overall, and considered that maybe this whole experience would turn out positive. Maybe it would help him appreciate all the small things—like having an appetite, what a luxury!—things he hadn't even noticed before.

When Genevieve asked him what he was up for—"I'll do anything you want," she said, and he felt she really meant it—Nick sheepishly asked if she liked video games. He feared he was pushing his luck, and that the suggestion would prompt Gen to say that actually she had to go. And Nick was desperate for her to stay. He'd been cooped up in the apartment for so long, visited only by a mostly distracted and often annoyed Emma.

"Ah, so then you aren't actually the perfect boyfriend," Gen said, winking. She grabbed a controller. "What the hell? I'll give it a try."

The two of them set about their mission with focus, eyes intent on the split screen as they worked on evacuating their players from underground. Gen was a fast study, and after each triumph she made contact with Nick's body—high-fiving him or rubbing his shoulder, though always gently, mindful of his wounds. After an hour, Nick felt more clearheaded than he had in a week.

And then it was happening: After all this time underground, his player was finally escaping into open air. Sweet victory! It was thrilling and amazing, and Nick stood up and cheered without reserve, pumping his fist. Apparently Genevieve also realized the significance of this accomplishment: She leaped up beside him, and then pulled Nick's face in and kissed him on the lips.

Nick's head buzzed. His mind emptied, and his thoughts were replaced with sensations: the lips that tasted of honey, the hair soft against his jaw, the skin scented with vanilla and soap. Sensory overload. Nick felt drugged. At some point he flashed on a memory or maybe a dream from the night before, his half-asleep body excited, Emma on top of him, repositioning his limbs this way and that like a rag doll. She'd seduced him out of sleep, his sick self so in need of rest. Was he angry at her? Maybe. Or maybe he just wanted Genevieve in that moment. Genevieve, that sexy French name that rolled off his tongue—his tongue that was now touching her tongue, which was exploring his mouth, so different from his girlfriend's, so new and exhilarating and . . . He pulled her toward him on the couch.

Later, after he'd found his unsent text to Emma, the one that wished her luck and love, and then rushed to the toilet to upchuck a hummus sandwich, Nick forced himself to look back on the afternoon. He reassured himself that he hadn't kissed Genevieve back, that he'd been the one to pull away. He told himself that they hadn't gone any further, that he was sick and hadn't been in his right mind, and that the incident had meant nothing, less than nothing. However, it was hard to reconcile this version of events with what else he remembered—Genevieve's gasp, her jumbled apology, her reaching for her shirt and the fast retreat. Had Nick tried to convince her to stay? Surely not. Probably not.

And what had he been thinking later that day when Gen texted him an apology and plea to forget the whole thing, and when he responded *Forgotten*, but then on a whim decided to add, *Even your honey lips?* And why had he then kept up the conversation, even as both of them swore up and down to erase the event from their memories and never breathe a word of it to Emma? Why had he even flirted, shamelessly and with stupid innuendos and emojis? Nick felt disgusted with himself.

And so, whatever had actually happened, and whatever his role in it had been, Nick numbed it all away with the pain meds that were running low and that he probably no longer needed. That way, those last moments with Genevieve seemed to exist out of time, separate from anything real in his life. After all, since when was he home in the middle of a Monday hosting Emma's friend for a visit? His mind continued along like this, denying and dismissing, so that he was still sitting slumped on the couch—having not even bothered to shower, possibly still smelling like Gen—when Emma swooped into the apartment that evening, face beaming. The sight stabbed at Nick's heart.

"Babe, I found our home!" she squealed. "It's huge and flooded with light, plus a two-minute walk to the train. I was lucky to see it first, since anyone would snatch this place up. There's this old fireplace—not functional, of course, but it's got the original detailing. There are a few cracks here and there, but nothing we can't fix up." Nick was working to keep up with Emma's words, the flurry of excitement after such a slow, low stagnancy. "Anyway," she said, "I filled out the application and paid the twenty-four-hour hold fee. Do you think you can manage to come see it with me tomorrow? No pressure, but this place is amazing."

"Okay, sure, Em. It sounds wonderful." Nick believed his words to be a variation on an apology. Emma was so happy, and if he'd blurted out a confession right then, she would've withered and collapsed. That's what he told himself, anyway; it was a kindness to stay quiet. And seeing his girlfriend so thrilled and full of life, he was reminded of all that he loved about her, all that made her the person he really did want to share a home and a life with. Laden with shame, Nick pulled Emma into his arms.

"Hey, you showered," she said happily, "and cleaned the apartment! I hope that means you're feeling a bit better. Do you even know how much I love you?" Nick held her tighter, hiding his face in her hair.

Nick was remembering those words—*No pressure, but this place is amazing*—the next evening when, along with his girlfriend and a broker whom she was already chummy with, he was climbing a flight of sloping stairs, looking at paint-peeled walls and smelling rotting trash.

"The halls aren't ideal, but wait till you see the inside," Emma said.

As Nick stepped into the space, he felt Emma's eyes fix on him with expectation. What he saw was a mess. Stained walls. Uneven floors. Cracked molding. Crooked shelves. Cabinets whose doors hung from their hinges. What could Emma possibly see in this den of squalor? He wondered it but he didn't say it. Somehow he felt himself to be on a precipice, like if he made the wrong move he— or maybe *they*—would be doomed. But after recent events, Nick no longer trusted his instincts. So he stood very still and stayed silent.

"Like I said, it's a bit of a fixer-upper," Emma said, still watching him. "But come look at the bedroom. The light is beautiful. Picture the walls painted, and we could have those holes filled. The broker said the landlord would probably pay for it, right, Paulo?"

Paulo nodded and shrugged. He consulted his clipboard. "You people have ten—no, nine—more minutes before I gotta open up the showing. Two other couples are waiting outside."

"Okay, come on." Emma led Nick down a long hallway—the apartment was spacious, he'd give it that. "Look at that sunset. It's stunning."

She pointed out of a window, which did offer a sweeping panorama of Brooklyn. But view or no view, the place was shabby.

"And come see the tub. We could take bubble baths!" Emma pulled him into the bathroom, which looked like it belonged in some fleabag motel—faded paisley wallpaper and a medicine cabinet whose gold veneer was flecking off into rust. "I know what you're thinking," Emma said. "The décor is awful. Paulo said the landlord would change out the light fixtures if we bought ones we preferred." Before Nick could respond, he was being dragged along. "Oh, and check out the kitchen. There's a ton of counter space."

She was right—a large island separated the room, and though its tiles looked as if they'd been slapped down by a drunk (and who tiled a kitchen counter, anyway?), it was a nice feature. Emma sat on the stool and began spinning herself in circles. Was she going crazy, or was Nick's brain processing still not up to snuff?

"Listen, Emma—"

"Nick." She came to a stop on the stool and faced him. "Before you voice all your objections, please hear me out. I've spent the past week pounding the pavement like a madwoman, investigating Brooklyn's every nook and cranny in search of a home for us. I've seen every variation of shithole and met every flavor of sleaze-ball landlord, and these were places that were just barely in our price range. That first apartment in Prospect Heights? It was a fluke. We can't actually afford a dishwasher and skylights and his-and-hers closets, all in such a nice location. Even if we did happen upon another miracle find like that one, guess what? There'd be a dozen other couples lined up right behind us, who all made more money and possessed some kind of magic relationship juju that we apparently don't have. The competition would blow us out of the water."

She took Nick's arm and drew him toward her. "I know this place isn't picture-perfect, but if we lived here, we'd make it into our home. Can't you see it?"

And for a moment, Nick could. Despite all his common sense, despite the fact that he knew Emma had put on her P.R. hat and was pitching him like a pro, despite a gut that was telling him this place was not for them, Nick felt himself giving in. Maybe Emma really did know better; maybe he was still in a fog from the injury; maybe they could fix this place up into a home. It was big—and the extra bedroom could serve as an escape from the too-close quarters Nick feared. Plus, the thought of escaping his own apartment, the place now soiled by yesterday's afternoon visitor, appealed.

"All right, let's do it," he said.

Emma leaped upon him with a kiss. "Yay! It's going to be great, I promise."

Paulo ushered them into his office to meet the landlord. A squat man with a shaved head and a soul patch beard introduced himself as Luis, then crushed Nick's hand with his grip. Paging through their financial documents, Luis kept flashing his beady eyes at them, as if they were intruders instead of potential tenants. "Fine," he said finally. It didn't exactly feel like a triumph.

Paulo pulled Luis aside and they started up in rapid Spanish; it sounded heated. "What are they saying?" Nick whispered to Emma, who spoke the language.

"Um, they're talking about a worker who'll come in and do some fixing up, like Paulo mentioned to us. And, let's see, they're discussing the bathroom fixtures." She smiled at Nick, but it was strained. The men's voices were escalating.

Finally Luis glanced in their direction. "My brother will patch up the holes. He lives upstairs. But I'm not changing the light fixtures. They're brand new. I'm sorry if they're not good enough for you." He snorted.

Emma jumped in: "Oh no, they're fine. Paulo just mentioned— never mind."

"You guys gonna pay the rent on time?" he asked.

Emma and Nick nodded.

"Fine. So I need first month, last month, one-month security deposit, and the broker's fee. You got all the cash?"

Emma produced a fat envelope. She'd figured out the finances the night before. Nick's mouth went dry as she handed over the money—nearly $10,000. Everyone shook hands. Luis didn't crack a smile.

Emma and Nick took turns signing the lease. "What's the date?" he asked her.

"The eleventh."

September 11—it seemed like another bad omen to Nick. He couldn't help his hands trembling as he penned in the numbers next to his signature; he wondered when he'd become so superstitious.

After the signing, Nick and Emma went out for a celebratory beer at the pub on the corner—their new neighborhood bar, Emma called it. But Nick didn't feel like drinking; his stomach hurt and he was tired. "Em, can we call it a night?"

"Oh." She took a sip of the pint she'd just ordered, then set it down. "Of course."

They didn't say much on the ride home. They watched through windows on opposite sides of the train as it soared out from underground and rattled its way across the Brooklyn Bridge and over the East River.

"We're done with the wake-ups, right?" Emma asked. "You're concussion-free?"

"Yes, we did the full week. I can't thank you enough." Nick noticed the stiff formality in his speech.

"Then I think I might head home to my place," she said. "It's been forever since I've slept in my own bed."

"Okay, Em." Nick felt torn between disappointment and relief. When the subway pulled into Emma's stop, he kissed his girlfriend atop the head, and she stepped off, leaving him to stew in his own doubt and regret.

Chapter 14

Emma pressed Redial for the sixth time, again trying the number Annie had given her for her international cell phone. She'd written a limerick for her friend's birthday: "My Annie, she once was so purdy./ Though time's passage is swift as it's sturdy./ Your hair's turning white,/ You've got cellulite,/ You're old now and married and thirty." But with each successive dial the possibility of reciting it seemed less and less likely. She was calling from her office phone to avoid the fees on her cell, and again Emma heard that unfamiliar series of beeps that signaled either a bad connection or a busy signal, she wasn't sure which. It wouldn't have surprised her if Annie were on safari, mere feet away from giraffes and elephants, and meanwhile chattering away on the phone to her mother. The image made Emma giggle, but then she felt a pang in the chest—missing Annie was a physical sensation. "Happy Birthday," she said to the dead line, defeated.

Emma couldn't remember ever having gone more than a week without speaking to her best friend; their gab sessions were usually multiple-times-per-day events. She was eager to tell Annie about the apartment, and all her clients' latest antics, and how Nick was finally cleared to go back to work. Being apart from her friend had been like stopping cold turkey on some vital medicine, and Emma would've done anything to get her on the phone—

spent a whole night entertaining a group of Hellis, reinstated the middle-of-the-night wake-up routine with Nick, continued her apartment hunt, anything.

Because Emma felt unsettled. She couldn't put her finger on why exactly, but it had something to do with her relationship. She knew talking to Annie would help her get it all straightened out, plus her friend would make her laugh and then suggest something stupid like meeting up for sangria and drunken Zumba. It was exactly what Emma needed. But all she got was that infuriating foreign dial tone, or busy signal, or whatever the hell it was. She slammed down the phone, prompting Genevieve to duck her head into her office and ask if everything was all right.

That was another thing—Genevieve. Her friend hadn't said hello this morning and had been distant all day; her claim of a doctor's appointment during their regular lunch date sounded invented, which was odd coming from the actress. Emma wondered if Gen's aloofness was because she'd been bailing recently on their nights out. But surely Gen understood how stressful it had been taking care of Nick. The strange situation made Emma miss Annie all the more. "Yeah, I'm fine," she said now, half hoping her friend would draw her out. But Gen just nodded and closed Emma's door.

Usually Emma didn't mind that her office was windowless—she hardly had time to look up, never mind stare out at some skyline panorama and ponder life's big questions—but today she was crawling out of her skin, cooped up in the small space. She only had one more client to endure before the two-hour window she'd cleared to meet Nick at the Museum of Modern Art; the excursion had been his pick for one last hurrah before heading back to school the next morning.

After an hour of drilling Isaac Goldstein on SAT vocab and trying not to recoil at the aggressive rash of acne that had sprouted up on the boy's face, Emma dashed out of her office and uptown to Fifty-third Street. She spotted Nick in MoMA's sculpture garden, tossing a coin into the water from the bridge.

"Wishing for something?" she asked.

"Luck, I suppose. Or a time machine."

"Aw, you don't want to skip over your first day back to school." Emma hooked her arms around her boyfriend's waist. "You'll be great tomorrow, as always."

"Oh right, of course." He seemed distracted. "I guess after having Carl as a sub for a week, the kids are pretty much guaranteed to like me."

"True." Those who knew Carl and his haphazard teaching suspected his bump up to assistant principal had been a ploy to get him out of the classroom.

"What do you think of that sculpture?" Nick pointed to a contorted figure of a nude woman. "Is she trying to hurl herself over the edge or just washing her hair?"

Emma studied the woman, who was dipping her hair into the pool, her body twisted in what could have either been whimsy or distress. "Hmm, hard to tell."

"I know, and it's giving me the creeps. I can't stop staring."

"How about let's leave her alone, then, and go see the exhibits?"

"Okay." Walking inside, Nick peered back at the sculpture, and Emma was bewildered to see an unfamiliar look in his eyes—a mix of sadness and longing and something else she couldn't quite name.

They zigzagged their way up five flights of escalators, landing at the entrance to an exhibit about play in the twentieth century. Immediately Emma felt herself transformed by the world of colored blocks and finger puppets. The first room's toys were wooden, made a half-century before the plastic Legos and Fisher-Price people of Emma's own childhood, but they transported her back to kindergarten nevertheless. She pictured playing house with Annie, both insisting on being mothers, cooking pretend food and dusting mini-furniture. Emma couldn't remember what kind of closet space their imaginary house had, or whether it had featured a dishwasher, although she knew for sure no sketchy landlord figured into the scenario; playing house had been predicated on the belief that having a home was their manifest destiny, sacrosanct and certain.

The exhibit's next room featured armies of toy soldiers, spinning plastic tops, and Radio Flyer wagons. "I'll race you," said Nick, eyeing a pair of scooters.

"I'd kick your butt," Emma said, "but I also don't want to get us kicked out."

"Party pooper. And you're mistaken, my friend. I had that exact scooter growing up and I was the fastest in the neighborhood."

Emma pictured Nick as a little boy, racing down a broad street in that small Ohio suburb he grew up in, probably screeching to a halt to marvel at a bug on a flower petal, or to point out a cloud in an otherwise blue sky. In her imagination it was seventy degrees, sunny with a breeze. "I wish I'd known you as a kid," she said, grabbing his hand.

They traipsed along like children, swinging their arms to and fro as they passed tin cars and rocking horses and model airplanes. Emma recited the singsongy chants that accompanied long-ago playground clapping games—*Ooh, aah, wanna piece of pie, pie too sweet, wanna piece o' meat, meat too tough, wanna ride a bus . . .* and on and on with the nonsense rhymes that had wholly captivated her during childhood recesses.

They moved forward through the twentieth century, eventually reaching the eighties and nineties, and all the toys that Emma remembered lusting after through toy store windows: Moon Boots and Beanie Babies and Skip-Its and, a little later, slap bracelets and Tamagotchi pets. "Remember these?" Emma asked Nick, pointing to Kid Sister and My Buddy dolls. She and her brother had owned a pair of them.

Nick started right in on the product jingle: "My Buddy, my buddy, my buddy, my buddy, my buddy and me." Emma joined in: "Kid Sister, kid sister, kid sister, kid sister, kid sister and me." A nearby woman glared.

"It's kind of bizarre to see the stuff of our childhoods on display in a museum, isn't it?" Nick asked. "Like our old toys are relics of some long-ago time."

"Yeah. Although in a way all of it does feel like ancient history."

Outside the exhibit was an oversized chair, and people were queuing up to sit on it and have their *Alice in Wonderland* moment. Emma wasn't interested, but Nick joined the line, saying he liked the idea of altering his sense of the world. At his turn, he hopped onto the giant chair, swinging his legs in the air, and asked Emma to take his picture. Emma found it off-putting to see Nick so out of proportion with his surroundings. He looked like a too-old child, or a too-young man. The photo she snapped was blurry, but she didn't try again.

As they boarded the down escalator, Emma read from the exhibit wall: "The 1900s: Century of the Child." "Funny," she said, "that was literally the century of my childhood. I turned eighteen in the year 2000." She pictured that birthday, when she and Annie had used fake IDs to get into a dive bar in Long Beach, and then spent the whole night exclaiming at how cool it was to be in a bar—not exactly a passage into maturity.

"So what are the 2000s?" Nick said. "The century of the old? Or of the tween?"

Emma thought of Nick posed on the oversized chair, and of herself trilling playground ditties from her past. "Uh, the century of the grown-ups who won't grow up."

Nick began singing, "I don't want to grow up, I'm a Toys 'R' Us kid. There's a million toys at Toys 'R' Us that I can play with."

"Come on, Peter Pan," Emma said. "I have twenty-five minutes before my next client, and we've got a very adult task to take care of: picking out paint colors for our new walls."

But Emma turned out to be wrong about the nature of the task. Scouring the hardware store for paint colors reminded her of picking out crayons to draw with as a kid.

Nick grabbed a handful of swatches: "For the bathroom, I'm thinking Pink Salmon. A nice, strong fishy smell will suit the place where we do our business."

"Seriously, who comes up with these names?" Emma asked. She was thinking she'd be a pro at that job, and made a mental note to look into it.

"Or let's see"—Nick flipped to a swatch of browns—"how about Dog's Ear? Or Puppy's Paw?"

Emma giggled. "Do they have Canine Slobber? That kind of iridescence would work better for the bathroom."

"Look at this one, Dorian Gray. Never ages or chips!"

"You're terrible." Emma sorted through the strips in her hand. "How about Chilled Chardonnay? Might be too cold in the winter, though."

"We could paint it over with Mulled Wine, hardy har. Here's Final Straw. Perfect for the spare room. When you're on your final straw, that's where you go."

"And our bedroom could be Lover's Lagoon." She held out a swatch.

"That awful color? I'd call it Swamp Vomit."

"Or maybe you prefer a more collegiate look—this one's Dartmouth Green."

"How about these for the kitchen? Brown Mustard. Crème Brûlée. Fig. Or Bagel."

"Bagel? Oy vey. Let's accent it with Pink Salmon, and then all we need is some cream cheese and strong coffee for brunch." Emma was laughing her head off. "You know who would love this? Gen. For a hot minute she worked at Revlon naming nail polishes. She called them things like 'Pepto Pink' and 'Cockroach Copper,' and was fired within a week." Nick looked funny. Emma was about to ask what was wrong, but then her phone jumped in her pocket, distracting her. She saw a text from Luis, their new landlord: *My bro not free to fix holes in apt. You should hire a guy.*

Emma tilted the screen to show Nick, whose face turned dark. "I thought he said his brother was the super."

"I know." Emma texted the question to Luis.

A moment later her phone buzzed with his response: *No super. Check your lease.* Emma's gaze went to the swatches of gray, with names like Storm Cloud and Rocky Slope and Coal Smoke. Where was Silver Lining? she wondered.

"Shady asshole," said Nick, and for a moment Emma thought he was reading out another paint swatch. Their playful game was over, and Emma had to return to work.

Emma's next client, Dylan York, brought in a printout of Columbia's application, and the two of them were now paging through it. "Your statement of interest is super-important if you're applying early decision," Emma said. "So tell me, why Columbia?"

"Well, it's Annabelle's dream school—that's my girlfriend. And I hear it's easier to get in early decision, so I think I may actually have a shot."

"That's what you're planning to write about?" Emma asked, incredulous.

"Yeah, I mean, have you heard how some schools let twins apply together, so that the one who's a stronger student can give a leg up to the weaker one? I'm hoping I can convince Columbia to do the same with Annabelle and me since we're a couple. She's got a perfect 4.0. Once she claimed she got a B-minus in Biology, but I found out she was just trying to make me feel better because she knew I had a B. So sweet, right?"

Emma didn't know which point to address first: the boy's ill-advised criteria for picking a college, his baffling approach to the admissions process, or the fact that his girlfriend was dumbing herself down in order to stroke his ego. "Dylan, look at me. You cannot tell Columbia that you want to attend because of your girlfriend of—what?—ten weeks?"

"Three months, actually. And fine. Then I'll write about the architecture, or the sense of tradition, or whatever."

"Sure." Emma knew admissions officers could smell that kind of fakery from a mile away. "And if I were you, I'd think carefully about this whole following-your-girlfriend-to-college thing." Emma couldn't believe what was about to come out of her mouth: "Do your parents know about this?"

Dylan rolled his eyes. "Isn't your job to help me get into whatever college I want, not to tell me which school that should be?"

"Touché. It's just—"

"If you're worrying about me, please don't. If I don't get in to Columbia, I'll just drop Annabelle. No point wasting time before she shacks up with some Ivy League douchebag next fall. I know of at least three freshmen girls who are dying to get into my pants tonight."

Emma was dumbfounded, even as she also knew that Dylan's sudden brashness was just an act born of nerves. He was clearly feeling inferior to his high-achieving girlfriend, plus terrified that he couldn't cut it at Columbia. About the latter point, he was probably right. But Emma restrained herself from saying so; she was the adult here, and it would behoove her not to rebut Dylan's adolescent outburst with an insult of her own. Emma felt thankful that she was thirty, not seventeen, and that she'd found a boyfriend who didn't seem threatened by her smarts. Then again, how intimidating could her intellect be when she spent her days getting ordered around by teenagers?

As if right on cue, Dylan blurted out, "Are you going to help me with my essay or not? I believe that's what my mother is paying you for."

"Yessiree." Remembering that Dylan did need her help—quite badly, in fact—refocused Emma on her job. She started up her shtick: Since he'd expressed an interest in architecture, he might care to know that Columbia had a strong major in the subject. Perhaps he might write about his lifelong fascination with the city's buildings. Or his excitement to take interdisciplinary courses with the design department and partner with Manhattan's elite architecture firms for projects. As Emma rambled on, Dylan scribbled down her suggestions word for word, replacing his honest (but objectionable) reasons for wanting to attend the college with Emma's facile inventions.

Chapter 15

"Okey-dokey," Nick said, consulting the same worksheet as the thirty students in front of him, "we've figured out the best deal on an apartment within our budget, so now let's look at our options for fixing it up. Joe the Handyman charges three dollars to patch up holes in the wall and five dollars to smooth out each bump in the floor, whereas Jack of All Trades charges four dollars for each. We've got ten holes in the wall and seven bumps in the floor. Work with your partners to figure out the best solution."

"Mister," one of the kids yelled out—Carl clearly hadn't trained them to raise their hands—"what kind of crappy apartment is this anyway, with so many bumps and holes? We shoulda rented the pricier one—it probably wasn't all ghetto."

"Interesting point," said Nick. "But for now let's focus on the task at hand."

Nick felt vaguely bad about using his students to help him think through his apartment problems. He'd promised Emma he'd find a worker by this coming Saturday, the fifteenth, when they'd get the keys to the new place—and then schedule all the repairs by their planned move-in the following weekend.

"Okay, who has an answer and can show us how they got it?"

Sierra's hand shot up, and she sashayed to the board, looking sure she was about to school all her peers. José let out a *"Psst."*

Nick swiveled around. "Mr. O'Hare, my dad could help you for cheap."

"Really?"

"Yeah, he does construction and all kinds of stuff. I can hook you up, big-time."

"You're his agent, huh?" The boy nodded proudly. "Let's talk after class."

Nick checked Sierra's work; she'd correctly chosen Joe the Handyman.

"Now let's furnish this pad," yelled Lawrence. "We need a pair of La-Z-Boys, and we best get curtains, too. Block all them nosy neighbors spying on our business."

Nick felt a burst of pride—the kids were into this. And it seemed like Nick might now have a deal, too. "All right, where should we go to buy furniture? Kmart?" He knew this would elicit moans and groans, and he relished the happy chaos.

Emma had offered to join Nick to pick up the keys to the new apartment, but she'd looked so content curled up asleep in his bed on Saturday morning that he left her to rest. She'd been working her butt off lately, taking on extra clients to fund their upcoming move. Nick had planned to start tutoring for the same reason, but he was still too tired, careening home after his two days back to school and collapsing for two-hour naps.

At the address Luis had given him, Nick pressed the bell—the shrill buzzer made him jump. The landlord appeared at the door with a cigarette hanging from his lips. "Hey, hey," he said, emitting a puff of smoke into Nick's face in a way that, while seeming unintentional, still made Nick suspicious. His eyes burned. "Come in, welcome to my home base," Luis said.

Nick had expected hoarder-level squalor, but Luis's apartment was as fastidious as a store display. "Wait here," Luis said, then disappeared into a side room. There was nowhere to sit, so Nick stood with his hands in his pockets, perusing the room. The only décor was a Mexican flag, which spanned an entire wall, and a framed photo of Luis with his arm around a woman in a sparkly halter top, the kind favored by preteens; the woman didn't look much older than that. The photo sat upon a sturdy bookshelf, and Nick crouched to scan the books' spines. He was surprised to discover all the heavy hitters of the Western canon: Geoffrey Chaucer, John Milton, William Shakespeare, George Eliot, Herman Melville, William Faulkner, Nathaniel Hawthorne, Henry David Thoreau, Mark Twain—all Americans and Brits. Nick wondered if perhaps Luis thought George Eliot was a man. If Emma had been there, she would've been fuming about the exclusion of Edith Wharton, whom she believed had never gotten the recognition she deserved.

"Ah, I see you're admiring my library," the landlord said, returning to the room. "Quite the collection, eh?" He stroked the spine of an essay collection by Thoreau.

"You're a civil disobedience man, are you?" Nick asked. "Ever been to Walden?"

Luis narrowed his eyes. "No, I haven't yet had the chance."

"It's beautiful. Very peaceful." Nick remembered back to his summers at B.U., when he and a few buddies would drive out to the pond, smoke joints, and spend whole afternoons back floating and cloud watching. "I can see how that kind of environment might convince a man to embark on a spiritual quest."

"Yes, Henry was a real man," Luis said.

"Think so?" Luis nodded brashly, and Nick let out a laugh. "I guess your idea of a real man includes slinking back to Mom's house whenever you've got dirty laundry or an itch for homemade pie. Thoreau was a real mama's boy. A bit of a hypocrite, some say."

Luis seemed to be searching for a response, and Nick couldn't help himself: "So which of the Bard's works do you favor most?" Luis adjusted his stance. "Mr. Billy Shakespeare, you have a favorite?"

"I like his early stuff."

"Right, *Richard III*: 'Now is the winter of our discontent' and all that. I can see that. Although I'd peg you more as a *King Lear* kind of man."

"Yes, a great book. You're a teacher, right?"

"Right. Fifth grade."

"My sister and two of my aunties teach. Speaking of real men, that's kind of a womanly line of work, no?"

"I suppose some might think so. Although I'm sure you know that certain traditions hail Aristotle as the First Teacher. Plato taught him, and then he tutored Alexander the Great. I don't think of those guys as too womanly, do you?" Luis was no longer making an effort to mask his scorn. Nick knew he was being an asshole, and getting himself into trouble, too. Had Emma been present, she would've diffused the situation minutes ago. "Anyway, I came for our keys."

Luis held them up and jingled them. "What'll you do for them?"

"I believe we already paid a pretty hefty sum."

"Just kidding, papi." Luis held out the keychain. Nick went to take it, but Luis snatched it back. He re-extended his hand. "Kidding again. Here you go, all yours."

Nick took the keys warily. "Thanks."

"The pleasure belongs to me." Luis's eyes bore into him, conveying zero pleasure. "I'll stop by the apartment sometime and we can continue our intellectual discussion."

"Sure, see you," Nick said, uneasy at the idea of Luis popping by for a chat. He decided he would ask Jose's dad to install an extra lock on the door.

"Everything's set," Nick told Emma, who lay sprawled across the three-seater, head in his lap. The Metro-North train was surprisingly sparse, considering the Jewish New Year began that evening. "I passed the keys to José's dad, and he'll fix it up while we're gone. He was so much cheaper than every other guy I talked to—José really hooked it up."

"I'm so glad your students are such skilled operators, pimping out their parents."

"Hey, whatever works." Nick ran his fingers through Emma's hair and surveyed the passing landscape through the window. Once again he found himself swallowing his thoughts—there was no need to tell her about the exchange with Luis. Emma had enough to worry about. They'd been on the train for less than an hour, on their way to her brother, Max's, for Rosh Hashanah dinner and an overnight stay, and already she'd gnawed her fingernails down to the quick. Nick got along with Max all right, his wife, Alysse, wasn't too bad if you ignored some of her more inane comments, and the kids could be fun in small doses. What Nick disliked was how Emma let her brother get to her, and how she sometimes acted around him. Usually so self-possessed, with Max Emma wilted into a wimpier version of herself; she was constantly rationalizing her life choices and apologizing for who she was, as if her brother were some kind of bastion of the right way to be. If you asked Nick, Max was the one who should admire Emma. While Max had taken the safe route of law school, married boring but dependable Alysse, and skulked back home to his parents' house, Emma had ventured out into the world and taken risks and bets and plunges of faith to figure out who she was and what she wanted to be. So what if she hadn't quite landed on all the answers yet? So what if she occasionally stumbled? She always got back up, and with a wry grin on her face. If Max were to trip and fall, he'd probably cry himself into a puddle of pity until Alysse came along to hoist him to his feet, then rebuild his confidence with a pep talk about how big of a man he was. The image made Nick laugh. He leaned over to kiss Emma. "I love you," he said.

"I love you, too," she said, jerking herself upright in the seat. She yawned and stretched her spine like a cat, extending her arms to maximum wingspan. Nick loved watching his girlfriend's movements, so guileless and unpredictable. She hunched over her bag, rummaged around, and then pulled from it Edith Wharton's book of Italian gardens, her comfort reading. She collapsed back in her seat, legs tucked into herself, and cracked the book's spine to its centerfold: an illustration of a lush garden in Florence. Her sigh was almost postcoital. Nick didn't get the book's appeal, but Emma said paging through it made her feel like she was living in another world. Some men might've been bothered by their girlfriends ignoring them to lust over an alternate existence, but Nick didn't take it personally, especially considering that most of the so-called gardens in their daily lives consisted of small squares of concrete at the backs of bars. Who wouldn't want to escape to a villa in Florence? As long as Emma didn't start poring over books of suburban houses with sprawling lawns, Nick felt fine.

The train slowed to a stop. "Hastings-on-Hudson," Nick read through the window, the sign's bold, italicized lettering like a frantic shout. "Two more stops."

"Are you ready for the wildest New Year's celebration ever?"

"Yep, and this time I even remembered my flask." Nick did think it was kind of a bummer that Jews celebrated their New Year by drinking bad wine, sitting through interminable services, then meditating for days on all their sins—pretty somber stuff.

"Oh goody, you can sneak some swigs to the kids, give them a first taste of the traditional New Year's Day hangover. Alysse would love that."

"It would give me something to repent during the 'I've been so bad' service."

"Kol Nidre. Because that would be your only sin of the year, right?"

"That's right." Nick smiled, but felt a lump in his throat.

When they pulled in to Ardsley-on-Hudson, Emma was barely off the train before her niece and nephew came charging at her and handcuffed their arms around her legs.

"Hi, guys," she said. Nick relieved her of her bag.

"Shanah Tovah," screeched Aimee, wishing Emma a happy new year in Hebrew.

"Look, I've got a shofar!" Caleb produced a child-sized ram's horn and honked it in Emma's ear. Nick was reminded of why he liked his kids older, and what a relief it was to wave them goodbye at three o'clock each day.

"Did you guys say hi to Nick?" Emma asked. Aimee hid shyly behind her leg.

"Poopyhead goy boy," shouted Caleb.

"What's that, buddy?" Nick smirked at Emma, not sure he'd heard right.

"You're a poopyhead goy boy!"

"That's not very nice, Caleb," Emma said, then whispered to Nick, "Apparently the reverse SS has arrived in Westchester, on a manhunt for non-Jews."

Alysse approached the group on the platform. "Hey, guys." She extended her signature minimal-body-contact hug to both of them in turn. "Did you kiddos give Auntie Emma and Mr. Nick a nice welcome?" Caleb nodded innocently, the little shit. "Good, good. Come on, everyone, it's almost sundown!"

For most of the drive to the house, Alysse went on about what a shame it was that so many people now resorted to using store-bought chicken stock in their matzo ball soup instead of making it traditionally with the carcass; Nick thought either way of consuming animal flesh was a shame, but he held his tongue. "Oh, and I hope you've thought through your Rosh Hashanah resolutions," Alysse said, a sparkle in her voice like she was the inventor of this idea. "Personally I'm hoping to keep our mudroom more organized. They say it takes ninety days to create a habit, so in three months we can have a group check-in to make sure we're all sticking to what we said we'd do."

Nick could tell from how Emma was working her jaw that she was on the verge of spewing some serious invective. He squeezed her hand. He was always encouraging her to stop looking for every opportunity to be offended by her sister-in-law and instead to focus on the humor of Alysse. For example, her driving. Nick had assumed Alysse would be one of those by-the-books obeyers of the speed limit—that is, until he'd first gotten in a car with her and discovered the woman's Danica Patrick alter ego. It turned out, Alysse was a speed demon, weaving in and out of traffic like a fiend. What Nick found most entertaining was how entitled she seemed about it, her nose wrinkled in perpetual annoyance, as if the cars around her were deliberately dawdling in order to hold her back.

"I think resolutions are a great idea, Alysse," Nick said from the backseat. "I certainly have some goals for my classroom, helping the slower kids get up to speed and all that." He nudged Emma at the word "speed," trying to get her to crack a smile.

In the rearview mirror, Nick saw Alysse set her lips into a line. Nick suspected she considered him a sort of prop, on the scene temporarily, someone to be tolerated only until Emma woke up and found her real partner—some kind of mensch-y, good-family-breadwinner Jew, like Max. Never mind that Nick had been around for years. It was obvious where Caleb had picked up his insult—well, at least part of it.

Nick braced himself as they stepped over the threshold of the Feit front door. It was Emma's practice to begin each visit to her brother's house with an updated inventory of everything that had been altered from her childhood, cataloging all the new blasphemies Alysse's homemaking had wreaked upon Emma's nostalgic vision of her former home.

"What's that smell?" Emma blurted out. Nick sniffed it, too, the air shellacked with a strange sweetness.

"Oh, it's a hoot," said Alysse, either not noticing or choosing to ignore Emma's tone. "Yankee Candle started a line of Judaica candles. This one's Apples 'n Honey. I bought Freshly Baked Challah, too."

"Do they also have Latke?" Emma said under her breath. "Miraculously makes your house reek of oil for eight full days!"

"It's very festive, Alysse," Nick said. Emma rolled her eyes.

Max appeared in the foyer, donning an apron that read, "Schmaltz happens." "My lovely sister and her beloved! Hello, welcome, make yourselves at home!"

Nick was glad Emma didn't take the bait, insisting that it *was* her home. "Hi, dork," she said, hitting her brother on the arm, then following him back into the kitchen. Nick was left behind with the two kids. Alysse had disappeared, too; she had a tendency to desert visitors with her children, likely assuming anyone would consider it a privilege to babysit her progeny. It was actually something Alysse and Emma had in common, a wholehearted devotion to their own agendas.

"What are we gonna do now?" Caleb asked. He and his sister peered up at Nick.

Nick dredged up the tricks he'd used ages ago as a camp counselor intended to simultaneously entertain and exhaust children: He bounced Aimee and Caleb around on piggyback rides, timed them in three-legged races around the living room, and challenged them to a dance-off; still they begged for more. With no sign of relief from either parent, Nick longed for a drink. From experience he knew that Max tended to make a big deal of drinks before dinner, acting as if it were a massive inconvenience to dig out a beer from the fridge. (This made Nick wonder if somewhere along the way Emma had complained to her brother about Nick's drinking.) The way Nick saw it, if you were going to pop out a few kids and set up house in Westchester, you may as well embrace the Cheever-Yates-Updike tradition of middle-class suburban debauchery, or at the very least treat yourself to an occasional five o'clock cocktail.

No booze in sight, Nick thought up an alternative remedy. Ignoring the kids' protests, he pulled their squirming bodies onto his lap, then whispered in their ears, "Can you two keep a secret?"

"Maybe," said Aimee, squealing as Nick tickled her belly.

"Just maybe?"

"Of course we can." Caleb said this with big-brother seriousness, setting his mouth into the same line as his mother's. "Trust us."

"All right, I'm going to teach you a song that's top-secret, one hundred percent classified, understand? So you've got to sing it very softly and never breathe a word about it to a single soul. Are you ready?" They both nodded somberly. Nick sang in their ears: "On the first day of Christmas, my true love gave to me a partridge in a pear tree."

Nick felt a perverse thrill as Aimee and Caleb repeated the line in their scratchy whispers, their eyes wide at the word *Christmas*. He took them through the ensuing verses, and they diligently sang along, giving in to the greed of requesting turtledoves and French hens and gold rings and more. Nick happened to know that for the kids' birthday parties, Alysse requested charitable donations in lieu of presents. Caleb and Aimee were having fun, and Nick congratulated himself on making a relatively harmless choice; after all, he could've taught them the much more religious "Hark! The Herald Angels Sing" or "O Come, All Ye Faithful."

Aimee tapped his shoulder. "What's lords-a-leaping and maids-a-milking?"

"Like Consuela, dummy," Caleb told his sister, then explained to Nick, "Consuela comes each Tuesday to vacuum and change our sheets and take Mom's old clothes. And the lord is like Hashem,

Adonai—you know, God. Duh. Leaping is jumping." The boy smiled with self-congratulation. It was clear he'd be a piece of work by the time he reached the age of Nick's students; Nick was glad he didn't teach in this area.

Now Nick was starting to enjoy himself. He was about to explain the concept of milking cows, when Max appeared, miraculously holding out a beer. "What are you hooligans up to out here?"

Despite Nick miming a zip-your-lips gesture, Aimee blurted out, "Nick's teaching us a secret song." Her brother bopped her on the head.

"I have no idea what she's talking about," Nick said, putting up his hands in surrender and winking at Caleb. Nick accepted the beer and clinked it against Max's.

"*L'chaim*, cheers," said Max. "Dinner's ready, folks."

In the dining room, Nick found Emma slyly chomping her way through a hefty chunk of mandel bread. He wiped a crumb from her cheek, then kissed the spot.

"Guess what?" She held out a stack of papers. "Alysse gave me homework."

"What is that?" Nick read the title: "My summer helping African orphans."

"Alysse's friend's son is trying to get into Princeton, so she thought I wouldn't mind taking a look at his personal statement. She even gave me background info so I could research the program the kid did."

"Oh no. I hope you told her no." Nick knew how much this bothered Emma. He'd listened to her rant about how people didn't approach dentists at parties and ask them to extract a sore tooth, gratis; and yet, Emma's most distant acquaintances felt comfortable asking her to review their kid's/cousin's/brother's college apps in her spare time.

"I told her I'd be happy to take a look, for my professional rate of one hundred dollars an hour."

"I'm proud of you, Em. Just—"

"I was nice about it, don't worry. I can be a goddamned saint when I want to be."

"My sweet angel." Nick drew a halo above her head, and she batted her eyelashes.

Dinner began with prayers. Nick assumed the stance he'd perfected over his years with Emma's family, eyes set at forty-five degrees to the ground, half humming along to show that he'd learned something from all his time spent witnessing the Feits' religious traditions. The final "Amen" set Nick into Pavlovian salivation. For all of Emma's complaints about visiting her brother's family, Nick always looked forward to Alysse's cooking. He didn't begrudge Emma the fact that she'd never learned to cook—he wasn't one of those guys who felt a woman had to know her way around the kitchen—but he did envy Max, who probably came home each night to a home-cooked meal. Plus, Nick felt grateful that Alysse prepared alternate vegetarian dishes for him. (Emma, of course, suspected her sister-in-law of martyrly motives, believing she wanted extra praise for specially accommodating her guest.)

The heaping plates made their way around the table: apples and honey, of course, then pomegranate coleslaw, matzo ball soup—with vegetarian broth for Nick, despite Alysse's comments in the car—sweet potato tzimmes, and eggplant kugel. Nick allowed himself a whiff of the brisket before passing it along. "This looks beautiful," Max said, and Nick nodded in agreement, his mouth already full.

Nick was savoring a bite of honey-glazed potatoes and buttery (although since the meal was kosher, probably margarine-y) noodles, when he felt the buzz of a text in his pocket. He discreetly pulled out his phone, and when he saw the name Luis, his mouth went dry: *Neighbor complaints about noise. Tell your guy to keep it down.*

Nick's throat erupted in coughs. He reached for his water, and drained the glass. What did Luis expect? Nick had instructed José's father to finish by ten p.m., but beyond that, he couldn't exactly tell him to use a silent hammer. Nick saw Emma's face contort into worry, so he shoveled more potatoes into his mouth—tasteless mush—to show he was okay. He felt another buzz: *The smell, too—bothering the residents. Not happy.* Nick fumed. Again, what was he supposed to do? He considered typing back, *If you don't want a worker there making noise and using chemicals, maybe you shouldn't have let your apartment fall into such disrepair.* He stilled his twitching thumbs and forced himself to put away the phone. He craved a drink—something stronger than beer.

"Nick?" Looking up, he saw everyone's eyes fixed on him.

"We were just talking about how the ten days between Rosh Hashanah and Yom Kippur are meant for reflection and repentance," said Alysse. "We're all sharing our hopes and regrets. Do you have something you'd like to contribute?"

Emma touched his elbow. "I said I was going to reflect on how to value myself more as a professional, and stop offering my services pro bono."

"Um," Nick said, "I guess I'm going to try and think more positive thoughts." He tried it right then, sending good vibes to this landlord who made his insides churn, and waves of forgiveness to himself for all his recent foibles. He took out his phone and typed back to Luis, *Worker will be gone soon. I'll ask him to open some windows.*

"Well, I've got something I'd like to share," Alysse said, squeezing Max's hand. "We're so excited to be telling you this in person. Here goes: Next spring, we'll be welcoming a new addition to the family." Her palm went to her stomach. Max beamed.

Silence. Nick glanced at Emma, urging her to offer her congratulations or say anything positive. And she did, about a beat too late: *"Mazel tov."* She raised her wineglass, then tipped its entire contents into her mouth. "Damn it," she whispered to Nick, "I thought she'd just put on some weight."

Nick shushed her. "Congratulations, Alysse," he said. "That's really great news." Emma reached for the bottle of wine, and now Nick was really jonesing for some whiskey. He scanned the room, unsuccessfully.

"Isn't that right, kiddos?" Alysse said. "Soon you'll get a little brother or sister."

Aimee, who'd previously been preoccupied with dragging an apple slice through a blob of honey, perked up. "I want a cat!" she screeched, flinging a handful of kugel in Nick's direction. The noodle mass plopped onto his plate, splattering custard in his face.

"Good arm," he laughed, dabbing at his chin with a napkin.

Max ignored his daughter. "It's a blessing, and it'll be just in time for Passover."

Alysse beamed. She turned to her fussing daughter: "Which do you want, sweetie, a baby brother or sister?"

"A cat! I want a cat!" Aimee was now screaming and on the verge of tears.

"No, a partridge in a pear tree," said Caleb to his sister, eyes wide with mischief.

"Yeah, a partridge in a pear tree!" yelled Aimee, and then the two of them were off and singing, an enthusiastic duet.

Nick, though impressed by the kids' recall, nevertheless intended to escape into his e-mail. But a glance at his phone revealed another text, this one from the worker: *Problem here, need to talk. Call me ASAP.*

"Where'd you learn that song, kids?" Alysse's brightness clearly masked fury.

"Mr. Nick," Aimee squealed, before launching into the sixth verse.

Alysse seemed about to speak, but then Caleb broke out with, "Poopyhead goy boy taught us. Poopyhead goy boy!"

Alysse's porcelain cheeks blotched red.

"Who taught him to say that? I wonder," Emma said, giddy at the drama.

"Please excuse me for a moment." Nick stood up. "I've got to make a call." Though he was certain no one believed him, Nick fled from the table down the hall to Max's study. This room was the only one that made Nick jealous of suburban living. Classically done with cherry wood and sturdy, stately furniture, it featured three walls of bookshelves—this was the kind of man cave Nick would want. Although his would feature a bar, too. Dropping into Max's ergonomic office chair, Nick dialed José's father.

"Bedbugs," the man spilled before Nick could even say hello. "I hate to give the bad news, but I had to say. The minute I put on the paint—I guess it was the chemicals bring them out. They're everywhere, the little guys in every room." Nick stopped listening. His brain buzzed, like the bedbugs had crawled inside his head. He flashed on all the horror stories—the furniture and apartments and whole lives ruined by the tiny, unstoppable blood-suckers. People with bedbugs went crazy, got shunned by their friends and cast out from society; they lost their jobs. And then Nick heard a voice carry from down the hall: Emma. What would he tell Emma? What would they do? They'd already scheduled movers for the following weekend.

When Nick realized the man had stopped talking, he tamped down his panic. "Mr. Valdez," he said, "why don't you take off? You shouldn't be exposed to that. Thank you for letting me know. I can pay you after school tomorrow—I mean, on Tuesday." Nick remembered he had the next day off for the Jewish holiday. At least he'd have time to—*what?*—celebrate Rosh Hashanah with the arrival of bedbugs? He thought he might be sick.

When Nick returned to the table, no one was speaking. The kids had clearly been silenced and were sullenly picking at their food. Emma was reaching for more wine. Nick tugged at her shirt. He was hesitant to tell her the news, but feared she might soon polish off the entire bottle. "Hey, can I speak with you privately for a minute?"

Secluded in the guest bedroom, Nick filled Emma in, and she laughed. Hysterically. Perpetually. She was drunk, and she set her woozy sights on the bed, which was made with military precision and featured mints in shiny wrappers atop each pillow. Before Nick could stop her, Emma lunged for the bedspread and flung it to the floor. Then she tore into the sheets, ripping them from their neat tuck and twisting them up into a maniacal tangle. Next she went for the mints, grabbing them one by one and chucking them across the room. One hit the television with a dull ding, and Nick winced.

"We don't deserve bedbugs," Emma whined, her voice wobbly. "They do. Max and his Jewish Martha Stewart and their two-point-five children and their perfect, happy little life. *They* deserve the bedbugs."

"Shhh." Nick worried their voices were carrying. Also, it looked like Emma was searching for something else to throw; clearly her tantrum-prone niece had rubbed off on her. Nick restrained her in a hug. "Come on, Em. Alysse cooked us a nice meal, and—"

"And what, invited me over to edit her friend's kid's essay, and then condescend to me about how I couldn't possibly begin to imagine the blessing of a newborn baby?"

"Well, those things, too, yes. But I bet there's a killer apple cake coming out for dessert."

"No ice cream, though." Emma had slumped onto the mess of sheets.

"What?" Nick sat down beside her.

"No ice cream. It's freaking dairy. And it's idiotic to eat apple cake without ice cream. It's dry and crumby and dumb. Stupid kosher laws, they don't even make sense."

"Okay, okay." Nick rubbed circles into her back. She seemed calmer, despite her anti-kosher tirade. "Let's go back out and have some dessert, and then we can deal with everything else in the morning. Please try and at least pretend to be happy for Alysse."

"Who, the reproductive robot? The busy breeder? The fertile female? The—"

"Yep, we all know you're good at alliteration. Come on, Em, let's go."

Emma let herself be led into the dining room. Nick didn't comment when she Hoovered up three pieces of cake, and he was relieved to hear her ask Alysse for the recipe. *Happy New Year,* he thought, thanking God or whomever that it was time for bed.

Chapter 16

The throbbing of Emma's head served as an alarm clock, knocking her out of sleep. She lay still, blinking her vision into focus, and then slowly, like the oozing of some poisonous molasses into her brain, the events of the previous evening returned to her. She rolled over to realize she was alone in bed, alone in the guest room, and the silence was total—no buses whirring by outside the window, no neighbors' voices muffled through porous walls, no horns or sirens or any of the other sounds that had formed the background to Emma's thoughts for all the years she'd lived in Manhattan. Overwhelmed by the quiet, she emitted a low groan.

Emma considered her choices: escape back under the covers and sleep it off for a few more hours, but eventually face Alysse's scornful glee at her late rising; or tough it out and force herself up. After a moment of thought, Emma opted for the latter, and one at a time she jostled her limbs to make sure everything was in working order—yes, barely. Getting dressed seemed too challenging of a chore, so she slipped on the bathrobe she'd packed in reluctant deference to her sister-in-law's morning modesty policy.

Emma padded downstairs and into the kitchen, where she was glad to find only her brother. He was at the counter, mixing.

"*Shalom*, sunshine," Max said.

"Hey." She kissed him on the cheek, not caring about her unbrushed teeth.

"Alysse is at her Pilates class, and I sent your man out with the kids for more OJ." Emma nodded. "I bet you could use some coffee."

Emma was still nodding as Max placed the coffee in front of her, with 2 percent milk and one sugar like he knew she liked it. She cradled the warm mug, breathed in the steam of roasted beans, and sighed with gratitude. Her eyes filled with tears.

"Hey, Max, I'm sorry about last night." He waved her away, but she continued: "No, really, you and Alysse invited us over, and you shared your big baby news, and I acted like an imbecile, and, um . . ." She'd told herself she wouldn't let Max know, but she couldn't stop the words from pouring out of her mouth. "We have bedbugs. The apartment Nick and I are supposed to move into next weekend, apparently it's overrun with bedbugs." She saw her brother recoil and inch away. "Hey, *I'm* not infected!"

"Sorry, gut reaction. Oy vey, that's a tough break."

"I know." The liquid brimmed over Emma's eyes, and she buried her face in her arms. "I don't know what we're going to do. Shit. Shit, shit, shit." She felt a perverse pleasure in repeating the curse in Alysse's squeaky-clean kitchen.

"You know"—Max placed a hand on her shoulder—"sometimes when I'm having a hard time and don't know what to do, what I do is go to shul, and something clicks."

Emma lifted her head. "Max," she said sternly.

It was as if he hadn't heard her. "Shul can really help clear your mind—the familiar songs, the sense of community, the mood of the service. And what's so mystifying is, the rabbi's sermon always seems to speak to whatever it is I'm struggling with. Whether that's God's mysterious workings, or luck, or what, I don't know."

Emma sneered at her brother. "My God, Max."

"What?"

"Can you stop being a Jewish missionary for, like, five seconds? Seriously."

"Oh." His voice was quiet. He sat down next to her, bringing the mixing bowl. "Sorry. I just thought it might help you."

She rolled her eyes. "What are you making, anyway?"

"Pancakes. Buckwheat raisin, with chia seeds."

"Ugh, you're such a good father." Emma groaned, but she didn't feel as upset. "Remember Dad used to make us Bisquick?"

"Yeah, with that Mrs. Butterworth that was all corn syrup and chemicals."

"And delicious. It was always on Sundays, when Mom was off Jazzercising. And sometimes we convinced him to make them with chocolate chips."

"Dad was such a pushover," said Max. "I think his strategy was to flood us with sugar, so after ten minutes of hyperactivity, we'd crash hard and nap the rest of the day."

"Then he could read the paper in peace."

"Exactly."

"You know what I could really go for right now?" Emma said. "A bacon, egg, and cheese. That's the best hangover cure in the world."

"Emmy, come on."

"You come on. I know you're Mr. Kosher now, but admit it, there's nothing better than a bacon, egg, and cheese. When's the last time you had one? Seriously?"

Max's sharp facial features relaxed as he considered it. "Years ago, probably. Definitely before Caleb was born."

"That's bonkers. Well, I have an idea. Let's sneak out and indulge in some big, fat, greasy breakfast sandwiches."

"Emma, be serious."

"Oh, do it for me, Max-y. We'll pick up some mouthwash and no one will ever know. I'll take it to my grave, cross my heart." From muscle memory, Emma performed the series of complicated hand gestures that had once made up their sibling swear.

That did it. Moments later, she and Max were sitting in the parking lot of the next town's deli (Max didn't want to risk being seen close to home), tearing into their eggs.

"Oh my God, that is freaking incredible," said Max, mouth full.

"Orgasmic." Emma began giggling. "Hey, you have egg on your face."

"So? You do, too." He lobbed a piece of food at her cheek and barked out a laugh.

"How dare you!" She tilted her coffee cup toward him in mock threat.

"All right, I surrender." Max held up his hands. "You know, we should do this more often. I mean, not you peer-pressuring me into breaking the dietary laws of my faith, but, like, hang out more. It's the New Year now, the time to look at our lives, to reflect, to think about what kinds of changes we'll make in the coming year—"

"But, Max, the problem is you're always doing that."

"Doing what?"

"*That.* Lecturing me to go to temple or to feel some Rosh Hashanah spirituality, or trying to convince me to take some class about the Talmud—whatever your latest campaign for the chosen people is."

Max was quiet, nodding. "I see. By the way, I'm sorry about what Caleb called Nick last night."

"Goy boy? I thought that was actually pretty clever. It has a nice poetic ring."

"It's Alysse, not me, who's so concerned about Nick not being Jewish. But you know it comes from a place of love." Emma arched her eyebrows. "Truly. She's just worried about you. She thinks it might cause problems down the road to have a partner with such an unfamiliar background, someone who grew up so differently from you."

"You make it sound like he was raised by wolves."

"You know what I mean. But, Emmy, an interfaith relationship isn't insignificant."

"Whatever you say."

"And I admit it makes me sad that you've turned your back on our faith. Make fun if you like, but Judaism gives our family a real sense of peace and purpose."

"Max, it's my instinct to make fun when I feel like I'm being proselytized. We're not the same, okay? It doesn't give me a sense of peace and purpose, for example, to wake up early on a Saturday and spend half the day singing along with that tone-deaf cantor, then kibitzing with all the perfumed old ladies of Westchester.

Look at little Maximillian, such a mensch, with such a sweet punim!" She
pinched her brother's cheek, imitating the elderly Jewish women
who were the mainstays of the shul's congregation.

Max swatted her away. "Cantor Cohen *is* kind of tone-deaf,
isn't he?"

"Completely! What kind of crazy person who can't carry a tune
decides to make a career out of singing?"

Max shook his head, laughing. "Let's make a deal, okay? I'll
stop nagging you about the Jewish stuff, if you stop treating my
devoutness like it's some kind of ridiculous, antiquated hocus-
pocus. How about it?"

"Fine," said Emma. They shook on it. "This seems like a good
time to invite you to my Islam conversion ceremony."

"Ha ha. Anyway, as I was saying before, we should be in each
other's lives more. I know I'm always on you to trek up to the
'burbs, but I could come into the city, too. We'll hit the bars like
we used to." He said it with enthusiasm, as if he really believed
this was something he'd do, so Emma nodded along. He'd made
similar proclamations before.

"Sounds good," she said.

"Bring it in." Max extended his arms, and their embrace was
tight and warm, not like those fake hugs his wife doled out. "Okay,
we should get back to the house. Everyone'll be waiting on us, and
I've got to get the kids ready for shul. Remember, you rat me out
about this sandwich to Alysse, I'll kill you."

"Noted." They drove back in silence, Emma thinking how,
bedbugs or not, she would never trade her life for Max's. She
guessed he was thinking the same about her.

It seemed like five days, not five hours, later when Emma and
Nick found themselves idling outside the building in which
they'd rented a space to live. They were waiting for their new
landlord, who'd communicated via text message that he'd arrive
Btween 2&3:30 and no, he could not be any more specific.

With her brother's help, Emma had successfully fended off
Alysse's insistences that they join the family for services, then she

and Nick had boarded Metro North, where they'd spent the whole trip back to the city researching bedbugs. Nick had quickly become captivated by a series of slideshows of the critters, eyes peeled like at a car crash, while Emma entrenched herself in housing law. She'd been heartened to discover that it was a landlord's responsibility—legally *and* financially—to act in the face of an infestation. She'd then read up on all the available extermination techniques, and built a spreadsheet organized by companies' supposed effectiveness, price, and user ratings; if they acted fast, they could get this taken care of by their move-in date. She'd imagined how relieved Luis would be to learn that she'd already gathered all this helpful info.

By 3:45, there was still no sign of their landlord. Nick had decamped to the corner bar a half hour earlier, but Emma was still standing in front of the building, optimistically scanning every passerby for Luis's face. She hoped their conversation would be finished by four, when she'd told Sophia to come meet her. She'd explained the situation over the phone (well, a version of it, saying services were running late and she wouldn't be able to make it up to Midtown in time for their appointment—she didn't want her client knowing about the bedbugs), and the girl had happily agreed to another adventure out to Brooklyn.

"Man, you can go to temple in sweats?" Sophia appeared, ten minutes early, eyeing Emma's outfit. Emma had never changed out of her pajamas from morning. "Lucky. For church, my mom makes me wear these awful Lilly Pulitzer getups."

"Oh, hey, Sophia. Um, no, I was uncomfortable, so I ran home and changed." Emma realized how little sense this made, and also what a bad idea it was to have Sophia there when Luis showed up; she scolded herself for this poorly planned attempt at multitasking. "I had to arrange a last-minute visit with my new landlord, so I'm thinking we should cancel today's appointment. I know it was a pain for you to get out here—I'll talk to your mom and credit you a session."

"Ooh, so these are the new digs?" Sophia asked, ignoring the part about the canceled session. She lunged for the front door and, discovering it unlocked, disappeared inside before Emma could stop her—or warn her about the bedbugs. Sophia was back outside a minute later, thumbs working her phone.

"What are you doing?" Emma asked.

"Instagramming. That is one insane rat trap in the hall."

"Excuse me?" Emma peeked at the phone screen, and her stomach flipped. "Surely it's a mouse trap. Practically every building in New York has mice."

"No way, José. Look at the size of that thing." Emma watched as the girl typed a caption: *Epic #rattrap. #grittybrooklyn #eek!!!*

Emma decided to excise this new information from her mind, figuring that if she didn't, she might have a breakdown right there on the street. "So about today's session."

"Oh, come on, please let me tag along to your meeting. I was excellent support the other day, remember? If it'll make you feel better, you can quiz me on vocab until he shows up."

Sophia made a good point about her support with the other landlord, so Emma considered the proposition. Well, why the hell not? Plus, part of her suspected that, as if to prove something, Luis would continue to keep them waiting well past four.

She was right. Emma and Sophia had made their way through nearly a hundred SAT words—"abjure" all the way to "winsome"—before Luis sauntered by the building at 4:25, as if his tenants hadn't been waiting on him for two and a half hours. His relaxed stance seemed like a put-on.

"Good afternoon," he said, shifty eyes playing over Emma and Sophia in a way that made Emma want to wrap her teenage client in a protective embrace.

"Let me grab Nick," she said. "He's just over in that bar."

"We'll all go to the bar," Luis declared. "I'm thirsty."

"Okay," Emma said. It couldn't hurt to meet in neutral, non-bedbug-infested territory. "Sophia, you can wait—"

"I'll come," she chirped, whipping out a driver's license that aged her five years and darkened her hair several shades. Sophia didn't even drive, Emma happened to know.

"All right, whatever, but no drinking. Come on." So the motley crew consisting of Emma, her teenage client, and her new landlord, set off to join Nick at the corner bar.

There were certain difficulties Emma had anticipated about this meeting—one, that they'd have to be delicate about their delivery, since no one wants to hear that his property is overrun with bedbugs; two, that the money part might get tense, since the treatments deemed most effective were also the priciest; and three, that they'd have to be pushy about the time frame, so everything could be handled before their move-in. But there were also certain assumptions that Emma had taken as givens about the meeting— one, that Luis would be as invested as his tenants (if not more so) in ridding his building of the bloodsucking parasites; two, that he would not argue with the letter of state housing law; and three, that he was a rational human being and would act accordingly.

But the longer Emma sat slumped in the bar booth, sandwiched between Nick and Sophia, and across from Luis, who between utterances sipped infuriatingly small quantities of club soda through a long straw, the more Emma was reminded of a childhood maxim: To "assume" is to make an "ass" out of "u" and "me."

"The reason we set up this meeting," Emma began, "was because it's come to our attention that the apartment we've rented from you is infested with bedbugs." At this, Sophia gasped, making Emma feel like she was starring in a soap opera before a rapt live audience—more and more she was regretting letting the girl tag along. The bigger surprise was that Luis began laughing.

"This is very interesting," he said. "None of my other tenants have ever had a problem with my walls, but then you two show up and the place isn't good enough, so you bring in your noisy construction crew." Emma wasn't sure how one worker could be construed as a crew, but she was too stunned to respond. Luis went on: "And none of my other tenants have ever complained about bugs, but then the two of you come around and suddenly my building is infested. Very interesting."

"Are you suggesting we're making this up?" Emma was indignant. She felt a hand on her knee—Nick's—so she softened her tone. "What motivation would we possibly have for inventing a bedbug infestation?"

"I'm just wondering, is all. I wonder, too, maybe the worker brought in the bugs?"

"This is rich," Emma said. "I sent you the pictures, right, of the bedbugs crawling out of the walls? Would you like to see them again?"

"Ooh, *I* would," said Sophia. Emma ignored her.

"Look," said Nick, "regardless of who brought in the bedbugs, they're there now, so we have to deal with them."

"Whatever you say, teacher man," said Luis.

Although Emma now felt less confident about her spreadsheet of solutions, she whipped it out anyway, and began explaining the different options to Luis—the sniffing dogs, the industrial-grade vacuums, the specially trained exterminators.

Luis snorted. "Last time I checked, dogs sniff out food and the assholes of bitches, not little bugs. Who exactly is going to pay for all this?"

On her phone Emma pulled up the housing law Web site; she scrolled to the statute about a landlord's responsibility to provide a bedbug-free environment for tenants, and how the expense of eradication fell to the owner. Despite her jumpy stomach, the legal jargon calmed her; this was official, government-decreed, indisputable.

"This is a joke, right?" Luis asked, waving the phone away. "You hire some handyman who comes in, makes a racket all day long, then tells some story about scary bugs, and now you expect me to pay a fortune to get rid of this so-called problem?"

Emma felt disoriented; it had never occurred to her that Luis would hear the law and simply consider himself exempt. Despite her doubts, she still thought she might appeal to his sense: "The legitimate companies charge by the procedure," she said. "So if they brought in the dogs and found nothing, you'd only get charged for the evaluation."

"Oh, how generous," Luis seethed. "Okay, I'm going to be reasonable with you." An unreasonable-looking grin spread itself across his face. "I'll go to Home Depot and buy a few cans of foggers, which are probably ten dollars a pop. That's on me, my treat."

"But." Emma looked to Nick for help, but he seemed paralyzed, his knuckles clenched white. Although she'd bookmarked the page on the Health Department site that explained how foggers were a scam and could actually exacerbate a bedbug problem, she sensed the futility of calling it up on her phone. In fact, she, too, found herself frozen. Here before her was one of those people she'd heard about but had never really believed existed—the ones who didn't subscribe to reason, who were suspicious of science, and who, based on ignorance or anger or Emma didn't know what, had invented their own set of rules for how the world worked. The worst part was, unlike a muttering nut on the subway whom you could escape by sliding a few seats away, Emma and Nick were bound and beholden to this particular nut—by contract.

Luis continued: "I'll tell you what else. I'll indulge your little fantasy about the creepy-crawler invasion. I'll hire an exterminator. But I'm not going to tell him about the so-called bedbugs, because then he'll do what any smart businessman would do: rip me off. Who wouldn't? He'll go along with it and charge me a fortune to get rid of the 'problem'"—here Luis made air quotes—"that was never there in the first place. So I'll have him look around and see what he finds. If it's bedbugs, fine, I'll get the foggers. Or if you two want to hire your fancy experts, that's on you. And that's final." Luis slurped up the last of his soda, and then placed his hands on the table. "Excuse me, I need to go relieve myself." He stood up, saluted them, and sauntered to the back of the bar.

"Holy shit," said Sophia, as soon as he was out of sight. "What a psycho. Is every landlord in New York like that?"

Emma's head was churning. She was working furiously to devise a more convincing tactic, to figure out an approach that would make Luis understand their perspective. A tug at her shirtsleeve jolted her from her strategizing. "Emma," Nick said. "We've got to get out of this lease."

"What?"

"Luis is dumb and dangerous. Do you really want this to escalate any more?"

"But—"

"Can you imagine if something goes wrong with the plumbing, or if the heat breaks down? We'd be living under that guy's reign of terror. We'd be held hostage by this lunacy."

"But both our leases are up in less than two weeks. We'll have nowhere to live."

"We'll find somewhere else." Nick nodded, as if to close the case. He signaled to the waitress with his empty pint glass.

Emma began rubbing her temples. She looked up to see Sophia's beseeching grin. "So this might not be the perfect time, but I'm curious, did you happen to save any of the bug carcasses? I bet I could make an awesome installation out of them."

Emma found herself giggling in a pitch an octave higher than usual. "Sophia, that's an excellent idea. Why don't you ask Luis? Maybe he can sponsor your exhibit, and write up the commentary. He can expound upon our culture's obsessive fear of bedbugs, and how the infestations are often just a product of our deranged, middle-class imaginations. He can theorize how this speaks to the guilt of the modern-day gentrifier, a xenophobic paranoia about urban living spaces, an uneasy symbiosis with nature, a—"

"Easy there," Nick said, cutting off her ramble. "Let's save the postmodern crackups for the privacy of our home, okay?" Sophia, who'd been furiously scribbling Emma's words onto a cocktail napkin, looked disappointed.

Luis had reappeared. "So, my tenants, what do you say? How are we going to handle this big, scary bug situation?" He wiggled his fingers in front of his face.

Nick tilted his head at Emma. She looked down in defeat. "Luis, we want to talk to you about ending our tenant-landlord relationship. We've realized this is not the right living situation for us, and we'd like to terminate the lease."

He shrugged. "Fine by me. I have the paperwork here—we can tear it up right now."

"Excellent," said Nick. "So you can just write us a check for, let's see, first month, last month, security, the broker's fee . . . We can call the repairs even."

Luis laughed. "Be serious, man. You wasted my time and energy, you terrorized my tenants with your construction, you made crazy claims about bedbugs, and now it's too late for me to find another tenant for October. I say you count yourself lucky that I'll let you out of our contract without penalty, instead of charging you twelve months' rent as I could definitely do. Let's say we tear up the lease, all shake hands, and walk away."

"Without all the money you owe us?" Emma asked, incredulous.

"Like I said, I don't believe I owe you guys shit. We had a deal, fair and square. You want to pull out of the deal? Be my guest, but you'll have to face the consequences."

"Emma," Sophia said. "You need to talk to a lawyer. I think I can help."

Without waiting for Emma's okay, Sophia turned to Luis, and said, "Hold your horses, mister. Don't tear up a thing. We'll get back to you soon enough. And we'll have the law on our side!" Despite the lines that seemed lifted from a bad cowboy movie, Emma welled up with gratitude for the girl's gumption—and for her fake ID.

After Luis fled from the bar, muttering on his way out about "the goddamn gentrifiers," Nick ordered them a pitcher of beer, then another one, and then several drinks in, Emma caved and let Sophia have one, too, and then it started to seem like a good idea to join Sophia at a party uptown where she claimed they'd find her housing lawyer friend. (Emma was reluctant to call her lawyer brother, for fear that Max would skew the story into an I-told-you-so opportunity.) It didn't occur to her to question why Sophia was going to a party on a school night, or to consider the inappropriateness of attending said party with her teenage client; although she did think to ask why, at age seventeen, Sophia was partying with someone who was old enough to have completed law school.

Sophia waved away the concern. "All my friends are older. High school kids are immature."

"She has a point there," Nick said, emptying the remains of his glass.

"Anyway, you should really come."

Nick shrugged his concession, and Emma, more than willing to spend the rest of the evening avoiding their current predicament, said, "Why not?" Her beer-fogged brain was still calculating the best subway route up to Seventy-second and Second when Sophia announced a car service was on its way. Moments later they were beckoned to the curb by a honk that sounded almost polite, as if to expose the car's prim Upper East Side origins.

Emma was expecting a stately high-rise with an equally stately doorman, vases of freshly cut flowers, and polished, shiny surfaces, but the car pulled up to a building as battered-looking as Emma's own Lower East Side tenement. "Thanks, Gordon," Sophia chirped. She reached to pat the driver on the shoulder, then shimmied her way out and guided Nick and Emma inside and up three sets of stairs.

The door swung open, and a waifish guy in his early twenties planted a peck on Sophia's forehead. "Darling, hello. Who's this, your nanny?"

"This is my tutor-slash-friend-slash-life-coach, Emma," said Sophia, giddy. Emma felt herself blushing. "Also her lover, Nick." Nick shot Emma a skeptical look.

Post-introductions, Sophia pulled them into a large room that resembled the set of a down-market Benetton ad: Each of the dozen or so people was an unusual take on attractive, and each projected a variation on a thrift-store-chic aesthetic. Genevieve would've fit right in, with her long blond hair and vintage wardrobe, Emma thought. Emma considered texting her, before she remembered with a twinge her friend's recent chilliness—although maybe Gen really was just busy with her nursing school applications, as she'd claimed. After a few moments, Emma realized that no one in the room had moved or spoken; they all lounged, wearing listless expressions and draping long, limp limbs across the furniture; she half wondered if there'd been a gas leak. Sophia made introductions, but Emma couldn't quite follow the names that either sounded like medications (Allegrina? was it Frescaline?) or else just things (Branch, Lyric, Bird, *did she say Nickel?*). The painted walls were accented with snaking lines of poetry, some of which Emma recognized as Langston Hughes and Pablo Neruda. Nick nudged her. "I need a drink, stat."

In the kitchen was a guy busy transferring most of a bottle of vodka into a plastic cup. "Aloha," he said, his marble eyes a hypnotizing hue of blue. "I'm Wade."

"Oh," said Emma, suddenly hopeful. "You're the lawyer Sophia told us about."

"Did she?" Wade raised his eyebrows, which made his eyes pop even more vividly. "Yep, I'm doing the legal education thing at Hunter—starting with Constitutional Law this semester, and I think I'll try Torts next. I'm taking it slow so I can really experience each class fully, you know? Also so I have time for my art."

"Your art—of course." Nick said it with an edge, but Wade nodded in earnest. "Mind if I pour myself a drink?"

"Be my guest, bud. And one for the lady?"

Emma grabbed a cup, her hopes of getting help from Wade dwindling. "So then you're not a lawyer." She didn't even bother phrasing it as a question.

"I'm not sure I'll end up taking the bar. It's, like, I definitely wanna help people who get screwed over by the system, but at the same time, I don't wanna be part of perpetuating the man's bullshit with some elitist degree. I mean, what does it even mean to call oneself a Juris Doctor?"

So that she wouldn't have to respond, Emma gulped at her drink—vodka with a trickle of tonic. She decided they should leave, and was about to say so to Nick, but then Wade set his electric-blue gaze upon her, and she understood how he could get away with spewing such nonsense. No straight woman could laugh those eyes out of the room. Wade draped an arm each around Emma's and Nick's shoulders, and asked, "But what's going on with you guys, I mean legal system–wise?"

Their whole sob story tumbled out of Emma, as Wade "mmm-hm"-ed along in sympathy and Nick freshened all of their drinks.

"Well, you're screwed," Wade declared after Emma finished describing the afternoon's altercation. "I hate to say it, but if this guy wants to bogart your money, your only real recourse is to sue his ass. And the government's slashed the shit out of the courts' budgets, so you're looking at a six-month wait time, minimum—and that's *if* you make it before a judge at all. Usually they triple-book the cases. Even if you go all cheapskate and rep yourself, and even if you do get your case heard and manage to win, if this dude knows anything about how fucked-up shit is in the law, he can just straight up not pay. Then it's on you to go all Sherlock on his ass and track down his assets, fill out a shit-ton of paperwork, freeze his bank accounts, and more or less mire yourself in a total cluster-fuck of governmental incompetence. Don't even get me started on appeals."

"They teach you all that in Constitutional Law?" asked Nick.

"Oh no, man. I sued my dad's ex-wife over these Rolexes I'm positive she lifted from my pad, so I'm mad knowledgeable about the courts and all their bullshit. The judge had my back, but two years later, that shit's still not resolved."

"Wow, I'm sorry," said Emma.

"Yeah, it's a major bummer. Anyway, want my advice?" Wade clearly knew the power of his gaze; Emma was suddenly eager for his input. "Drop it. I know it's hard as fuck, but try and get Namaste about that shit: Just let it go. So you're out a few Gs? Tough shit. That's life, man." Wade raised his cup, and they all drained their drinks.

Nick leaned into Emma and whispered, "Escape route, please, now."

Out in the living room, Sophia beckoned them to a couch. "How'd it go with Wade? Was he helpful?"

Emma nodded, not wanting to get into it.

"He's really magnanimous, isn't he?" Sophia winked; they'd re-viewed the vocab word earlier that day. Emma's pang of pride un-fortunately also instigated a burbling of the alcohol in her system and an accompanying shot of shame; despite her knowing that Sophia would never say anything to her mother about tonight, it really was not okay for Emma to be out drunkenly fraternizing with her client. Once again she planned to announce that it was time for Nick and her to leave, but once again she got sidetracked.

"Hey, I've got some sweet news." The soft voice came from a girl on the futon, whose long strands were being twirled around the fingers of the boy next to her. Her hair was mesmerizing—it fell to her waist, and was jet-black but bleached in such a way to resemble dappled light through tree branches. "Zeke and I just decided to get married."

Sophia and the others cheered, but the girl and her hair-twirling friend—Zeke, presumably—remained placid, like they'd just announced their plans for lunch.

Emma must've not been as quiet as she thought when she said to Nick, "How old do you think they are?" because the boy turned to her and said, "We're seventeen."

Emma was shocked. As one of two card-carrying adults in the room (she didn't count Wade), she felt a responsibility to say something sensible, like about the reverse correlation between marital age and divorce rate. Still, another part of her sensed the futility, and really didn't want to delve into a sociological debate with someone from this crowd. Nick, likely feeling similar, excused himself for the bathroom.

Despite Emma staying quiet, the newly engaged girl launched into her theory of marriage: "The way I see it is, if you're going to get hitched, the only way to do it is super-young, like shockingly so, because then you're still giving the finger to societal conventions. If you hit, say, twenty-five and you still haven't made it to the altar, then you've gotta say, 'Fuck it!' to the whole thing. Because the last thing you wanna do is give in to the marriage-industrial complex that says your late twenties is *the* time to shack up, spend a shitload on some stupid white dress, and invite everyone you know to buy you blenders and crap. You can't be a slave to that bullshit."

"Totally, just like Emma and Nick," Sophia exclaimed, slapping Emma on the thigh. "You've been together for years, right? You've never asked anyone to buy you a blender!" Sophia was definitely buzzed and, oddly, Emma felt relieved; she couldn't bear it if her whip-smart client were engaging with such nonsense sober.

"Hear, hear." This from Zeke, who was now teasing his fiancée's lovely hair into a horrible nest. "To not following anyone else's expectations. To paving your own path."

"So what are your plans?" Emma asked, mostly to steer the talk away from herself.

"Well, I get access to my trust fund when I turn eighteen," the girl said, "then we'll elope to South America, and embark on an epic trip around the southern hemisphere. You know, have a grand adventure and see the world!"

Emma glanced around to see if anyone else was horrified by this so-called plan. But what she noticed was something else: What she'd first assumed were everyone's thrift-store clothes she now saw lacked the shabbiness, the slightly off fit, the occasional loose seam characteristic of secondhand attire. Instead, Emma detected buttery cashmere, delicate silk, velvety leather, and what she now realized was probably real fur. Unlike a different kind of well-heeled crowd who would flaunt their duds' designer labels, this group had selected their pieces to conceal their expense; their seemingly bohemian styles belied what closer investigation revealed to be fine materials and expert cuts. Next Emma turned her eye to the mismatched furniture. Again, no discolorations or signs of wear like one would find in Salvation Army stock. In fact, Emma could've sworn she'd seen that end table in the Restoration Hardware catalogs that had mysteriously begun appearing in her mailbox; she'd been disgusted to discover the company's two-hundred-dollar throw pillows and forty-dollar mugs, wondering who would possibly pay such prices.

She turned to Sophia, whispering, "Who lives here?"

Sophia shrugged. "No one, really. Branch's parents keep the place for when they have out-of-town guests, but mostly we use it to party."

All at once Emma realized that she'd had too much to drink. Through bleary eyes she squinted at Sophia, who was trading swigs from a bottle of Dom Pérignon with the boy who was maybe named Nickel, and Emma felt a sting of sympathy with a woman she'd previously dismissed as dreadful: Sophia's mother. Mrs. Cole was dead set on her daughter attending college, preferably outside of the city, meaning far away from this posse of overprivilege. Everyone who was hanging around, using this perfectly good apartment purely to party, seemed devoid of perspective or real-world knowledge (with the exception, perhaps, of Wade's expertise in how to sue your stepmom). Emma felt a pang then for Genevieve, who was the real version of what these people were posing as. Her friend had worked every odd job, had subsisted for weeks at a time on bananas and black beans to save money, and had always lived on the city's fringes with a slew of roommates, all to support her dream of acting—what this crowd would call "her art"—and who, Emma now realized, was likely not filling out nursing school applications. Gen's recent distance seized at Emma like a stomach cramp.

Emma couldn't tolerate the party for another minute. She had to escape this ridiculous crowd and this beautiful space where no one lived. She charged into the bathroom to find Nick and demanded they leave.

"Oh, good. I've been waiting an hour for you to say that." He zipped up his fly.

Emma caught her image in the mirror, and saw she was fuming. "We just have to make a stop on the way home."

Outside the bathroom, she pulled Sophia aside. "Come on, we're leaving."

Sophia protested, but Emma stood firm, citing Sophia's school day that would begin in just seven hours. "God, you're turning into my mother," the girl moaned, which made Emma smile.

Together the three of them staggered the four long blocks west to Park Avenue. Before delivering Sophia into the hands of the doorman, Emma instructed the girl, "For next week, take an entire practice SAT and write a personal statement—a serious one, I mean it. No excuses." Emma wasn't going to cut Sophia any more slack; it was time for her to face reality. Emma waved good-bye, thinking she, too, should take her own advice.

With that, she and Nick boarded the downtown subway, both headed to their respective apartments, which they could each call home for a few more precious days.

Chapter 17

Recess patrol under normal circumstances required an extra-large coffee, and this week, when Nick had hardly slept at all thanks to the Luis crap, plus everything else he'd mired himself in, he could've used an IV drip of caffeine. Nick had requested library duty for his afternoon free, but it was probably his friend Carl's idea of a practical joke to stick him instead with policing the post-lunch hordes set loose on the "playground." Just as New York City bars called their concrete backyards "gardens," New York City schools called their fenced-in strips of pavement "playgrounds." Nick observed the urban recess with pity, feeling nostalgic for his own suburban school's lush playing fields. But city kids didn't seem to know what they were missing—they looked high on something as they darted across the blacktop in games of football and keep-away. Their small lungs released a series of screeches that made Nick want to scale the fence and flee.

Nick mostly kept out of the mayhem. Although he didn't sub-scribe to the "boys will be boys" attitude that ignored certain cru-elties, he'd learned years ago that trying to micromanage the kids' play tended to result in an "accidental" baseball to your gut. Still, when he spotted a notorious troublemaker swinging a metal bat way too close to a classmate's head, Nick thought of his own recent head injury and felt a twitch of solidarity with the targeted boy. "Hey," he yelled, jogging over, "knock it off."

The bully was slow to stop his bat's rotations, and when he did he played it off like he was simply done working on his swing. "Whatever," he snorted, strutting away. The picked-on kid looked mortified; Nick patted him on his back—narrow and bony—then returned to his post at the picnic table.

He sat down next to Mrs. Gould. "Boy, could I use a smoke," she said for the second time in ten minutes. Mrs. Gould's desire for a cigarette was always a palpable presence on recess patrol. (Her other one-liner was "I sure wasn't expecting weather like this," which made Nick wonder if the existence of meteorologists had somehow eluded her notice.) Nick felt sorry for the woman, whose fidgety fingers were making him more desperate for a nap. He went for the next-best thing, coffee—*hot!* His tongue tingled with a scald that he knew would remain for days. Now Nick felt sorry for himself, too.

He scanned the blacktop for the bullied kid, hoping he hadn't suffered a bat to the head while Nick's back had been turned. The boy was alone in a corner, kicking the shit out of a stick. Nick had imagined him to be a shy, sweet type, but now he realized the boy was no angel. If he were bigger he probably would've happily kicked the shit out of the bully, too. *How terrible people are to one another,* Nick thought, realizing even he wasn't immune; he drowned his own guilty gut in gulps of coffee.

That's it, Nick thought suddenly, Luis must've been bullied as a kid. Who else grew up to be so angry, so haughty, so irrationally convinced that others were out to get him? It made sense. But Nick didn't feel sympathy for the landlord. Everyone had their shit from the past, and part of being an adult was moving on and deciding to do the right thing; Luis clearly hadn't learned this lesson. Nick brought two fingers to his mouth and blew a shrill whistle. "Hey, cool it over there," he shouted. "Yeah, you with the stick."

Deciding to do the right thing. Nick was always drilling the importance of this concept into his kids' heads, and yet he himself had been hanging out with Emma for days and not mentioned what had happened with Genevieve. With every interaction they shared, with every word he uttered, Nick was aware of the omission. Still, it never seemed like the right time, and it pained him to imagine Emma's devastation. Plus, Nick was exhausted. He'd lain awake all last night, never managing to set aside his anxiety and fury for long enough to slip into sleep. He'd thought of Emma, then Genevieve, then Emma, and when he occasionally found himself replaying the hookup with Gen and fantasizing about another, he was overcome by a new wave of self-disgust. Now he downed the rest of his coffee, wishing he had more.

Also there was Luis. Luis, who, after their disastrous confrontation at the bar, had taken three days to respond to Nick's and Emma's texts, and who'd then only begrudgingly agreed to meet up again last night. Although the couple had read up extensively on housing law—and they'd even drafted an official document to break the lease, based on a template they'd found on a tenants' rights site—Luis had barely budged on his terms: He'd agreed to refund them the last month's rent, and not a penny more. Plus he'd brought along his steroids-happy brother, a savvy move; when it came to intimidation, Nick's knowledge of the Western literary canon was no match for the brother's bulging muscles. More than anything, Nick and Emma had been terrified of *not* breaking the lease, and then getting a monthly bill charging them for rent to an apartment where they'd never even moved in. So they'd agreed to Luis's preposterous offer, figuring they could sue later. And while Nick had been busy doing the math in his head of all they'd lost—first month's rent, security, the broker's fee, plus the cost of repairs—Emma had flung the pieces of the torn-up lease to the ground, stomped on them, and yelled, "We'll see you in court, mister!" It was a bit dramatic for Nick's taste, but he knew Emma just needed to vent. (Luckily the jacked-up brother seemed amused and not affronted by her antics.)

So now, here they were, more than eight thousand dollars in the hole, and Nick, broke and exhausted from insomnia and worry, with twenty minutes still remaining of recess. Nick's phone beeped in his pocket, reminding him of a saved voicemail. It was his current landlady, asking for the third time if he still wanted to renew his lease, insisting it was urgent he let her know. Nick had kept the message for seventy-two hours now. The beeping reminder soothed Nick, even as it made him burn with shame. He watched the kids all around him—the athletes diving to score a point, the dancers gyrating to their iPods, and the indoor kids huddled around a stack of Pokémon cards—everyone escaping into some kind of fantasy. They were playing, and in a way Nick felt like that's what he was doing, too—playing with the idea of staying put, of not embarking upon this next step of cohabitation, of wondering whether the Genevieve incident was some kind of sign, of letting Emma down and thus safeguarding himself.

It was cowardly, of course, but Nick had been raised to always have a Plan B. It was why he invariably looked up an alternate subway route and why he stored a week's worth of canned goods in his pantry (for which Emma made merciless fun of him, often forecasting imminent disaster). You never knew what might happen to derail your plans. Nick needed this particular Plan B. Because what if they really didn't find another apartment? Or what if Emma found out about Genevieve and not only bagged the cohabitation idea but the whole relationship, too? Or what if Nick decided to give in to the part of him that was paralyzed with anxiety by the idea of moving in with his girlfriend?

Commitment-wise, Nick understood that moving in wasn't getting married, and it certainly wasn't having a baby—that truly unbreakable bond with another person. Most of his friends from childhood had long since tethered themselves to a wife, taken on a mortgage (although, to Nick's credit, that was much more manageable in suburban Ohio than in New York City), and were now onto their second or third kid, coaching their sports teams and limiting their socializing to weekly football with the guys. But contrary to what some people claimed, Nick felt moving in *was* a big deal. He'd heard enough horror stories of couples who'd jumped into it too soon, broken up, and then had to keep living together since neither person could afford the lease solo. One acquaintance had thrown out his back from sleeping on an air mattress; another's ex had had the nerve to bring home one-night stands to their studio. Not that Emma would ever do that to Nick (and he hoped he wouldn't do such a thing to her, although who knew, considering recent events?). But the point was, Nick was scared. He knew he would eventually tell his landlady no, that he wouldn't extend his lease, but he wasn't yet ready to make the call.

Nick went to chuck his coffee, careful not to get tangled in the undulating jump ropes nearby. Along with their fancy footwork, the double-dutchers were chanting what sounded to Nick like: "Divorced, beheaded, died, divorced, beheaded, survived." Weird. He asked his student Jasmine what it was all about.

"Ms. Mitchell taught us," the girl said. "It's about a king who married a whole buncha wives, but he ditched each of 'em in crazy ways. We like jumping to it."

"Ah, Henry the Eighth," Nick said, wondering why playground rhymes were always so absurd. He remembered the girls in his elementary school had sung a song praising the taste of Winston cigarettes. Jasmine executed a particularly deft jump as she yelled out, "Beheaded!" How morbid. Nick imagined Emma's head on the chopping block, and immediately felt guilty. Of course he wanted to live with her. He asked Mrs. Gould to cover for him, and then slipped away to call back his landlady and say he was moving. Where, of course, and how they would afford it, he still didn't know.

On his way to Emma's, Nick stopped home to check his mail: catalog, *Vegetarian Times* magazine, and—*shit*—a thick packet from the hospital in D.C. Nick tucked the unopened envelope into his bag, too terrified to find out what his insurance hadn't covered of the three-day stay. That was reason enough to move, he thought, to dodge the bill collectors. Nick's bank account had dwindled to nearly nothing, and he wouldn't get paid again until October first. To calm his nerves, he ducked into a deli and grabbed a six-pack, charging it to his card.

That night, as Emma compiled a list of apartments to look at that weekend, Nick couldn't get the double-dutch rhyme out of his head: *Divorced, beheaded, died, divorced, beheaded, survived.* It seemed like a bad omen, although at least it ended somewhat positively—"thrived" would've been better. "Emma," he said, "we need to talk."

She looked up from her scribbling.

"I'm in trouble here. I don't know if you can front the money for renting a new place, but I just don't have it."

"Well," she said, not skipping a beat, "hopefully we can find a place where they only ask for first month's rent. And, let's see, I get paid next Friday, the twenty-eighth, so maybe a landlord would let us wait to pay until then. I'll go down to the court next week to start our case against Luis. Hopefully we'll get our money back soon."

"Before October first? As in ten days from now?"

"You never know."

"Em."

"What?" She'd gone back to her list. Her talent for denial was almost admirable.

"Come on, Em, you know none of those things is going to happen."

When she looked up, Nick saw that her eyes were glassy with tears. "Shit," she said, "Shit, shit, shit." It seemed she'd been working so hard to stay positive that, now that she'd abandoned the act, she was falling apart. Nick felt himself copping out of the other piece of his confession.

"Hey, it's okay," he said. "We'll figure it out."

"I feel like we can't win. I mean, how many weddings did we have this summer—*five?* And do you have any idea what I spent on Annie's bridal shower and bachelorette party, not to mention that Versace maid-of-honor dress? I won't even get into my monthly student loan bill—I'll be paying for grad school till I'm fifty. But still, I bring lunch to work every day. I put money aside every paycheck. I hardly ever buy twelve-dollar cocktails, no matter how delicious they look. I've been so good! How was I supposed to know I'd have to save up for two moves, not just one?" She was trembling, and Nick pulled her onto his lap. "You know what's crazy? Last time I talked to my parents, they went on and on about how free they feel now that they've cashed in all their savings, and how amazing it's been to just start over and live simply. To them being broke is romantic."

"They think everything is romantic, don't they?"

"Yes! They really do live on a totally different planet from the rest of us."

Nick rubbed Emma's back, thinking how inconvenient it was, considering their predicament, that her once-wealthy parents had gone bohemian. Personally he found it crass how openly the Feits talked about their finances, but to them it was a hobby. They still lived better than most everyone he knew, with their sprawling pied-à-terre and extravagant wine collection. Still, Nick knew that if Emma went to them for help, they'd start preaching about silver linings, supposedly to buck her up, but then provide no actual help. Nick had supported Emma in the aftermath of many such previous lectures.

"Emma, we need a backup plan." Nick had already given this a lot of thought. After abandoning his other Plan B of staying put in his apartment, he'd considered who might lend them money. His parents were not an option. They'd always made it clear how proud they were to help Nick through college, but graduation was the end of the line, period; when he visited home, he and his dad split nine-dollar diner tabs right down the middle. But there was another relative of Emma's: "So I know you don't love the idea of asking your brother for help—"

"*Max?!* Are you kidding me? No way in hell am I turning to Max for money."

"Well, it would just be a loan."

"To think of Alysse lording that over me every time I saw her. To have her look at me with her sad doe eyes and say, all fake-concerned, 'So how are you guys doing, *really?*' as if she wouldn't love every minute of us being her charity case. No. I'd honestly rather be homeless than ask them for a pay-out."

"Well, we may just end up homeless then."

"How about I ask Annie? Eli is loaded, and I'm sure they'd help us out."

Nick bristled. Eli was no more than an acquaintance, plus he considered himself such a hotshot. Nick couldn't imagine involving him in their finances. He'd probably tell his asshole buddy Connor all about it, too. "No way," he said.

"Why not? Annie is my best friend."

"I don't have a good feeling about it."

"You're being inflexible."

"Max is your family. I think *you're* being inflexible."

"Fine."

"Fine."

Emma stormed out of the room, murmuring something about a client. Nick sighed, thinking the only way that conversation could've gone worse is if he'd added, "By the way, I hooked up with Gen." He popped open a beer and pulled out a stack of student papers on America's thirteen colonies, determined to use grading as a distraction.

That night in bed, Emma squeezed herself into a tight ball, making no physical contact with Nick's body. Nick lay awake on his side of the mattress, fantasizing about being Christopher Columbus, coming to America, and laying claim to the land, natives be damned. Of course the so-called founding of our country had been chauvinistic and inhumane, Columbus Day a fraud—Nick knew these things and taught them to his kids. But at the moment, the idea of colonization sounded quite appealing to Nick, arriving and declaring a space your home, no talk of landlord or rent or lease, simple and done.

"What kind of person sells their hair?" José yelled out.

"And who would *buy* human hair?" Sierra chimed in.

"They sell combs for a dollar on the subway. That's a pretty cheap-ass present."

"Watch your language, Lawrence. Everyone else, calm down." This discussion was not going the way Nick had intended. He'd asked his students to respond to O. Henry's "The Gift of the Magi." They were all always talking about jeans they simply *had* to buy or a cell phone upgrade that would transform their lives, and Nick wanted them to consider the importance of relationships over material things. It wasn't working.

"Mr. O'Hare, this story is dumb." José again. "Della and the dude shoulda just asked each other what they wanted. And what's a fob anyway? Sounds like a you-know-what." He gestured to the front of his pants, and the class erupted in laughter.

"Guys, it's supposed to be ironic," said Nick. "Remember irony? Della and James love each other so much that they're willing to sacrifice their most prized possessions—her hair and his watch—in order to buy each other something special. Even though they each end up with items they can't use, a comb for Della, and a watch part for James—José, a fob is a kind of chain—they see how much the other one loves them."

Blank stares all around. Nick decided to cut the lesson short and move on to math.

At lunch, he called Emma—on her cell, not through Genevieve—to vent.

"You read them 'The Gift of the Magi'? Of course they hated it."

"What do you mean? It's romantic!"

"No, it's depressing," said Emma. "The couple is broke and then they end up broker, plus the girl gets her hair chopped off. And it's horribly sentimental. Also, isn't that a Christmas story? It's September."

"Yeah, but . . ." Nick trailed off. He realized now that, more so than his students, he wanted Emma to get the moral about love prevailing over money. Maybe he wanted to convince himself, too.

"I have an idea for your next lesson," Emma said.

"Yeah?"

"Cue up cartoons all day. I bet you won't get any more complaints from the kids."

"Ha ha, very funny."

"My point is, you're not there to entertain them, right? So don't take it so hard when they're hard on you. News flash, Nick: Most kids don't like school."

"I know," Nick sighed. He appreciated these pep talks.

"So have you thought any more about us asking Annie for money? I'm sure the wedding bucks are pouring in—all she'd have to do is redirect a few checks our way."

"Emma, no, sorry. We'll figure something else out."

"Okay." She sighed. "Gotta run, client calling."

* * *

Nick paced the block around his school, over and over chanting to himself the Henry VIII playground rhyme: "Divorced, beheaded, died, divorced, beheaded, survived." Striding to its beat, he indulged himself in what ifs: What if he'd gone to law school and now pulled in six figures? What if he robbed a bank and never got caught? What if he played the lottery, won, and—*poof!*—all of their problems disappeared? This last option was the only mildly feasible one. The lottery was a terrible Plan B, but Nick figured it was worth a shot. He ducked into a bodega and eyed the scratch-offs. He was about to order five Lucky 7s when he heard, "Mr. O'Hare!"

Two of Nick's students tailed him in line. "Oh, hey, guys."

So instead of the scratch-offs he bought a pint of milk, which he then chucked in a corner trashcan, cursing his kids for forcing him to always set a good example. Feeling despondently out of options, he dialed Emma: "If you really want to ask Annie for help, go ahead. But make sure she gets that it would be a loan, that we'd pay interest, and—"

"Listen, I have an even better solution! I spoke to Annie—she was literally watching a lion sleep while we talked; it sounded amazing. They have a week more of safari, and then they're doing the whole city thing before they're back in town on the eighth."

"Their honeymoon is over a month long?"

"You know Annie. Anyway, she said we could crash at their apartment until then, and after that we can stick around in the guest room for as long as we need. Plus they have basement storage where we can keep all our stuff. I know it's not ideal to live at their place, especially once they're back, but this way we'll have time—we'll both get another paycheck—and we can look for a place for October fifteenth."

Nick wanted to jump up and down like a lunatic. As usual, Emma had solved everything. "That's perfect. I love you."

"I know you do. And I gotta go, babe. My next appointment."

That night, Emma used her spare key to let them into Eli's SoHo dream apartment, and they took a look around their new temporary digs as of next week. Despite Emma's protests, Nick snuck into Eli's closet. Among the designer suits and perfectly shined wingtips and other items that even smelled expensive, he discovered a red velvet robe. Nick threw it over his shoulders and strutted into the bedroom, where Emma was laid out on the bed flipping through a magazine.

"I am Henry the Eighth," he proclaimed on a whim, hoping Emma was game to role-play. She usually was. "And you, my adulterous wife, deserve to be punished."

Emma yelped, "No, I didn't do it! Don't hurt me!" and ran from the room. Nick chased her to the living room, where she'd draped herself dramatically across a couch. Nick hesitated a moment—the couch was white leather—but then pounced upon his girlfriend, berating her for her inability to bear him an heir.

"Give me another chance," she cried, tearing off her clothing. "I'll give you a son, I know I will, the future king of France!"

"England."

"Yes, the future king of England."

"I don't believe you, you unfaithful lout. After I ravage you one more time, I'll have to behead you."

"Oh, how I'll shame my family, the, um, the—"

"The Boleyns."

"Ah yes, the whole Boleyn clan will be cast out of high society. That's a fate I couldn't bear."

"You better bear it, Anne."

"*Anne?*" Emma said, out of character, pausing her hips' movements. "As in *Annie?* Is that what this is about, you have a thing for my friend?"

"Silence, my minx of a wife," Nick said, his voice cracking. His heart pounded. "I'll chop off your head!"

A devilish smile appeared on Emma's face. Just as Nick finished, she cocked her neck to the side and enacted a dramatic death by guillotine, titillating and terrifying both.

Chapter 18

"Bunking up with Annie for a few weeks, how fun!" Emma's mother's eyes popped; this was a frequent occurrence in their Skype conversations, and Emma suspected it had something to do with the screen's pixilation. Still it made her recoil. "It'll be like your sleepovers from the old days."

Emma was taking a break from packing, which she'd been doing for hours, and her stomach groaned. As her mom chatted from her bakery, she picked at a flaky pastry, and Emma wished she could reach through the Internet to tear off a piece. "Yeah, it's super-generous." Emma could hear that she was doing "the voice." Before meeting Nick, she'd never noticed that when talking to her mother she raised her pitch and added a singsongy lilt. It drove Nick crazy, and now it caused Emma to cringe, too. Despite this, Emma couldn't control it, and it made her annoyed at her mother, unfairly, she knew.

"Well, isn't everything working out nicely for you two, after a few little hiccups." This last phrase grated on Emma. "You're such New Yorkers, navigating this crazy apartment rental process. And now you'll get free rent for a couple of weeks, right?"

"I guess so," said Emma, "but we lost a ton of money on the other place."

"Oh, but you'll get it all back in court. I can just picture you arguing your case, a total natural. I always thought you, not Max, would end up being our family's lawyer. My feisty little Emma! Can't you see Emma being a star before a jury, dear?" She was shouting to Emma's dad, who now ducked into the frame to wave. On-screen, he always looked squinty and flummoxed.

"Hey-a, Em. I'm off to my Spanish conversation class, but all's well, I presume? Gotta run. *¡Adiós, hija mía!*"

"Isn't that sweet?" her mom said. "It's taken him weeks to get that far. This group has really built up his confidence. He likes to drag me to the markets now just so he can ask for *el precio* and name the vegetables he's learned. Although last week we ended up with a dozen tomatoes when he confused *dos and doce*. We were eating gazpacho up the wazoo. Of course I was fluent ages ago, but we all learn at a different pace, right?"

"Right." Emma hadn't made a Skype date with her mom to talk about tomatoes or varying rates of learning, but somehow she felt incapable of steering the conversation back to what she'd intended to discuss: Nick's head injury. Emma hadn't told her mother about the hospital visit, and it was eating at her; withholding something that had caused her such fear and worry for the past few weeks seemed like lying. And now that Nick was almost entirely healed, the whole fiasco felt safe to bring up. But the topic seemed out-of-bounds of this airy chat so it sat unmentioned, heavy in the pit of Emma's stomach.

"All right, give me Annie's address so I know where to send your next care package. I'll throw in a few extra goodies for the newlyweds." Emma read out the address, the swanky SoHo location lost on her mother. "*Perfecto.* And when you guys land on a fabulous new place, make sure you send me that address pronto, too. I wouldn't want you to miss a package amid the hubbub of a move."

"Sure, Mom. Listen, I have to finish packing."

"Ooh, I read an article in the *Times* about these companies that'll come in and pack up all your stuff for you, and then when you get to your new place they'll unpack everything and set it up exactly where you want it. It sounds fab. I'll send you the link."

"Thanks, Mom." Emma knew about these services—Eli had hired one for Annie when she moved into his place earlier this year. The cost was exorbitant.

"Anything else, Em?" Her mother popped the last piece of pastry into her mouth, then licked her fingers one by one. Again Emma thought of Nick in the hospital, and how scared she'd been. She shook her head.

"Okay, sweetheart. I love you more than anything. *¡Hasta luego!*"

Emma shut her laptop and slumped against the boxes she'd filled that morning. Dipping into her mother's world, so bright and European and pastry-filled, often made Emma's own feel dull and dark. She reached to turn on a lamp. It didn't help. So she got up and pulled a pint of ice cream from the freezer, then settled back onto the floor, where she soothed herself with spoonfuls of the cold sweetness until her mouth went numb.

Emma remembered back to when she was little, when her mother had meant everything to her, when she'd truly believed she had the best mom on earth. There had always been something to celebrate—after a school play a candy bar would await Emma on her pillow, and at the end of a softball season she'd be allowed to stay up late and watch *A League of Her Own*, brand new on VHS. For the temple's Purim festival one year, her mom had helped her build a ball-toss game with life-sized photos of Blossom and Six from Emma's favorite TV show; at the news that her game had drawn the longest lines all day, her mom had high-fived her, as if she'd never doubted it. Then she'd surprised Emma with a replica of Blossom's outfit, matching scrunchie and all.

But at some point, her mother's enthusiasm had stopped seeming magical and started feeling overbearing to Emma. Did everything have to be cause for celebration? she wondered; did every day have to be extraordinary? She'd started to resent all the goodies and the fanfare, which, for their ubiquity, came to feel not so special at all. And then she'd begun to suspect that maybe something was wrong with her when she sometimes felt sad or upset. Consciously or not, her mother had confirmed this suspicion when, in reaction to Emma crying over a poor grade or a fight with a friend, she'd descended upon her daughter as if the world had ended, offering up so much solace that Emma felt she might drown in it. Eventually she'd learned to monitor her feelings around her mom, shielding her from the extremes so as not to feel so overcome by her mom's responses.

Emma's thoughts tilted toward Lily Bart. She knew it was childish to identify with the tragic heroine (an orphan, no less). But Emma couldn't help comparing her impending stay with Annie to Lily's sojourns to her wealthy friends' estates, the people who'd taken pity on her and given her shelter when she was broke and in need. (This daydreaming had ultimately gotten Emma in trouble in grad school, when she'd started viewing Wharton's novels as fairy tales to slip into rather than scholarly texts to be studied.) But the imagining was a pleasure like ice cream, sweet and simple and soothing.

Scraping up the last bits of ice cream from the pint, Emma sighed. She wondered if her brother felt this same strange gloom after talking to their parents. Probably not. Max was often declaring (a little too adamantly, if you asked Emma) that he was just as happy if not more so than their parents. Although who knew? Maybe he was. After all, the trickle of loneliness now infecting Emma was the kind of thing Max had been talking about when he'd gone on about the power of religion. His answer to uncertainty and anger and despair was Judaism. Emma knew her brother felt part of a tight-knit community—both of his congregation and of Jews all across the globe (not to mention throughout history). Emma couldn't imagine that kind of comfort. Although she also had her heritage—you didn't just stop being a Jew because you ate cheeseburgers—it didn't possess the same power as what Max had, that total commitment and giving over of yourself, that impervious bond of belief. Agnostics like Emma sat on the sidelines. She was envious, not of religion itself but of what it provided for its faithful. "Oy vey," she said, then burped loudly.

And then Emma remembered what her brother had said to her when she'd visited, how he wanted to make more of an effort to hang out together. She was dialing his number before her idea was fully formed. "Max!" she yelped, surprised that he'd picked up;

he'd described early evenings as chaos with the kids. "I'm so glad you're there."

"Yeah?" He sounded both flattered and skeptical. "I was just going to call you to wish you happy break fast."

"Oh, right, Yom Kippur. *Chag Sameach.*" Emma was proud to remember how to say "Happy Holiday" in Hebrew, although she guiltily pushed away the empty ice-cream container; apparently her parents had blown off the high holiday, too.

"So what's up, Emmy?"

She related a truncated version of the apartment drama, downplaying the more traumatic parts, then asked if he was free that weekend to help her move.

"Ah, so you need my car?"

"Yeah, and also your brute strength. I've heard Alysse brag about your bench-pressing skills, and even flimsy IKEA furniture is heavy." Emma was only half joking. "Come on, I'll pay you in pizza and we can hang out."

"Sure, I'll work for food. As long as we can do it on Sunday, and no pepperoni, it's a deal. I'll drop the kids off at Hebrew school, then drive down to the city."

"Excellent. See you then." Emma felt good about this, spending time with just her brother, far away from his wife and kids and his home turf, which had formerly been both of theirs, and which could make Emma so uncomfortable. Finally she felt that uplifting closeness that family is supposed to make you feel. It was a feeling she always hoped for when she set up the Skype dates with her parents, but one that rarely materialized. Satisfied, she set about configuring another box, aiming to fill five more that night.

By Thursday evenings, Nick was usually almost brain-dead, so short on energy and mental resources that the oasis of Friday afternoon started to seem like a mirage. But only on Thursdays was the Kings County courthouse open late enough for both Emma and Nick to make it there before closing time. And Emma had insisted they file their grievance against Luis together—"as a team," she'd declared with pep, as if suing their almost-landlord were an intramural softball tournament. Nick would've preferred they drop the whole thing altogether, just leave it be and move on. But Emma was determined for justice. So there they were at rush hour, battling hordes of commuters and the smoggy downtown air in search of the address among a row of identical municipal buildings.

It should've been simple—according to the court's Web site, they'd check a box on a form to indicate their grounds for suing, pay the fifteen-dollar fee, and then get assigned a court date. The first complication came at the metal detector, when Nick's backpack was flagged for containing scissors, which meant he had to stop in the security office to register the "potential weapon." Nick asked whether he might abandon the scissors in lieu of registering them, but was informed that that would not be permitted: "We can't just have people leaving weapons willy-nilly on our premises, can we?" replied the guard, arms crossed against an ample bosom. Nick wondered aloud what kind of damage he might do with the childproof tool's blunt edges. The guard didn't crack a smile, so he figured it wouldn't help to show her the nonviolent pursuit for which he'd been using them—to cut up goods and services cards for a lesson about bartering in colonial America. To make Emma laugh, on the weapon registration paperwork Nick filled in his name as Edward Scissorhands. They quickly fled the office.

Next came the elevator, which was packed with people and all their various odors, and which lurched violently to each floor's stop, so that by the time they reached their destination, Nick, never one for carnival rides, felt ill. The guard had told them Floor 9, but when the doors opened to a hushed hallway, well lit and sparsely populated, Nick thought, no way was this Housing Court. And he was right—several surly officials had to redirect them several more times before they found the right floor, where they joined the end of a line snaking down a long hallway. The mood reminded Nick of an airport terminal after a several-hour delay. Their neighbors' chatter, in what Nick could identify as at least three languages, clashed in a cacophony of noise, and two babies seemed to be competing to outfuss each other. Worst of all, it smelled as if the invention of deodorant had not reached this part of town, or perhaps like Nick, most of these people had worked a very long day and were overdue for hygiene refreshment.

"We don't belong here," Emma whispered, clutching at Nick's arm.

"Excuse me?" he said, feeling strangely defensive.

"We don't belong here," she repeated, now in a whine. "You know what I mean."

Nick didn't respond. He wasn't going to be cruel and make Emma articulate what he guessed she meant: that they were the only white people, or that it never would've occurred to them to wear torn sweatpants to court, or that their haircuts and shoes were clearly more expensive than the ones all around them. Especially when a moment earlier Nick had been doing some judging of his own. In truth, he wasn't thrilled to spend his evening among this crowd, either. But he was ashamed of this judgmental part of himself, and he never would've given voice to it; he couldn't help feeling contemptuous of Emma's brazen complaints. Still, he had to remind himself that Emma spent most of her time in a sleek highrise among Manhattan's wealthiest families, or else with Annie and her platinum credit card at the city's trendiest restaurants. Whereas for Nick, back-to-school night in his classroom had more in common with this courthouse scene than it did with any setting Emma was familiar with; it was a miracle if he could get half his students' families to contribute five bucks to the classroom tissue fund.

But beyond demographics, the truth was that Nick and Emma *did* belong here. They'd gotten themselves into a sorry legal snafu just like everyone else in this line, and just like everyone else they weren't above pursuing their right to recoup what they'd lost.

"How long do you think we'll be waiting?" Emma asked, and then she assumed that faraway actress-y look that Nick knew all too well; she was imagining herself as that pathetic Edith Wharton character. The line hadn't budged for fifteen minutes, but Nick noted that no one else but the babies was complaining.

"Are you doing the Lily Bart thing, feeling sorry for yourself?"

"Oh, give me a break, Nick," Emma said, forgetting to whisper. "Here we are, two decent, hardworking people surrounded by who knows who, in this interminable line that shows zero sign of moving. There's this scene in *The House of Mirth* where Lily hits rock-bottom and has to start working as a hat maker, a job that's far below her class—"

Nick could feel people staring. Now he was the one to whisper: "Emma, stop it. You are not some society lady-who-lunches stuck in a terrible tragedy. You're not above anyone here. And *you're* the one who wanted to pursue this in court, remember?"

"Well, I just thought—"

"What, that you'd get special treatment? That you'd be able to skip to the front of the line?" Emma pouted, and Nick realized he was being harsh; he was exhausted and taking it out on her. There was a reason he usually spent Thursday nights home alone, sans girlfriend. He worried what Thursdays would be like once they were living together.

A half hour later, when it was finally their turn at the window, Emma nudged Nick, pointing to a sign: CASH ONLY. MUST HAVE EXACT CHANGE! NO EXCEPTIONS! ATM AT MCDONALD'S AROUND CORNER. "I don't have cash," she said. "Do you?"

Nick felt so exasperated that he began laughing. "Of course not. And of course they wouldn't think to mention this on the Web site, or at the start of the line."

"Next!" snapped the clerk behind the glass. "I don't have all day."

"Come on," Nick said, taking Emma's hand. "Let's go get some money." Reluctantly they abandoned their hard-earned spot at the head of the line.

As the elevator bumped its way to the ground, Nick held his head between his legs. "This ain't Edith Wharton territory, by the way. It's Kafka."

Emma was suddenly scratching at Nick's back and arms. When he glanced at her, startled, she said, "I've metamorphosed into a cockroach. I'm crawling all over you."

"Ah, Kafka." It was a feeble attempt at a joke, but Nick went along with it. "You better disguise yourself before we hit Mc-Donald's. I don't think they're too fond of large existential bugs on their premises." He kissed her on the forehead.

At the ATM, Nick avoided looking at his bank balance as he withdrew twenty dollars. He broke the bill on an Oreo McFlurry, a treat he knew Emma secretly preferred over the organic tart yogurt she often ate with Annie. Back upstairs, and back to the end of the line, Emma slurped at her dessert, which drew envious stares from the cranky kids; Nick was relieved when it was gone. The line did creep forward, although at the rate of a DMV, and occasionally Nick caught Emma re-afflicted with her Lily Bart look. "Cut it out," he'd say, pinching her. "Return to real life, please." In Nick's opinion, Emma had been leaning on this escapist crutch for far too long; instead of facing life's unpleasant and uncomfortable moments, instead of feeling them and dealing with them like a mature adult, Emma had the bad habit of slipping away from reality and envisioning herself as the heroine of some long-gone society with black-and-white rules, good guys and bad guys, and a beginning, middle, and end already written and memorialized. Nick felt that it would do Emma a world of good to give up her obsession with Wharton's high society, once and for all.

After an hour of waiting the second time around, Nick and Emma finally reached the front of the line, only to discover that they could've completed the whole process online. "Although I'm not sure if we've updated the Web site to let you know that," mentioned the clerk, double-checking that they'd handed him fifteen dollars. Their court date was set for October twenty-fifth, exactly four weeks away. Nick considered how, by then, they would've come and gone from Annie and Eli's apartment, and they'd be settling into a new home, wherever it might be. It seemed not quite believable.

It was not until the next morning when Nick, hoping to finish the Barter Day preparations for his fifth graders, realized he'd forgotten to retrieve his scissors from the court. He imagined the officers issuing a warrant for the arrest of Edward Scissorhands, with the charge of "abandoning a potential weapon, willy-nilly, on the premises." This made Nick snort out a laugh, although he did worry, irrational as he knew it was, that they'd dust the scissors for fingerprints.

"So Emma's a racist, huh?" Carl asked, sucking at a juice box.

"Not racist, exactly." Nick had visited his friend's office to vent about the courthouse experience. He'd brought along his pet, Mensa.

"I mean, you're either racist or you're not, right?"

"I think it's more like, everyone she works with is in the top one percent—superwealthy and privileged and, yeah, for the most part Caucasian."

"So she's classist, then. Almost as bad." Carl tossed a handful of animal crackers into his mouth, then held out a giraffe for Mensa; the gerbil grabbed at its neck in nibbles. Carl had clearly stolen his snack stash from the kindergarten supply closet.

"It's not that simple," said Nick. "I dunno, the whole thing just made me uneasy."

"Because you're secretly a racist and a classist, too, obviously. Don't deny it, dude. I know you get nervous walking to school early in the morning in the winter, when it's dark out and the streets are empty and at any moment someone might jump out and mug you like, POW!" Carl leaped forward in his seat and mock-punched Nick. Nick's breath caught in his throat and Mensa emitted a squeak, then scurried down his leg. Carl erupted in laughter, cracker crumbs spewing from his mouth. "Just screwing with you, man. I know you're not like that. But seriously, dude, fuck the courts. After working for the goddamned government all these years, I can't believe you haven't learned your lesson that everything in the public sector is a total cluster-fuck. Maybe Emma doesn't know any better, but you should. If I were you I'd forget about the few Gs you lost and save yourself the hassle of dealing with the system's bullshit."

"That's exactly what Wade said."

"Who's Wade?"

"Some Upper East Side trust-fund kid. From a party."

"Ah yes, Wade. Anyway, my point is, I don't think this is about the money. Emma needs this court case to pursue some sense of justice, and I'm guessing that's because her job of abetting rich people who throw mountains of money at the college process is not very fulfilling. You, my friend, are toiling on the ground day in and day out in pursuit of social justice, so you don't need to stick it to one shitty landlord to feel like your life has meaning. If you ask me, you should talk to Emma and convince her to drop the case. Otherwise you've got a whole load of crap ahead of you."

Nick wasn't used to Carl saying anything of any value, never mind sharing actual wisdom. "I'll think about it," he said. And he would.

"Want some more advice?"

"I know you're going to give it to me either way, but be quick because the kids are back from gym in four minutes."

"It's a fucking cesspool out there, and soon it's gonna be flu season. Load up on Vitamin C while you can." Carl tossed Nick two juice boxes. "One for you, and one for the furry guy. Now get the hell out of my office. Scram."

When Emma burst into Nick's apartment that night, bearing an armful of flattened boxes she'd gathered from the curb, and speed-talking about the document she'd gotten José's father to sign about bearing witness to the bedbug infestation, Nick knew there was no point in suggesting they drop the case. Plus, it was easy to get caught up in her excitement—she'd already organized and filed all the relevant documents into an accordion folder, like his own personal Julianna Margulies from *The Good Wife*. She seemed confident they'd make Luis look like a fool before the judge.

Emma went on about all of this as she reconstructed the boxes, wielding the packing tape like a pro, and Nick was grateful for his girlfriend's energy. All week he'd been putting off packing. Not only would Emma's brother be arriving in two days to haul their stuff over to Annie and Eli's, but on the same day Nick would have to forfeit the keys to his apartment. It was hard to imagine, after seven years in the same spot. He'd tried to convey to Emma how big of a deal this was, how his stalling on packing was out of sentimentality and not just sloth, but she'd gone directly to his gaming console and touched the top; her frown indicating it was still warm. The disappointed-mom look was not becoming on her. Nick knew she wouldn't understand that the video games and the sentiment were connected—yes, Nick had given in to giving up his single life, but he felt a right to cling to it until the last possible moment.

Nick watched helplessly as Emma refolded each of his shirts and sweaters—somewhere she'd learned to do this in the fancy department store way—and then stacked them into boxes. "I cannot believe you still have some of these," she said. "Surely it's time to ditch the 1992 Science Fair T-shirt with a hole in the armpit."

"Don't you dare get rid of that," Nick said. "My wind-powered rollercoaster won second place in '92."

Emma raised her eyebrows and made a show of folding the shirt extra carefully. Nick knew she was joking, playing the part of the exasperated girlfriend—but he feared part of her was more serious than she let on. He changed the subject: "So listen, Em, my school's launching this new tutoring program to help kids apply to the city's top middle schools. Carl of all people issued a survey, and it turns out eighty-four percent of our students don't get any help on their apps. That means almost all of them get funneled into the crappy local schools, even when they could get into better ones."

"Uh-huh." Emma had moved onto Nick's pants, tugging out each pair's crotch before bending the overlapping legs into thirds. She wasn't really listening.

"So they're looking for a coordinator," Nick went on. "It's a part-time position—"

Emma wheeled around. "Nick, you are not seriously thinking of taking on another activity at that school, are you? What is it, a five-hundred-dollar stipend for five hundred hours of work? Is Carl pressuring you into this? I am so sick of them pushing you around."

"Oh, well, I was thinking of it for you."

"Me?" She stopped folding. "What do you mean?"

"You're always talking about how your clients are spoiled and overprivileged, and how ridiculous it is that their parents hire them a tutor for every single subject—"

"I'm not always saying that." Nick knew she would act defensive. He waited, and eventually she put down the pants. "Some of them, fine, but most of them are just kids. With those kinds of parents, anyone would grow up spoiled."

"That makes sense. But what if you did both, if you cut back at *1, 2, 3 . . . Ivies*, and took on this position, where the kids could really use your help?"

"My kids can use my help."

"I know, but—"

"Just because they're wealthy doesn't mean they don't need help. Most of the Hellis believe throwing money at a problem makes it disappear, and that approach makes their kids totally unfit for the real world, or just plain terrified. They think because their parents are sinking tens of thousands of dollars into college prep tutoring that if they don't get into Harvard then they'll be total failures, doomed to mediocrity, unable to ever afford the army of staff they've grown up to believe is essential to managing their lives. I help them with their SATs and essays, but more than that I'm their source of support, their counselor and big sister and cheerleader. I assure them it'll be okay, Ivy League acceptance or not, despite the company name. And these kids need that. Plus, I figure if they're going to be running the world someday, with all their inherited money and influence, they might as well have some empathy and humility, too—and I'd like to think I have something to do with teaching them those things."

It felt like the end of a speech, and Nick began slow-clapping. He was impressed.

"What?" Emma blushed.

"That's the first time I've heard you talk about your job without apologizing for it or making fun of it or denigrating it as total B.S. Turns out my Emma Feit is providing a real service, and you're proud of yourself. I like it!"

"Plus," said Emma, smirking, "if I worked with your students instead of mine, what kind of holiday presents would I get?"

"One kid once got me a five-dollar gift card to Popeye's."

"Hmm, tempting."

"But seriously, think about it. You could do both jobs, really."

Now Emma changed the subject. "Next up is to pack your comic books. Where'd you put them?" Nick's stacks of comics had been a contentious topic for the move—Emma hadn't been shy in grumbling about how much space they'd occupy in their new place, wherever the two of them ended up. Nick had planned to surprise her with the bookshelf he'd set up in his classroom: a comic book lending library for the kids.

"Come here." He pulled up a photo of it on his phone.

"Aw, sweet," said Emma. "Too bad I sold my soul to the devil to get you a new comics subscription." Nick had no idea what she was talking about. "O. Henry, get it? It's a gift of the magi."

"Ah, I see. Well, I got you a welcome mat, but you no longer have an apartment."

"Not funny. Anyway, that's so thoughtful. The kids are going to love your comics collection." She wrapped her arms around him. "Ugh, I'm sick of packing all your stuff. I can't believe you roped me into this."

"Hey, you roped yourself. I didn't ask you to do a thing."

"Either way, I'm done for the night. How about Scrabble, a tournament for the final weekend in our single-person apartments?"

"Bring it."

And so, among the boxes and half-packed contents of Nick's apartment, they each took seven tiles and began arranging and rearranging them into viable words on their racks. Distracted as he was by this being their last round of Scrabble in his soon-to-be-abandoned bachelor pad, Nick knew he didn't stand a chance.

Chapter 19

⁓

The noise that came through Emma's speaker when she pressed Listen was like a pack of laughing hyenas. She wondered if her buzzer system was broken, and pressed Speak. "Excuse me?"

"Sorry, Emmy." Max's voice. "Aimee and Caleb were screaming their hellos."

"The kids are here?" That had not been part of the plan. In addition to the problem of how all of her and Nick's stuff was going to fit in Max's van with two extra bodies, Emma was nervous about those bodies entering her apartment, which was currently all sharp edges and dangerous implements. She pressed Listen, hoping for an explanation, but heard only chaos. "I'll buzz you up," she said, then ran around picking up loose nails and tacks and an X-Acto knife while Max and his kids climbed the flights of stairs.

They burst through her door like a sweaty storm, the kids squirming free of their father's grasp, then scurrying away to investigate the apartment's corners and hiding spots. With so many people present the space felt even more cramped than usual. This might make it easier to say good-bye, Emma reasoned.

"So sorry about the kiddos." Max sounded exhausted, like it was midnight instead of nine a.m. "Alysse wanted to keep them out of Hebrew school because of the bomb threats at that temple."

"You mean the one in Crown Heights?" Max nodded, and Emma

felt a prick of pride at knowing this Judaism-related news item, which she'd heard an hour ago on NPR.

"Apparently they're planning to install metal detectors at the entrance to the sanctuary. Can you believe that?"

"But, Max, that's, like, fifty miles from where you live."

"More like thirty."

"Well, it might as well be a world away, considering how different the two places are. Crown Heights is a pretty poor area, with Hassids and a black community basically living on top of each other. The clashes have been going on forever. Isn't Irvington still, like, ninety-five percent Jewish and a hundred percent upper-middle class?"

"Look, I'm not defending Alysse's decision. It's what she wanted, and she'd already planned a JCC fund-raiser today, so here we are, the kids and me. Sometimes there are things you just go along with. One day when you're married you'll understand."

"All right-y." Emma felt belittled by the implication that she didn't know how relationships worked. She reminded herself that Max was here doing her a favor. "Nick's on his way over. Why don't you two load up the car, and I'll take the kids to the park."

"Thanks, Emmy, I could use a break. You know that Christmas carol Nick taught them at Rosh Hashanah? They've been screaming it on auto-repeat all morning."

Serves you right, she thought. "I'll stick to Hanukkah songs at the park."

Passing through the gate to the park's play area, Emma felt a thrill, as if she were accessing a club's VIP room. Adults had to be accompanied by a child to enter, and while in theory Emma understood the rationale of keeping out creeps and perverts, she'd always felt weirdly excluded; if she wanted to swing on the public monkey bars, she thought it should've been within her rights to do so. Before she had a chance to warn Aimee and Caleb to stay within her view, they were off, swallowed into the swarm of city kids.

Alone now, Emma examined her surroundings. Aside from the children, there were two main clusters of women, plus a stray man or two—one group was mostly late-thirtysomethings, mostly white, mostly holding coffee cups from Ost or Ninth Street Espresso, all well dressed in that fashionable-but-not-trying-too-hard way; the other group was a livelier, more diverse crowd, mostly non-white and of varying ages, some speaking Spanish. Each group gave off an intimate vibe, like these were their people and this was their hangout: the moms and the nannies, Emma assumed. She herself wasn't sure where to stand. That is, until she spotted a lone woman in a corner, who looked a bit like Annie, only heavier and with curlier hair. Emma missed her friend, which may have been why she approached the woman.

Emma waved hello, and the woman introduced herself as Rosie, then launched into a mile-a-minute monologue, as if this were her first opportunity in weeks to speak. "That's my Chaz over on the slide. He'll be five next month. He looks older, but he's just big for his age. I can't decide if that's going to help him or hurt him in the kindergarten application process. What a nightmare, right?—all those tours and interviews and IQ tests, as if they're applying to college. Have you started all that with yours?" Rosie didn't wait for an answer, so Emma couldn't clarify that she was just an aunt. "Of course my ma wants us to ship out to the suburbs, move into her leaky basement in Jersey, and send Chaz to the schools out there. Someone shoot me if I have to move back in with my ma." Rosie popped a piece of gum into her mouth. "Want one? It's Nicorette." Emma shook her head. "Remember when they used to let you smoke in here? Some of the snooty types would give you the stink-eye, but screw 'em; I always exhaled the other way."

Rosie snapped at her gum. "Anyway, I may just end up out in Jersey. Chaz's dad doesn't give us a dime unless I shake him down like the Mafia, so we're stuck in a crappy studio over on Avenue C. But it makes me feel better, living in the city, like I'm not being totally robbed of my twenties. What a ball and chain kids are, am I right? You gotta get a sitter to go out, and the kid doesn't care if you've got the worst hangover of the twenty-first century, you still hafta get up and take him out to play the next day. On the plus side, I'll only be thirty-six when Chaz is off to college, God willing, and then I get my freedom back."

After this torrent of information, Emma felt tongue-tied. "He's

very fast on the slide," she said moronically, then did the math:
Rosie must've had her son when she was eighteen, which put her
at twenty-three now; she looked older, her eyes heavy with bags.

"Who's yours?"

Emma pointed to her niece and nephew, who were swinging
side by side on the monkey bars. It seemed too late to mention
that they weren't really hers. Rosie nodded. "Confession: I kind of
can't stand other people's kids. No offense, it's nothing personal."

"None taken."

A moment later a teary Aimee rushed up to Emma, exhibiting a
freshly scraped knee. Caleb followed closely behind: "That girl
pushed her," he announced, a little too gleefully, if you asked
Emma. Emma followed his finger and landed upon a kid who was
small but seemed older than Aimee—age four? five?; she was
headed for the swings. Emma knew she was supposed to do something, but what—yell at the girl? Tell Aimee to go work it out on
her own? Find the mom or nanny associated with the girl and talk
it through? She felt woefully uninformed and feared that whatever
action she chose, she might violate some complicated bylaw of
playground politics.

Rosie, who'd been swiping at her phone, humming what sounded
like a Justin Bieber song (Emma was embarrassed to even recognize
it), stepped in. "Hey you," she yelled at the offender. The girl
turned away, casting down her eyes. "Yeah, you, I know you can
hear me. Get your butt over here and say you're sorry. No one likes
a bully. Come on!" The girl did as she was told, looking frightened, and Aimee stopped her whimpering. "It's okay," Aimee
mumbled.

Rosie returned to her screen, waving away Emma's thank-you.
Emma then watched as the girl ran across the playground and collapsed her body into one of the nannies. The woman shot a dirty
look in Rosie and Emma's direction, which Rosie seemed to ignore. Although under her breath she spat, "Stupid cunt," in reference, Emma hoped, to the adult and not the little girl.

It was exhausting trying to keep track of Caleb and Aimee
among all the small bodies flitting around at a fever pitch, and it
seemed like hours later when Max finally appeared at the park

gate. He waved to Emma, and Rosie looked up from her phone, as if she had a radar for the arrival of testosterone in the estrogen-heavy play space.

"Holy shit, is that your man?" she said, then whistled. "Lucky you."

"My brother, actually."

"Ooh-la-la."

"Hey, Em," he said, oblivious to the woman next to him who was now thrusting her chest forward. "We're all packed. How's it going out here?"

Aimee and Caleb must've heard their father's voice; they tumbled over, yelling, "Daddy," and flinging themselves into his arms.

"Did you guys have fun? You're covered in filth!"

"That's city living for you," said Emma.

"I got into a fight, and my knee is scrapened up, and Auntie Emma watched me go down the slide, and Caleb found a brokened glass bottle in the sand."

"Wow, Aims." Max's eyes widened. "Let's go clean you guys up."

"Nice meeting you," Emma said to Rosie, but the woman barely glanced up. Emma felt a funny stab of hurt, like she'd been cast out of the mom club (a club she'd wanted no part of in the first place). She hoisted her niece into a piggyback, and they set off to find Nick and the van full of all of Emma's belongings.

Annie's building featured on-call daycare, so they dropped off the kids then set about hauling their things, some into basement storage and some into the guest room, which was already crowded with parcels from Barneys and Tiffany and Jonathan Adler—the wedding gift bounty.

"You know, it looked a lot like this when Alysse and I first moved in together," said Max, rolling a suitcase into the guest room. "We were staying in her parents' basement while we looked for our own place. We had nowhere to put any of our things, so we just lived among the boxes. It was still a thrill." That's right, Emma remembered—the day after their wedding, Max had moved into Alysse's childhood home in New Jersey, where she'd still been living while commuting to the city for work. They'd wanted an apartment in Hoboken—Alysse's parents would've never stood for their daughter living in big, bad Manhattan—when the Feits announced their move to Spain, and Max and his new wife swooped in to claim the house in Westchester. It seemed odd and old-fashioned that the two of them had only ever lived in their parents' houses.

"It's a real adventure, living together for the first time," Max said. Emma nodded dismissively. Max and Alysse had gotten hitched and moved in after one of those formal courtships straight out of *Fiddler on the Roof.* Emma doubted they'd even had premarital sex. Max continued: "It's funny, even with Cindy—"

"Wow, Cindy," Emma blurted. "I haven't thought of her in years." The name of Max's college girlfriend seemed out of a different lifetime. Cindy had been non-Jewish, but willing to convert, if Emma remembered correctly.

"Yeah, well, even though she'd been sleeping over at my dorm for months—her roommate was an epic snorer—when we officially started living together, it felt different. We learned so much about each other."

"Huh."

"Like how her room was always a mess, but she kept the insides of her dresser drawers freakishly neat. And how she liked a beverage in the shower—she kept juice and seltzer by the towels."

"That's bizarre."

"Cindy was a trip." Emma wanted to ask her brother if he missed her, that girl she remembered as a spark plug, always up for an adventure, pretty much the opposite of Alysse. Even back then, Emma recalled thinking Cindy had been much too interesting for her brother. Max looked immersed in thought, so she didn't interrupt.

"I don't know, though. I feel like I already know everything about Nick."

"I bet not. It'll be interesting to see. I'm psyched for you guys."

"Someone talking about me?" Nick appeared in the room, shouldering the body pillow Emma liked to sleep curled up with.

"Geez," said Max, "I thought it was bad having a three-year-old show up in my bed at night, but that thing's crazy. A serious cock block, eh, Nick?" Emma smirked at the comment her brother never would've made in front of his wife.

"We manage with an occasional ménage à pillow," said Nick. Emma blushed at the dorky joke, and chucked a pillow at Nick. He deflected with the larger pillow.

"If this is some kind of foreplay, I'm out," Max said. Emma rolled her eyes.

"Well, I think that's everything," said Nick. "All that's left in the van is a layer of Goldfish crumbs and a stuffed penguin."

"You sure the penguin isn't yours, Emmy? Need more company to go beddy-bye?"

"Oh, shut up," she said. "So should we grab the kids and order pizza, as promised in your mover contract?"

Max consulted his watch—Emma noticed he'd swapped out his usual Cartier for a sports kind on a fabric band; it looked good on him. "I actually think we'd better get going. Alysse is making tacos for dinner, and she'll have a fit if we come home full of pizza."

Emma was surprised to feel disappointed. "Okay, next time then. I still owe you."

"For sure." While they hugged, Emma went for the back of Max's neck, where she knew he was most ticklish. Predictably he began convulsing with giggles, looking like his ten-year-old self; his laugh sounded just like his son's.

"Pathetic, as usual," she said.

"My sneaky sister," he said. "I better scram before you launch another attack."

Watching him go, Emma thought about how today had felt like the old days, the two of them just hanging out together. And it was fun to be with her niece and nephew in the city. Maybe once she and Nick settled into a new place, she'd suggest hosting them for a sleepover; they could go to one of those trendy origami work-shops or a kid yoga class, then hit up the Central Park carousel and overload on sugar at Dylan's Candy Bar.

Alone now with Nick, Emma looked around at all their boxes. "We should probably unpack and relaunch our apartment search."

"You're right, we probably should."

"But I don't really want to, do you?"

"Nah."

"If I know Annie, they've got cases of fine wine stashed somewhere in this place. How about we hunt one down and go unwind on the roof deck?"

"I like it. You find the wine, I'll order the pizza. But in just a minute." Nick pulled Emma close and together they toppled onto the borrowed bed that was temporarily theirs.

Chapter 20

In that split-second fog between sleep and waking, Nick made out a blue-and-white pattern, sniffed gourmet coffee shop, and heard the low whir of a fan. He barely registered his panic—the fear of the unfamiliar, the disorientation, the longing for his own bed—before he heard Emma's voice, blinked fully awake, and spotted his girlfriend entering what he now remembered was the guest room in Annie and Eli's apartment.

"I made you a vanilla cappuccino," she said, holding out a mug. "And look, I used a stencil to make a foam flower on top."

He took a sip. "Holy shit, that's good."

"Apparently Eli gets his beans shipped from Colombia. And that espresso machine has a larger skill set than I do. I made myself a mocha granita. I feel like we're at the Ritz!"

She said it with excitement, but as Nick stumbled around the space trying to approximate his Monday morning routine, he, too, felt like he was in a hotel—though in a cold, detached way. He straightened out the high-thread-count sheets, remade the bed with all its embroidered pillows, and then showered under the rain-forest spigot that Emma said was designed to soothe, lathering up with the lilac soap. He tried the shower's steam feature and got momentarily lost in the air, then dried himself with a towel two inches thick. He'd planned to grab a bagel on his way to the subway, but Emma intercepted him with a bowl of granola, the kind they sold at the farmers' market for twelve dollars a bag. Someone had sent a Harry and David fruit basket, so he chopped a pear into his bowl, perfectly ripe. Leaving the building, the doorman handed him the *Times* and tipped his cap in a way that made Nick wonder what he'd done to deserve it.

It was all a little unsettling. So when Nick commuted up to East Harlem and arrived at the crumbling school and entered his slightly sour-smelling classroom, then turned on the halogen lighting whose one bulb always flickered, he actually felt relieved. Here he belonged. And as the day progressed, and he led his students through science and reading and math, Nick realized he'd hit his groove; he'd made it through the shaky first few weeks of the year, and the class was becoming a community, almost a home.

Nick had been dreading the relaunch of their apartment hunt. But that evening, as he joined Emma at the computer and she loaded up Craigslist and typed in a move-in date of October fifteenth, Nick surprised himself by feeling fine. Popping open beers and scrolling through their options, they may as well have been perusing cute puppy gifs for how comfortable Nick felt. Calmly he urged Emma away from the listings that looked too good to be true—suspiciously spacious or too well located for their price range—nudging her instead toward spaces that seemed exactly adequate. Nick realized he didn't care much anymore about having a dishwasher or a full-sized bathtub or central air; all the fancy gadgets in Eli's apartment were nice, but to Nick a dollar coffee and an egg-and-cheese from the deli were just as satisfying as a gourmet latte and designer granola. He didn't even need to be in a choice location. So long as it was safe for Emma to walk at night, it would be fun to get to know a new neighborhood. Nick's revised priorities were affordable rent, functional plumbing, a lack of bedbugs, and a decent landlord. As long as these conditions were met, he was sure he and Emma could thrive. It was amazing how many listings fulfilled these simpler needs.

So Nick wasn't surprised when, just three nights later, he and Emma found themselves perusing yet another lease, pens poised for signing. For both of them it was their first foray into Red Hook, the South Brooklyn neighborhood they'd previously heard about mostly in relation to its IKEA. The walk from the subway to the apartment in question had been long, but it took them across cobblestone streets and past an occasional bar or restaurant and just a handful of other pedestrians. Though they were only six miles from Nick's Manhattan neighborhood, it seemed worlds away. Nick dug the sparse, even stark feel, and he noticed that Emma had relaxed her usual clip to an actual stroll. She went on about her research of the area—the waterfront views of the Statue of Liberty, the world-class supermarket, the free pool in the summer that attracted a field's worth of food trucks outside—and Nick half listened happily. A block from the apartment, the aroma of espresso lured them into a coffee shop and, lidded cups in hand, they arrived at their destination. Maybe it was the rush of caffeine, but Nick's heart began racing when they entered a plain hallway— no uniformed doorman or fancy lobby like at Eli and Annie's place, but no smell or garbage and dying animals like at Luis's place, either. It was average, nondescript, exactly fine. Nick squeezed Emma's hand.

The landlady introduced herself as Shelley, then announced that she would start with the downsides. She proceeded to tour them around three small rooms, pointing out little cracks in the shower's caulking and a kitchen sink whose faucet had to be positioned just so to stop the drip. "First-floor apartment, so no stairs, yay!" she said. "But you get tiny black ants when it gets warm outside, but they don't bite and they gone in a week. We spray each month." She shrugged. "What else? Small closet space. But, a five-minute walk to IKEA, which sells excellent wardrobe. Here, I got you catalog to look." The cover bore a sticker: "For tenants!!" Shelley seemed like a long-lost aunt.

The landlady left them alone to browse, and Emma pulled Nick into the corner closet. Pressed against each other they barely fit, and Nick's head bumped up against the hanger bar. "Cozier than those walk-ins, right?" Emma said, starting to nibble on his neck. Nick would've undressed her right then if Shelley hadn't been waiting in the next room. Back in that first apartment with the pair of closets, he'd mostly been thinking about how much sports equipment he could fit. "Should we sign?" she asked. He kissed her in agreement.

Moments later Nick watched as Emma looped her signature onto the lease, feeling none of the nausea he'd experienced while signing Luis's lease. He added his own name, and Shelley extended them a thumbs-up. Nick felt like they'd won the lottery.

"Now, go celebrate." Shelley handed them a laminated index card entitled *Shelley's best ratings!!!*, which listed several local bars, followed by descriptors such as, *Best for friends and fun! Good times for all!* and *For romantic lovers—candles and roses! Drink up!* Emma pointed to the description that read, *Attention **PARTY** animals, this spot's for you!* next to an address on the same block, and they set out.

Shelley's idea of party animals was apparently small groups of twenty- and thirtysomethings nursing beers and nodding along to St. Vincent songs played at a reasonable volume. Nick, who'd already decided this would be their neighborhood spot and that he'd establish a signature drink, asked for a Dark and Stormy and imagined the bartender—cute in that dirty-haired hipster way—mixing it up each time she saw him come in.

In the spirit of party animals, Emma ordered them shots of whiskey. "Cheers, love," Nick said. As he tilted back the drink and felt that back-of-the-throat burn, the sky outside erupted into downpour. They watched the falling water through the windows, which soon fogged up, making the space even more charming. Nature seemed to be releasing a sigh of relief along with the two of them. Everything seemed like a sign.

They didn't have umbrellas, of course, and the rain was relentless. So they stepped outside naked to the elements, and raced through the flooding streets, sheets of rain and gusts of wind pounding against them. Nick imagined they were in Venice, or somewhere else he'd never been—Mars, maybe (his students would correct him, saying Mars was dry as a bone). This was the beauty of New York, Nick thought: Every neighborhood was a world unto itself, and every season, every shift in weather transformed it totally—a new iteration, a new scene to explore. And the person you were with, of course, made it all new again, too. There was Emma beside him, soaring over sidewalks and splashing through puddles, hair matted to her head and eyes sparkling with rain, miserable and thrilled all at once. They'd signed on for a home here during a cool and dry golden hour, and now they were flying through a wet, cold twilight. Nick had navigated the city's streets for years on his own, and now he had this beautiful, bright companion. Anything seemed possible.

Distracted by Emma's off-key rendition of "Singin' in the Rain," Nick's foot caught on a newspaper, soaked to a slimy pulp. He slid across the cobblestone and, in attempts to regain his footing, groped at Emma's arm. His grab was rough, and Emma, too, lost her balance. The two of them lurched forward, tumbling to the ground. They landed hard, both acquiring the beginnings of bruises that Nick imagined would remain black and blue for days, eventually fade to yellow, and only return to healthy pink after they'd settled into their new apartment and made this street their home. It was a strangely thrilling thought. Lying with Emma on the sidewalk in a wounded heap, the rain pounding, Nick experienced a surge of adrenaline—excitement for all that was to come.

Now that they'd secured a home that Emma could conjure up concretely (moving there would be another matter, but for now she chose not to dwell on it), she was free to devote her full emotional energy to missing Annie. They'd been apart for more than a month, with just two staticky phone calls to sustain them—a record, ever since their parents had gifted them their own phone lines for their respective tenth birthdays. Emma dug into her friend's bureau, searching for traces of her scent. Mostly everything smelled of Tide Fresh, but Emma managed to find a ratty sweatshirt and baggy Lehigh sweats that smelled of Annie. She pulled them on to pad around the house in, tricking herself that her friend was nearby. Nick catcalled her, praising her new hobo look.

As crucial as it was to have a place to live, Emma had always found her home in people—first her parents, later Annie, and finally Nick. These were the ones who gave her a sense of comfort, and whom she longed for when they were far away. But now Emma had everything she'd wanted—Nick, an apartment, a home together—and still she yearned for Annie, feeling as if her friend had taken a chunk of Emma with her to Africa and left a gaping hole in its place. It didn't help that Gen was still acting distant— Emma kept inviting her over to grill on her borrowed roof deck, but Gen had rain-checked twice.

Maybe Emma's sense of home was more complicated than she'd assumed, more fragmented. With the latest iteration of the apartment hunt, Nick had turned placid, totally at ease with shipping out to an unfamiliar area and into an apartment much smaller than what they'd initially hoped for. Emma had gone along with it because Nick seemed so certain, and also because she'd started doubting her own judgment. But she was worried about being so far out in Brooklyn, so isolated from the familiar. And Nick's sudden assuredness troubled her, too—would he eventually snap out of it and turn resentful? Would he go on another drinking bender then? Part of Emma feared the brain injury had fundamentally changed Nick, although the doctor had assured her that was very unlikely. Plus, ever since she'd delivered her self-righteous rant about the integrity of her job, Emma had been feeling slightly sick about how little the reality matched her description. She felt ridiculous for stressing over all this stuff that was small potatoes compared to the potential homelessness they'd faced a week ago, but Emma couldn't help it. And as much as she knew how if she voiced these concerns to Nick, he'd listen and nod his support and kiss her with care, she wanted Annie, now, here in New York, home with her.

And then, as if she'd never even left, Annie was back in Emma's life, returned to New York in all her suntanned, bug-bitten, African-print-donning glory. "Hellooo!" she bellowed upon entering the apartment, and then flung open the bathroom door to reveal Emma inside, nursing her wounds from her recent spill in the rain.

"Holy shit, did Nick become a girlfriend beater while I was off newly-wedding?"

"Yes, and where have you been when I've needed you most?" Though she said it melodramatically, Emma really meant it. She flung her arms around her friend.

"Well, I'm glad I could provide you with refuge here at the Blum Center for Battered Women. Sorry, not funny—I'm jet-lagged and famished. I haven't had a decent meal in weeks. Let's get burgers and catch up on everything, including how you got that nasty bruise."

"Five Guys?" Emma was already salivating, thinking of their favorite comfort food; for weeks she'd been subsisting on Nick's abstemious vegetarian fare.

"Obviously." Emma took a look at her friend, who was now all grown-up, a wife and a home owner, but still her same five-year-old self, with the same long nose, the same full lips, the same— wait—"What is *that?*" Emma spat, pointing to a blue line snaking its way around her friend's wrist. Annie lifted her hand, revealing a curlicue design like an ornate wristwatch, which ended in a flourish at the base of her palm. "Ta-da! Eli got one, too. Like it?"

Emma remembered when she and Annie had hoped to get matching tattoos in high school—symmetrical butterfly wings, one on each of their ankles to symbolize their connection no matter how far apart they flew. But Annie's mother had gotten wind of the plan and intercepted them at the mall before any needles pierced skin. Emma hadn't admitted it then, but she'd felt relieved to be caught, and spared the permanent marring. Now she felt the absence of that wing on her ankle.

"Well?"

Emma realized Annie was waiting for an answer. "Oh, it's cute," she said. "The squiggles complement your freckles. Is there any significance?"

"Besides my eternal bond to Eli, you mean? Well, we met a few locals on safari, and some of the women had the pattern sewn onto their dresses. I thought it was beautiful, and they said it was their tribe's symbol of love. So we just went for it. Although for all I know it's just a brand logo, or some creepy anti-American thing."

Emma laughed along with her friend, but it was hollow, not the kind of laughter she'd been pining for during Annie's absence. "Come on, let's eat," Annie said, hooking her elbow through Emma's. And as they walked arm in arm through the streets of SoHo, Emma wasn't sure if the goose bumps she felt were Annie's or her own.

In the restaurant booth, Annie tore into her cheeseburger with a vengeance. "Wow," said Emma, "your honeymoon changed you. You eat like an animal now."

"Listen, between all those jeep drives over bumpy dirt roads and the water that was supposedly safe to drink (I don't buy it), I was sick nearly every day. I'm thrilled to have good old American fare—meat and cheese and a sesame bun. Mmm!"

"Says the Jew from Westchester."

"*L'chaim!* So, Ems, did you open any of my wedding gifts? I saw that Babeland box in the foyer—I think my sorority sisters pitched in on that new diamond-encrusted dildo."

"Seriously?" Emma choked on a gulp of beer.

"Yeah, I registered for it." Emma must've looked as incredulous as she felt, because Annie said, "Oh, lighten up. You and Nick might still have a smoking sex life, but old married ladies like me need some toys to spice things up." But it wasn't the dildo that shocked Emma; it was the diamonds, which seemed absurdly wasteful. What was the point? "Anyway, I was hoping you'd be bunking with me for longer than a week. I can't believe you're moving to Red Hook, which may as well be Philly for how far it is."

"I know, but you have no idea what we went through."

"So spill. Tell me everything."

And Emma did, not editing out or softening parts of the story like she would've with her parents or even with Nick, and Annie gasped and grimaced and cheered at all the right moments. This was what Emma had missed. They were halfway through chocolate shakes when she got to the final lease, the fall in the rain, and the resulting bruises.

"Well, now we have to plan you the perfect housewarming," said Annie.

"Lemme guess, you'll handle it?" Annie nodded, and Emma was glad to cede control—and any party planned by Annie was sure to be epic. Emma had wondered how her friend was going to channel her famous event-planning energy post-wedding; she was glad to provide her with a fix. Emma sucked up the dregs of her shake, feeling fortified by the thick sweetness lining her stomach.

Although apparently Annie didn't feel the same—a moment later a hand flew to her mouth and she fled for the bathroom.

"Don't tell Eli," Annie said afterward. "He kept saying to avoid the fruit stands. I thought he was being overcautious. I don't want to hear his 'I told you so' about picking up some parasite." Emma nodded, happy to know she and Annie shared a secret from her husband.

Back in the apartment, they found Eli working his way through a bottle of wine, and Nick hunched over a stack of papers. Eli reached for one. "Ah, the good old spelling test," he said. "I never realized what power teachers have, like you could claim some word's spelled the wrong way, then all those kids would all grow up believing it."

"Why would I do that?" Nick said, looking disturbed.

Eli shrugged. "I dunno, because you can."

Nick gathered up his papers in such a way that made Emma nervous about both paper cuts and the prospect of cohabitating with Annie and Eli until the fifteenth.

"I wish I had the excuse of some teacher screwing with me," said Annie, diffusing the tension as usual. "My spelling's horrendous. Anyway, Eli, why don't you let Nick grade in peace? Ems is gonna help me open presents."

As Annie went at the packages, ripping wrapping paper, flinging ribbons, and sending tissue paper flying, Emma stood by and filled in the spreadsheet: what the gift was, whom it was from, and whether or not Annie would keep it. Soon the room looked like a ransacked Party City. From a hefty parcel Annie pulled out several serving platters—"Perfect for your party," she said to Emma, who was looking forward to what would clearly be the classiest housewarming ever. She unwrapped monogrammed towels, his-and-hers iPods, and Tiffany silver in ten different forms. There were silk bathrobes, designer bath products, and bottles of Johnnie Walker in labels blue, red, and black. The sheer quantity of stuff was staggering. All brand new, all top-of-the-line, all for a couple that already had an apartment and a life fully stocked with everything they could've ever wanted. At each item, Annie squealed, and Emma diligently recorded the details. Only Emma seemed stressed about where they'd possibly put all of these things. The temporary solution, it turned out, was the guest room, meaning that when Emma and Nick went to sleep that night, their bed was an island in a sea of wedding gifts.

"Are you still awake?" Emma asked, nudging Nick. He made a noise. "How about we keep our new place minimalist? Just a few pieces of furniture, no knickknacks."

"I was thinking the same thing." Between snores, he murmured something that sounded like, "I love you." Emma drifted to sleep happy, knowing she was under the same roof as both her boyfriend and her best friend.

Chapter 21

In addition to Nick and Annie, the apartment's luxury espresso machine became Emma's other source of comfort, and she intended to savor it during her remaining time at her friend's place. Each morning she treated herself to a different concoction—*café au lait*, soy cinnamon mocha, extra-frothy chai—and Annie taught her to pour the milk into flower and heart patterns without the stencils. Nick denounced the machine; he started buying his coffee, black, from the truck on the corner, as if to make a point to Eli, who happily let his new wife serve him his gourmet cup each morning without ever offering to reciprocate. But for Emma, the daily fix of fancy caffeine, along with Annie's company at the breakfast table, made her thrilled to wake up. Each morning she left the apartment cheered, full of vigor and purpose, intent on making the most of her day at *1, 2, 3 . . . Ivies!*

In the office Emma waved a tentative hello to Genevieve, who was on the phone, and then checked her schedule: First up was Sophia Cole. Emma was determined to reinstate the professionalism she'd let lapse in recent weeks. No more giving in to the girl's whims about how to spend the sessions or letting her tag along on personal errands, and certainly no socializing. Upon arrival, Sophia admitted she'd done exactly none of the work Emma had assigned.

"Oh," she added nonchalantly, uncapping a Sharpie and beginning to embellish a henna-like design on her forearm, "my alarm acted up on the morning of the SATs. But sleeping was such a better use of my time than standardized testing. I've been so exhausted lately. So what's new with you?"

It took all of Emma's restraint not to scream. Instead, in a very calm voice she said, "Sophia, what exactly do you plan to do with yourself after high school?"

The girl looked up from her drawing and batted her eyelashes. "Continue being my charming self, of course."

"Meaning what, going to parties and saying clever and cute things, like all of those layabouts I met at your friend's fake apartment the other night?"

"Hey, I brought you there as a guest."

"I'm just saying, if that's what you want, fine, but I can't imagine it really is. I can't think of anything more tragic than you ending up swallowed by that crowd." Emma flashed on the parties in *The House of Mirth*, the fashionable, vapid affairs thrown by the pillars of high society, so valued by Lily Bart even though they bored her to tears. In contemporary New York, Sophia was one of the few people who still had access to a sort of society life, changed as it was. At one point this might've made Emma jealous, but now she was going to make it her mission to rescue the girl from it.

Sophia aimed to distract: "How about we Google the worst examples of common app essays and laugh at how idiotic people can be?"

Emma had let this relationship go way off the rails. To avoid funneling her frustration toward her teenage client, she decided she needed a breather. "Sophia, I'll be back in a minute. Sit here and work on that practice test. I mean it."

On Emma's way to the bathroom—she must've been stomping—Genevieve called out, "Everything all right?"

"Yeah," she said tentatively, trying to discern whether Gen was back to being her friend or still the weirdly polite person she'd become in the last couple of weeks. Her air seemed friendly. "Actually, no, I'm not really all right. I'm trying to figure out what the hell to do with Sophia Cole"—*and with you,* Emma thought but didn't say. "She's brilliant, but has zero motivation. All she wants to do is hang out with me."

Genevieve tucked her long hair behind her ears. "Well, the clients aren't your friends, as I know you know; though I bet it's hard to remember that when they're so smart and well spoken. And of course New York City teens are all freaks of nature who look and act like they're twenty-five. But they're still kids, you know?"

"Yep, you're totally right." *Smart and well spoken* . . . It occurred to Emma then that Sophia, whom she'd slipped into thinking of as some sort of sidekick or little sister, reminded her of her actual friends, Annie and Genevieve. Though neither was book-smart like Sophia, they all shared a similar spark. No wonder then, that while Annie had been off honeymooning and Gen had retreated mysteriously from their friendship, Emma, feeling lonely, had slotted Sophia in as a kind of substitute. Well, no longer.

"Hey, Gen," she added, gathering up her nerve, "are we okay? I feel like I did something wrong and I don't quite know what it is."

Gen looked like she might cry. "Ugh, I'm so sorry. It's not you; you're perfect. Though maybe that's part of it. I'm feeling so less-than-perfect lately, with my acting career a bust and this stupid joke of a job." She glanced at their boss's door—closed.

"But the nursing school thing—"

Gen waved her away. "I know, I know. But *blech,* what a pain to start over from scratch at thirty. Especially when so many people we know are killing it in their careers these days. And now that it's getting cold outside, all I want is someone to cuddle up with. Two of my roommates just got boyfriends, you know. They're head over heels."

"I didn't know. I'm sorry."

"No, I mean, I'm happy for them. It's just, I had this new guy over the other night, and when we were going to bed, he warned me that spooning made him break out in hives. I couldn't tell if he meant it literally or metaphorically."

"Yikes."

"Exactly. So I dunno, I've had a hard time around couple-y friends lately."

"Right. Are Nick and I that couple-y?" Genevieve shrugged.

"Huh, okay." Emma was struck by how much harder being single must be at age thirty than at twenty-five.

"Don't worry about it. It's just me being stupid. I'm an idiot. It hasn't made me feel better to ditch my friends, believe me. All it's meant is me staying holed up at home, bored and clicking through Instagrams of everyone else's fabulous lives."

"That's the worst." Emma thought of the cheesy, overly posed engagement albums on Facebook that made her seethe simultaneously with condescension and envy.

"It's masochistic is what it is. I'm always half considering renouncing all of social media, but then I catch myself fantasizing about when I land the lead in some killer Broadway show, and how then I can post tons of my own braggy photos." Gen smiled, and Emma welled up with feeling for her friend; she'd really missed her.

"How about this? As soon as I move into my new place, I'll kick Nick out for the night and the two of us can stay in and cuddle up in front of a bad movie. We'll make fun of the acting, then we'll go out and find you a guy in some hip bar in my 'hood, okay?"

"Sure, it's a plan. And in the meantime, I'll try and stay off Instagram."

"Good luck with that." Emma knew Gen spent most of her workday bored online.

"And good luck with the girl in there," Genevieve said. "Stay strong." Emma nodded, jutted out her chin, and marched back down the hall. She was feeling very mature, having faced a friend issue head-on and resolved it, instead of letting it fester under the surface, as she definitely would've done at Sophia's age.

In her office, Emma found her client using a Scantron to create a pointillism-style drawing of a leaf. "Here's a question," Emma said, snatching away the paper. "What does your mother want you to do after high school?"

"Besides attend Smith, join a sorority, wear pearls and cardigan sets, and learn how to set a table for tea?"

"They don't have sororities at Smith, which I bet you know. And your mom isn't a total idiot, either. Seriously, I'm curious."

Sophia sighed. "She thinks I should work for Annie Leibovitz or Jeff Koons or one of the three other world-famous artists she's actually heard of. As if that's at all realistic. So yeah, she pretty much *is* a total idiot."

"Okay, so she thinks you should get your feet wet in the art world. If it weren't totally unrealistic, would you want to work for an artist, like as an apprentice or an intern?"

"I dunno, I guess." Sophia's voice wavered, sounding stripped of some veneer. "But not here. What I'd really like to do is study at the Prado—there's this Velázquez scholar who writes for *Artforum* and he's always talking about the collection there."

"You mean the Museo del Prado, in Madrid?"

"Yeah. My mom says my dad used to take her there in the eighties and they'd draw together in the portrait galleries. I still have some of his sketchbooks." Emma could picture her own parents doing the same thing—they'd raved to her about exhibits at the Prado. "It would be cool to retrace their steps."

"Wait, you've never gone?"

"No, I've never been abroad." Sophia blushed, as if this were a mortifying confession. And Emma *was* shocked—she'd assumed the girl from Park Avenue was a well-seasoned worldwide traveler. "Oh," was all she could think to say.

"Yeah, well, my mom goes to Europe all the time, but she always leaves me behind. Tells the doorman to keep an eye on me." The edge was back in her voice, and Emma realized her client was a real-life Eloise. "She comes back showering me with souvenirs, most of it stupid, expensive stuff. But a couple times she brought things from the Prado—a Goya poster I have up on my closet door, even though it's torn now. Mom's constantly threatening to toss it. And this silk scarf with little pink birds on it." Emma was nodding enthusiastically—she'd seen Sophia wear that scarf. The girl suddenly scowled. "Anyway, why are we talking about my stupid mom and her guilt gifts?"

"We're not—well, not anymore." Emma had an idea; she made a mental note to e-mail her parents later. "But speaking of your mother, I'm sending her a progress report this week. So if I were you, I'd spend the rest of today plowing through that practice test."

"Boo, you're no fun. I thought we were friends."

"Nope, we're not. I'm your tutor and you're my client."

Next up was Dylan York, who strutted in sporting a Columbia University T-shirt, still stiff with lines from what was probably the store's folding. Emma had practically written his early-decision application herself, and yet she knew it wouldn't be enough. Dylan's parents had forwarded her his SAT score report: 1,800. Way too low for that ivory tower.

"I have some materials for you." Emma laid out a pile of brochures—to NYU and Rochester and Skidmore, perfectly decent schools that Dylan had an actual shot at.

"What the hell are these?" he asked. "I'm going to Columbia with my girlfriend, remember? Or if not, probably Cornell. Did you forget the name of your business?" Dylan's sneer reminded Emma of something, and she realized it was the initial meeting with the boy's Hellis; when Emma had mentioned the importance of applying to safety schools, Mr. York had assumed the same look. "That won't be necessary for Dylan," he'd said. "My son's IQ is off the charts."

Behind Dylan's scoff must've been real fear—that he wouldn't get into Columbia, that his girlfriend would abandon him, that his parents would think him a failure instead of a genius, that he'd be doomed. "Dylan, I'm going to let you in on a little life wisdom that I doubt you'll hear at Dalton."

"I go to Trinity," he spat.

"Trinity, sorry." Emma sometimes had trouble keeping straight all of Manhattan's elite prep schools, those $40K-a-year breeding grounds for entitlement. "Anyway, you're going to get into college. In fact, you're going to get into a great college, although it probably won't be the number-one or even the number-ten school in the country. Also, there are always going to be people who are smarter than you, and more talented than you, and yes, even richer than you. But guess what? That doesn't make you a loser, or stupid, or any less worthy. It's just life, and it's perfectly okay. There are more important things than where you go to college. Like whether or not you're a good person."

Dylan's scoff deepened, aging him ten years. Emma could almost picture what he'd look like middle-aged, a bloated banker type who talked down to his secretary. "Here's a little life wisdom for *you*," he said, words thick with sarcasm. "Read your job description. My dad isn't paying you to dole out some two-bit psychobabble crap. Your purpose is to get me into the Ivy League." He flung the pamphlets aside and stormed out.

"Do yourself a favor," Emma called after him. "Apply to a safety school." She knew she would get an angry Helli call, and that this would likely be the last time she'd see Dylan York. But she didn't care. She hoped that maybe when the boy was panicking over his rejection letter from Columbia, getting berated by his parents, and watching his girlfriend gloat over her acceptance, he'd remember her words. Beyond that, there was nothing Emma could do.

Chapter 22

"And this is my china. Ems, tilt the screen this way." Annie held up a bowl and a plate, and beamed at Emma's parents through the Wi-Fi connection.

"Ooh, beautiful," said Emma's mother. "Honey, we should think about investing in some new dishware, don't you think? That pattern is *perfecto*."

"How much longer are we doing this show-and-tell?" Emma asked, tailing her friend with the laptop. "My arms are getting tired."

"Come on, Ems. Be a good sport and come to the bedroom. I wanna show your folks the sculptures we got in Johannesburg."

Emma endured ten more minutes of gift ogling before Annie finally acknowledged her pout. "Poor Ems, have I hijacked your Skype session? Okay, Mr. and Mrs. Feit, here's another object for your inspection: my beautiful best friend, gifted to me by you, many years before my wedding, as beautiful and stunning as any antelope I spotted on the South African reserve."

"Cheers," said Emma's mom. "Lovely gifts, darling. Happy wedding!"

"Ta-ta, Feit fam!"

With Annie out of the spotlight, Emma waved to her parents.

"Oh, Emma, I found a great program for your little friend."

"She's not my friend, Mom, she's my client."

"Well anyway, it's an intensive year of art history and painting classes at the University of Madrid, designed for students taking a gap year. I'll send you all the info."

"Wow, thanks." It sounded perfect for Sophia.

"So do you have a new address for us yet?"

Emma experienced one of her parents-specific mood swings, snapping instantly from grateful to annoyed. Why couldn't her mom phrase the question in a way that implied she cared whether or not they'd found a new home, instead of what was in it for her? But Emma chose to let it go, and began describing the apartment, glossing over the aspects that worried her and focusing on its interesting location and the decent landlord.

"Sounds great, dear—and you can receive packages there?"

"I dunno, Mom."

"*Por supuesto*, she can. *Claramente.*" Her dad furrowed his brow as he attempted to roll his "r." "What kind of *casa* can't receive *correo?*"

"Isn't he darling? He's working on exclamations. He's dying for a language partner at his level, so in the meantime he's been torturing me. Haven't you, *querido?*"

Huh, Sophia had mentioned how Spanish was the one subject she struggled in. And if she got to know Emma's parents, they could be like surrogate parents for her while she lived abroad. "Dad, how would you feel about having a teenager for a language partner?"

"*¿Porqué no?*" he said.

"Okay, I'll talk to her."

For once Emma ended a Skype chat with her parents feeling invigorated instead of defeated. She left a voicemail for Sophia, filling her in on the Spanish art program—if she wanted they could fill out the application together next session—and proposing the language exchange with her dad.

Emma relayed her evening plans to Annie via text: She and Nick would "measure the hell out of" their new place, as Nick had put it. *Thrilling Friday night!* Annie replied. *Can Eli and I come? Double date? We'll bring beer. Dying to see new hood!* It was a sweet gesture from the person who'd gasped in horror when Emma had first mentioned Red Hook. Emma found Nick loading up his bag with graph paper and two types of measuring tape. "Okay if Annie and Eli crash our party?" she asked. He groaned; despite his gratitude toward their hosts, Emma knew he'd been getting fed up with spending so much time with them. "They'd bring booze."

"Ugh, fine." Nick stretched out one of the tapes to a foot, then snapped it back at Emma's butt. She swatted his hand with a nearby ruler, then ducked out of his reach.

As their subway car tunneled downtown and under the river to Brooklyn, Nick went on about the tutoring program his school was planning to pilot; at a recent meeting, he told Emma, he'd floated her name as a possible director. "No one knows what they're doing yet, and you have so much experience," he said. "We could really use your help." Emma smiled noncommittally, not wanting to put a damper on his excitement. "Plus, it might be fun to work together."

That was an interesting point, though Emma was still skeptical. She'd been to Nick's school just once, as one of two total audience members at the fifth grade's performance of *West Side Story*. It was the farthest north she'd ever traveled on the subway, and despite Nick's assurances that the neighborhood was safe during daylight, she'd found herself striding quickly from train station to school, head held unnaturally high in attempts to radiate confidence. The kid actors had been cute, but the school was a mess: In the girls' bathroom Emma had had to try three stalls before she found one that wasn't clogged, and someone had desecrated the bulletin boards, scrawling Fs just to the left of the "Art Show" announcements. When, as a Good Samaritan, Emma had reported these items to the main office, the secretary had rolled her eyes so dramatically that Emma had wondered if the woman was all there in the head. She was impressed that Nick battled that scene day in and day out. It also made her realize how lucky she had it at work—the resources, the facilities, the capable coworkers. And for all her complaints about the Hellis, Emma had to give her clients' parents credit for being on the ball and caring about their kids—or at least about their kids' entrance to a top college.

As if Nick had been reading her mind, he said, "Think about it: The parents at my school are the anti-Hellis; they'd be falling all over you with gratitude."

"Hmm, that is tempting," she said, and Nick lit up. "Okay, calm down. I am considering it. But please lay off the pressure for now."

Nick obliged, and they spent the rest of the ride riffing on the ads plastered across the subway car. Emma did her best Dr. Zizmor, lending the infamous dermatologist a nasally whine while raving about miracle cures for bunions. Nick explained how he'd managed to earn an associate's degree online, all while working full-time and raising three kids; "now I'm a proud medical assistant!" he beamed. The two of them tested out new taglines to frighten people away from obesity-causing soft drinks: "Soda: 9/11 in a bottle," Emma said, and Nick grimaced. "Ingredients: sugar, carbonation, death," he tried. In this way they entertained themselves, nearly missing their stop.

Emma and Nick found their friends in Fairway's juice aisle, where Eli was trying to persuade Annie to step away from the packages of lemonade powder.

"Ooh, Emma's here, she'll understand," she said. "Remember Country Time from when we were kids? You'd pour the powder in your mouth, add water, shake it all up, and then bam, instant lemonade! They've got the gourmet kind here."

"Gourmet powdered drink?" Eli said. "For some reason I'm skeptical."

"I always preferred the chocolate milk version," Emma said.

"Right," said Annie, "with milk and a squirt of Hershey's! I bet they have that, too."

So while Eli and Nick picked out practical picnic supplies— bread, cheese, meat (portobellos for Nick)—Annie supplemented the cart with items chosen for nostalgia's sake: an organic take on Cheez Whiz and a jar of half-sour pickles. Eli paid for the whole haul despite protests from Nick and Emma, and the quartet carried their bounty to the nearby riverside park. Emma stretched out on the blanket, and happily took in her surroundings: the sparkling bay beyond the pier, the sun bleeding soft, peachy streaks into the horizon, and Annie performing somersaults around their blanket. The breeze tickled Emma's skin as she listened to the lazy lapping of water against the rocks.

Annie stopped tumbling to catch her breath. "Not exactly Tompkins Square Park, right? No junkies or crusty kids or crazies. It's like we're on the other side of the world."

"I guess," said Eli, "except for the Statue of Liberty staring us in the face."

"Good point," said Emma, who'd been thinking the same thing as Annie.

Eli produced nips of bourbon. "Here's to you guys for finding a new home—and for finally leaving us alone in our place." On three, they threw back their shots.

"I'm gonna miss you guys as roomies," Annie said.

They ate and drank as the light drained from the sky. Nick pulled Emma toward him, pointed at Lady Liberty's twinkling torch, and whispered in her ear, "Give me your tired, your poor, your huddled masses yearning to breathe free, the wretched refuse of your teeming shore. Send these, the homeless, tempest-tost to me. I lift my lamp beside the golden door." Emma thought about her journey with Nick and their impending emigration from Manhattan to Brooklyn. They'd pushed their move back a few days, so they could go in ahead of time to paint, and then have a whole weekend to unpack. One week from today, they'd both cut out of work early to meet up with the movers, and then finally arrive at their home. Tired and tempest-tost indeed.

While the rest of them topped their crackers with the Gruyère they'd picked out with the help of the store's *fromager*, Annie insisted on reviving the art of Cheez Whiz towers from their youth. "That is revolting," said Eli. "I hope you're not going to eat it."

"Of course I am," she said. "Ems, too."

"Speak for yourself. Jeez, you're good at that."

"How many coils you pile up is how many boyfriends you'll have, remember?"

Annie was up to at least fifteen coils. "Looks like we've got a real player on our hands, folks," said Eli, who then knocked down the tower with his finger.

"Hey!"

"Just preventing you from getting too cocky. Remember the Tower of Babel?"

"So does that make you God?" Nick asked Eli. Annie guffawed and went for Eli's fingers, licking them clean of Cheez Whiz.

Next up were the lemonade shake-ups. Emma went first—shaking her head like crazy, she was transported back to her childhood kitchen. The first time she and Annie had orchestrated a coed hangout involved inviting boys over for lemonade shake-ups; Emma's first kiss was with Jonathan Siegel, fizzy-headed and dusted with sweet-and-sour powder. Max had come home and, as uptight back then as he still was now, insisted they clean up immediately. After that, he'd asked their mom to buy actual lemonade, instead of the mix.

"Me next!" Annie opened wide as Eli shook the powder onto her tongue and added water. She spun around, tossing her head, then slowed to an unsteady stop. Her eyes went wide and she bolted to the park's edge, where she leaned over the fence. When Emma ran over, her friend was hurling the contents of her stomach into the river. Emma rubbed her back and focused on the horizon, trying not to look at the foamy vomit polluting the water.

"I guess I'm a little old for the lemonade shake-up," Annie moaned. The color had faded from her cheeks, like a reverse sunset.

"Annie, have you seen a doctor yet? You seem really sick."

"I'm sure it's just a bug. It needs a few days to work its way out of my system."

"But you've been home almost a week." Emma couldn't believe how nonchalant Annie was; what if some parasitic worm was eating up her intestines, killing her from the inside out? Emma pushed the thought from her head. "Promise me you'll see a doctor."

"Fine."

When they returned to the blanket, Nick was stuttering and red, and Emma soon realized why: Eli was drilling him about the budget of the school's new tutoring program.

"You know," said Eli, "my company has been looking into funding charitable ventures. The shareholders want us to seem more humane." Emma saw Nick bristle and then try to hide it. "We could probably throw at least ten grand your way."

"Ten grand would be great."

"I bet you'd make it count more than our corporate team. They blow that kind of money on a couple of boozy lunches at Le Cirque." Eli slapped Nick on the back, and Emma could see him battling between wanting to reject Eli's offer and realizing how much good ten thousand dollars could do for a program with a budget of a tenth of that.

"Maybe that could pay for Emma's consulting stipend," said Annie.

"So does Annie get a recruiting fee if I join up?" Emma asked. "Or did you bribe her, Nick, to help convince me?"

"I think Emma would prefer we pick another topic of conversation," Nick said, squeezing her arm. "Like politics, or religion, or the weather."

"Speaking of which, it's getting chilly." Emma pulled her cardigan closed, shivering. It was now nearly dark and the wind was picking up. They'd been pushing it to picnic that evening, when summer was already long gone and fall was in full swing. It always made Emma sort of sentimental, the shifting of seasons. "Should we ship out?"

They gathered up their garbage, and Emma pulled Annie in for a good-bye hug. "Make that doctor's appointment, okay? I mean it." Annie nodded.

"We're changing the locks," said Eli. "Good luck squatting at your new place."

"Very funny," Emma said. "See you in a couple hours."

Emma and Nick left to size up their future home, though Emma knew the exercise was pointless—it would be a while before they could afford any new furniture (and they certainly wouldn't be buying anything used, considering the recent bedbug scare). They'd be moving with what they had, working to make it fit however they could. Still, there was something soothing about mapping their new home with numbers and measurements. It was a balm to imagine they could quantitatively capture what it all might mean.

Chapter 23

Moving day was upon them in a blink. Rather than operating on her usual autopilot, Emma had spent the week devoting as much thought to each of her clients as she had to Sophia. In addition to assigning the required test-taking drills, she'd conducted interviews with them that were different from the usual mock admission interrogations inviting them to humble-brag about their accomplishments and goals; now, Emma asked them to picture a world without the pressures of college or parents and to consider what they truly enjoyed. Her questions sounded corny but yielded results: *What would you do with a free hour, endless money, and no responsibilities?* Some kids looked at her blankly, like the scenario was terrifying, maybe even impossible, to imagine. But it was a start—Isaac Goldstein opened up about his obsession with video-game art, and Emma was able to direct him to animation programs at the Museum of Fine Arts in Boston and R.I.T. upstate. Paul Spencer admitted he'd had a panic attack taking a practice PSAT (and he was only a freshman), so Emma introduced him to Hampshire and other schools that didn't look at test scores or give grades; the look of relief on his face was reward enough.

Emma realized how much more satisfying than usual her work felt, and that perhaps this was her own answer to the kinds of questions she was asking her clients. She flashed on Lily Bart, and how having to stoop to work as a hat maker had horrified the heroine; whereas once Emma had sympathized with Lily's despair, it now struck her as sad. Because being useful—whether by making hats or helping kids figure out what they really wanted to do—seemed like the simplest, most decent way to feel fulfilled. Between clients, the idea of working with Nick's school kept popping back into her head.

As gratifying as the workweek had been, it left Emma exhausted for the move. She'd anticipated an emotional day. But as the movers arrived and transferred all the boxes from Annie and Eli's storage space to the truck, and then she and Nick hopped aboard, Emma felt like a zombie. As soon as the vehicle began its rumbling, she drifted off to sleep. She slept hard, nestled among their belongings, not stirring as they rode downtown and over the Manhattan Bridge then onto the BQE, or even as they bumped across the cobblestone streets of Red Hook. Nick had to nudge her awake upon arrival. It was through a drowsy fog that Emma observed the two tall men empty the truck and then stack, floor to ceiling into the small space of their new home, her and Nick's whole lives.

Emma's usual approach was to unpack immediately, as she always did within five minutes of returning home from vacation or the Laundromat. But in this case the lure of inertia after a long day—and a very long week—felt too strong to overcome. Plus she was starving. Nick offered to get a pizza, and when he returned with a large, there was a FedEx carton perched upon the box—a care package from Emma's parents, no doubt. Emma's annoyance gave way to gratefulness when she discovered the contents: a huge array of paper goods, plates and bowls and cups, plus plastic utensils, meaning they wouldn't have to dig out the boxes labeled *Kitchen* in order to eat dinner.

Nick held up a plate. "This looks just like Annie's china pattern, doesn't it?"

Emma would've questioned why Nick had noticed their friends' china pattern, but she was distracted by the fact that he was right—the swirls of baby-blue flowers around the paper plate's rim made it look like a knockoff of Annie's new dishware. Emma pulled out the card: *Until we get you the real thing someday, enjoy and happy housewarming! Love, Mom and Dad.* Again, the annoyance seeped back— must her parents' housewarming gift also include a dig at the fact that Emma wasn't yet married? She tucked the note away without showing Nick.

The next day, Skyping with her parents, Emma again found herself cycling between those two emotions: grateful as her father described his recent Spanish exchange with Sophia and how she was teaching him about *el arte* and he was teaching her about Madrid's various neighborhoods, then annoyed as he poked fun at Emma for still being surrounded by boxes; grateful when her mother praised their choice of neighborhood (she'd apparently been researching Red Hook online), then annoyed when she said that working with Nick's school sounded "cute" (although, Emma admitted to herself, she'd originally thought the same thing). Emma cut the conversation short, claiming she had to go unpack; but as soon as they signed off she felt guilty for having been so abrupt. She headed out on a walk to make herself feel better, leaving the boxes untouched.

So Emma was dismayed, come Sunday night, to realize that she and Nick had spent the entire weekend eating takeout on flower-rimmed paper plates, admiring their new views of picturesque brick buildings, giddily referring to *"our* apartment" (Emma was more interested than Nick in this last activity), and talking about but not actually doing any unpacking. As a result, on Monday morning Emma found herself yelling, "Shit, shit, shit!" while frantically searching for something, anything, decent to wear to work. In a suitcase's side pocket she eventually located a frumpy maxi-dress she'd been meaning to toss for years. She also happened upon her jewelry box and, while shoving down a slice of leftover pizza, dumped it out onto the kitchen counter. The contents went careening across the counter—the charm bracelet Nick had been adding to for years, a bunch of costume necklaces, and a dozen pairs of studs. Emma grabbed a string of faux-pearls, one of the only items not tangled up with other pieces, and then inexpertly twisted her wet hair into a clip. Forgoing coffee to save time,

Emma arrived at work disheveled and un-caffeinated—and, for the first time ever in her year-plus at *1, 2, 3 . . . Ivies!*, late.

In retrospect, it was hard to understand how little Nick had paid attention to the news that week. But at the time, he was plenty preoccupied: by the new apartment that they had yet to settle into, by the upheaval of trying to launch an after-school program, and by the court date with Luis, which was scheduled for that Thursday, October 25. Nick had planned on reviewing the paperwork for their case against the landlord, but every time he approached the accordion folder that Emma had smartly kept separate during the move, his stomach seized. The thought of seeing Luis again in the flesh—those beady eyes, that stupid soul patch—filled Nick with dread. And now that he and Emma had moved on, literally to another apartment, Nick wished they could move on from this mess, too—accept their losses and leave the rest in the past. But Emma was adamant about recouping what was rightfully theirs; and though Nick wished he could've given her a good-luck kiss and sent her off to court solo, he knew that opting out would result in worse repercussions to his relationship than was worth it. So for better or, as Nick suspected, for worse, they were in this together.

He planned his Thursday school day according to how anxious and distracted he knew he would be; instead of teaching, he kept the kids busy with worksheets and video clips. He'd worn a suit and tie, but the outfit was itchy and constricting, making him fidget and sweat. More than one student asked him if he was okay.

Nick didn't realize quite how resentful he'd been feeling toward Emma for spearheading this ordeal until he met her at the courthouse, where she greeted him with a granola bar and he felt his anger recede. "You knew I'd be too nervous for lunch," he said, gratefully tearing into the snack. It calmed his stomach, both the sustenance and the reminder that his girlfriend understood him so well.

Luckily their case was number two out of nearly fifty on the docket, so when Luis still hadn't appeared halfway through roll call, Nick let himself hope that he would arrive too late to testify. But after the announcement of two separate cases against one management company and the calling of a plaintiff and defendant who shared the same unusual last name—Nick didn't want to look to see if they appeared related—Luis showed up, sauntering up the aisle to find a seat. Even from half a room away, Nick could feel the landlord's eyes like lasers through his back. His hands grew clammy and, as if sensing this, Emma reached for one; her cool grasp soothed him.

They had to sit through the first case as observers. It involved a landlord claiming his tenant had broken and/or stolen his refrigerator, and the tenant countering that the fridge had been broken to begin with, and that since the landlord had refused to replace it when it started "stinking to high hell and leaking like a nursing mom's ti—" (here the judge had cut her off), she'd tossed the thing. Nick felt bad for both parties and mostly tried to tune them out, but a glance at Emma revealed she was rapt. They didn't learn the verdict—judgments got mailed out—but it was pretty clear the tenant had won. When the judge, a middle-aged woman with dyed red hair and a thick Queens accent, asked the landlord how old the fridge was, and he answered twelve years, she gave him a withering look and then launched into a lecture about how everyone knows the shelf life of a refrigerator is seven years (Nick didn't know this), and that no decent homeowner should expect to keep one humming along for so long. Case closed.

Nick was trembling as the judge called them to the stand. Luis stood inches away, and Nick smelled his musky cologne. "So what's your story?" she asked. "Not another dud appliance, I hope."

Mercifully Emma did most of the talking, laying out a succinct version of the events that had transpired between them and Luis, the landlord shaking his head and laughing under his breath throughout. When it was Luis's turn to speak, Nick was surprised at how similar his account was to Emma's (in Nick's mind the landlord had morphed into one of those street bums who twitchily spurts out nonsense); only in Luis's version Nick and Emma were the villains, expecting him to spend a fortune to get rid of harmless little bugs, acting too fancy for a reasonable solution like foggers, and turning their noses up at his floors as if their feet were too good to walk on them. Nick could tell Emma was relishing the drama—her eyes went wide when Luis mixed his metaphors—but all this rehashing of their trauma sickened Nick. Luis talked about how "man to man, me and Nick had an understanding" and how Emma "was a trickster with a capital T." Emma was likely thinking Luis's sexism would tip the judge in their favor, but Nick simply wanted it to be over. When the judge asked Luis to confirm whether this—she pointed—was his signature on the lease, which stipulated that he would pay for his tenants to redo the floors, he claimed he'd been forced into it. "As in physically forced, like with a gun to your head?" the judge asked, wearing a wry grimace. Luis seethed. For another half hour they rehashed the last month's events, point by painstaking point, the judge interrupting the he-said, they-said with her sassy commentary. In the end, Nick was pretty sure they'd prevailed, although he didn't feel very triumphant.

Out in the hallway Luis appeared as if from a shadow. He stalked up to Nick. Nick tried to retreat but ended up trapped against a wall. "You know this is fucking bullshit," he whispered. Nick's eyes darted around in search of a court officer, but none was near; plus, Luis had a smile on his face that might've looked friendly from afar. "Buddy, if you win this case, I'll never pay. I'll appeal your ass, I'll sue you, I'll do whatever it takes to wear you down and make your life miserable. You and your stupid girlfriend will be so sorry you ever messed with me."

"All right, enough. Let's go." Emma stepped between them and tugged at Nick's sleeve. He found it hard to pick up his feet.

"What a crock of B.S.," she said on the walk downstairs. "He knows he lost, so clearly he's feeling helpless and angry. But he's so obviously all talk. Wanna get a drink and take our minds off all of this?"

No, Nick didn't want to get a drink. He didn't even want to open his mouth to say so. Emma was doing her best—she'd taken charge, whisking them into the stairwell so they wouldn't have to wait for the elevator with Luis, and then rubbed Nick's back in a way that usually eased his tension—but Nick didn't want a drink. He wanted Luis out of his life, and to live somewhere that wasn't covered in boxes. He wanted to be back in his old apartment, alone, playing video games. "I'm gonna take a walk," he mumbled, and took off, pretending he didn't hear Emma ask after him whether she should wait or go.

Nick had made the Herculean effort to hook up the TV and then clear off a small area of the couch so that he could assume his Friday post-school position of half conking out and channel surfing. He flipped past the BBC version of *Pride and Prejudice,* one of Emma's favorites, wishing the cable was set up so he could DVR it for her. Nick thought about how strangely all over the place he'd been feeling. Last night after the run-in with Luis, he'd retreated to a bar and played round after round of pinball, letting the flashing lights and the balls' movements lull him into a stupor. When he'd finally snapped out of it, it was much too late for a school night. And although hours had passed, he'd still dreaded going home to Emma, facing her questions and looks of concern. And yet, after several minutes of jiggling his key in the lock he still wasn't used to, Nick had realized what a comfort it was to return to his girlfriend. She'd already been asleep, curled up on top of the covers, and when he'd climbed into bed beside her, her warm body instinctually found its way to his. She smelled exactly like herself, and their bodies fit together just so. Nick thought of this now and, aware of Emma's absence on the couch, threw a blanket over his legs. He flipped to another channel. The screen flashed onto what looked to be *The Perfect Storm,* a perfectly decent movie for his end-of-the-workweek ritual. Just as he tossed aside the remote, his cell phone rang: Carl's dopey mug accosted his screen.

"So sorry to interrupt your daily masturbation hour," Carl began, "but I just got set free from an epic meeting with our beloved principal. The one time I dared glance at my phone she shot me that ice queen death glare. It was brutal."

"Sounds like a real tragedy." Nick felt impatient. "So, to what do I owe this call?"

"Lara wants to finalize the budget. Is it true your moneybags friend is going to bankroll the tutoring deal? And is Emma still considering gracing us with her presence? Lara wants a résumé and all that; it's just for show, of course—she likes to pretend well-qualified candidates are beating down her door dying to help our crappily educated kids get into good middle schools, all for a grand jackpot of twenty-five bucks an hour."

"Nice attitude for a school leader." Nick could hear Carl snapping his gum. "I'll know everything by Monday." He felt a twinge about following up with Eli on his offer.

"Thattaboy. See ya, dude." He'd hung up before Nick could say bye. Nick turned back to the TV. Again it was the storm images, but when he realized it wasn't a movie but the news—*boring*—he flipped it off and called Emma.

"Hey, so according to Carl, you have to officially apply for the tutoring position."

"Ah, so you're calling to say you're volunteering to ghostwrite my cover letter?"

"If that's what it takes to get you, then of course."

"Although first I should probably have a serious sit-down with Carl. I'd like some answers, like, what'll be the criteria to recruit kids? And which pedagogy will we use to teach essay writing and test prep? How about textbooks, and parental involvement? Is there a snack budget? And will there be student liaisons at the target middle schools?"

"Carl would adore this conversation. We'll get it on his schedule— a two-hour window, minimum. So does that mean you're really up for the gig?"

"Hm. Hey, have you heard about this storm they're predicting for the weekend?"

"Are you purposely changing the subject to the weather?"

"Well, yeah, but—"

"Good-bye, Ems. I have very important Friday afternoon relaxing to attend to."

Chapter 24

Emma started to freak out in the bottled water aisle, where the shelves were so deserted it didn't even look like a supermarket. "What if this storm is actually a big deal?" she said to Nick.

"Oh, come on." He tossed a green pepper into their cart. Most of their items were perishable, meaning they'd quickly rot if the power went out. Emma thought of the court battle over the broken refrigerator, which now seemed like an omen. "Remember last year for Hurricane Irene? Everyone freaked out and bought flashlights and first aid kits and weeks' worth of canned goods, and then it rained for, like, an hour."

That was true, and Emma was happy to latch onto the comforting comparison. Plus, Nick was usually the cautious, overprepared one, so if he wasn't worried, then she probably shouldn't be, either. "Remember that little twig they kept showing on TV?" she said, more breezily than she felt. The local news, seemingly desperate for footage of Irene, had broadcast a loop of the so-called damage, and Emma and Nick had laughed their heads off at the repeated appearances of one twig rolling down a windy avenue.

"See? Exactly." Although as Nick threw a pint of mint ice cream into their cart, Emma made a mental note to eat it within the next day.

"I'm going to get some supplies just in case." She added cans of soup and beans and fruit to their haul, plus shelf-stable milk that

Nick claimed he wouldn't go near even in case of apocalypse. Emma wanted candles, too, but Fairway was sold out, along with batteries. The lines for the registers wrapped all the way around the store.

"Should we abandon ship and just eat out?" Nick said. They'd come in for dinner ingredients—Emma couldn't put up with any more takeout—although seeing all the panicky people clutching at their disaster supplies, her appetite had been replaced with a case of nerves.

"Let's split up our cart so we can both stand in '15 items or less.'"

"Fewer," said Nick. "And I really think we should leave."

"What? Oh, thanks, smarty-pants. What do you think'll be more useful during a hurricane, proper grammar or a cabinet full of canned food?" She divided the groceries between them, thinking they still needed to find somewhere to buy bottled water, then ducked over to the express line and stuck out her tongue at Nick.

Emma slept poorly that night. She dreamed of running from a tidal wave, surrounded by her clients and their panicked parents, plus her niece and nephew. Emma ran and ran, until it suddenly occurred to her to wonder where Nick was. Had he tripped and fallen? Was he okay? Eventually she reached a ship, which she somehow knew was Noah's ark. But when she tried to board, she was denied entry: Couples only, someone said, and it was a moment before she realized that that someone was Luis, apparently the ark's bouncer. As others raced past her to embark, she was trampled.

Emma bolted awake—it was early morning. She'd sweated through her T-shirt. Nick's breath was even against her cheek— there he was, safe beside her in bed, not caught up in some tsunami— but still Emma couldn't calm down. She got up and flipped on the news. The mayor and the governor were giving a joint press conference, warning of the severity of the coming storm—the winds could hit ninety miles per hour, the mayor said, and the water surge might reach twenty feet, the governor added. Schools would be closed tomorrow, said the mayor, and subways would shut down this evening, added the governor. It was like a battle of who could make the most shocking statement. The city's flood zone map appeared on-screen, and Emma searched for her new neighborhood among the color-coded sections. There it was, smack in the middle of the red, like it was bleeding: Zone One.

But when Nick awoke, he didn't want to evacuate. He was convinced that once again the politicians were overreacting and the media was feeding the hype in an effort to boost ratings. "Anyway, it'll be fun to be all cooped up inside in the rain," he said. "There'll be nothing to do, so we can finally unpack. Plus, where would we even go?"

"Gen's place up in Harlem is outside the flood zones."

Nick looked outraged. "You mean her five-hundred-square-foot pen that she shares with three roommates?"

"Good point. Or Annie and Eli's. They're in Zone Five, which is supposed to be much safer than our Zone One."

"Zones? So you know all the lingo now? What is this, *The Hunger Games*?"

"That's districts." Emma's voice was sober; it seemed easier to feel upset about botched *Hunger Games* terminology than about the possible coming mayhem.

"Em, I know you're scared, but I really don't want to go lean on Annie and Eli's hospitality again. We did it for weeks and now we finally have a home of our own. Come on, we survived apartment hunting in New York City; we can survive anything." As Nick pulled her into his arms, Emma considered whether she would evacuate without him.

She spent most of the day staring out the window—the air was heavy, so that the tree branches seemed to be straining against it, their leaves hissing with effort. The birds sounded louder than usual, like they were issuing warnings. Emma was on and off the phone with Annie, who was begging her to come stay with them. "Seriously, Ems, your apartment is, like, ground zero."

"Please don't say 'ground zero.' "

"You know what I mean. It's supposed to be a total shit show. Plus, Monday's a full moon. The tides are going to be wacky."

When Annie started in on her horoscope, Emma tuned her out in favor of the mute TV; President Obama was standing at a podium as a banner of text flashed across the bottom of the screen: *Emergency declared in the state of New York.* Nick, meanwhile, was sprawled out on the couch devouring a can of corn, which he must've pulled from their disaster supply; Emma burned with fury. Annie was still talking: "Our apartment has extra-thick storm-proof windows, plus we're on the twenty-sixth floor—as in, twenty-five floors higher than you guys. I bought pretty much all of Whole Foods, including rum and grenadine so we can make Hurricanes."

The reminder that they were on the ground floor, plus the sight of Nick lying about eating his way through their storm food, was the breaking point for Emma. "All right, I'll come," she told Annie. She found her overnight bag and called out, "Nick, I'm going to Annie's whether or not you come with—although I hope you will." No response.

An hour before the subways were set to shut down, Nick was still planted on the couch watching the news. "Holy shit," he said, turning up the volume, "IKEA's closing until at least Wednesday." At which point he got up and began packing, too. Emma would make fun of this comment for the rest of the week—the fact that it wasn't the president's declaration of emergency or the mayor's call for mandatory evacuation, but IKEA's closure that finally convinced Nick to haul out. But Emma suspected it was really the fact that she'd be leaving; Nick had put on a good front, but he, too, was scared.

So in what must've been one of the last rides before the mammoth MTA machine cranked all of its trains to a halt, Emma, Nick, and dozens of other Zone One residents boarded the F train headed to Manhattan. One guy had a boom box and was blasting Bob Dylan's "Hurricane." Unusually for the train, no one gave him dirty looks or shouted to shut the damn thing off. Several people actually sang along—Emma mouthed the lyrics without quite realizing she was doing so—and two kids got up and began that subway-specific dance genre of pole swinging and fancy footwork in the aisle. Despite the song's ominous melody, and the fact that the train was filled with people in practical clothes toting backpacks and duffel bags, rather than the usual fashion show of the Manhattan-bound F, it was hard to remember this wasn't just any New York moment, everyone nodding along to the same song. One of the dancers performed a one-armed pull-up using the bar directly over Emma's seat, and she dropped a dollar in his hat.

"Hey, guys." Eli greeted them at the door. "Be prepared: There's nothing like an impending storm to whip Annie up into a party-planning frenzy."

"What he means is, welcome to our Hurricane Sandy bash!" Annie spun around to model her dress, which featured Dorothy and the rest of the cast of *The Wizard of Oz* being lifted away in a tornado. "I know it's the wrong natural disaster, but it's all I had."

"Shoot, I left my flood-themed ball gown at home," Emma said.

"And my blizzard bow tie is still at the cleaners," said Nick, kissing Annie hello.

"Damn it, guys, you're always letting me down." Annie ushered them inside. "Anyway, I got *The Ice Storm* plus *Twister*, both the movie and game. And I made a hurricane!" No wonder "Blowin' in the Wind" was playing; Annie usually couldn't stand Bob Dylan.

Also weird was the thought of playing Twister as a foursome, especially if they were going to see a movie about swingers and key parties. Emma glanced at Nick, who met her gaze with a your-friend-is-batshit look. "You mentioned drinks?" he said to Eli.

"Follow me, my man," said Eli.

Although Nick probably wouldn't have wanted her to, as soon as he and Eli were out of earshot, Emma couldn't help dishing to Annie about their dramatic night in court. Which is why, when the guys returned from the kitchen, they found the girls hysterical over Emma's terrible impression of Luis trying not to lose his temper before the judge.

"Let's just hope the judge found him as laughable as we did," Nick said, handing Emma a cherry-red drink.

"It's so obvious you'll win," said Annie. "How about I throw you a victory party? I could serve appetizers on little scales, you know, like the scales of justice."

"Yep," said Nick. "And we could get a piñata that looked like

Luis and wear blindfolds like Lady Justice and take turns hitting at it. We'd have to fill his head with some really shitty candy. Or better yet, just hot air."

Annie pursed her lips, like maybe this didn't sound like the best idea. After a moment she seemed to realize he was kidding. *"You're* full of hot air."

Emma kissed Nick's cheek. "Thanks for putting up with my need for revenge."

After the entirety of *Twister*, the movie, and two Hurricane cocktails apiece, the rain still hadn't started, but the wind had grown powerful. Emma thought of Genevieve, who, despite being in a supposedly safe area of the city, might've been all by herself. She texted her: *Are you OK? Wanna come hunker down with us at Annie's?*

Gen texted back: *Thx I'm good. Watching My-so-called-life marathon, then hitting the sack. XO.* That sounded lovely to Emma, but still she hoped Gen's roommates weren't all off at their boyfriends' places.

"This storm better not be a big letdown," said Annie. "Ems, remember our adventure during Hurricane Bob?"

"You mean, sleeping on smelly cots and eating stale bologna sandwiches? Quite an adventure." Two decades later, the debacle was still branded in Emma's memory.

"Yeah, and my mom went up to the cook and asked if they had anything without pig products, remember? He thought she was totally nutso."

"To be fair, we were sharing a shelter with all those patients from the local mental hospital. Your mom could've been one of them." Emma explained to Nick: "The summer before fourth grade, or maybe fifth, Mrs. Blum took us on a trip to Plimoth Plantation."

"For some reason," Annie said, "it's pretty much a requirement for kids who grow up in the Northeast to go witness pilgrims make artisanal pots and churn butter and stuff."

"Very Brooklyn Flea Market," said Eli. "The original hipsters, these ten-year-old girls."

"Anyway," said Annie, "then Hurricane Bob hit, and the B and B where we were staying had to be evacuated. It was too dangerous to drive home, so we were shipped over to this awful shelter. This one creepy old dude kept asking if we needed private tutoring since we were probably missing school. I mean, it was the middle of August."

"God, I had nightmares about that guy for weeks afterward," said Emma.

"What a blast we had. It was all-you-could-drink soda—someone had donated, like, a warehouse full of Coke—and we got to stay up until midnight."

"Yeah, because the people all around us were crying and moaning in their sleep. It was not a blast." Emma remembered how, when they were finally cleared to leave, Annie and her mom had spent the whole drive home recounting all of the colorful details of the weekend, while she'd sat in the backseat quietly trying not to throw up. Back home, when Emma had complained that they'd never gotten to see the pilgrim village, her mother had responded, "Yeah, but you got something even better—a real adventure. And now you're a hurricane expert!" It was exciting to be called an expert in anything by her mom, but Emma had wanted some comfort after the trip's trauma. And in the coming weeks, when she'd woken up at all hours from nightmares of howling wind through her windows, she'd felt too ashamed to seek out her mom. In the two decades since, Emma had had several opportunities to return to Cape Cod, but she'd always made excuses not to.

"We must've filled out three full books of Mad Libs in that shelter," Annie said.

"You two haven't really matured much since then, huh?" said Eli. "Emma, Annie told me you helped her write her wedding vows, Mad Libs–style."

Emma was thankful for the change of subject. "Well, in the end Annie pulled through like a champ, no Mad Libs needed."

"Pretty much anything great I've done is because of Ems," said Annie. "I never thanked you for that poem, by the way." Right, the poem she'd recited at her ceremony.

"Emma wrote that?" Eli asked.

"No, dummy. Edith Wharton, whom Ems worships. It's, like, her favorite poem."

"You didn't tell me that," Eli said.

"Look, if it was wedding-appropriate to recite a commercial jingle, I would've been golden. But love poems? No way. So it's a good thing I have a bestie with such sophisticated sensibilities to help me out in a time of need." This was the reason Emma had put up with Annie for so many years; even when she pulled a stunt like stealing the poem Emma would've liked to recite one day at her own wedding, she always apologized with grace and panache, making Emma feel like the world's best person.

"I was happy to help." And just like that, Emma revised her memory of standing by as maid of honor fuming to standing by feeling thrilled for her friend. "More drinks?"

"I'll help you," Annie said. In the kitchen she measured out the juices and grenadine into four glasses, and then Emma began splashing them with rum. When she reached the fourth glass, Annie held a hand over it. Emma gave her a puzzled look.

"So I went to the doctor like you insisted," Annie said, her eyes going glassy with tears, and Emma knew right away what was coming. Her stomach was already swishy with drink and nerves about the storm, but the understanding of what was about to be revealed hit Emma's gut like a whirlpool. "I'm pregnant."

Emma clutched at Annie and hooked her chin over her friend's shoulder. It was a gut reaction that seemed appropriate no matter what Annie's state of mind. Plus, it conveniently hid Emma's panic. Her mind hummed in shock, and whatever expression she wore, she was sure she wouldn't have been able to mask it.

Emma felt Annie trembling against her. What was her friend thinking? she wondered. They'd never even talked about pregnancy, motherhood, the whole shebang—at least, not in any serious way. She considered how impossible it was that Annie's stomach, pressed against her own, was now home to a tiny growing creature, a speck of a future person now literally coming between them; the last thought barely flickered in her consciousness before Emma banished it. Of course she'd already partly known, and so had Annie—Annie, who was usually a total hypochondriac, running to the doctor at the slightest sign of a cough, and who'd been so flippant about her imagined African parasite. Annie, who was a pro at anything she put her mind to, in this case denial.

"I'm so sorry, Ems." Annie was now crying.

"*Sorry?* What do you mean, sorry?"

"Sorry I didn't tell you before. I was so scared, and . . . I don't know."

"Shh." Emma stroked her friend's curls. "So was this, um, planned?"

Annie shrugged. "Eli was pushing for it even before we got married, and I knew it took my mom more than a year to get pregnant with me. So I figured it wouldn't happen right away. I mean, we were sleeping in tents in Africa, un-showered, and wearing pleated khakis, for God's sake—we only had sex, like, twice." She nuzzled her head back into Emma's neck. "Ems, I'm not ready for this. I'm completely terrified."

"Hey, I'm sure everyone's scared when they first get pregnant. You'll be a great mom." She stared at Annie's stomach; the Tin Man smiled stupidly back at her. Together she and Annie had spent the better part of two decades doing crunches and planks and a hundred other trendy workouts with the goal of attaining flat abs; now Annie's stomach would go a different direction, growing and distending to create new life.

"Please don't tell Nick, okay? Eli doesn't know I'm telling you. He wants to wait until twelve weeks to share the news, but I can't keep a secret from you or my mom."

"Of course." Emma framed Annie's face with her hands. "And listen, as soon as you pop that thing out, we'll get the guys to babysit and you and I will go out on the town for a big old glass of wine, same as always."

Emma barely paid attention to *The Ice Storm*. She couldn't help thinking how her friendship with Annie was now stamped with an expiration date. They'd still hang out once Annie became a mom, but it wouldn't be at all the same.

By midnight the rain had started up, and Eli suggested they strap on boots and go for a walk. "We might be stuck inside for who knows how long." Emma wasn't in the mood, so she stayed behind, carrying Annie's laptop into the guest room. Sprawled out on the bed, she was intent on visiting celebrity gossip sites and turning off her brain.

Emma quickly tired of the vapid news bytes, and logged onto her e-mail. Her brother had written detailing the predicted storm damage in her neighborhood and asking if she was okay and whether she'd evacuated; Emma replied that she and Nick were safe and bunking at Annie's. She jotted off a similar note to her parents. In her work in-box, among the Helli cancelations, Emma was surprised to see a message from Dylan York; after he'd fled in fury from her office the previous week she'd assumed she'd never hear from him again. The subject line was *Suck it!* and the e-mail's body featured only a photo of Dylan's fist, middle finger raised, in front of an application to what Emma assumed was Columbia. "Oy vey." She clicked Delete. A note from Sophia invited Emma and her "beau" to come stay with her on higher ground for the hurricane; also, she wrote, she was halfway through her application to the University of Madrid program, Emma's dad was hilarious, and she was looking forward to meeting him in person. Emma considered replying that she was cabbing up to Sophia's place stat, but then she reminded herself that the girl was a client, not a friend.

What happened next was one of those things that seemed insignificant at the time, almost laughably so in retrospect. Yet, that small moment, a single click, would set in motion a series of revelations, which would each etch themselves permanently into Emma's mind. It must have been a preference setting, the cartoon red flag that popped up on Annie's computer dashboard. Emma didn't think of herself as a snoop. When she'd heard stories of girls ransacking boyfriends' pants pockets or browser histories, she'd always felt shocked and a little disgusted, like where was the trust, and why would you want to expose yourself to every little thing about your partner anyway? But when the flag began waving and then flashing from the bottom of the screen, Emma couldn't help but click. Up sprang Annie's e-mail, the first subject line practically shouting: *We're pregnant!!!* The message was to Annie's mother. With little hesitation, Emma opened it.

Hey, Mom . . . I mean, Grandma (!): It's true! Eli, the
little rascal, knocked me up on our honeymoon and we
could not be more THRILLED that we're gonna become
Mommy and Daddy! YAY!!! Love you and talk soon! Hi
to Dad! —A.

Emma was paralyzed. The exclamation points danced before
her eyes. Maybe Annie was playing up her excitement for her
mom's benefit. Even still, there was no denying that Annie had
been faking it earlier, putting on an act about how distressed she
was just to make Emma feel better, her poor, pathetic, unmarried
and childless friend. Emma wanted to crumple up from sadness.
In their decades of friendship, she'd never known her best friend
to lie to her. Also she was furious. How childish for Annie to pull
this kind of stunt—and if it hadn't been for Emma, she never
would've gone to the doctor in the first place! If she couldn't even
take care of herself, how was she going to care for an infant? Sure,
she could throw some brilliant baby shower with the perfect appetizers and the best party games, but what about when it came to
actually bearing responsibility for a human life? The diaper changing and the middle-of-the-night feedings? Knowing Annie, she'd
probably just farm it all out to some high-end nanny—probably a
couple of them—and of course she could, thanks to Eli's bottomless bank account.

Emma was still stewing in a swamp of anger and self-pity when
she heard the faint chime of a text on Nick's phone—he must've
forgotten it, or maybe he'd left it behind, hoping to preserve its
battery life. Thinking back on the moment, Emma wasn't clear
about her state of mind or motivations: Had she been worried
about the hurricane and the possibility of an emergency, of someone needing to get in touch? Or, reeling with hurt and mistrust
over Annie's e-mail, did she feel entitled to invade her boyfriend's
privacy, to check up on his loyalty, too? Or, had she simply *not* been
thinking and acted on impulse? It was a hard thing to piece together and pinpoint in retrospect. In any case, in fewer than ten
seconds Emma had swiped open Nick's phone and read the text: *I*

hope you & Emma are OK. I'm scared up here. Wish I had company ;)
The sender tag read, *Genevieve.*

Emma stared in a stupor, blinking at the screen. After a while
the message became gibberish, a pile-up of letters in haphazard
order, plus that moronic emoji. She didn't even know Nick had
Gen's number.

After one minute or ten, it occurred to Emma to scroll up. She
was more curious than angry—there must've been an innocent explanation, since surely if her friend were coming on to her boyfriend
via text message she wouldn't have included Emma's own name a
mere sentence away from her flirtation. Then, in reverse order,
Emma found herself uncovering what had apparently been an on-
going conversation. First, another stupid wink from Genevieve.
This was a relief—although it revealed a side of her friend that
Emma didn't know existed. (Gen never would've communicated
to her in smiley faces.) Emma figured Nick would find it ridicu-
lous, too. But the previous message, this one from Nick, made
Emma newly nervous: *Of course. Lips sealed.* Before that, from Gen,
But totally a mistake. Pleeeease don't tell Emma. No need to hurt her.
Emma felt her lungs contract; she was having trouble getting
breath through. From Nick, one of those emojis of a kissy pout.
This, from the Nick she knew? Emma began panicking, scrolling up
with a numb thumb. Gen: *Although it was fun . . .* Nick: *Forgotten.
(Even your honey lips.)* This stabbed at Emma. She pressed together
her own lips, bare and chapped, taking in the cheesiness she
couldn't imagine her boyfriend capable of. It seemed a mercy that
there was only one more missive, this one from Gen: *I'm so sorry
about today, no idea what I was thinking. Let's forget it ever happened.*

Rain pounded like fists against the windows, and Emma felt
suddenly unsafe. She yearned to flee, to dash out of the building
and into the fresh-aired storm, to run free into the night, far from
her loved ones' deceit, and from her own fear.

But she didn't. Instead, she stayed very still, moving not a muscle, feeling her feet on the ground to reassure herself that it was
still there beneath her. It was the weak part of her winning out, the
part that insisted on staying dry and warm, in a familiar place, and

close to the people she knew and loved best, however vile and deceptive she'd just discovered them to be. So although Emma felt as if the storm had already ripped through the walls and swept her up in a ferocious gust, that the wild wind was now inside of her, whipping through her veins and blowing apart everything she'd known mere minutes ago, there she sat on the edge of the bed, quiet and still and perfectly postured. Someone happening upon her at that moment might have believed her to be at peace.

Chapter 25

Emma was still sitting in a stupor, head roaring with wind and not much else, when she heard the front door creak open. "Yoo-hoo, Ems, where are you? We found an open deli and we got your favorite—Swedish Fish!"

"In the guest room," she called out, trying to sound casual and despising herself for it. "Just a minute."

"Hey." Annie appeared in the doorway.

"Hey." Emma was pathetic, she knew, feeling as though she had to act breezy—why?—because giving in to her true feelings, all the rage and turmoil, felt too dangerous and unwieldy, because expressing these things would make her look like a fool. "I'm just answering some e-mail."

"Cool. It's like the surface of the moon out there, totally deserted. It's really creepy. So, are you up for another movie? *The Day After Tomorrow*'s on demand."

"Nah, I think I'll turn in for the night. I'm exhausted."

"Okay. Love you, Ems." *Yeah, right.*

"You too. Good night." Emma felt her insides crinkle.

Perhaps even more pathetically, when Nick slid into bed beside her, to him Emma feigned sleep, while to herself she pretended that everything was just as it had been. The rain struck like a machine gun against the glass and the wind howled like a tortured animal. The part of Emma that she deemed her common sense understood that the only way to survive the night was to push from her mind all that she'd discovered, to instead focus on how nice it was to lie skin to skin against her boyfriend, to feel his chest pressed into her back and his arms around her waist as permission to slip into a deep sleep.

There was no question of going outside the next day. The four of them were housebound, watching the whipping wind and rain through fogged windows, listening to the disaster coverage on the radio, and sipping mimosas. Annie made a show of declaring the champagne delicious, which at this point was only for Nick's sake; with great restraint Emma resisted rolling her eyes, and instead kept topping off her drink.

Never in her life had Emma felt more anxious. There was the storm news—the power had already gone out in parts of Brooklyn, including Red Hook, where trees were down and streets were fast flooding—plus the Annie news, and of course the news of whatever the hell had happened or maybe was still happening between Nick and Gen. Emma had done all she could to avoid the storm, camping out in this apartment on the twenty-sixth floor, and now she tried to avoid her boyfriend and friend, too, sequestering herself in the guest room supposedly to work, then offering to make lunch when the rest of them hit up the building's gym. While she spread eight pieces of spelt bread with some kind of designer Dijon, Emma spun scenarios in her head—Nick and Gen had been sleeping together for years, laughing at Emma's naïveté during their steamy trysts; or they'd only recently realized their deep love for each other and, pitying Emma, were trying to find a gentle way to let her down; or Nick, desperate to escape buzz-kill Emma who was forcing him into cohabitation, had run into the arms of fun-loving Gen for relief and commiseration, and now was plotting how to weasel his way out of their new lease.

When this line of thought became too overwhelming, Emma moved on to Annie. She conjured up every stereotype of new moms, picturing Annie's designer purses replaced by diaper bags spilling forth with rattles and pacifiers and picture books, her Insanity workouts replaced by Mommy and Me Yoga, the silly romance novels she read and then related to Emma plot point by steamy plot point replaced by how-to books on babies and breastfeeding. What would the two of them talk about? How would they relate? Would Emma, too, get replaced by Annie's new mom friends?

Finishing the sandwich prep but feeling too troubled to eat one, Emma retreated back to the guest room. Eventually Nick appeared in the doorframe. "Knock, knock," he said. "We're starting Monopoly. I saved the iron for you."

"I think I'll sit this one out."

"Hey, are you okay?"

"Yeah, fine."

"I know this is a scary situation, but we're safe here. You were right to make us evacuate. And even if we can't go home for a few days—"

"It's not the storm." As soon as she said it water began pooling in her eyes. Nick sat down next to her and Emma couldn't help nuzzling into him. (God, she was pitiful.) So she chose the easier thing to say: "Annie's pregnant." She no longer cared about her friend's request to keep the news under wraps.

"Wait, seriously? Hasn't she been drinking the whole time we've been here?"

"Drinks minus the booze, yes. Virgin." The word "virgin" in relation to Annie made Emma scoff.

"Oh." Nick looked like he was trying to gauge Emma's reaction; Emma wondered if he feared she'd launch into a tearful speech about her ticking biological clock. It wasn't that this hadn't occurred to her, but there were a dozen more pressing things on her mind.

She clarified her upset: "I'm worried for our friendship. Within basically a year Annie will have changed from my fun single best friend to someone who's totally settled down, married with a kid. Maybe that sounds selfish."

Nick shook his head. "Hey, do you seriously think a baby has the power to break what you and Annie have? When we were living here, do you know how many times I walked in on the two of you having what I thought were choking fits, only to realize you were actually hysterical with laughter? Do you realize what most people would give for a friendship like that? Most of us are stuck with the likes of Carl for friends." At this Emma laughed. "You and Annie are bonded for life. God, Em, pretty much the only thing Eli and I have in common is that we've both been trying to worm our way into your and Annie's number-one spots for years, to no avail. And if *we* can't do it, what chance does a baby have? A newborn's like eight pounds and can't even roll over."

What he was saying was mostly bullshit, especially considering all Emma had recently discovered, but it made her feel better nonetheless. "How about you take a break from pouting and come play Monopoly," he said. "I know you love being the iron, hiding your sneaky little self behind properties to dodge the rent." *Sneaky little self*—the words pricked at Emma. "Come on, play with us."

She felt incapable of making a decision, so she let Nick pull her up. "Oh, and the pregnancy's a secret," she said.

"Lips sealed." *Lips sealed. Your honey lips.*

"Oh God." Emma bolted from the room to the toilet, where she proceeded to cough up the contents of her stomach—all that pulpy champagne. Nick was behind her then, stroking her back, at which point it would've been easy to reveal what she knew. Instead, she heard her rationalization: "Too many mimosas." For the rest of the afternoon, she let herself be the target of the group's jokes about her daytime drinking problem, and how she was too much of a lightweight to hold her fancy brunch bubbly.

Through a daze Emma ferried her iron around the Monopoly board, landing on others' properties and paying a steady stream of rent, somehow never getting it together to buy up her own places. Just as Eli was about to clean them all out, the lights flickered, they heard a whining sound and then a pop, and they were thrown into darkness. Annie squealed and grabbed Emma's hand, and then all was silent—no hum of electronics or pedestrian noise from the street; for a moment even the wind stilled.

They lit candles and gathered around the crank radio to hear the news: A ConEd power station at Fourteenth Street had exploded, leaving nearly all of Manhattan below Forty-second Street in the dark. Most of Alphabet City was flooded. So was the NYU Hospital, and since backup generators had failed, patients were being evacuated to other area hospitals, although those weren't in much better shape. These devastating facts were followed by on-the-street interviews, which Emma mostly tuned out—that is until the reporter introduced an artist from Red Hook, whose studio had already been ruined. "The water started off as a trickle," the woman shouted; you could barely hear her over the sound of rushing rain. "But then it burst in through my windows, like some kind of power hose, dousing all of my paintings. It kept coming and coming, filling the studio. I had to wade through a foot of water to get out. Now I'm just trying to save myself, walking north until I can find a cab or someone willing to give me a lift."

"Let's turn that off," said Nick. "Come on, it's late anyway. How about bed?"

That night she and Nick had desperate sex. As Emma slammed her body into her boyfriend's, fueled by fear and rage and anxiety, she imagined that the pounding rain outside was moving through her, the wind slapping at her skin and knotting her hair. So powerfully did she feel connected to the storm that she fully expected with her own release would come one final flash of light, one concluding crack of thunder, and then a petering out of the rain. But the elements pounded on long after Emma and Nick had finished, long after Nick had fallen into sleep. Emma stayed alert, listening. The water and wind, relentless against the windows, were oblivious to the two of them inside Annie's guest room twenty-six floors up from street level, just a couple of the probably hundred thousand people in Lower Manhattan holed up at home in darkness.

At some point she must've drifted off, because Emma awoke with a bolt, eyes swollen and cheeks wet with tears. Her sobs woke Nick, and before she could reconsider, she blurted out, "I know about you and Genevieve."

In a flash Nick's expression morphed from fuzzy with sleep to wide-awake and miserable. Even in her anguish, Emma was relieved to see he wasn't going to deny it. "Oh, Emma, I was such an idiot." He sputtered out everything she realized she'd been desperate to hear—the apologies, the I love you's, the fact that it was one time and that it had been little more than a kiss. Emma believed every word. She had to. "Considering you and me and everything we've done and built and have, that one stupid moment hardly registers," Nick said, his forehead scrunched up like a shar-pei dog's. "What I mean is, it didn't mean anything. Gah! I don't know how to say this stuff without sounding like a soap opera. But I'm being sincere, I promise." This made Emma smile despite herself; it was so rare for Nick to be tongue-tied. "Listen, if you want we can talk all night about it. Or I'll shut up immediately."

"Let's not talk," Emma quickly responded. As much as part of her wanted a play-by-play, a script of all that had happened along with Nick's internal monologue, another part knew that would be the worst thing to hear. Also, Emma was exhausted. Nick nodded, and she could see he was hesitant to touch her. Emma didn't feel better exactly, but she no longer felt like she was plummeting into a bottomless pit. She felt about like she did after Nick said he'd help her with her taxes but then spent the afternoon smoking pot and playing video games, or when he hinted that going vegetarian might be a good way for her to lose that layer of belly fat; she was angry, yes, but she wasn't doubting the very foundations of their relationship.

Without her asking, Nick took his pillow to the floor. Emma harmonized her breathing with his, inhaling when he exhaled and vice versa, and in this way she tricked herself back to sleep.

The second time Emma awoke shivering, she saw that the sky was glimmering with a thin light, so she wrapped herself in a blanket and went to the window. The rain had stopped, but water was swishing through the streets. No one was out. Every window was dark. Emma switched on her phone, and scanned the news and her e-mail: The city's power would likely be down for a week or more, and schools would stay closed through Friday. Her boss, Quinn, wrote that *1, 2, 3 . . . Ivies!* was out of commission until further notice, and her mother had sent a one-liner: *Stay dry and warm! XO*. Genevieve had texted Emma a selfie from her bed, surrounded by stuffed animals, along with the message, *My cuddle buddies during the storm!* Emma winced, and jotted off a reply: *Screw you! The way to get a guy is NOT by stealing mine!* She quickly deleted it. She sat there trembling, thumb poised over keypad, but before she could come up with an alternative, she noticed her phone had just 10 percent left of its juice. Relieved, she powered it down.

Emma climbed back into bed, still shivering. Nick, a potential source of body heat, was still on the floor. Eventually she pulled him back up under the covers.

"Hi," he said, hesitant.

"Hi." She pressed her chilled feet into his shins; he didn't even flinch.

"You know," he said at last "when I was laid out after my injury, I finally got around to reading that favorite book of yours."

"*The House of Mirth?*"

He nodded, and Emma was torn between declaring that sweet—Nick usually liked modern sci-fi, not century-old novels of manners—and saying something cutting like, *That's not all you got around to.* Instead, she said nothing.

"You've talked about the main guy, that Selden dude, as some kind of romantic hero, as Lily's great love interest who got away." Emma shrugged her assent, then waited curiously. "Well, I think he's an asshole."

"What do you mean? Selden is the only character with any ethics, the only one who's not willing to give up his principles for riches or popularity in that small-minded society. He refuses to play their petty games." Emma was indignant; it actually felt good to get worked up about a fictional character and fictional events.

"Yeah, but only because he can get away with it. Because he's a guy. He's so judgy of your girl Lily for trying to trade her looks for a marriage proposal and security, but it's different for her. Unlike a man, a woman in that world can't stay single and still be accepted. She can't just live alone with her high moral code."

"Fair point," Emma said, "but Selden is always trying to save Lily from those silly societal values."

"Not quite. Didn't you notice how he only makes himself available to her when she's fallen on her face? And then he can be the knight in shining armor who swoops in to rescue the damsel in distress. Selden doesn't want to be the day-to-day guy; he wants to be the hero. The hero is a much sexier role. It's classic macho dude stuff."

Emma considered the point. "I suppose that's true. Um, why exactly are we talking about this?"

"I've been thinking about why you're so drawn to this Lily Bart character, the ambitious thirty-year-old New Yorker."

"She's twenty-nine," Emma said; the distinction seemed important.

"Okay, twenty-nine, whatever. My point is, obviously Manhattan society has changed a lot in a hundred years, but maybe not as much as we'd like to think. It seems to me that the pressures on a Lily Bart are pretty similar to the pressures on an Emma Feit—to have a kick-ass social life and relationship and home and career (maybe the career part's new), to have a certain amount of money in the bank, to look a certain way, et cetera, et cetera. And then there's the struggle to figure out exactly what the world expects of you and also what you really want, and to understand the difference between the two. That's a ton of pressure. Obviously things don't work out in the end for Lily. But even without some grand tragic ending to your story, it still seems like a lot to deal with."

"Okay . . ." It was interesting to hear Nick rant about the hardships faced by female New Yorkers of Emma's age group, especially in connection to Edith Wharton's masterpiece, but Emma still didn't understand what he was getting at.

"The thing is," Nick went on, "I kind of get Selden. It can be hard to see you so ambitious, wanting a certain kind of life—your fancy job and us moving forward in our relationship in this one specific way, looking for the perfect place to set up our couple-y little life. It's honestly hard to not feel resentful sometimes." Emma felt her cheeks burn. She remembered that Gen had also used the word "couple-y" to describe Emma and Nick, back when she was trying to explain her own recent distance. *Ha,* Emma thought bitterly, recalling how she'd sympathized with Gen's words—all lies, she now realized.

Her voice was harsh: "Nick—"

"Hold on, please hear me out. My point is that I'm the jerk, not you. I'm saying it's hard, sometimes, to remember the kinds of pressures you face—because this stuff still isn't nearly as intense for a guy. It can be difficult to be compassionate and patient and understanding and all the other things a boyfriend is supposed to be."

"But, Nick, you're assuming that I'm just mindlessly giving in to stupid societal conventions. What if I really do want these things?"

"You're right. That's not fair. Which actually brings me back to Selden. He can't be bothered to get mired up in Lily's complications. She's working so hard to figure out how to exist in that society without totally succumbing to its more ridiculous elements, to live genuinely without also becoming a social pariah." Emma was thinking this was a quandary more or less everyone faced: how to be true to oneself while also getting along in the world. Nick continued: "Selden only wants to be the hero. And I get that, I do: It's exciting to be the hero, and it can be fucking hard to be the day-to-day guy, the grown-up in the serious relationship. That's shitty to say, but it's true." Even as she was trying to wrap her head around Nick's literary analysis, Emma was starting to understand where he was going with this; she felt nervous. "I'm not at all making excuses, but on that particular day with Genevieve, I'd been feeling like a useless lump in our relationship, failing at all the practical day-to-day stuff and frustrated with my recovery. And there was Gen, looking at me like I was that hero. And I gave in to it. It was a crappy thing to do, no question—childish and selfish and hurtful to the person I love most—and I take full responsibility for the crappiness. But I guess I'm hoping this is making me seem less like a monster, and more like an idiot guy who sometimes finds being a grown-up kind of complicated and overwhelming. A guy who messed up big-time in one specific moment."

Emma nodded, not quite in understanding, but in acknowledgment. She'd often suspected that Nick found all the trappings of adulthood more daunting than most; it was a relief to hear him admit as much, despite the consequences it had led to. But it was a lot to take in, too much. "Okay," she said eventually.

"The other thing is, no matter how you end up taking my stu-

246 Lindsey J. Palmer

pid lapse in judgment, you have to know that, unlike Lily Bart, you have tons of people in your life who love you like crazy. Me, duh, your family, and Annie. You can't begrudge her the fact that she's having a kid." Emma interrupted to explain about the e-mail she'd found—how after confessing her supposed misery to Emma, Annie had gushed to her mom like the pregnancy was the best thing ever. "Em," Nick said, "I'm sure she feels both those things, and a dozen other ones, too." For some reason this hadn't occurred to Emma.

"Look, it's not fair to you that I acted like an asshole, or that your friendship is inevitably going to change—"

"And don't forget that our home might be flooded and destroyed."

"Right, that, too. But—"

"I forgive you." Even if she didn't totally mean it, Emma knew she would eventually, and she'd had enough of this conversation.

Nick nodded, looking unconvinced. "You know I love you, Em."

"Yeah, yeah." Emma batted away his kisses. "I'm ravenous, suddenly." Her only sustenance in the last day and a half had been orange juice and wine.

"Great. Let's locate our storm benefactors and track down some breakfast."

Chapter 26

As it turned out, Annie was not the fun-loving party hostess she'd been for the previous two days. "My cell phone's dead, all our good food is rotting, and I'm fucking freezing," she complained to Eli, who comforted her as if these problems were unique to her. Emma knew Annie would've been melodramatic even if she weren't pregnant, and she steered clear of her all day.

By Wednesday, day four of being stuck inside, even Annie and Eli's six-room apartment was starting to feel cramped. Emma awoke early, hoping for some alone time, but Eli was already up and dressed, setting the table with a platter of peanut butter sandwiches and a bowl of apple slices. Emma knew this was the last of the fresh fruit. He'd also mixed up a pitcher of lemonade from the powder Annie had insisted they buy at Fairway for their picnic. The spread almost made up for the lack of coffee.

After everyone ate, Eli explained his plan: "I went down to the storage unit and found our old rain boots. Thank God for flashlights and intuition, right? Our newer ones are up here, so that's enough pairs for all of us. Apparently there are makeshift charging stations above Fourteenth Street. So let's venture out for a walk to the wonderful land of electricity. We can power up our phones and maybe find some decent food."

"And hot coffee!" said Emma, thinking it was a great idea. She craved fresh air and space. Although she'd half decided she could move past Nick's slip-up, she was feeling claustrophobic with all that had been revealed in the past few days.

But Annie snapped, "And then what? Ems and Nick can go crash with Gen uptown"—*Yeah, right,* Emma thought—"but what are we supposed to do? Come back to this dark, freezing place? They're saying the power could be out for a week or more. I want to go to my mom's."

"And get there how, honey?" Eli asked. Emma was impressed by how patient he sounded; Annie really had found the right guy for her.

"We'll figure something out, right?" Which, as they all knew, meant Eli should figure something out. And miraculously he did: Within an hour he'd worked his magic (or connections) and found a car service that, if they could get themselves up to Midtown, was willing to drive them to Westchester. God knows how much money Eli had offered.

"The car can take us another three blocks to my brother's, right?" Emma asked. A couple of months ago she would've dreaded the thought of crashing indefinitely with Max and Alysse, and might have even opted instead to stay in a dark, cold apartment with a dwindling food supply. But now Emma was sort of looking forward to it (though Max didn't yet know she was coming). They likely had heat and light, yes, but Max was also one of her few loved ones who hadn't recently betrayed her.

As they marched north along the dark, ravaged streets of NoHo, then the Village, and then Chelsea, Nick felt like he was in a dystopian video game. The few other pedestrians were all headed in the same direction, everyone on the same journey, off to face some final enemy and reap the ultimate reward. Nick was handicapped by the too-small boots—Eli had seemed embarrassed admitting they were size 8.5—and the noises they made as he walked with pinched feet were like a soundtrack: *squish, suck, squish, suck.* Nick thought of their home in Red Hook as of another land and another time, left behind in the quest for—*what?*—light, power, dry earth, civilization, peace. His despair at imagining all their things still packed in boxes on the floor of their street-level apartment, maybe now ruined, was punctuated by waves of lightness; he had the clothes on his back and his girlfriend at his side and the strength in his legs to walk forty blocks north. He and Emma had persevered through some big battle, and although who knew what other villains lurked around the corner, at least they were moving forward, trudging together away from the worst of the wreckage. Nick felt equipped to crush this game.

Annie's complaining interrupted Nick's fantasy. Apparently she *didn't* feel she had the strength to walk: "I'm getting blisters," she whined. "Honey, will you carry me?" God, that girl could be grating. After three full days cooped up with her, Nick kept catching himself spinning violent scenarios targeting Annie, her generous hospitality notwithstanding. He didn't know how Emma, or for that matter Eli, put up with her in large doses. He felt a new respect for the guy he'd previously pegged as just out for a trophy wife, a guy who was now lifting his full-grown pregnant wife into a piggyback.

"Let me know if I can relieve your burden," Nick said, patting Eli on the back.

"Thanks, dude. I think I can stick it out. Luckily we're less than ten blocks away."

"Fewer than," Emma whispered, elbowing Nick. He smiled, and didn't mention that distance could be an exception to the less-versus-fewer grammar rule. "Wow, look."

She was pointing to Macy's, the flagship store that took up an entire avenue block. What was arguably the city's epicenter of commerce and capitalism was now, at ten a.m. on a weekday, dark and deserted—an incredible sight. Emma had once dragged Nick inside Macy's to shop for couches, but he'd felt so overwhelmed by the crush of shoppers and sheer quantity of merchandise that he'd fled down the street to Sbarro. Now, all across Herald Square people were trekking together toward safety and power, talking to one another and taking in this strange new iteration of their city. No one was checking a cell phone (they were probably all dead) or brushing past others in a race to get somewhere important. Everything had slowed. Nick gaped like a tourist, in awe.

It seemed as if the whole world order had shifted. After weeks of distress over whether or not to tell Emma about his lapse with Genevieve, and if so how exactly to broach it, she'd found out on her own. When she'd discovered the text messages, Nick couldn't believe how stupid he'd been not to have deleted them; but now looking back on it, he wondered if perhaps he'd saved them on purpose, partly hoping Emma would stumble upon them and bring everything out into the open. Because when that had finally happened, it hadn't spelled total disaster. He and Emma had talked it through like adults. Nick wasn't exactly sure where he stood with her, but there she was by his side now. And in a way he'd never felt better about the two of them.

In the spirit of camaraderie, he approached Eli. "So the other day you mentioned how your company might be able to help fund my school's new tutoring initiative."

"Oh yeah, man. Though now is probably not the best time to ask."

"Right, no, of course. I figured the chances were probably pretty slim."

"Nah, I mean right now, as in today. When no one has power and the whole city's flooded, I don't think I can call the board together to discuss your after-school program."

"Oh, right." Nick laughed nervously. He knew this kind of conversation was called fund-raising, but to him it felt like begging. He inhaled sharply, trying to shore up his confidence: "Well, when business is back up and running, I'd love to talk. Ten thousand would be great. Twenty thousand would be even better."

"Look at you, driving a hard bargain. I didn't think you had it in you, buddy."

"Whatever I can do for the kids. We could mention the sponsorship however you'd like. And maybe I'd lay off on teaching my class about the evils of Wall Street."

"Really?"

"No, probably not."

Eli laughed. "That's cool. Well, I'd say it's as good as done." He shook Nick's hand and then hoisted Annie higher on his back. "Fuck, you're heavy, honey."

"She starts gaining weight that early, huh?" As soon as he said it Nick realized his error.

Annie glared at him and then at Emma. "Ems, did you tell him?"
Eli craned his neck to face Annie. "So then you told Emma?"
Simultaneously they said, "But you promised."

"Shit, sorry," said Nick. "I fucked this up."

"So did everyone else, apparently," Eli said. "I guess I'm the only one around here who can keep a secret."

"Sorry, hon. It's just, Ems is my BFF. I told my parents, too."

Eli rolled his eyes and patted his wife on the butt. "Of course you did, naughty girl. Oh, well, now that it's out, we may as well tell the world. Hey, world," he shouted. On any other day a guy screaming on a street corner in Midtown would be either ignored or scorned, but now in the midst of the biggest natural disaster ever to hit the city, several people actually turned to look. "My wife's pregnant! We're going to have a baby!"

A group of people clapped; someone whistled.

"Congrats, dude!"

"Woo-hoo!"

"Hey, a hurricane baby. Name it Sandy!"

"That's as good a reason as any to drink!" one guy yelled, and then pulled a beer from his backpack. He popped it open. "To the baby!"

Among the cheers and huzzahs, someone barked, "Whoop-de-fuckin'-do. Shut your goddamn piehole!"

"So we're still in New York City after all," Eli said. He yelled out, "Whoop-de-fuckin'-do yourself, dude! Screw you!" and then set off in a run to escape any consequences of the retort, Annie still hitched on his back.

They'd been passing homemade charging stations all through Manhattan, Good Samaritans with electricity who'd strung power strips out their windows for passersby to juice up their electronics. On Christopher Street they'd witnessed an argument between one man charging a large pink dildo and another wanting to plug in his iPad; the fight over which device was more essential devolved into a battle of pseudo-ethics, iPad Guy citing Aristotle and Dildo Guy citing "my motherfucking libido." Nick insisted they stay to watch the outcome: Unsurprisingly, Dildo Guy eventually won out.

A block before Times Square they found a free power strip and plugged in their phones. Nick checked his e-mail, which was mostly junk. He scanned a *Celebrate Halloween with Style!* newsletter from something called Big Apple Fun (oh, right, today was Halloween); it was full of party tricks, like how to give guests a fright: "Try strobe lights; or better yet, turn off all the lights and hand each person a candle when they arrive." Jesus, Nick thought, the image of people huddled in the dark with candles no longer sounded like a fun Halloween party gimmick. He moved on to an e-mail from Carl, subject line, *Wish you were here!* The attached photo was of Carl in his Hoboken condo, donning flippers, a Speedo, and a sun hat, his baby wading in water that was already up to Carl's ankles. *Jesus*, Nick thought again.

He heard Emma on the phone. "There's no way *you* installed it last winter," she said in the impatient tone she reserved for Max. "You hired someone to install it, right?"

"*Psst*," said Nick. "Don't antagonize him. We're asking for a favor, remember?"

She rolled her eyes. "Anyway, that's awesome that you guys have a backup generator. Congrats on your foresight. Is it possible we could come crash at your place for a couple of nights? Nick and I could babysit and give you and Alysse a break."

"There you go," Nick whispered.

An hour later the car service showed up. When the driver opened his door, people all around pounced, spewing sob stories and begging for a ride. "Mr. Eli Silber?" the driver called out. Nick felt embarrassed as Eli pushed past the crowd and shook the man's hand, acting as if he'd won some award. The four of them piled into the car, and with a slam of the door separated themselves from the community of people in the streets.

"Peace out, New York City," Eli yelled. "I can't wait to get out of this shit storm."

It was possible Nick was imagining the hostile, jealous glares from the throngs outside, but he slid down in his seat nevertheless, his stomach swirling with equal parts shame and relief as the car peeled off, ferrying them out of the storm-ravaged city.

Chapter 27

As Nick and Emma fidgeted on Max's doorstep, Nick took an inventory of their appearance—their slick, grimy skin made it clear that they hadn't showered in days, their clothes were matted with dirt, and Emma's hair was doing that frizzy-wavy thing she hated. They probably smelled, too.

"You made it!" Alysse appeared at the door and ushered them inside. "I'll tell you right away that I'm feeling very self-conscious. At fourteen weeks I always just look fat, not pregnant." Emma might've found the comment narcissistic, but to Nick it was a kindness for Alysse to ignore the fact that he and Emma looked like homeless people.

"You look great, Alysse," Nick said, then he blinked at Emma until she added, "You really do."

"Before you two tell us everything, I bet you're dying for showers. I set out hand towels and bath sheets, plus sets of clean clothes. Nick, I think Max's things will fit you all right. Sadly I don't have your long legs, Emma, so my jeans will probably be capris on you. But those are trendy now, right? Aimee wanted you to borrow one of her sundresses. When I tried to explain how size might be a concern, she threw a fit, so I said you'd wear her barrette. I hope that's all right." Her chatter continued as she led them to the spare room, what had been the Feits' office during Emma's childhood. Nick knew the bed would be made with sweet-smelling sheets and that toothbrushes and little bottles of water would be set out for them; it felt nice to be mothered, even by a woman his own age. "Max and the kids are down at the school gym trick-or-treating. Trees have been toppling everywhere, and half the houses still don't have power, so they moved the whole production inside. It's a sad approximation, but at least the kids will get their sugar high. If you ask me, I'm not sure why we're encouraging our children to celebrate a pagan holiday, but Max was insistent." This one was new to Nick—Halloween's incompatibility with Judaism. "All right, I need to start dinner so I'll leave you two be. I hope you're up for burgers. Don't worry, Nick, I've got a veggie one for you."

Under the shower's steady stream, the water running cloudy with his body's grime, Nick felt happier than he had in days. "Yoo-hoo." Emma stepped into the tub and pressed herself against him, a pleasant surprise; they hadn't showered together since the beginnings of their relationship.

"Pretty great, right?"

"Yeah," she said, "except look at all the bath products: nontoxic, dye-free, and a hundred percent organic. Also, zero percent fun and probably smell like armpits."

"I bet they smell better than you do right now." That began a splashing fight, which quickly led to kissing. The tub had those no-slip treads in rainbow colors, which were surprisingly conducive to shower sex—Nick made a mental note to buy some. He put his hand over Emma's mouth to shush her moans, which were maybe meant to reach and shock the ears of a certain sister-in-law. This thought conjured up an image of Alysse in Nick's mind, which he couldn't shake as he pressed himself into Emma's back. He found Alysse not at all sexy, although maybe there was something alluring about her plump arms and efficient smile. Jesus, he thought, there was no accounting for desire. He came quickly, then slid down to sit in the tub, letting the water pound against his shoulders. This was what water was supposed to be: refreshing and restorative and safely confined to a specific space, not out of control and wreaking havoc on an entire geographical region.

The two of them patted each other dry with plush towels, then Nick pulled on Max's track pants and NYU Law T-shirt. "Hey, gang," he said, attempting an impression of Emma's brother, "how about a friendly game of Wiffle ball? Afterward I'll whip up flaxseed pancakes and cups of Sanka for everyone."

"I don't know, Max-y," Emma said in an approximation of Alysse's voice, modeling her pair of elastic-waist jeans. "I reserved the morning for family Torah study, and I think we better find a way to include some v-e-g-g-i-e-s in our meal." They fell onto the bed giggling. "We're both terrible at impressions, you know," she said. "Also, I think these are maternity pants."

"Holy shit, is it nice to be dry and in clean clothes in a warm place," Nick said.

"I know."

"And together with you." He was practically bursting with the sentiment.

They lay there luxuriating in their simple good fortune, until the silence was pierced by a squeal: "Auntie Emma! Mr. Nick!" Little footsteps came padding down the hall, until Emma's niece appeared, beaming, in a beige bodysuit adorned with leafy vines. "I'm Eve!" she shouted, leaping into Emma's arms. "But I ate my forbidden fruit and lost my serpent." She pronounced it *suh-print*. "I filled my whole bag with candy!"

"Good job, kiddo!" Emma gave her a high five. "Who knew the Garden of Eden was so great for trick-or-treating?"

"Mommy says come down to dinner when you're ready."

"Yum yum," Emma said, tickling her niece's spandex belly. "Let's go eat."

In the kitchen, Spiderman, né Caleb, latched onto Nick's leg. "Hey, buddy," Nick said. "I would've thought you'd be dressed as Adam."

Alysse raised her eyebrows. "Someone had a meltdown when he realized his costume was supposed to make him look naked. So we switched plans last minute."

"Spiderman and Eve, my two beloveds." It was Max, who

crouched down to hug his kids, and then righted himself to plant kisses on the cheeks of Emma and his wife.

Nick shook his hand and marveled: Max was the ultimate day-to-day guy and he seemed to relish the role. "Thanks for the clothes, man. I'm feeling very styling."

Alysse served Nick the same packaged veggie burger he ate several nights a week, but it was the first warm food he'd had in days, so it tasted gourmet. Aimee and Caleb seemed less interested in their burgers than in their candy hauls, which they were now inventorying aloud, talking over each other and unfazed by the fact that no one else was paying attention. "So let's hear your hurricane tale," Alysse said.

Nick and Emma tag-teamed the telling of the events of the past four days. (They skipped the Gen part, of course—and in editing that out of what would become their official Sandy story, to be told and retold again and again in coming months, part of Nick felt that maybe his slip-up hadn't happened at all.) Emma finished with their walk uptown that morning: "You could just feel the fact that everyone had been through something tough, and there was this amazing spirit—we were all in it together. It was like a cheesy movie, but it didn't feel cheesy at all."

Nick thought she'd summed it up well, conveying precisely how he'd felt, too. But Max snorted. "It sounds like you think this whole thing has been romantic," he said. "You do know there's been billions of dollars of damage. People have died."

"Yes, of course. All I'm saying is that out of this awful disaster came some moments that were kind of wonderful." Emma squeezed Nick's hand.

"Okay, sure. Can you pass the ketchup?"

Nick sensed Emma wasn't going to let her brother's comments go, and he was right: "Max, believe me," she said, "I know this has been devastating. While you've been up here safe and sound with your backup generator, our neighborhood has been totally pummeled. Our apartment might be ruined. It's possible we lost all of our stuff."

"But you guys have renter's insurance, right?"

"Well, it was on my to-do list. There's been a lot going on, you know."

"Unbelievable." Max shook his head. "Maybe that's what you get for moving to Red Hook. Did you think that would be romantic, too?"

"Excuse me?"

"I've been out there. It's all industrial warehouses and run-down lots, right? A total shithole." Nick saw Alysse wince at the last word, but she said nothing. The kids, meanwhile, had stopped talking about trick-or-treating and were now spellbound watching their father and aunt. "Plus, it's totally cut off from the rest of the city. I don't know what you were thinking, moving all the way out there."

"When were you last there, like a decade ago?" Emma said. "The idea of you knowing anything at all about neighborhoods in New York City is totally laughable."

"Oh, I'm sure they've put in some cool dive bars and overpriced coffee shops, just like every other crappy area of Brooklyn that's supposedly now hip. My point is, leave it to you, Emma, to seek out some difficult, cutting-edge housing situation so you can revel in how complicated and hard your life is."

Emma scoffed. "You have no idea what you're talking about. And only someone who lives in boring, yuppie Westchester would think Red Hook is cutting-edge."

"Em." Nick placed a hand on Emma's shoulder, but she shook it off, not looking away from her brother. For the third or fourth time that meal, Nick instinctively reached for the beer that he assumed would be in front of him; once again he withdrew his hand, empty. The adults all had glasses of water, and the kids had mugs of milk. It was a novelty, to eat dinner without drinks. Although maybe it was like any other eating ritual people accustomed themselves to—keeping kosher or swearing off meat. Still, Nick thought a bit of booze could do this party good, loosen everyone up, and take the edge off this argument that didn't seem to be dissipating.

"After everything we went through trying to find a decent place to live," Emma fumed, "are you actually blaming me for not check-

ing the height above sea level of a potential apartment? Are you
holding me responsible for not foreseeing that the biggest hurricane in the city's history would swoop down a week after we
moved in?"

"I'm just saying—"

"What *are* you saying exactly, Max?"

In the brief silence that followed, Nick tried again: "Hey, guys,
Spiderman and Eve are looking a little put out. Should we change
the subject, maybe ask them about their friends' costumes?"
Alysse smiled pityingly at him, and both sets of siblings ignored
him. He squirted a ketchup smiley face onto his plate and tilted it
toward Caleb, but still couldn't win the boy's attention.

"What I'm saying," Max went on, "is that isn't it notable, and
maybe not such a coincidence, that it always seems to be you having the problems and me bailing you out? Maybe if you grew up a
little and didn't change course every two seconds, maybe if you
stuck with any given career long enough to make some real money
and be able to live—"

"Oh, so that's it, I don't make enough money for you, Max? I
don't have the right career? Is that what growing up means to you?
Well, I have news for you: There are other ways to be an adult than
becoming a fancy corporate lawyer, popping out a new kid every
couple of years, and slinking back home to live in your parents'
house in the suburbs."

"You know, you're just like Mom and Dad, doing whatever
pleases you and never even considering how your actions affect
anyone else. They were so giddy about their stupid Spanish bakery idea that they were practically going to give away the house to
the first people who expressed interest. It was totally childish and
irresponsible."

"So you did them a big favor by taking it off their hands?" Her
sarcasm seethed.

"Yes, to keep the house in the family, Emma. You think I was
thrilled to move out to the suburbs in my mid-twenties? No, but I
felt certain responsibilities and obligations. Sometimes there are
decisions to be made, and someone's got to make them. It's not always about what you want."

"Fuck that, Max. It's bullshit, and you know it." Alysse's chair squeaked as she stood up suddenly; taking her plate, she excused herself to the kitchen. Emma was oblivious. This verbal battle was spinning out of control, and Nick worried that at any moment Emma would throw out the fact that Max had no clue what she was dealing with: namely, infidelity. Instead she said, "You think you're so mature and responsible, but I think you're too scared to even consider what it is you want in life. You hide behind being a self-righteous prick because maybe you're terrified to discover that what you actually want *isn't* to be the good little Jewish boy with the picture-perfect family."

Alysse had reappeared, her face inscrutable. "So, who wants dessert?"

"Dessert!" Aimee yelled. "Candy, candy, candy!"

"You can each pick out two pieces from your pillowcases," she told her children. "But none of those chocolate creams. They're dairy, and you just ate meat."

"Two whole pieces of candy on Halloween? Lord Almighty," said Emma. "And you," she said to Nick, her voice trembling, "why can't you ever show that you're on my side?" She fled from the table in a huff. Nick, shocked at the accusation, stayed put. He suspected she'd want to be alone; or no, if he was going to be honest with himself, he wanted to give her time to cool off before going to face her. This conversation had confounded him, each sibling accusing the other of absurd things, both of them responding cruelly and irrationally.

Max got up calmly, kissed his wife on the forehead, and said, "I'll clear my plate later," before stalking off in the opposite direction from Emma.

"Well," said Alysse.

Nick felt awkward and a little panicked. At a loss for what else to do, he began clearing the table with Alysse. They did so in silence while the kids whined for more candy, and Alysse eventually gave in, sanctioning one more lollipop each.

At the kitchen counter, she handed Nick a sponge. "Here, you wash and I'll dry."

It was a relief to be assigned a task. Watching the suds gather in the sink as he stood beside Alysse, Nick thought about how both of their partners, in insulting each other and each other's way of life, had by extension insulted the two of them, too. "I don't know what to say about what just happened," he offered eventually. "It's been a tough few days. I'm sure it hasn't been a breeze out here, either."

"I think we're all just tired." Alysse dried and stacked several plates before continuing: "A lot of our neighbors have their power out, so we've been hosting people for meals all week. And then last night some kids were out playing and a tree came down. It fell on this little boy, one of Caleb's friends. Max took him to the hospital so his mom could stay with her other two kids. The dad was out of town, and the airports are still shut down so he can't get back. Turns out, the boy broke both legs. Anyway, so Max was up most of the night—I think he came home around four, and then our kids are up by six."

"Wow, what a mess."

"Exactly. We haven't told Caleb yet about his friend—he'll be in a wheelchair for weeks. The kids are already so freaked out from the storm and the power outages."

"I can imagine."

"I'm really sorry about your apartment. We'll do whatever we can to help. I don't think Max meant most of those things. . . ." She petered out.

"There's no need to apologize to me. It sounds like you've had a hell of a week. For some reason Max has a way of getting under Emma's skin. She doesn't act that way or say those kinds of things to anyone else." Nick wondered if he was betraying his girlfriend in speaking so candidly, but he also believed he was doing his part to repair the Feit family relations. Plus, it felt good to talk about the Max-Emma rivalry with someone who probably understood it as well as or even better than he.

Alysse shrugged. "Classic sibling stuff. Do you have any?" Nick shook his head. "Ah. Well, I was a hundred times worse with my sisters."

"But that was when you were kids, right?"

"Yeah, but still. Those childhood relations die hard. I want so badly for Aimee and Caleb to get along. Max thinks I coddle them, that I interfere too much when they're fighting. But he's not exactly an expert on sibling harmony, is he? I feel like the kids were taking notes tonight. Hopefully they didn't quite put together that their father and Emma are related in the same way that they are."

"I think it'll be a few years before your kids start criticizing each other's major life choices," Nick said. "Anyway, maybe that all sounded harsher to us. Emma and Max are so used to it." Though truthfully, Nick had never heard them go at it quite like that.

"Maybe." Alysse didn't sound convinced. "And Max is still really wrapped up in being the older brother. Ever since their parents moved abroad, he feels this huge responsibility, like he has to take care of Emma, well, at least until she's married and settled." She glanced down. "Oh gosh, I shouldn't have said that."

"No, it's okay."

"Sorry, I guess I'm more exhausted than I realized." She patted her belly pooch.

"I'll give you a pregnancy pass. The bottom line, I think, is that Max and Emma are just very different people."

"Yes, and not always so accepting of each other's differences." Nick handed Alysse a platter to dry. "Look at that, you're quite the scrubber. Max isn't so reliable on the tough stains."

"You sound like an ad for dish soap."

"What can I say, I guess I'm just a boring suburban housewife and mom."

"By the way, Emma found out yesterday that her best friend's pregnant, hence the anti-procreation remarks."

"You mean Annie Blum?" Alysse said. "Gosh, that was fast!"

"Exactly."

"You know, I read an article the other day about the earth's population. It's seven billion now, and they're saying it could reach ten billion by 2100. Ten billion! That really makes you think about bringing new people into the world, doesn't it? Especially when they're saying we're going to have more and more crazy storms like this one."

"Huh," said Nick.

"Sometimes I feel guilty being pregnant."

"Well, I guess I won't be out of a job anytime soon."

"Good point: All my baby making is keeping you teachers employed. I'm a job creator, as the politicians like to say." Alysse giggled girlishly.

Nick handed off the last dish, then wiped his hands. "I'd better go check on Emma."

"Thanks for helping. You're a mensch." Nick took the comment as a kind of olive branch; it was a given that Alysse would've preferred Emma to be with a Jewish guy, but maybe she wasn't quite rooting for Nick's ouster, either.

Nick found Emma facedown in bed. He tapped her on the shoulder and she turned her head, revealing eyes swollen from crying.

"Nick, the landlord left me a message. I was too upset to tell you before."

"Oh God, what does that asshole want?"

"No, not Luis, Shelley. She must've called when my phone was dead. She said she checked in on our place and things were floating."

"What do you mean?"

"Floating. As in, the water was a foot high. She said we were lucky since most of it's receded by now and other places on the street had flooding up to five feet. A foot of water in our home and we're lucky, can you believe it?" Nick wasn't sure what to believe; he pictured a pile of his stuff all scattered like flotsam across a wading pool. "Anyway, she has our mail. Like, thank God, all of our belongings are waterlogged but the catalogs and credit card offers have been spared."

"That was good of her to call." Emma gave him a look like *Really?*, but it was all he could think of to say. His head was reeling. "So that's what's been on your mind all evening, when you were laying into your brother?"

"I guess. And I don't know, everything else, too." Emma waved her hand, as if to swat it all away. "But also, I'm sick to death of Max treating me that way, like I'm a complete imbecile." Nick began rubbing circles into her back. "And yeah, yeah, I was an asshole, too. I'll apologize."

"You know, they've actually had a hard time this week, too. Alysse has basically been running a soup kitchen out of their home, and Max was up all night in the ER with Caleb's friend, who broke both legs from a downed tree."

"Shit, really?"

"Yeah. But, Emma?"

"Uh-huh."

"I'm always on your side. You know that, right?"

Her brow was knit, her eyes distracted, but Nick detected a hint of a nod.

Chapter 28

Emma had passed out by nine p.m., so it didn't surprise her that she was tossing and turning by three, and though she willed her body to reverse course into sleep she was wide awake by four. So she tiptoed downstairs, stretched out on the family room couch, and, taking a chance on one of the four remotes, pressed Power in hopes of finding a distracting TV show. *Dora the Explorer* clicked on from the DVD player—not what she'd had in mind. Emma eyed the remotes, clueless, and wary of screwing up the entertainment system and giving her brother the satisfaction of yet another grievance against her, she resigned herself to the cartoon. Dora and a monkey sidekick had set their sights on an ice-cream truck, which they were now busy chasing to Coney Island. Emma preferred the show's sparkling ocean and golden sand version of Coney Island to what she imagined the storm-ravaged beach looked like now, post-Sandy. All the talk of ice cream eventually made her peckish, so she wandered into the kitchen to forage.

The cabinets were stocked with Tupperwares of grains, canned vegetables, and beans, and an entire shelf of herbal teas. Where were the snacks? Emma wondered. The fridge was a disappointment, too—there weren't even any leftovers wedged between the fresh produce and organic yogurt. The freezer featured bags of peas and chicken breasts, not a pizza or pint of ice cream in sight. Emma kept searching, thinking Alysse must have a weak spot, that surely a pregnancy craving had made her cave and buy something processed or yummy for middle-of-the-night noshing. Finally, in the small space above the oven, which Emma used a footstool to access, she hit on her treasure: the kids' Halloween pillowcases. Gold mine!

Emma returned to the couch carrying a handful of chocolates. Dora was now venturing across a crab-infested sand dune, and Emma set about stuffing her face with the fun-sized treats, filling her pockets with the wrappers. She didn't even bother to keep the TV volume low; everyone sleeping was upstairs, and she had the whole downstairs, four large rooms, to herself. This was the life! Growing up, Emma had taken it for granted that her four family members might all be under the same roof but each in separate spaces, doing their own things. Now, it seemed incredible that they'd had so much space. Any apartment Emma had lived in as an adult could fit in its entirety in this family room. No wonder it felt like such a big deal to move in with a boyfriend in New York City; apartments were sized so that you couldn't just coexist. If you were both home, you were necessarily together. In Brooklyn if Emma woke up at four a.m. to watch TV, she'd either have to make the volume barely audible or use her laptop with headphones to avoid waking Nick. She supposed there were some perks to suburbia.

Emma was so absorbed in her candy consumption and in trying to estimate the house's square footage that she didn't notice her niece's presence until the girl began cuddling up to her on the couch. Aimee wore pajamas covered in unicorns and she smelled like talcum powder.

"Hi," she said simply. "May I please have a Milky Way?"

Emma hesitated before remembering that it was Aimee's candy supply she'd been siphoning from. "Okay, but don't tell your mother."

"Thanks. This is a good episode. They walk across the boardwalk"—*bud-wuk*—"to get Boots's floatie and then they go swimmin'."

"Aw, man, did you just spoil the ending?"

Aimee grinned wickedly. She kicked her bare feet against the couch cushions. "Mommy says I can watch one show a day."

"Oh yeah? That's good, so you won't become a couch potato." Aimee squirmed and repeated the phrase "couch potato" quietly to herself. "So tell me, besides watching *Dora the Explorer* in the middle of the night, what are your hobbies?"

Aimee looked thoughtful. "Painting. And dancing. And mac and cheese."

Emma laughed, tearing open another candy bar. Aimee's gaze followed the chocolate's trajectory from hand to mouth. "Oh, what the hell," Emma said, and tossed a second Milky Way to her niece. "We're gonna brush our teeth after this, okay? We've got to cover our tracks."

"Also I like the Torah and *Cat in the Hat*."

"So you're into the classics. And what are you gonna be when you grow up?"

Aimee shrugged. "I'm just three, you know."

"Wise girl."

"You're still wearing my barrette," Aimee said, beaming.

"Yes, I adore it." Emma touched her hair; the clip was adorned with a row of strawberry decals. "Thank you so much for lending it to me."

"Aimee and Emma. Emma and Aimee. Aimee and Emma. That's a tongue twister."

"You're right."

"Auntie Emma, I'm sleepy."

"Okay, let's go back to bed." She lifted her niece, who was surprisingly heavy for her size, and carried her upstairs. They brushed their teeth with Aimee's bubblegum toothpaste, then Emma tucked the girl into bed.

"We have to do *Goodnight Moon*," Aimee said. She began reciting the words to the children's book, and Emma added what she could remember—*goodnight house, goodnight mouse*—until Aimee declared it was okay to make up their own words. Aimee wished goodnight to Dora and Boots and Emma and Mr. Nick and hamburgers and Halloween, and Emma wished goodnight to Aimee and Caleb and Milky Ways and Aimee's barrette. Then Aimee closed her eyes and tucked her thumb between her lips, apparently satisfied with the ritual. Emma fluttered her lashes against her niece's cheek, feeling a pang of envy toward her sister-in-law, then tiptoed back to the guest room.

"Hey, babe," she whispered, nuzzling into Nick's sleepy scent. He emitted a noise that was adorably incoherent and it made Emma well up; how sweet and kind and patient Nick was, despite his flaws, and how lucky she was that he was hers. On a whim she asked, "Are you going to love me forever?"

"Probably," he mumbled, still seeming to be asleep. "But no promises for now."

This made Emma snort out a laugh, which woke her boyfriend. "Huh?" he said, blinking in confusion. "Oh, hi, Em."

"Go back to sleep, babe. It's nothing."

Emma could feel her heart pumping as she descended the stairs in the morning, but it calmed as soon as she realized Max was already gone for work—at a satellite site, since his Manhattan office was still closed. She waved to Alysse, who was helping Caleb with a Lego structure while talking on the phone about a food drive. "Yep, I'll do today's drop-off," she said, then whispered to Emma, "Can I make you some coffee? Tea?"

Emma shook her head, sitting down with Caleb to take over Lego duty. Aimee attached herself to her mother's leg and complained of a stomachache, and Emma blushed with guilt; maybe a strict limit on Halloween candy wasn't such a bad idea for a three-year-old. Alysse made two more calls—phone tree duties, she explained—before hanging up and turning her full attention to Emma. "Oh, you're still in those same clothes from yesterday. Just give me a few minutes and I'll scrounge up some clean ones. I haven't had a chance to get these guys fed yet, and I just have to call the plumber about a pipe in our basement. As if our little leak is going to be a priority this week!"

Emma felt a surge of sympathy toward her sister-in-law, who clearly didn't ever get a break in her job, even—or especially—after a hurricane.

"How about Nick and I take the kids out for breakfast and you can have a couple hours to yourself?" Alysse looked skeptical, so Emma added, "I'd really like to help. You've been so generous."

"Oh, um, thank you. You can take my car to the diner in town." She sounded tentative, which gave Emma a pang of shame, realizing she'd maybe never before offered a favor to Alysse.

Apparently the whole town had the idea to take their kids out to eat. A half hour later, Nick and Emma found themselves entrenched in a mob scene of children climbing across booths and screeching at random, like animals on the loose. It was clear they'd all been cooped up inside all week, with school canceled and little opportunity to play outside in the hurricane's aftermath. But Caleb and Aimee seemed oblivious to the chaos, thrilled as they were by the novelty of an outing with adults who weren't their parents.

A ball flung over the booth divider bounced directly onto Nick's head. Aimee tittered and Caleb pumped his fist. "Bull's-eye!" he yelled.

"This is horrifying," Nick said.

"I know." Emma noticed Aimee was drawing on her brother's shirt and wrestled the crayon from the girl's grip. "Thank God these guys are just on loan."

"For real."

And yet, Emma was enjoying herself. She played referee to the siblings' brawls over the green then the red then the yellow crayons, at first lecturing them about the importance of sharing, then when that didn't work, meting out three-minute increments for them to take turns. And when Nick again got bonked by the ball, he gave in and began a game of catch with the boy from the next table.

"For real!" Aimee shouted, parroting Nick, and then her elbow knocked over a water glass and soaked the table.

"Mommy always gets us sippy cups," Caleb said with authority.

"Okay, smarty-pants. And what does Mommy usually make you for breakfast?"

"Bacon," he said. Emma nearly ordered it before Nick interjected that there was no way Alysse cooked up bacon for breakfast in her kosher kitchen.

They managed to make it through the morning with only minor

additional catastrophes—a glob of jelly in Aimee's hair and, upon leaving the restaurant, Caleb sprinting across the parking lot and almost getting himself run over. ("Mommy always holds our hands when we're near moving cars," he declared when Nick caught him.) Driving home, Emma felt ready for a nap.

All afternoon Emma dreaded her brother's return home, and when he finally arrived she was glad to be on the floor playing with his children like a good aunt.

"Hey," he said. "I let Mom and Dad know you're here. They want to Skype with us at six."

"Okay." God, the thought of dealing with Max and her parents all at once was overwhelming. Maybe the two stressors would cancel each other out.

Max murmured something about a shower and shuffled upstairs. He remained absent through their early dinner—a slew of neighbors who were still without power showed up, and Alysse made chicken Marsala, plus pasta for Nick and the kids. Emma was amazed at her sister-in-law's composure serving dinner for a dozen; it had once taken Emma a week to prep a dinner party for eight, then another week to recover.

Max resurfaced at 5:55, grabbed a leftover drumstick, and launched Skype. Emma sat down next to him. In silence they waited for their parents. Emma kept wanting to say something— that she hadn't meant half of what she'd said the night before, that in fact she was in awe of her brother and the life he'd built, that she couldn't imagine the responsibility of feeding and caring for and raising two, and soon three, kids. She wanted to ask him about what he'd said, too—like at this point did he like living in their childhood home? And was he excited to have another child? But Emma felt tongue-tied, unable even to ask after the boy with the broken legs, the one Max had taken to the ER.

At 6:10, their parents signed on. "Hey-a, kiddos," said their mom, cheeks flushed. "We're just in from a night of salsa dancing. Your father's almost got the moves of those sexy Spanish men. They say it's all in the hips." She shimmied before the screen.

"Are you drunk?" Max asked. Emma realized it was after midnight in Spain.

"Oh no. Well, maybe just a little," she tittered. Max seemed irritated, like he was the disapproving parent and their mom the naughty kid.

"Hola, mis hijos." Their dad appeared, hair matted with sweat to his forehead. "That hurricane is the talk of the town around here. All of our regulars have been asking if you guys are all right."

"It's nice to hear that *your customers* are concerned about us," Max said. Emma shot him a side smile. Their parents either missed or ignored the comment.

"I'm just so glad you two are safe and sound. You both look healthy and happy!"

Max filled them in on the neighborhood—the downed trees, the power outages, and how it was a good thing he'd installed a backup generator last winter.

"Well, isn't that lucky!" their mom said.

"It's not luck, Mom, it's preparation."

"Sadly I wasn't so well prepared," Emma said. "Only thanks to the generosity of Annie and then Max and Alysse did we not basically drown in our home. Our landlord says our things were floating in our apartment."

"Really?" Max said. "Wow."

"You'll figure it all out, Emma. You always do." Their father flashed a thumbs-up. "It's just great that the two of you are together. It's so important to lean on family at a time like this." Emma and Max exchanged a tentative glance; she couldn't read her brother's expression, but she felt a twinge of remorse.

"Oh, that reminds me of a segment I heard on the news about a group of urban farmers in New York," their mom said. "Apparently they'd set up a whole bunch of beehives at the Brooklyn Navy Yard along the East River, and the storm completely destroyed them. One million bees have lost their homes!"

"Homeless bees, huh?" their dad said, winking. "Let's hope they don't go swarming after you guys."

"The worst part is," their mom continued, "they were donated by some retired bee expert who'd made certain their genetics were top-notch."

"Meaning what, they were of Aryan descent?" Max asked. "How tragic, the beekeeper's dream of a master race of bees doomed. What will we possibly do without all that genetically superior honey?"

Emma laughed. She thought how she should always team up with her brother to talk to her parents; he made the experience much more bearable.

"Oh, Emma, have you met with Sophia recently?"

"No, Dad, my office has been closed this week."

"Because the entire city shut down!" Max said impatiently. "Not just the beehives! Did you not hear Emma? Her whole neighborhood has been obliterated, and after all she went through to find an apartment." So this was Max's apology, his standing up for her to their parents. Emma felt grateful.

"And you guys should see Alysse," she said, trying to return the favor. "She's been cooking for the whole block, like, restaurant-style. She could be a professional chef."

"That Alysse has always been resourceful," said their mom. "It's a good thing we installed that high-quality oven back in the nineties."

"*El horno está bueno,*" said their dad. "Anyway, Emma, Sophia and I have been having a ball practicing our Spanish, and she told me all about her application to the art program. That girl thinks the world of you." That was flattering to hear. Emma missed Sophia; in fact, she was surprised to realize that she missed many of her clients. After a week out of the office, she was itching to get back. "Mom and I were thinking how fun it would be to get more involved with teenagers, how energizing they can be."

"Not all of them," Emma said. "Sophia's sort of an exception."

"Ooh, maybe you guys could start an after-school beekeeping club for at-risk teens," Max interjected. "I bet all those stings would be very character building."

"You could sell honey cakes at the bakery and donate the surplus," Emma added. "Food banks are probably dying for shipments of top-notch, artisanal honey."

"That's an idea," their dad said, smirking. "Your mother and I would look dashing in those beekeeping suits. The hoods are very hip now, right, hon?"

"All right, enough," said their mom. "That's the last time I tell the three of you an interesting news story. But, Emma, seriously, if you're up for it, we were talking about investing in you to start up your own tutoring venture."

"And then you could call the shots on the type of clientele. Not just kids from Park Avenue."

"You could expand to Madison and Lexington, perhaps," Max said.

"Well, my point is," said their dad, "you could broaden beyond the rich families who you say are always trying to buy their kids' way into top colleges. And maybe you wouldn't have to deal with those—what do you call them?—Hellios?"

"Hellis," Emma said. She was surprised to hear her dad repeat back all of this information; she'd never been sure he was listening when she talked about her job.

"Right, Hellis. It was actually Sophia's idea, investing in a company for you. She thought you might hire her on as an online tutor so she could earn some extra cash next year." Emma smiled at Sophia's savvy. She would actually be quite a good tutor.

"Well, it's something to think about," Emma said. The idea of being her own boss was intriguing, although she thought of Max's accusation, that she never stuck with any job for very long. She'd only been with *1, 2, 3 . . . Ivies!* for a year.

"Max-y, did the kids get our Halloween package? We sent it last week."

"Yes, thanks, Mom. They really loved it."

"Oh, good. Emma, I don't think there's any hope of your receiving our recent goodies for you, considering the weather and all." She looked stricken. Emma thought again of Shelley saying she had their mail, how absurd it was that she'd probably get the knickknacks from her parents when the rest of her stuff might be destroyed. Hopefully the package included a water damage restoration kit. "All right, kiddos. We've got to get up early. The challahs won't bake themselves. No rest for the weary."

After they signed off, Max began laughing. "God, they're obsessed with those idiotic care packages."

"Speaking of which, I haven't heard a peep from the kids about the package you claimed they loved so much."

"That's because it went straight in the trash. Mom sent face paint that's totally toxic. Plus enough candy to fill a convenience store. The kids, not to mention their teeth, don't need all that junk."

"You're kind of nuts, you know," Emma said.

"I'm not the one considering going into business with Mom and Dad. You're the crazy one."

"No, Mom and Dad are crazy," Emma said.

"You're right. Mom and Dad are crazy." After a moment Max said, "So would you really do that, have them invest in you?"

"I don't know, maybe. It would be nice to be able to take on other kinds of clients, and charge them on a sliding scale. Nick's starting this tutoring program at his school that he wants me to help run. Maybe this would allow me to do that, join forces somehow."

"I bet you'd be great at running your own business."

"Really? That means a lot."

"Well, it's true." It felt strange to be so polite with each other, but at least they were working their way back to solid ground. "I'll help you with any legal stuff, as long as you agree to take on the kids as clients one day, with a family discount, of course."

"We better get on that. In my professional opinion, kids do best on the SATs when they start studying by age three—four at the latest."

"Darn, I guess Caleb's already screwed. Maybe we just forget the whole thing and resign ourselves to third-tier state schools. That would save me a few hundred grand."

"Yeesh, the cost of college tuition."

"Yeah, it stinks. Every once in a while I think of cashing out the kids' savings accounts and blowing it all on a Ferrari."

"Alysse would be thrilled."

"I'd get her something, too. A necklace, maybe."

"She deserves more than a necklace for spending all day, every day with those nutso kids of yours. One morning alone with them and I was kind of ready to kill them."

"Nice, Em. If Caleb and Aimee get murdered, now I'll know who to blame."

"What's *muh-duh?*" Aimee appeared at the desk and climbed onto her dad's lap.

"Ah, that explanation seems most fitting for a father to give," said Emma. She mussed her niece's hair and got up. Max flung a pen at her back as she walked away.

Chapter 29

By Saturday, Emma felt as if she and Nick had moved in with Max's family. She'd been helping Alysse with a food drive, and Nick was making progress teaching Caleb his letters. But Emma knew they were stalling the inevitable return to Brooklyn, avoiding going home and facing reality. Nick's school was set to reopen on Monday, as was *1, 2, 3 . . . Ivies!* So on Sunday afternoon, they all piled into the minivan, along with a box of clothing and food that Alysse had packed for them, and set out for Red Hook.

They were quiet for most of the ride—even the kids seemed to sense the foreboding. Eventually Max flipped on NPR. They were airing an interview with a Brooklyn Grange beekeeper about his destroyed hives. Max and Emma began laughing hysterically. Caleb and Aimee caught the mood and started giggling, too.

"What's so funny?" Alysse asked. "I think it's pretty sad about the bees."

"Who knows?" said Nick. "Apparently a Feit inside joke."

Their laughter died down as they turned off the BQE and the smell of gasoline kicked in. "Mommy, it stinks," Aimee whined. Alysse shushed her. Entering Red Hook, Max slowed the car and they all peered out the windows at the wreckage. The scene didn't seem quite real, as if it were a series of dioramas in a museum instead of Emma and Nick's own neighborhood. The sidewalks were littered with debris, waterlogged furniture, and the occasional overturned car. The sides of buildings featured watermarks sometimes higher than the heads of passersby. Emma wasn't sure if she was imagining that everyone looked exhausted, beaten down. Certain street corners were mobbed with people—those handing out supplies and those taking them. It felt like a third-world country, and Emma remembered Max's comments, how he'd ridiculed her for moving to such a shithole. Now he said nothing.

When the car pulled up to their address, the noxious odor had become intense. "You guys can come back to Westchester if you want," Max said. "You could commute into the city with me. There are early trains to get you to school on time, Nick."

"Thanks, but no, we'll be all right," Emma said. Aimee had started whimpering again, and Caleb was becoming agitated, asking over and over what they were doing there. "You better get going before the troops revolt."

"I can come inside for a few minutes to help if you want."

"Daddy!" Aimee shrieked. "I wanna go home!" Max shot her a stern look.

"I think the people have spoken," Nick said, shaking Max's hand and then scooching out of the car. Emma leaned in to hug her brother, and they each held on for an extra beat. The great thing about siblings, Emma thought, was that no matter what you said or how much you pissed each other off, your bond was like an elastic, snapping you inevitably back together.

"Nice hair piece," Max said. Emma touched her head and felt the fuzzy fabric of her niece's barrette.

"Oh, this is Aimee's." She unclipped it and handed it over. Aimee shook her head.

"That's a present for you. You're a wise girl."

Emma touched her niece on the nose. "No, you're the wise girl."

"Aimee and Emma, Emma and Aimee."

"That's right. Aimee and Emma, Emma and Aimee. Bye, you guys. See you very, very soon." She bonked her niece and nephew on the heads, one per "very."

Emma and Nick stood there waving even after the minivan had

pulled out of sight. If they could freeze themselves in this moment, Emma thought, then they wouldn't have to face the next one. Eventually Nick turned toward her. "Ready?" he said. Emma felt a twinge in her stomach, but let him take her hand. She realized it had been over a week since they'd been alone together.

Inside the apartment, Emma felt as if it was her first time there. It smelled musty and the wood floor had warped into sloping hills. It didn't seem like a space where they, or anybody, might live. Nick flipped on the light switch and it took a moment before the main bulb flickered on, revealing pockets of water bubbled behind the wall's paint and items scattered around the floor. Mostly their moving boxes were still stacked where they'd left them, although now they slumped in various states of damp and collapse.

Emma felt the need to tiptoe as she surveyed the scene, as if wary of doing more damage. The place was in bad but not terrible shape—the couch and chairs were soggy, but the metal table and bed frame looked fine, solidly standing and rust-free. The electronics were obviously done for. Emma nearly broke down imagining her waterlogged laptop, until she considered Nick's video-game console, now caput, and how much she'd stressed about the possibility of him spending all his time in their shared home gaming. It was funny how the things you worried about rarely materialized; it was the things you never could've anticipated that actually went wrong.

Emma glanced over at Nick, who was poking at a pocket of water trapped in the wall and whistling—actually *whistling*. She felt a flash of anger and, in sudden despair, tore at a rip in one of the moving boxes. The box split open and out tumbled a pile of shirts and sweaters, and along with it a strong stench of mold. Emma spotted her purple tunic, and reached to pull it out. Her favorite top was now damp and distended, and splotches of discoloration lined the hem.

And then Emma lost it. Her knees buckled and her throat clenched with sobs. She clutched at the ruined shirt, which she'd bought years ago, long before she'd met Nick. She ran through a slideshow of all the times she'd worn it, its delicate silk swishing like little kisses against her skin, its sleek silhouette making her feel pretty and glamorous. She pictured nights out with Annie and department parties at Cornell and those early-on dates with Nick, so heady with promise.

Nick. Emma reeled around to find her boyfriend surveying a shelf of books. He was still whistling, his tune jaunty and light, like at any moment he might start tap-dancing. Emma felt furious. "Do you not even care that our lives are ruined?" she spat.

"What?" He turned to face her, his eyes going suddenly sad; Emma had started whimpering again and she held out the tunic. "Oh, Emma. Hey, shhh, it's okay. Our lives aren't ruined. This is all stuff." He made a sweeping gesture. "It's all just stuff."

"It's not just stuff," she said. "I had this on when I told Annie I was leaving grad school to move here. And I wore it the first time we went to the Botanic Gardens—you said the color made my eyes look violet. It means something to me. All of it does."

Nick was nodding, but he didn't look sympathetic; he looked impatient. "Okay, so you can take it to the dry cleaners, baby." The term of endearment made Emma flinch.

"You don't get it, do you?" She darted into the bathroom and slammed the door shut. She flashed on an idea of Nick as a hurricane, intent on destroying their lives—and not just their stuff. For the past week Emma had pushed from her mind the images of him and Gen, focused as she was on the storm and staying at Max's. But now that she was back in their wrecked home, the place where the two of them were supposed to start a new chapter together, the nausea returned: Nick had cheated on her. Yes, he felt awful about it; Emma didn't doubt that. But the fact was, he'd done it. It's not like it was always easy for Emma to be in a relationship, like she never felt stifled or bored by monogamy, like she wasn't sometimes tempted to fall into bed with a cute guy who gave her a certain look across a bar. But the point was, she'd never given in to those whims. She'd never lost sight of the wreckage and hurt that such a misstep would cause. She'd never been so selfish or stupid.

Nick was knocking on the bathroom door. "What?" she shouted.

"I found something behind the counter." Emma cracked the door. Nick was standing there, holding up her charm bracelet, the one he'd been adding to for each of her birthdays and other special occasions. A part of Emma wanted to say something nasty, like that the next charm should be a cell phone so they'd never forget his dalliance with Gen, another great milestone in their relationship. But Nick looked more than repentant; he looked devastated. So Emma held out her wrist. Nick's fingers were delicate with the clasp, and the charms clinked against one another like wind chimes. The silver was shiny, as if the storm water had polished it; the star, the miniature book, the thimble-sized champagne flute, and the Edith Wharton figurine all glinted in the light. "Beautiful," Nick said, kissing her hand.

"Nick," Emma started, water again pooling in her eyes.

"So much has been ruined, I know," he said. He took her shoulders and met her gaze. "I'm going to do everything I can for us to rebuild what we had." Emma nodded, and he wiped the tears from her cheeks. She nodded again, resolving to let him try.

For dinner they opened a can of pineapple rings and another of peaches in syrup. As Emma stabbed at a slimy peach with her plastic fork, she thought of all the elaborate meals her sister-in-law had fed them that week. Now she and Nick were perched on a countertop slurping at juice from tin cans. But it didn't feel awful, exactly. It felt like starting over. Emma glanced at Nick, who was poking his tongue through a pineapple ring. She leaned in and bit off chunks until the remainder fell away and slopped to the ground. "Storm debris," she said. "We'll clean it up later." Nick kissed her, his mouth pineapple-sweet, and Emma felt a surge of love. For the moment this all felt okay—her boyfriend, their relationship, this mess of an apartment, their life.

When the doorbell's mechanical beep sounded, Emma started—it was strange that the buzzer system still worked, considering the collapse of everything else. Peering through the peephole, she saw their landlady, Shelley, waving energetically. She opened the door and Shelley lunged in for a hug. "You're okay!" she yelped.

"We are, we just got back. Are you okay?"

"I'm okay, too." Shelley handed Emma a laminated index card, nearly identical to the one she'd given them when they first moved in, the one labeled, *Shelley's best ratings!!!* This card also listed local venues, but instead of bars and restaurants it was supply pickup spots and pop-up soup kitchens. Emma read from the *Bonus!* section at the bottom: *IKEA serving breakfast all week. Free! Cinnamon buns so sweet!*

"Also, you have not had good time as tenants so far," Shelley said. "No heat, water everywhere, electricity on and off—they say for many more weeks, maybe." As if on cue, the apartment went dark. They heard someone yell, "Goddamn it, again?" from across the airshaft. A moment later the lights flickered back on. "Let there be light," Shelley said, slapping her knee. "Anyway, I decide to give you free rent for the first two weeks, okay? And here's your mail. I like *People* magazine, too."

"Thanks," Emma said, not quite believing what she'd heard. "For everything. I'd offer you a drink, but all we have is bottled water."

"No, no, I get out of your hairs. Got to go give out my little cards." And then Shelley flitted away, like some kind of fairy spirit.

"Is she for real?" Emma asked.

"I think we may have found the one decent landlord in all of New York City," said Nick. "Speaking of which . . ." He pointed to the two letters on top of the stack of mail—both from the court. "I can't look. You better do the honors."

As Emma tore open the letters, Nick flipped through an L.L. Bean catalog, his nonchalant air clearly an act. Emma peered over his shoulder; nearly half the pages were filled with rain jackets and water-resistant gear, which seemed like a practical joke.

Emma turned her attention back to the court letters and scrutinized the legal jargon. "Well," she finally said, fairly certain she'd gleaned the correct meaning. "We won every penny we asked for. Yay! But Luis is appealing. Boo!"

And then they were both laughing. Of course this would be the result; of course they would win, only not really; of course Luis would continue to cast a cloud over their lives. Emma thought of that silly friend of Sophia's, the one who was making his way through law school one course per semester, who'd warned her of the long, painful, paperwork-filled process these court cases always were.

Nick swatted the letters from Emma's hand, and they flitted to the floor. "Storm debris," he said.

The electricity cut out again, and Nick laid one of their borrowed blankets across the damp couch. He took Emma's hand, and reluctantly she let him pull her down beside him. Without the hum of electronics, all she could hear was the sound of their breath and the tinkling of her charm bracelet. Emma felt happy. When it was time for sleep, she pulled another blanket on top of them, tucking it tight like a cocoon. "How's this for being socially conventional," she said. "Just how you imagined our shacking up together, right?"

"Exactly. You know, we could get some cats and a few creepy knickknacks and open a bed-and-breakfast. We already have the musty smell and the rotting furniture."

"Emma and Nick's Ramshackle Paradise."

"Emma and Nick's Storm-Ravaged Haven."

"Emma and Nick's Waterfront Wasteland."

"Emma and Nick's Happy Home."

Emma fell asleep in Nick's arms, the names of all these imaginary places pinging merrily about her head.

When Emma arrived at work the next morning, she was so focused on slipping past Gen's desk undetected that she nearly tripped over the basket in her office doorway. It was filled with bottled water, batteries and candles, plus several kits meant to dry out wet electronics. Her boss popped her head in. "Oh, good, you saw our little care package."

"This is so generous, Quinn."

"Oh, everyone pitched in. The rest of us live uptown, where Sandy was just a little rainstorm." Tucked among the supplies Emma spotted a bag of Swedish Fish, and pulled it out. "Genevieve said those are your favorite," Quinn said. Emma felt a pang, no longer wanting the gummies. "Anyway, let me know if you need to cut out early this week to deal with whatever. I can cover your clients."

"Thanks. You're really the best." Emma was touched by her boss's kindness. Although she felt a tad paranoid, too, as if Quinn somehow knew she was considering leaving, and was reminding her of the benefits of working there.

All day long, Emma heard tales of her clients' storm dramas. Some lived on the Upper East Side, set off from Sandy's most intense rage, but others hailed from Tribeca and the East Village and spoke of freezing nights without power, broken windows, and dogs forced to do their business inside. Unlike what Emma had heard of Hurricane Katrina—how it had wreaked havoc precisely along socioeconomic lines, preying on New Orleans's poorest while sparing its wealthiest residents—Hurricane Sandy hadn't discriminated in its damage. One client, Paul Spencer, said his family would have to stay indefinitely with cousins up in Queens; this boy who, two months ago, had slunk into Emma's office timid and terrified, now stood up and delivered a hilarious impression of his socialite mother discovering she'd have to sleep on an air mattress. All of Emma's clients had done their homework, too—some by candlelight, it sounded like. Emma was sure this was due to her recent revised strategy of finding out what the kids actually wanted out of their tutoring.

Sophia was the last client of the day, her last-ever session. Emma had scheduled it this way on purpose, so they could linger. Sophia rolled in, greeted Emma with a double-cheek kiss, then launched into rapid-fire Spanish—she'd clearly advanced more than Emma's dad in the few weeks they'd been Skyping. The torrent ended with an upward inflection, implying a question. Emma shrugged. "My Spanish is kind of rusty, sorry."

"So listen," said Sophia, switching back to English, "I want your feedback on my Madrid app, which I brought, but I also want to talk about my future as the best part-time tutor you could hire. If you want me to sit for the SATs and actually take them seriously so you can advertise your star tutor as having aced some stupid test, I'll do it. Gladly."

"All right," said Emma. Sophia had thought this all through.

"So are you really gonna go for it, then—start your own business?"

"Shhh." Emma went to close her door. "I don't know," she

added, but even as the words came out of her mouth, she thought, *Yes, I'm really going to go for it.*

As Emma read over Sophia's application, dazzled as usual by the girl's writing but also impressed for the first time by her passion for the subject matter, Sophia sat sketching. Emma made a few notes and then handed the papers back to Sophia. "If they don't accept you, I'll have my parents personally go and beat up the admissions team."

"Deal." Sophia passed her sketch to Emma. It was a picturesque, Disney-style scene: a cartoon of a cozy home, two figures embracing in the doorway, and friendly animals flitting all about. Hanging from the mouths of a pair of bluebirds was a banner reading, THANK YOU, EMMA!

"That's you and Nick," said Sophia. "And look at the clouds." Emma glanced up at the cumulus formation at the paper's edge, where she spotted a girl in a flamenco outfit standing before a museum, two wizened faces smiling behind her.

"You and my parents?"

"Yep."

"They're going to drive you kind of crazy, Sophia. I'm warning you."

"Oh, they're the best—they said they'd teach me how to bake. I've never even turned on the oven!" Emma pictured Sophia whipping up rugelach and mandel bread, exclaiming "Oy vey" when the kitchen overheated. "And wanna know what your dad said when we were talking about the tutoring business?" She stated this as if a business already existed. "He said, 'Emma is so strong and capable and brave that we never worry about her.' Apparently that's not the case for your brother—what's his name, Matt?"

"Max."

"Anyway, my mom would never say something like that about me."

Emma thought about this, how sweet it was, and yet, how maybe it wouldn't hurt for her parents to worry about her occasionally. "If it makes you feel better," she said, "I think you're strong and capable and brave, and I don't plan on worrying about you at all when you skip off to Spain and embark on your illustrious new life as an artist ex-pat."

"That does make me feel better," Sophia said.

"I'll hang this drawing in my new office. That is, if I get a new office. And you're hired, no SATs necessary, on the contingency that I actually start up a business."

"You'll do it, I know it."

It seemed like the shortest session ever, and before Emma realized it Sophia was trilling, *"Adios, mi amiga,"* and flitting away. Emma felt like a proud parent, launching her child out into the world.

It was late, so Emma was surprised to find Genevieve still at her desk. When Gen rushed up to her, bubbling over with exclamations of "Oh my God, are you okay?!" and "How's your new apartment after the storm?!" it was a shock to remember that she had no idea what Emma knew. Emma realized she'd been steeling herself for a tense reunion. But all of Gen's hugging and concern derailed her from her original plan to confront her friend and curtly demand an apology. Instead, she found herself recounting her Sandy saga like the plot of some steamy TV drama, then asking after Gen's own storm story.

"Well, I had a revelation!" This was practically Gen's catchphrase. "As the water was pounding down on my roof, I started thinking, What if this was it for me? What if my ceiling suddenly caved, and kaput, I'm gone? Would I want to die knowing I've spent my days answering phones, or even taking sick people's pulses and drawing their blood? Hell, no. I'd want to know I've given my all to my dreams. So, I'm moving to Los Angeles!"

"Wait, what?" Emma had half expected all of it, except for the last bit.

"For pilot season. Well, first I have to get my headshots together and do a boatload of research on directors and producers and the kinds of scripts that are coming down the pipe for the season. Which is why I'm here so late."

"So you're going permanently?" Emma asked. Even in the

shock of the moment, Emma was aware that maybe she should feel relieved; with Gen relocating thousands of miles away, whatever had happened between her and Nick would now be 100 percent through. And maybe there was a flicker of relief, but it was accompanied by sadness. Despite recent events, Emma couldn't conceive of her life without Gen.

"Not necessarily. I mean, if I get cast in a part, then obviously yes."

"Or if you meet some dreamy Venice Beach surfer dude, right?"

"Eh." Gen wrinkled her nose. "I'm over men for now—I feel like a guy would just get in the way of my career."

Emma smiled, thinking about how Gen had spoken just last week about yearning for a boyfriend. She watched her friend move manically about the office, showing Emma the research she'd done on scripts, and what to wear for auditions, and which non-seedy L.A. neighborhoods had the cheapest rent. Gen looked happier than she'd seemed in months, back from a thousand whims to the inevitable place of trying to make her dreams come true. It was her one constant. This made Emma realize that Gen's attention on Nick had likely been just another fleeting fancy, a momentary conceit in a whirlwind of changeable passions and interests. In that moment she forgave her friend.

Plus, Emma thought of the conversations she'd had with Nick since she discovered his deceit. They existed in what she thought of as their relationship vault—that private cache of intimacy shared by the two of them and no one else. Genevieve had no place there. In a weird way, Emma had felt closer to Nick in the past couple of days; she'd realized they were stronger than she'd known.

"So what do you think?" Gen flashed her bright eyes.

"Sorry, repeat that."

"I was just saying I think The Genevieve has the potential to be as big as The Rachel from *Friends*." Gen was vamping, tossing her hair from side to side and batting her eyelashes. Emma giggled, thinking her friend was delusional, if always optimistic.

"Sure, Gen, I can see it. Everyone with long blond hair, very elegant."

"A girl can dream, right?"

"Absolutely." Emma glanced at the pile of audition notices on Gen's desk. "Hmm, this evening I'm casting for a story of female friendship, a comedy, but one with heart. Would you be interested in the role of dinner date? It's a hot part, and many young ingénues are vying for it. Your costar's a relative unknown, though there's a lot of buzz about her potential to blow up big-time."

"You're such a dork," Gen said. "I'd be delighted." She hooked her arm into Emma's, and they left *1, 2, 3 . . . Ivies*, off to dine *à deux*. As they strolled together through Midtown, Emma found herself caught up in Gen's dream, spotting several women with long bleached hair and imagining them mimicking the look of TV megastar Genevieve Pine. It felt good to fantasize with her friend.

Chapter 30

The next evening, Emma got a call from a man who identified himself as a mold-and-water-damage expert. Apparently he was a friend of Max's and said he owed her brother a favor. Max had arranged for him to come assess their apartment, and to provide cleanup and restoration. "You can wait for the building owner to take care of it, but experience tells me they'll be squabbling over FEMA funding for months. So as long as your landlord's okay with it, I can handle the cleanup much sooner."

Emma thought of Shelley, and how this would be a favor to her as well as to Nick and herself. "Great, let's do it." They made an appointment for that weekend.

A series of horn honks sounded from outside, and Emma leaned out the window to see Annie hanging from the door of a taxi, the annoyed-looking driver slumped at her side. "Get Nick," she called up. "I need help, fast! The meter's running."

Nick and Emma found Annie by the curb, pointing to an espresso machine secured with a seat belt in the cab's backseat. "Ta-da," she said.

"You know, you don't have to transport your own supplies out here to get a latte," said Nick. "Coffee shops do exist outside of Manhattan."

"Ha ha. Eli made the same joke. But, guys, this is your house-warming gift."

"Oh, sweet." Nick gave her a high five. "Thanks, Annie."

"Seriously?" said Emma. "Is it the same one you and Eli have?"

"Yeah, except this one's got a built-in bean grinder, and some sort of laser-fast heating technology, plus all kinds of other features that Eli could talk your ear off about."

"Annie, it's too much." Emma's idea of a housewarming gift was a basil plant or a bottle of wine. Leave it to her friend to show up with a luxury appliance probably worth thousands of dollars.

Annie waved her off. "We got it as a wedding gift, but we already have one. Plus, I'm off caffeine for the next eight months, which is a total tragedy." She patted her belly.

The cab driver cleared his throat, and Nick went to lift the load. "Jesus."

"Yeah, it's ninety-two pounds. But on the bright side, you get to show off how strong you are."

Inside the apartment, Nick set the sparkling new machine down on the kitchen counter. Annie perused the wreckage. "Well, I won't say it fits right in." She and Emma burst into laughter.

Nick said he'd get the machine set up, and the girls decided to go for a walk. They were subdued, passing a supply drop-off full of down-and-out-looking hordes. Annie pulled Emma into a playground up the block. "God, was that depressing," she said as they hopped onto side-by-side swings. "We really should sign up to volunteer."

"We should." Emma pumped her legs, relishing the funny feeling in her stomach as she soared above the sand. She'd spent a lot of time this past week feeling sorry for herself, but not everyone had a friend who would gift them a luxury coffeemaker, or a brother who could call in a favor and potentially solve their storm damage. Although Emma was fairly certain the favor was really from Max, who was probably paying full price for the supposedly free restoration.

"The donation drives are a good excuse to go through my closet and pare down." Annie swung in arcs higher than Emma's. "I'm sure it won't be long before I don't fit into any of my clothes."

"Nah, you'll probably be one of those annoying pregnant women who gains, like, ten pounds, then loses it within a month of giving birth."

"Let's hope. Eli's hot little secretary put one of my OB appointments into his calendar, so now she knows about the baby. I'm sure she's having a ball imagining me blow up like a blimp."

"So this pregnancy is really real, huh?" Emma let her legs go limp and hovered idly above the sand.

"Yep. And really terrifying."

Emma felt a pang, remembering the overjoyed e-mail Annie had written to her mother. "But it's not all terrifying, right?"

"I'll put it this way." Annie swooped past her and up into the air. "I was on the subway the other day, sitting across from this woman with a baby. Of course as soon as the baby looked in my direction, I started playing peek-a-boo and making those little kissy faces. What is that, some kind of biological impulse? You never see men doing it—it's only women of prime baby-making age. Anyway, I'm thinking, like, oh, right, this is great, I'm gonna adore being a mom. But then it got old after, like, two minutes, and I felt like an idiot for making all these dumb expressions in public. And then I was panicking, like, is this what the next few years of my life are going to be like, making stupid faces at a drooling person with a brain the size of a pea? Will I never again be able to take the subway and play Candy Crush in peace?"

"First of all, babies' brains are larger than a pea." Emma began pumping her legs again and caught up with her friend. "And secondly, I can't exactly picture you riding the subway with a baby."

"Good point. I'll definitely be an Uber mom. But anyway, then the baby cooed up at his mom and she kissed him on the head, and my heart totally swelled, like practically burst open right there on the Q train. My hormones are bonkers, if you can't tell. Within five minutes, I went from having a complete crisis over becoming a mom to, like, praising the heavens that I was with child."

"Oh, Annie. It'll all be fine."

"I know it will. Or at least I hope. I'm just so happy I can talk to you about this. With everyone else I have to be like, 'This is the most thrilling news in the universe!' because otherwise I seem like some kind of heartless bitch. And it is exciting, but it's also horrifying." So Nick had been right about that.

"I'll babysit whenever you need a break."

"Even on New Year's?"

"Well . . ."

"I thought so."

"Just promise me you won't move to the suburbs, at least not for, like, five years."

"Are you kidding? Eli would have to drag me by my hair out of Manhattan. But I'll tell you one thing, because only you won't think I'm being obnoxious. Though it'll be hard for you to understand, since you're always so good at everything—"

"Excuse me?"

"Oh, come on, when did you ever even get an A-minus in school? And every career you try you're immediately the best. I've never had that. And now it's sort of worse being married, like everyone's always saying 'Eli's wife' and 'Mrs. Silber' and I'm thinking, Wait, is that me? What happened to 'Annie Blum'? Who am I, and all that crap. But, my point is, I think I'm really going to kick ass at this motherhood thing. Think about it, I'm awesome at multitasking, I love to puree food, and I genuinely enjoy playing all kinds of silly, stupid games. Also I'm a pro at picking out adorable clothes."

"And you're a rock star on four hours of sleep."

"I am!"

"You're gonna kill it, no question."

"You're the best, Ems."

"No, you're the best, bubeleh." She said it in her best Jewish grandma voice.

Annie did her analogous impression: "Oy, I'm kvelling!"

They began swinging in synch. "What did we used to say, that if you stay in tandem you'll end up married, right?"

"Or how about best friends?" said Annie. "Ready? One, two, three." And then, just as they'd been doing for the past twenty-five years, they leaped off their swings and landed together in a heap in the sand.

A navy envelope stamped in yellow block letters with "IKEA" slid out of Annie's pocket. "Oh, right," she said. "I got something else for you guys. I know you'll have to get rid of a lot of your stuff, so hopefully this will help with redecorating. It's another wedding gift, from one of my mom's friends."

"No! She got you a gift certificate to IKEA? Eli must've been outraged."

"Exactly. I don't think he would've stepped foot in IKEA even to furnish his college dorm room. What a snob, right?"

"A snob with beautiful leather furniture, soft like buttah." Emma revived the Yiddish accent.

"Like buttah! Only the best for my little prince." Annie rolled her eyes lovingly. "Anyway, hopefully you can use it." She handed over the envelope.

"Thanks, Annie. You're always here for me."

"You know it, Ems." And then they both spotted the seesaw, and ran like lunatics over to play.

Carrying the gently used clothing and books that his students had collected, Nick followed the directions on Shelley's card to the nearest donation drop-off. He'd instituted a show-and-tell in his class, giving each student five minutes to share a hurricane story. Normally the kids would've dismissed the activity as too childish, but they'd gotten into it. They'd passed around the two-liter bottle one kid had filled with storm water, and a photo of the fish that had ended up in another kid's kitchen, and a comic book one boy had read with a flashlight when his electricity was out— "the first book I ever finished," he said, taunting Nick with his grin. Mostly they'd been fine, living in Upper Manhattan, and when Nick shared a news article about the kids in the projects in his neighborhood and how they'd lost everything—yes, even their cell phones and favorite kicks—the class had decided to organize a donation drive. Nick was proud of them.

Along the main stretch of Van Brunt Street, where most store-fronts were still shuttered post-storm, Nick came across a small jewelry stand. Its owner, a man perched on a stool making earrings, paused his work to take in Nick. "Howdy, my man," he said. "All profits go to Sandy relief. Take what you like; give what you can afford."

It turned out the man was a local artist, and most of his soldering studio had been destroyed. "I'm taking the opportunity to scale down my operation," he said, stringing a glassy bead onto a wire. "Back to basics."

Nick homed in on a smattering of silver charms. Among the hearts and moons and stars he spotted an umbrella, its handle a red hook—the same symbol he'd spotted all over his new neighborhood. "I'll take that one," he said, and dropped a twenty-dollar bill in the metal can. The man wrapped the trinket in finely woven fish netting, and Nick tucked it into his pocket. "Thanks, buddy."

Walking home, Nick considered the charm bracelet he'd been assembling for Emma, piece by piece, over the course of their whole relationship. He knew the bracelet was quaint, the sort of thing girls wore back when he was a kid, and by now Emma's had become heavy and cluttered, not exactly practical for wearing. But it meant a lot to Nick, and he hoped to Emma, too; he could remember the reasoning for selecting each charm, what had been going on between the two of them when he'd given it to her. Nick had never been a big fan of fancy jewelry, but the idea of the charm bracelet appealed to him. It was a slow amassing, like their relationship had been, a growing and building and accumulating of stories and emotion and quirk. The bracelet had character and it even made a noise—sometimes the delicate ringing of a bell, sometimes an uglier clanking—plus it required the upkeep of frequent polishing or it started to go dull and tinny. It seemed to Nick like the opposite of the diamond rings so many guys gave to propose marriage, the betrothed's ring finger at first bare and then— *boom!*—glimmering with a big, showy rock, their relationship suddenly switched from boyfriend-girlfriend—so juvenile sounding—to affianced—a word so frilly and French it seemed fake. That transformation struck Nick as unnatural. He much preferred the gradual giving of small symbols of his love to Emma. Might someone accuse him of being cheap or timid or safe in his preferences? He supposed so, but he didn't see it that way.

In his pocket now Nick carried the latest charm, an umbrella with a red hook. He remembered that old Rihanna song, "Umbrella"; he'd found it sort of catchy despite its clunky lyrics, and during the hurricane he and Emma really had been each other's umbrellas, and in its aftermath, too. Nick also liked the idea of the flash of red on the otherwise silver chain—this moment in their life, their coming together to share a home, captured by a bold streak, the color of passion and love.

When he stepped in the apartment door, Emma charged at him, holding out the IKEA gift card from Annie. "I opened it," she said. "It's five thousand dollars."

"What do you mean?"

"There are three zeros after the five; I double-checked the decimal point. For five thousand bucks we can buy all of IKEA!"

"Emma, we can't take that kind of money from Annie and Eli. Especially since you know that wasn't just some wedding gift."

"What do you mean?"

"Oh, come on." Surely Emma wasn't that naïve.

"Well, I know it's a lot, but for them it's practically nothing," Emma said. That was a fair point. "And we could have all new furniture to replace the rotten stuff. Granted it'll be made of clapboard and probably take us months to put together, but we have time, right?" She explained that a neighbor had told her about a moving company doing volunteer work, taking away furniture that had been ruined by the hurricane, recycling what they could, and dumping the rest, all free of charge.

Nick felt himself slowly giving in to the idea of accepting charity. His sense of pride, and his resentment toward Eli and all of his money, were fading into a simple appreciation for their friends' generosity. He felt himself readjust to this new position of acceptance. It was an adjustment he recognized—it happened to his students when they finally set their minds to learning a new concept or when a grammar rule suddenly clicked: that moment of understanding, followed quickly by a sense of wonder that they hadn't known it all along. Nick could already see their apartment furnished with the affordable Swedish pieces, and he could picture the party he and Emma would eventually throw in honor of their benefactors: They'd serve Swedish vodka and lingonberry juice, cabbage rolls and meatballs, and they'd play old-school Ace of Base and ABBA. It would be right up Annie's alley and mean much more to her than a check of reimbursement. Nick agreed to visit the furniture warehouse that weekend.

Of course Emma knew all the jokes about couples on outings to IKEA, how the store guaranteed a fight, how it was responsible for more breakups than Internet porno. But to Emma, IKEA felt magical, offering up every possible iteration of home, every fantasy of cohabitation one could dream of. As she and Nick traversed the showrooms, wandering through this beachy bedroom and that sleek kitchen, this modern living room and that cozy reading nook, Emma imagined it all. It was all for the taking—literally, in that a five-thousand-dollar credit was tucked snugly in her pocket, but also in a larger sense. Emma and Nick could create any of these homes and build any kind of future together. They were pure potential.

The store was set up according to life stages. When they'd walked past the dorm accessories—pop art posters and corkboards for photo collages—but hadn't yet made it to the baby stuff—cribs and diaper pails and pastel blankies—Nick and Emma nearly smacked into a sign advertising the store's new wedding registry. A saleswoman lured them over. "It's fun and easy," she said. "I can give you the scanner to try. Everything you beep automatically uploads to your list. See, it makes this cute little sound." The woman touched the contraption to a pillow's tag and it emitted a *badoop* that was admittedly adorable. She cooed with delight, doing an admirable job of acting like this was the first time she'd heard it. Emma was nearly taken in—it did look fun and easy.

"No thanks," Nick said, pulling Emma away. He smirked. "Lucky us, we can get a bunch of free stuff and we don't even have to throw a wedding."

She laughed. "Lucky us."

For a while they entertained each other mock-fighting about what to buy, bickering about whether to get the EKTORP or the POÄNG or the SÖDERHAMN, enjoying the feel of the unfamiliar sounds on their tongues. Emma thought this could be a funny kind of foreplay. But when it came to picking out a couch for real, Emma was surprised to discover that they really weren't on the same page—that Nick's preference for the EKTORP over the SÖDERHAMN was genuine and not a joke. To Emma the EKTORP looked boxy and old-fashioned, not at all what she imagined for their home. They agreed on several mirrors and compromised on throw pillows, finding a pair they both felt good but not great about—"B-plus," Nick said—but even after a break for cinnamon buns, they made no further progress on the couch. It occurred to Emma that one trip to the store, and one appointment later that day with the storm restoration guy, wouldn't be enough to make over their apartment into somewhere settled and comfortable, a real home. It would take time.

"Wanna take a break?" she asked, eyeing the beds section.

"Meet me on the FJELL."

Emma had heard that you were supposed to lie on a mattress for at least twenty minutes to determine if it was the right match for you; nearly every bed felt comfortable at first, but it was at the fifteen-minute mark that the mattress revealed its true essence, or something like that. After five minutes on the FJELL Emma could already determine that it wouldn't work for the long haul—it was too soft, with not enough support—but she stayed put, lying supine next to Nick, content for the moment.

Nick rolled on his side to face her. "So I have something for you," he said, reaching into his pocket.

Emma felt the air slow to a stop. The noises around her no longer penetrated her ears. All was still and quiet. And then the questions started up, running like a ticker tape across her brain: Were they on a verge of a huge moment? Was Nick going to propose to her right here in the mattress section of IKEA? Wouldn't that be odd and hilarious? Or would it be terrible? Was that even what Emma wanted? Wasn't it all a little too quick? Though, wasn't everyone always joking about what was taking them so long to get engaged? But still, wasn't it all a little too fast? Weren't they in a good place just where they were? And just starting to recover from so much turmoil? Or maybe Nick was just reaching for a tissue? But if he really was ready for this, shouldn't Emma take a leap, too, and say yes? She couldn't say no, could she? Surely it was just a tissue, right? Why would she even think of saying no? She wanted to be with Nick forever, right? But even still, wasn't it a little too soon?

"Emma?"

"Oh, huh?"

"I thought you'd passed out on me. You got very pale all of a sudden. Are you okay? Should we get some DRYCK FLÄDER to revive you? I hear it's very refreshing."

"Oh, ha," she said mechanically. "No, I'm fine, really."

Nick took her hand, jangling her charm bracelet. She hadn't taken it off all week, ever since Nick had found it on the kitchen linoleum among the hurricane wreckage, and ever since she'd decided once and for all to forgive him. At times she'd thought the piece too bold, or annoyingly heavy, but this past week it had suited her mood. From his pocket Nick pulled out a pouch of what looked like netting. Emma immediately relaxed. She could feel the color reenter her cheeks.

He opened the pouch to reveal a beautiful charm—*of course*. Emma examined the piece, overjoyed. The umbrella was delicate, a fanned circle of silver panels joined in the center by the nub of a clasp. The handle was a hook, colored red—*ah, Red Hook*—a stylish swoop. It was just the right memento of this moment in time, just the right thing for Nick to gift to her while lying on a trial mattress in a mock bedroom in the middle of a furniture warehouse. He really was the right guy for her.

"Hold out your wrist," Nick said, and then hooked the new charm onto the chain.

"Babe, it's gorgeous." Emma shook her arm and added to the clanking of silver was a new kind of clink from whatever material the red hook was made of. "It's perfect."

Nick and Emma didn't end up buying anything that day. They abandoned their half-filled cart and decided to return another time—the next day, or the next week, or the next month. Others were exiting the store loaded up with bags and boxes, buried by their stuff, but Emma, empty-handed, felt light and happy stepping out into the daylight with Nick. At one end of the parking lot a small group of volunteers was busy cleaning up the free breakfast, and across the grass the East River lapped up against the shore, the midday sun igniting its surface in sparkle. Soon it would be winter, but today was lovely, crisp, and almost warm, autumn's last hurrah. Nick took Emma's hand, and they walked together, the flash of red from Emma's charm catching the afternoon light, glinting like a wink. They strolled through their new neighborhood, walking mostly in step all the way home.

Acknowledgments

I never would have made it past my initial panic about this book's deadline, on to hope and excitement and eventually a first draft and then all the way to today, without the following lovely people:

Max Apple, my lifelong teacher, whose writing workshops are magic and manna. Tom DePeter, my senior year English teacher, whose lessons live on with me all these years later, and whose memory I hope to honor each day in my own senior year English classes. My writing students at NEST+m, whose enthusiasm and creativity are infectious (and my friends and colleagues who regularly reassure me that taking a break from my students' writing in order to work on my own is necessary for my soul and my sanity). Kerry McKibbin, whose multi-genre project assignment was not only the highlight of my grad school experience, but also became the beginnings of this novel. Zick Rubin, for being a font of wisdom and guidance. Paula Derrow, a generous first reader, whose suggestions added sensitivity to an early draft. My brilliant agent, Joëlle Delbourgo, whose orbit I feel so lucky to have been pulled into, and who possesses the dazzling skill of turning what I think is casual conversation into sudden, savvy insights about revisions. My whip-smart editor, Martin Biro, whose delightful notes make me giggle even as I'm hard at work. Vida Engstrand, whose talent for spreading the word about my writing is top-notch, and the rest of the team at Kensington, who once again get all the credit for turning my scribblings into this beautiful book. My family, for their unconditional love and support and pride—and especially my mom, who has been offering sensible feedback on my writing since I was a kid, and who also was the one to suggest that a particularly harrowing home hunt might make good fodder for fiction. And Damian, who has been there for me through every clause and comma, and through everything else as well, and who has wholeheartedly built a home and a life with me.

With immense love and gratitude,

Lindsey